Books
by
Paul W. Feenstra

Published by Mellester Press.

Boundary

The Breath of God (Book 1 in Moana Rangitira series)

For Want of a Shilling (Book 2 in Moana Rangitira series)

Gunpowder Green

Into the Shade

Falls Ende eBook series
Falls Ende – The Oath   *eBook 1*
Falls Ende – Courser   *eBook 2*
Falls Ende – The King   *eBook 3*

Falls Ende – Primus Book 1
Print version of eBook compilation 1, 2 & 3

Falls Ende – Secundus Book 2

Falls Ende – Tertium Book 3

Falls Ende – Quartus Book 4

Falls Ende – Quartus
First published in 2022 by Mellester Press

ISBN 978-0-473-61378-5 Softcover
ISBN 978-0-473-61379-2 Hardcover
ISBN 978-0-473-61380-8 epub
ISBN 978-0-473-61381-5 Kindle

Published in New Zealand. A catalogue record of this book is available from the National Library of New Zealand.Kei te pātengi raraunga o Te Puna Mātauranga o Aotearoa te whakarārangi o tēnei pukapuka

With heartfelt thanks.
Cover Design - Mia
Edited by Mathew Walters

http://www.paulwfeenstra.com/
Falls Ende © 2017 Paul W. Feenstra

Published by
Mellester Press

Falls Ende

QUARTUS

by

Paul W. Feenstra

Published

by

Mellester Press

Part One
Sagittarii

CHAPTER ONE

The lone Templar knight raised his head, anxiously looked skyward, and saw that the break of dawn was fast approaching. Already, a smear of yellow seeped above the horizon from the east, and he knew within a short time it would be light, and with it, the Saracen[1] would come.

With hands on his hips, he carefully surveyed the dusky area around him as best he could. At just over six feet tall, the knight had long, unkempt, sandy coloured hair and piercing blue eyes. Unlike his fellow bearded knights, he preferred to be clean-shaven. A personal preference mocked by a daring few, but not in earnest, as Sir Odo Brus was not a man to be trifled with.

He stood in a narrow, dusty pass devoid of trees and underbrush. The only cover was from large wind-worn boulders scattered along the sides of a ravine that may once have been an old riverbed. Here it was desolate and forbidding, and when the sun fully rose, he knew the oppressive heat would follow.

---

1 *Saracen – Followers of Islam.*

On either side, the ground sloped steeply upwards. Still shrouded in the lingering greyness, man-sized boulders sat precariously balanced on rocky, shale covered ground and offered perfect places of concealment for the twenty or so Templar brothers[2] that were anxiously waiting for his instructions.

Sir Odo raised an arm and pointed. "Ye, to the right, more, more..." He leaned forward, squinting in the half-light as the brother obediently repositioned and moved to hide behind a protective boulder. Satisfied at his placement, he yelled, "Hold fast!"

Most unusually for Templars, each brother carried a bow, quiver, and a bundle of spare arrows. Additionally, he had a few men in reserve, and three more brothers would act as messengers when called upon and were safely out of sight and harm's way. The knight strategically positioned them to be ideally situated and, as part of a Templar counter offensive strike against a much larger force of approaching Saracen.

Odo turned, pointed to another archer on the narrow chasm's opposite side, and instructed him and others on where to move. It was growing lighter and becoming easier to see, and he knew he needed to hurry.

Eventually, he was satisfied, and all the archers were situated to their best tactical advantage. He turned and again carefully surveyed the landscape before walking towards his sergeant and taking the reins of his destrier before mounting. Once astride, he urged the grey stallion into an easy canter and rode from the gorge for a short distance before stopping

---

2 *Brothers – 3rd and lowest class of the Templar order. Most were men-at-arms, sergeants, squires, and blacksmiths, etc, that supported the knights.*

and turning. Again, he scrutinized the positioning of his archers to double-check. It still wasn't light enough to see clearly, but then, he didn't have the luxury of time. He nodded; he was satisfied. To his eye, the archers were all undetectable and well hidden.

Two non-descript rocks were carefully moved and placed, one on each side of the track, where they would be easily visible to the Templar archers once it was fully light. They were markers and would assist the bowmen in determining the range to their targets.

From the far side of the narrow rocky chasm and unseen around a bend, he heard the jingle and clatter of forty mounted knights. They would ride a short distance away, remain out of sight from Saracen scouts, and reveal themselves only when the main Saracen force arrived. Odo felt reassured as they began preparing.

A solitary knight, followed by a sergeant, emerged from the far side of the gorge and cantered towards him.

"Hail to ye, Sir Odo, it will be another glorious morn," greeted the knight when he pulled alongside.

"Aye, Sir Piers, but I live to see the beauty of a setting sun, fer then I know I have survived another day."

The Templar leader, Sir Piers de Aubert, laughed. "Fer a young man, yer outlook on life is always most refreshing." His expression grew serious. "Are they all positioned?"

"Of one thing we can be sure, Salah al-dins[3] warriors, will not expect

---

3 *Salah ad-Din – Saladin. Kurdish leader who fought the crusaders.*

Templars to deploy archers." Odo pointed to the boulders concealing his men. "This location is perfect for an ambuscade, but your decision to use archers will catch them unawares."

The Templar commander nodded as he scanned the boulders looking for any sign of his concealed archers. "If it weren't fer yer fine skill and abilities, then it wouldn't be possible." He turned back to face the young knight. "Are ye ready?"

"God willing," Odo quietly responded.

Sir Piers leaned across and patted him on the shoulder. "Launch yer first volley after the first twenty or so Saracen come through."

"As we planned, Sir Piers," Odo Brus confirmed.

"May God be with ye, Odo." Sir Piers squeezed his legs, and his destrier shot forward, and with his sergeant following, returned to his men.

"Be ready, soon as the Saracen break and the gorge is clear, bring my horse." Odo dismounted and handed the reins to his sergeant. Immediately he was given his bow and a quiver full of arrows in return.

His sergeant dipped his head in acknowledgement. "As ye wish, milord."

Odo had previously selected a suitable boulder, elevated high enough to give him the best possible vantage point to command the counter assault. He ran for the boulders and scrambled up to conceal himself as his sergeant rode through the gorge trailing his destrier. Not a Templar was visible as the first brilliant rays of sunshine speared over the rugged and harsh terrain. All was quiet as the Templars waited.

Led by Sir Piers de Aubert, the contingent of forty Templar knights and their support personnel, which amounted to another eighty men, had been riding towards Frankia[4] after departing Jerusalem six weeks earlier. Sir Piers had deployed two knights who then trailed his contingent by about a two-day ride. They reported back to him that approximately one-hundred Saracen warriors were following and fast catching up. For three days, the Templars rode onwards and gave no indication they knew they were being stalked. On instructions from Sir Piers, scouts ahead had been frantically searching for an ideal location to turn the tables on the approaching enemy.

Templars knights were heavy cavalry and fought their adversaries on horseback, one-on-one, and ideally on open ground, while archers were not typically part of their regular arsenal. Some years earlier, the young Templar knight, Sir Odo Brus, had convinced his commander to allow him to train squires and other eager personnel on how to use bows. For two years, he patiently taught and guided them, and during that time, their skills had improved, and Odo had reported to Sir Piers that they were ready. Heavily outnumbered by Salah al-Din's warriors who pursued them, Sir Piers acquiesced and readily agreed. There was no better opportunity.

The bow Odo used was remarkably different from the bows issued to the Templar brothers. Theirs were smaller, lightweight recurve bows, and easier to master. Odo had been carefully instructed to use the powerful and much larger Welsh yew bow for hunting from an early age.

As tall as a full-grown man and challenging to draw to its full extent, the yew bow required incredible strength and many years of practice to

---

4 *Frankia or Kingdom of the Franks is modern day France.*

become adept in its use. To the delight of the Templars, Odo had provided numerous demonstrations of his skills, and the visionary Templar leader, Sir Piers, had placed a lot of faith in the abilities of the young and talented Scottish knight.

As the sun continued to rise, the Templars waited. Occasionally someone coughed or moved, the inadvertent sounds drifting into the empty gorge. They remained hidden, and from horseback, were completely invisible. The dark tunics typically worn by Templar brothers blended superbly into the dull sandy hues and shadowed rocks they hid amongst. The knights, who all wore white surcoats emblazoned with the familiar red cross, were some distance back and well out of sight and hopefully wouldn't be detected by Salah al-din's scouts or the approaching warriors until it was too late.

The Templar's patience was rewarded when a vigilant lookout reported a small dust cloud rising in the distance. Preceding the dust and riding hard, four Saracen scouts materialized. They cautiously slowed and then reined in as they approached the gorge with boulder-strewn sides and pulling their horses to a stop. As experienced warriors, they knew this was a perfect location for an ambuscade, but they also knew the Templars preferred open spaces to fight and not the narrow, limiting confines of a gorge. While this narrow chasm between large boulders was perfect for an ambuscade, they believed it wouldn't suit the Templars, and they foolishly didn't dismount to investigate further.

On the other, far side of the gorge, and some distance away, hidden beyond the crest of a low rise, three Templar brothers on horseback dragged branches backwards and forwards over the dry ground. A significant amount of dust rose, caught in the gentle morning breeze, then slowly dissipated.

This was another part of Sir Piers' clever plan. The deception was simple; the Saracen scouts would see the dust cloud and believe the Templars were close, riding northwards and oblivious to the approaching threat. Sir Piers wanted the Saracen to ride into the gorge where his archers could let loose, and then in the ensuing chaos, his cavalry would charge in.

First, one Saracen warrior nudged his horse forward and warily entered the gorge; the others, now emboldened, cautiously followed. They walked slowly, line abreast, through the chasm and looked up at the terrain, either side at the shadowed boulders, and saw nothing untoward. The gorge was wide enough for six mounted men to ride side-by-side and was about one furlong in length. A slight bend near the end, caused by a rockfall, prevented anyone from seeing down its entire span.

Slowly the Saracen scouts rounded the bend and immediately saw a cloud of dust rising above a low hill in the distance. As one, they stopped and began chattering. They believed it could only be a dust cloud created by the Templars. In agreement, two scouts separated and turned to gallop back from where they'd come and update their commander on their discovery.

This is what the Templars wanted. Under orders from Sir Piers, the scouts were permitted to leave the gorge, and any remaining scouts would remain alive a little longer to maintain the deception.

For now, Sir Piers' ruse was working.

It was a bit uncomfortable remaining crouched and hidden in the rocks, and Odo desperately wanted to stand and stretch his legs. When he heard two galloping horses thunder past, he waited a moment and then cautiously raised his head to observe. Odo turned and looked back down the gorge, but the two lingering scouts were still out of sight. If they became aware of the Templar trap and tried to flee, he would immediately order his men to launch a volley of arrows and bring them down. Under no circumstances would they be allowed to escape and warn the Saracen commander that they rode into an ambuscade.

Sir Piers had earlier stated that any of the Saracen scouts that loitered behind should not be killed. The approaching Saracen force would feel reassured when they saw their scouts in the gorge, and it would further dispel the notion that they were heading into danger.

However, the two remaining scouts were not comfortable and appeared agitated and nervous. Rather than linger at the rear of the gorge, they turned their mounts and began walking back to wait for their leader at the other entrance.

Odo heard them coming and ducked back down. He was poised and ready to raise his bow and shoot if they became aware of the Templar trap.

As before, the scouts scanned the boulders and rocks on either side, but they still did not attempt to dismount and search on foot.

Someone stifled a sneeze. Odo didn't know who. Nonetheless, it was loud enough to be heard by everyone, including the two enemy riders. Immediately the two Saracen scouts responded and panicked. They were experienced enough to know the Templars had prepared an ambuscade, and they fled. Leaning over their horses' necks and with flailing arms and legs, they urged their mounts into a gallop. In fear of their lives, they bolted through the gorge to warn the approaching force of the Templar deception.

Odo didn't wait and yelled to his archers. An arrow was already notched, and the bowstring partly drawn as he stood fully upright. Without pause, he sighted, made a minor adjustment for the slight breeze and the movement of the swiftly moving horse, and then let the bowstring gently slip through his fingers. A heartbeat later, the leading scout was violently flung from his horse with an arrow embedded deeply in his upper back.

His archers obeyed his order and launched a volley of arrows. Only seventeen of the twenty Templar bowmen managed to let loose as three archers fumbled their arrows. Of the seventeen archers, only six arrows found their target.

The second scout suffered a worse and more painful fate, as three smaller arrows suddenly appeared sticking from his back, with another three in his legs. Luckily, the horse was spared. With the dead warrior laying across its neck, the horse immediately slowed and then stopped and began nervously pawing at the ground. Despite the inaccuracy of his archers, Odo was pleased; they had held themselves to good account and obeyed his instructions perfectly. He knew nerves played a part in the fumbling, and he wasn't overly concerned. The sneeze was unfortunate and, sadly, ill-timed, but it wasn't deliberate. The man would be spoken to, but not harshly, for it was just luckless.

Leaving his bow, Odo scrambled over the boulders, slid down into the gorge, and cautiously approached one of the Saracen horses, speaking calmly to soothe the anxious animal. He called for two men to remove the robes worn by the dead scouts and don them along with their conical helmets. Others were assigned to hide the bodies while a few searched for and retrieved fallen arrows. They had to hurry and remove all traces of the brief skirmish.

Soon as the brothers had donned the Saracen garb, Odo gave them instructions to ensure they were easily visible to the Saracen force when they arrived. Then, he told them, "Calmly ride back through the gorge to safety. All had to appear normal."

Odo hoped that a lookout had observed what happened and reported to Sir Piers. To be sure, he sent a messenger back to guarantee that the two pseudo–Saracen scouts weren't killed by eager Templar knights. They didn't have much time; he knew the Saracen would soon be upon them.

The plan was simple, and Sir Piers had outlined his daring ploy the previous evening to confirm that everyone knew their role. About half the Saracen force would be allowed to enter the gorge. At that moment, the archers would unleash their lethal arrows at the middle of the Saracen horsemen who'd entered, essentially splitting the group of twenty or so warriors from the rest. At that moment, the Templar knights would appear from the far end and charge, six abreast through the narrow chasm, to engage the leading Saracen horsemen. Odo's archers would continue to target Saracen at the front of the second group, who, Sir Piers hoped, would be in a state of confusion and trying to turn and exit. Even though the Templars were outnumbered, he believed they would easily overcome the disorganized Saracen and engage the survivors outside the gorge on open land that the Templars preferred, and God willing, with only minimal casualties.

Safely behind his boulder, Odo waited.

CHAPTER TWO

It wasn't a long wait before a telltale dust column became visible and announced to the Templars that the Saracen warriors were quickly approaching. The Saracen were riding hard, and intent on overhauling the Templars, who they believed were unaware of their pursuit and only a short distance away. Already, sunlight glinted off sharpened lances and the lethal curved, scimitars the Saracen warriors preferred to use.

A messenger had been dispatched down the gorge to advise Sir Piers, and Odo felt the familiar feeling of fear and anxiousness begin to overwhelm him. It always happened before battle, and he quelled the urge to be sick with steady breathing and a quick prayer. His mouth was already dry, and he licked his lips in fear. Again, he looked down to ensure the arrow notched to his bow wasn't damaged. His wildly thumping heart threatened to leap from his chest as he nervously waited.

Predictably, it was times like this, immediately before battle, that he questioned his faith and devotion and wondered if God was paying attention to him or would today be the day he was forsaken? He detested waiting; during those times, unbidden thoughts entered his head, creating doubt and uncertainty.

The Saracen slowed, and a lone warrior separated and rode forward, ahead of the mounted pack and pointed down the gorge. Everyone could see the two scouts near the gorge entrance and felt reassured. Resisting the urge to flee, the faux scouts turned and casually began riding down the gorge. Reassured, the Saracen commander yelled a few words of encouragement to his men, dug his heels into his horses' flanks and cantered into the chasm. His men eagerly followed.

The sound of men and horses charging through the gorge was deafening. Already a cloud of choking dust rose, making it difficult to see clearly. But from Odo's elevated position, he could still observe unseen and counted the Saracen as they passed his position.

Fear and anxiety quickly disappeared, his heart settled and slowed, his vision sharpened, and his other senses became acute. Time seemed to slow, and with no thought to his safety and wellbeing, Odo Brus stood like a spectre, his ghostly form rising above the dust, the red cross on his white mantle like a beacon, a harbinger of death.

Odo's first arrow hit a Saracen in the neck and knocked him from his horse in a spray of redness. As he quickly notched another, he saw his men respond. Missiles flew across the chasm. Struck by arrows, warriors began screaming; some fell only to be trampled by the horses behind. Those behind who were untouched saw the carnage ahead and tried to stop and wheel their horses around. As Sir Piers had predicted, the Saracen were panicked and in total disarray.

Twenty archers were not a significant number of men. But in the confines of the gorge, their concentrated efforts at targeting only a handful of warriors were having a devasting effect. Perhaps their accuracy needed improvement, but their rate of fire was impressive.

When Sir Piers emerged on his destrier, followed by thirty-eight Templar knights, Salah al Din's devoted warriors were in a state of turmoil. The Saracen knew they must retreat and exit the gorge or die inside. The first one or two managed to turn safely, then others. Once outside in safety, they attempted to regroup with those who had yet to enter. It was pure pandemonium.

Inside, Sir Piers and his men bore down on the leading group of Saracen who remained in the gorge. In formation and with lances fully extended, the knights crashed into the first twenty Saracen. The smaller Saracen horses stood no chance against the highly trained and much larger, armoured Templar warhorses. The Templar knights were accurate and lethal with their lances. Sergeants brought up the rear with spare horses and weapons, and killed any fallen Saracen warriors still fortunate to be alive. With Sir Piers leading, the Templar knights scythed through the gorge and hoped to break out the other end and fight the remaining Saracen on open ground that better suited them. Already, the Saracen had lost over forty men, and the Templars had yet to receive a scratch.

Odo and his archers could not release any more arrows in fear of hitting Templars. Sir Piers' orders were clear; the archers must retreat down the chasm to safety once the gorge was clear.

Odo turned to spare a look, back towards the fighting at the front entrance of the gorge.

The Saracen were clever; they knew their best chance of surviving was to attack the Templars at the opening of the chasm where the close confines would work against them. Sir Piers was fully aware of what the Saracen wanted, and with urgency, rode hard to break through and exit to open ground. He was stretched out over his horses' neck with his lance fully extended and shield raised as he thundered past Odo.

When his archers could no longer target Saracen warriors without fear of hitting Templars, Odo ordered his archers to withdraw to safety. Needing no encouragement, the brothers quickly scrambled over boulders as he watched to ensure none were injured or attacked during their retreat. With relief, Odo saw his sergeant round the distant bend leading his horse. As soon as he arrived, he would quickly mount his destrier, exchange his bow for a lance, and enter the fray outside.

The ground was littered with bodies, arrows, and discarded weapons. It was never learned what caused Sir Piers' horse to stumble, but the result was terrifying. His destrier's right front leg gave way, and immediately the other leg buckled, and the heavily laden horse dropped, skidding on its knees. There was only one outcome for a Templar rider, with one hand gripping a lance, the other a shield. Sir Piers was catapulted forward, over the horse's neck and crashed heavily to the ground. He lay winded and unmoving.

Seeing the mishap, the nearest Saracen warrior urged his mount forward to drive his lance into the defenceless Templar knight. Odo watched in dread. Without thinking, he leapt from the boulder he stood on and ran towards the stricken Templar knight commander.

Momentarily dazed and unaware that a Saracen warrior was quickly charging towards him from behind, Sir Piers stirred and tried to sit up. His back presented an easy target for the opportunistic Saracen.

Odo launched himself forward and dove for the Templar leader. He crashed hard into his shoulder and sent him sprawling onto his back as a Saracen lance shot past Sir Piers by a whisker, spearing nothing but air until it struck Odo's exposed leg, bounced off his thigh bone and embedded into the rocky ground.

On seeing Sir Piers' horse stumble and his sudden and very unorthodox dismount, then combined with Sir Odo's unexpected appearance, the knights following immediately behind, barely managed to avoid trampling and colliding into them.

Upon seeing their leader's mishap and fretful of his survival, the two closest knights desperately tried to intercept the attacking Saracen warrior. They were too far away to prevent the first thrust of the lance at Sir Piers, but they were close enough to prevent a second attempt. With renewed purpose, the enraged knights quickly dispatched the warrior and trusted that those behind would come to the aid of Sir Piers and Sir Odo.

The Templars poured from the gorge in a cloud of dust, immediately spread out, and wreaked havoc on the remaining and disorganized Saracen with clinical precision. Overcome by the intensity of the Templar attack, many Saracen fled when they saw their leader succumb to a fatal sword blow. The fight was brief, but for the victorious Templars, they spent no time celebrating.

Three Templars suffered minor wounds from Saracen arrows, two more received minor injuries from Saracen blades, but thankfully, none were killed or seriously maimed, except for one. Sir Piers was unharmed and mainly suffered from a head bump and a loss of dignity from the incident. However, his life was fortunately spared due to the selfless act of bravery from Sir Odo Brus, but jovial they weren't; each man knew the wound to Odo's leg was critical.

As soon as was conveniently possible, a wagon was brought forth, and Odo was gently hoisted and placed onto it. Priests in green robes immediately began cleansing the deep wound. They had learned from the Saracen surgeons of the Holy Lands, whose medical skills were far superior to their own, and began dousing Odo's injured leg with an antiseptic tincture known as the Elixir of Jerusalem. Made from aloe vera, hemp and palm wine, the potent cocktail was renowned for its curative and restorative properties. Once clean, they used plant fibres to sew the wound closed.

As a result of his fall, Sir Piers suffered minor lacerations to his head, but he brushed away any attempts to help him. His immediate concern was for Odo Brus, and as everyone knew, the chances of surviving such a severe injury without proper treatment were doubtful.

"We must make haste, Frankia isn't far away, and if we hurry, Sir Odo may yet be spared," he solemnly informed his men. There wasn't a soul amongst them who didn't enjoy the pleasure and company of Odo

Brus, and no one had cause to disagree with their leader. Young Odo was dedicated, pious, intelligent, and fought with remarkable and unique skills. His infectious laugh gladdened the hearts of many, yet he took life seriously and was fully committed to the order of The Poor Fellow-Soldiers of Christ and of the Temple of Solomon.

The day was still young, and rather than make camp, preparations were made to continue northwards immediately. While Sir Piers needed to meet with the King of Frankia urgently, his primary concern was for the survival of the young knight.

Sir Odo Brus had unselfishly risked his own life to save him, and Sir Piers privately conceded, his own near-death experience burdened him somewhat. He was eternally grateful and knew that God had blessed Odo and thus enabled the young man to come to his aid and save him when he should have died. Sir Piers looked down at his trembling hands and prayed. He gave thanks to the All-Mighty for sparing his life and asked his Lord for another selfless boon; to protect and spare the injured young Templar knight from misery and a painful death from a corrupted wound.

Other Templars also prayed for Odo's speedy recovery, but none more than the legendary leader of the Knights Templar, Sir Piers de Aubert.

Every jolt in the wagon caused him unbearable agony, and with some awareness, he knew his wound was more than severe. He had seen others with similar injuries and believed that, in most likelihood, it would kill him. Priests gave him undiluted wine, a rarity indeed, but it did little good to ease the pain. He tightly closed his eyes and desperately tried not to scream when the wagon rolled over a rock or bounced into a rut. The hours passed in agonizing slowness, the days and nights lasted an eternity, and Odo suffered. Despite the administrations of the well-intentioned priests, the wound festered, and as feared, corruption set in.

Commanded by Sir Piers de Aubert, the Templar contingent made good time and entered Frankia sooner than predicted and headed directly for Clugny, just north of Lugdunum[5]. However, Odo's condition continued to deteriorate, and Sir Piers hoped that it wasn't too late and ensured he would be afforded the best medical care available to recover and convalesce.

The Benedictine monks at the *Abbaye de Clugny* greeted Sir Piers and his exhausted knights warmly. The abbey was enormous, and most knights marvelled at the size and number of buildings that occupied the extensive grounds. Without delay, Abbot Eduin had Odo moved to a hall with other afflicted men and promised Sir Piers the young knight would be seen to by his best medical specialists. Feeling reassured by the abbot, Sir Piers and his contingent quickly departed Clugny and made directly for Lugdunum, where he had matters to attend to with the king and promised to return soon.

------

5 Lugdunum - Modern day, Lyon, France

CHAPTER THREE

"Take the leg, cut it off!" Odo screamed. He lay bathed in sweat and writhed in agony.

The monk looked down at him in sympathy and nodded. "It will be so. We have already called for a surgeon. Once he arrives, we will prepare."

Odo's eyes closed, and again he was inconscient. A state he drifted in and out of that afforded him some respite. The monk looked on in pity for a moment, mouthed a few silent words and walked away to attend to another ailing man.

The hall where Odo lay was situated near the abbey's gate entrance and the expansive grounds beyond. Villagers came and went. Some delivered food, others were labourers performing work, repairing rooves, buildings, or whatever needed fixing. Others came for guidance or to pray. People were everywhere, and the abbey was typically busy.

A woman entered the abbey grounds with her son straggling behind. She slowed a little, waited for him to catch up, then placed a hand on his back, ushered him close, and walked towards one of the buildings. His head swivelled from side to side as he marvelled at the structures and sights that interested a boy of about five years old.

She knew which building to visit, as she'd been to the abbey a few times in the past. As always, she sought to offer solace and comfort to the sick and injured men who lay in woeful despair. Less frequently, she offered advice. Initially, the attending monks were reticent about allowing a woman to enter their domain. However, she was observant of Christian tenets, kept her head covered, and did not talk unnecessarily. Her son was well behaved, respectful, and his demeanour affirmed to them that she was a moral, Christian woman of virtue.

She entered the dark hall and frowned. *The shutters should be open*, she tut-tutted again, as she did every time she visited. Immediately she paused, allowed her eyes to adjust to the gloom, and walked to the nearest cot and, with a kindly manner, began to speak to the ailing man. After a few moments, she reached into a bag and handed him an apple. She moved to another bed, then another, and always with her son at her side. The men who spent lonely days and nights in the dark hall welcomed her visitations and kind, uplifting words.

Twelve of the twenty cots positioned around the perimeter of the small hall were occupied, and a few dedicated monks tended to those who needed treatment with genuine care. Primarily, they ministered to the sick, sometimes an injury and, more infrequently, a battle wound. They replaced the straw that covered the earthen floor every few weeks or so, dispensed water, food and wine to their patients and cleaned them when needed. Above all, they ensured visitors were kept to a minimum and did not disrupt their orderly and structured routine.

The woman stood beside the bed of a man whom she'd never seen before, a new patient. He lay bathed in sweat and moaned incoherently. Her eyebrows furrowed as she examined his body and settled on the filthy bandages that wrapped his thigh. Her son obediently remained at her side and watched with equal fascination.

She spoke quietly, words intended only for her son to hear. She turned her head and looked around the hall. No one was paying her any interest. With utmost care, she sat on the cot and began to remove the bandages. Her touch was gentle, and if it bothered the man, he gave no indication. Slowly the festering wound became visible, and she leaned forward to inspect it more closely. She sniffed and peered at the redness and foul liquids that seeped from the gruesome gash. She looked thoughtful and again spoke softly to her son. She was so engrossed that she never heard the footsteps of approaching men and jumped when they spoke.

"What is it ye are doing? This isn't permitted," the monk said quietly. He never raised his voice in the hall, but his disquiet was evident.

With her hand, she moved aside a strand of hair that fell over her eyes and looked up at the monk intently. "This wound is devilish; it must be–"

"We will attend to the leg and remove it, forthwith," interrupted the monk.

The other man with the monk, a surgeon, stepped closer and looked at the exposed wound. He didn't react to the ghastly inflamed slash that oozed foulness.

No one saw Odo open his red-rimmed eyes except the boy.

The woman took a breath, "I can save his leg. I have not much time, but save it, I can," she offered with unwavering conviction.

Both the monk and the surgeon shook their heads simultaneously. "Nay, it is too far gone; he will die if it is not removed," the monk responded.

"He may not survive the amputation," she replied.

Neither man couldn't disagree with her assertion.

Odo groaned, the involuntary sound escaped his lips, and all heads turned to him. "Cut it off, please. The pain…"

"It is not too late, I can save it," she pleaded. "Allow me two days. In two days, ye will see an improvement. If I fail, then do as he wishes, but two days is not much to ask."

"Not if ye are him," the surgeon moved his heavy bag of surgical tools to his other hand and pointed to Odo. "Fer two days in agony is a lifetime, is it not?"

"She can, she can heal ye, kind sir," said the boy speaking for the first time." He nodded his head in naïve childish support of his claim.

The woman reached over and pulled her son closer. "Sir, with the Lord's guidance, I can heal him." She turned from the monk and looked down at Odo. "I know ye are miserable with torment, but grant me this, let me heal ye?"

Odo swallowed with difficulty and focused his watery eyes on the monk. He wouldn't communicate directly with her – he wasn't allowed. His Templar vows prevented him from speaking to women. He shifted his gaze and then looked at the boy who stared back at him with wide, open eyes. Odo didn't know why but felt the woman could be trusted. Slowly he exhaled. "Grant… grant her two… two days."

She rose from the cot. "I will return soonest." Without waiting for the monk to challenge her or the patient's decision, she grabbed her son's hand

and strode quickly from the hall.

The woman returned not long after, and without seeking permission, she again carefully removed Odo's soiled bandages and gently cleaned the exposed gash as best she could. Someone had roughly sewn the wound together with plant fibres, but in a few places, the fine strands had separated, and the gash had reopened. Once she'd cleaned the corruption and the surrounding area with clean water, she placed leaches along the length of the gash and then wrapped the leg with a clean cloth. The boy watched the process in fascination.

Odo occasionally opened his eyes but was delirious and totally unaware of her administrations. When she was finished, she sought the monk and explained that in two days, she would return. "Until then," she resolutely stated, "do not remove the cloth or touch the wound." While she spoke softly and respectfully, the tone of her voice was firm and left no room for misinterpretation.

The monk saw no reason to argue with her. In his opinion, the knight would most likely die either way. He nodded his head in agreement. It will be as ye ask."

The following two days were pure agony for Odo, and had he been capable of rational thought, he would have questioned his decision to allow the leg to remain. The monk had spoken to a superior about the woman's outlandish claim. It was agreed that they should allow her the opportunity to do what she could for the Templar knight, after all, they admitted, the leg should have been removed days earlier, and there was no guarantee that he would even survive the traumatic ordeal of amputation. There was nothing to lose by allowing her to continue.

On the afternoon of the second day, the woman arrived with her son, and she began making her rounds and visiting the patients in the hall. She gave fruit to those who could eat, offered words of encouragement with a smile, and moved on to the next. Eventually, she arrived at the cot of the injured knight.

She looked closely at his face. While his eyes were closed, she could see the young man was still afflicted and deeply troubled. Gently, she leaned forward and placed a hand on his brow. His skin felt hot to the touch. She frowned and turned her attention to his leg, and began to carefully remove the bandages.

Her expression never changed when the wound was revealed. Carefully the leeches were removed, and she leaned forward and examined the gash. As she was apt to do, she spoke to her son, pointed to various places of the injury, and explained what she observed. She was succinct and, with patience, carefully instructed him. Although still young, he would acquire all the knowledge and skills she imparted to him over time.

Much of the redness and swelling had decreased, while still inflamed, the leeches had done their task and eaten the dead skin and toxins; the miracle of their unusual gift never failed to amaze her. "Man kills, nature heals," she simply told her son. "Never forget."

She reached into the large bag she always carried and removed a small parcel wrapped in cloth that she had prepared earlier. She unfolded the package and carefully placed it on the bed, removed various items, and meticulously arranged them over the exposed wound. Captivated by her administrations, the boy closely observed.

Earlier, she'd pounded roots into a pulp, and with the utmost care, she placed the mash directly over the gash and sutures. Then, over that, she positioned moss, lichen, and an assortment of crushed leaves of various sizes and descriptions. Finally, she rebandaged the leg. Her patient hadn't stirred.

With her son's assistance, she cleaned her mess, and with her boy following, she began to leave the hall when the monk approached. "How fares our sufferer?"

She averted her eyes as she knew her presence made the monk feel uncomfortable. "There is improvement, but he still ails. I have replaced the dressing and, I ask, please, do not remove it fer another two days. He will recover."

The monk looked thoughtful. "Let me see." He walked towards the Templar knight to observe. It was plainly evident, the knight rested and appeared less troubled. Indeed, there had been some improvement, as she claimed, and notwithstanding his prediction, the wounded knight's condition had not deteriorated. He nodded. "Very well."

She respectfully dipped her head and, clutching the boy's hand, hurriedly left the hall.

Odo opened his eyes and felt terrible. After a few deep breaths, he was able to slightly move his head, and he looked down, wondering if he'd see his leg. He'd dreamed a surgeon had placed his leg on a chopping block, and with a hefty axe, lopped it off. To his surprise, the leg remained.

The torment had eased considerably, and although he still felt the effects of the trauma with exhaustion, thirst, ague, and of course, pain, he felt significantly better than he had.

The past days were lost to him, there was little he remembered, and he was unsure if what he recalled was real or just part of his troubled and tormented dreams. He tried to make sense of it... a woman... a boy... He wanted to cast his thoughts aside, it was wrong to be thinking of women, and he felt the guilt. He closed his eyes and fell into a restful sleep.

She returned with the boy, and this time, she saw the knight was awake and attentive. Acquainted with Templar protocols, she did not speak to him and dipped her head to avoid eye contact. Rather than act familiar and sit on the edge of the cot, she lowered herself onto the straw-covered earth as she softly began to hum a melody and focused on his leg.

As carefully as she could, she slowly unwound the bandage and peeled the remains of the moss, leaves and pulp from the gash and studied it.

Ever curious, the monk wandered over, stood behind her and looked over her shoulder at the wound. He crossed himself and muttered a few words of prayer. "T'is but a miracle," he said and shook his head in disbelief.

"What? What has happened?" Odo asked the monk.

From the folds of his robe, the monk produced a cross and clutched it tightly to his chest. "God has seen fit to spare yer leg and life, milord. I believe it not, but my eyes do not deceive." With the realization of a new thought, his eyebrows furrowed together. "Did ye cast a spell, use sorcery?" he took a step backwards and raised the cross protectively to ward off evil spirits.

The woman shifted position slightly to better see the monk. "Did ye see what I removed from the wound? They were from plants and roots, and ye did not hear incantations fer I uttered none. This man is healing because of medicaments from the earth." She ignored the ridiculous allegations and turned back to the knight's leg.

The monk gave her reply some consideration. He had not heard her cast a spell... If she had, then indeed, someone would have told him. He relaxed and exhaled, then swallowed away his fear and turned to the knight who looked at him inquisitively. "Yer wound is healing, milord. I believe it not, but this woman has given ye back yer leg and life."

"Then I offer my gratitude and thanks to her and God," Odo stated. He took a few deep breaths to steady himself. He still felt weak and slightly disoriented.

The boy watched and listened to the exchange with curiosity and then turned his attention to his mother, who began repacking the wound with her unique combination of root pulp and leaves. The monk continued to observe as the woman finished her task and rewrapped the leg with a clean, unsoiled cloth. When completed, she eased herself back to her feet, reached inside her bag, and handed the boy an apple.

"Milord?" asked the boy.

Odo blinked open his eyes.

"Ma says I should give ye this." he handed the apple to the knight and took a step closer to his mother.

This was awkward for Odo. He wanted to offer thanks, but his vows prevented him from speaking directly to her. "Tell yer *maman* I am very grateful fer all she has done to help me. God has blessed her with this gift of healing. I am forever in her debt." He looked at the apple. "Thank ye fer yer help too."

Imminently pleased at the compliment, the boy looked up at his mother, and she smiled with pride at him.

"My name is Odo Brus; what is yer name?"

The boy turned his head, squared his shoulders, and stood a little straighter. "Milord, my name is Cathal," he said proudly.

Odo was exhausted and wanted to sleep. "I hope to see ye again, Cathal."

The woman reached down, grabbed her son by the hand, turned and began to walk from the hall. The monk watched a moment, then called after her. "Wait!"

She stopped, and the monk approached.

"Why is it ye do this and come to these men and help?" he asked.

With his eyes closed, Odo slightly turned his head to better listen.

"Because I can," was her simple reply.

The monk laughed, "So can I, but that is not an answer."

She sighed softly. "If ye saw a man, a woman, or a child fall to the ground before ye, would ye stop to help?"

The monk looked puzzled, "If they weren't heathens or unclean… then, er, of course."

"Then how is it ye know if they are heathens or unclean?" she asked.

The monk thought of a suitable response.

Undeterred, she continued. "Ye pass judgement on them, I do not judge, fer *all* are worthy of help, and because I can help them, then I do."

The monk scratched at something on his neck and found himself staring at her back as she departed the hall. The boy, a step behind, looked over his shoulder at him.

Three days later, a commotion caused Odo to look towards the door. With a broad smile, he recognized the six Templars who strode confidently inside.

CHAPTER FOUR

Against the advice of the monks who administered to Odo, Sir Piers decided to relocate him. The journey from *Abbaye de Clugny* to *Château de Caen* took its toll on Odo's already weakened body. While the roads were not as rough, and he experienced far less discomfort than the last time he was transported on a wagon, he was poorly when the Templar contingent arrived at the grand *château,* and Sir Piers was distraught.

Before Odo departed from the abbey, the monk told Sir Piers that the spear had hit the bone of his leg with some force. The lingering pain was the result of the brutal impact on his thigh bone. "By a miracle of God and sufficient rest," he assured, "Sir Odo will experience a full and complete recovery." Removing the young knight was ill-advised, and he vigorously protested Sir Piers' decision to take Odo by wagon to another town.

On arrival at in *Caen,* Odo was immediately taken to a *hospitium*[6], called *Hôtel-Dieu,* which was conveniently close to *Château de Caen*

---

6   *Hospitium – A place of shelter most often administered by monks or priests.*

where Sir Piers and the other Templars would be residing as guests of Duke William X. Ongoing care at the *hospitium* would be provided by laymen overseen by a priest.

Sir Piers ordered the young knight to remain bedridden at *Hôtel-Dieu* and gave instructions to Priest Francis that Odo should be well fed and gave his permission to ignore the Templar rule where meat was only eaten three times a week.

Priest Francis was inherently uncomfortable in the presence of Templar knights; he didn't trust them and felt their power and grandstanding was far removed from the tenets of the Church. However, Sir Piers had convinced him that Odo's care and recovery were proportionate to the generous gratuity the Templar's would bequeath on his departure. The heedful priest readily agreed, and with his personal objections to the Templars cast aside, welcomed Odo Brus and set about ensuring the young knight regained his health expeditiously.

Before the Templar leader departed for the *château*, he stood at Odo's bed and said, "Ye will feast like a king. Rest and recover, Sir Odo."

Sir Piers returned to *Château de Caen*, which was only a brisk, short walk away and made final arrangements to meet with William X, who held the titles, Duke of Aquitaine, Duke of Gascony, and the Count of Poitou. An important and influential noble. Duke William had requested guidance from the Templars about a pilgrimage he wished to take to *Santiago de Compostela* in northwestern Spain. In return, the duke promised, the Templars would receive his loyalty and support, which, as Sir Piers knew, was vital if he wanted to bolster Templar recruitment.

While the *Hôtel-Dieu* was diligently managed by a priest, its day-to-day operation was quite relaxed and far removed from the order Odo experienced at *Abbaye de Clugny*. People came and went with unusual frequency, and there were times when all he sought was quietness to reflect, pray, reaffirm his devotion to the Church, heal, and recover his strength. It wasn't to be.

It was early evening, and darkness had begun to settle over Caen. The shadows lengthened, and spluttering smoky candles lit the room. A constant stream of visitors was coming to see him, and not long earlier, Odo's sergeant had visited and only recently left. Totally exhausted, Odo managed, with some difficulty, to roll onto his side to sleep. He felt the presence of someone nearby and opened his eyes and rotated his head to complain. Instantly, he shut his mouth and turned away. A young woman stood at his cot.

She held a candle, and its flickering flame lit her face. In the briefest of instants, he saw her, and he was taken back. She was beautiful. He swallowed and instantly felt shame for allowing his mind to acknowledge her beauty. His heart began thumping madly, and he sought the resolve and willpower to think of something that didn't provoke his imaginative impure thoughts.

"Why are ye here?" she asked. Her voice was soft and mellow, and to his ear, she was well-spoken.

Thankfully, she couldn't see his face. He kept his eyes tightly closed and didn't reply.

He felt rather than heard her move slightly. There was a lengthy pause before she spoke again. "I come here to talk to the sick… many who are here are lonely…."

Odo wanted to answer but couldn't; Templar vows were clear, he wasn't permitted to communicate to women. He wanted her to leave – to go away. His heart pounded.

"I will return tomorrow," she said. "I hope ye fare better."

Again, he felt her move, and to his relief, she walked away. Then there was silence and eventually sleep.

She returned to visit every day, always at the same time, and just as the sun descended. Like the woman and boy from *Abbaye de Clugny*, she spoke to all the ailing men in the house and offered words of cheer to them all. Each time she came to his bed, Odo ensured he faced away from her.

"I'm told ye are a gallant knight and suffered a critical wound to yer leg?" she said on the third evening of her nightly visits.

Odo remained unresponsive.

"And ye saved the life of Sir Piers at risk of yer own."

How did she know, and who had she spoken with? He wanted her to go away and allow him peace. *Doesn't she know what she is doing?* he wondered.

"I know why ye won't talk to me," she suddenly said as if reading his mind. "I find it absurd; God gave ye a voice, a gift, and with yer voice, ye can make others feel good. To not speak is rude and unkindly…."

Odo wanted to scream and felt his face redden.

Again, there was a pause. It seemed to him that she wanted to say more but didn't – like she held back. "…I wish ye well."

He heard a swish of skirts, and she walked away. He turned over and saw her at the door. As it opened, a man-at-arms appeared. Then she stepped through and was gone.

His heart and breathing settled, and he began to relax. *Who is she?* he wondered.

No one he asked knew the young woman's identity who visited each night, and he didn't feel it appropriate to push the issue. It would be unseemly if a Templar knight were seen to be inquisitive about a beautiful young woman.

With a good diet, his strength slowly returned, and each day saw a moderate improvement. He'd lost significant weight and muscle over the past weeks, and on the recommendation of Priest Francis, was permitted to begin walking. At first, it was just a few steps. It felt painful to put weight on his injured leg, but the hurt lessened after a day or two, and he began to exercise in earnest for short periods daily.

The beautiful young woman still came each evening, and he was always the last visitor she spoke with. She'd stand quietly at his bed for a few moments and then always ask a question or two. He never replied and, as before, always made sure he turned away from her. After a while, she'd say farewell and leave, always with the man-at-arms who waited outside.

She persisted with her visits, although it mattered not, tomorrow he'd leave this dreary place and would stay at the *château* with the Templars. He couldn't wait and longed to be back with the others in full health and resume his life as a Templar knight and not as an invalid.

The injury to his leg had robbed him of strength and stamina. Although he was regaining weight, he could only walk for short periods, and while sitting on a horse proved to be quite painful, riding was out of the question. With a sense of foreboding, Sir Piers probed and asked questions about his fitness in some detail.

After leaving *Hôtel-Dieu,* and arriving at the *Château de Caen,* Sir Piers took him aside and spoke succinctly. "Brother Odo, in three days, we depart fer Jerusalem, and ye are not yet able to travel with us. Ye must remain here a while longer."

Odo opened his mouth to protest, but the look on Sir Piers' face spoke volumes. Wisely, he closed it.

"Ye don't need me to tell ye that ye can't fight. Ye can't even sit astride a horse," Sir Piers shook his head. "Ye have to regain yer health and cogency. Ye will remain here, as a guest of Duke William until ye are strong enough to mount yer destrier and defend yerself. Templars will come here from the north in six months, and then ye will travel with them to Jerusalem. Ye have time to prepare."

Odo was thoroughly disappointed but also knew Sir Piers spoke wisely. He nodded in reluctant agreement. He'd expected as much.

The older Templar clapped him on the back. "On the morrow, the duke is honouring us with a feast. There will be many important people in attendance. We need their support, Odo. Ye can assist me by talking with them."

Odo nodded. "As ye wish, Sir Piers."

Sir Piers smiled. "It gladdens my heart to see ye alive and regaining yer health." He turned and walked away.

The feast was all it promised to be. Duke William had invited nobles and knights who arrived with pomp and splendour. *Jongleurs*[7] sang of battles past and storied victories. Wine flowed, and food aplenty was distributed in abundance to all. It was reported that some knights would contend in games of martial skill, but for the Templars, they would observe only; they didn't compete for sport.

Again, Sir Piers allowed his men to eat all they could and refrained from enforcing Templar vows of non-indulgence. "We need our strength. Eat heartily, for the road to Jerusalem is fraught with danger and hardship," he exclaimed to all.

Duke William allocated an area where the Templars could eat and enjoy themselves in relative privacy. Sergeants and Templar brothers kept curious womenfolk from straying too close and creating an unwelcome distraction for the devout and pious Templars.

Odo sat uncomfortably on a wooden seat, as his wound caused him discomfort when he sat for any length of time. Around him, men were becoming increasingly loud and boisterous and heartened by wine and good cheer, tongues and observance loosened. Seeking peace and solitude, Odo quietly excused himself, and with the aid of a staff, exited the area and limped around the side of the sprawling *château* and its massive walls, to where he hoped to find seclusion to pray and reflect.

---

7 *Jongleur – Minstrel or singer.*

Château de Caen was enormous and sat atop a low hill that overlooked Caen. It was truly spectacular, and Odo had never seen such a large castle before. Slowly he walked away from the festivities, around the outside perimeter and approached the rear of the *château.*

Below, fields of golden wheat swayed in the warm afternoon breeze, and he stopped to look at the panorama laid out before him. A small cluster of trees stood sentinel beside a small decorative structure that looked to be used as a place to sit in shade and comfort. He heard voices, and rather than disturb them, made his way to the trees to enjoy the vista and beauty before him.

The voices grew louder, and in annoyance, Odo decided to leave when he heard a woman's yell of admonishment, then a cry of fear. He pried himself from the tree he leaned against and walked curiously towards the structure surrounded by small decorative plants. Odo navigated around the garden with the utmost care, cautiously approached the front of the structure and then saw her. He recognized her at once; she was the young woman who came to visit him every evening when he lay bedridden in *Hôtel-Dieu.* However, and most alarming, an unknown *chevalier* was attempting to force his will on her.

Odo took in the scene at once. The *Chevalier*[8] was tall and presumably a guest of Duke William, but his behaviour was most unbecoming and totally improper.

As yet, no one had seen him, then she screamed when the knight roughly pulled her head back to kiss her.

Odo took a step closer. "What goes on here, explain yerself!" he fumed.

---

8 *Chevalier - French knight.*

The knight immediately turned to face the unexpected voice. The young woman who'd been forced against the wall quickly scooted away out of reach of the amorous knight.

CHAPTER FIVE

"Are you hurt?" Odo asked her. Her wellbeing took precedence over his vows.

"Thank ye, Sir Knight, your appearance is most welcome."

Odo turned back to the Frankian *chevalier,* who had taken an aggressive step closer towards him. He could see the knight was perturbed by the red cross emblazoned on the white mantle he wore that identified him as a Templar. But his dark eyes gave his violent intentions away. Odo raised his staff and pushed it onto the knight's chest, preventing him from approaching closer. The young woman stepped behind Odo to safety.

"You interfere, Templar, take yer leave," stated the Frankian knight and thrust out his chest in challenge.

A sword swung from the knight's belt, while other than the staff, only a walking aid, Odo was unarmed. Regardless, he felt no fear. However, his leg was causing him some pain, and the knight was astute to see the Templar was injured and weakened.

Odo met the hostile gaze of the knight, and despite the pain from his leg, didn't turn away.

It was a stand-off. After a dozen heartbeats and with a curse, the knight pushed aside the staff and strode angrily away. In the distance, he saw a lone man-at-arms approach and step around the angry *chevalier* as he stormed past.

Odo almost fell; he needed to rest and stumbled towards a seat in the structure. The young woman held his arm and helped him to sit.

"You must report this," Odo said after gathering himself. "Do ye know who he is?" He wouldn't look at her and instead gazed over the crops and fields below.

"Aye, he is *Chevalier* Jean Courteney, from Burgundy. An unpleasant man who seeks my hand in marriage. Father does not hold him in high regard." She sat down beside him.

"Ye must inform yer father of this, and he should enlighten Duke William. Such behaviour is…."

She laughed. "I will not say anything. In two days, he will take his leave, and until then, I will be more wary." She turned from him and looked out across the countryside. "I come here to this place because of the quiet and beauty. The sights below are truly magnificent, and I rejoice in the view… he sent my guard away.

"Yer guard…" Odo stated

"Aye, father assigns a man-at-arms to watch over me, but he is intimidated by the *chevalier.*"

Odo's eyebrows knitted together, and without thinking, he turned to face her. "Who is yer father?"

"Fer a man so unwilling to talk to me while ye lay bedridden in misery, ye are happy to speak now," she laughed.

Odo felt his face flush and looked away. If his leg weren't causing pain, he would have walked off.

She felt his reaction. "Fergive me, oh gallant knight, I am Josceline Poitiers, but I have not had the pleasure of yer introduction."

Odo couldn't help himself and turned towards her. Her beauty struck him hard in the chest and rendered him speechless. He coughed. "Then, then, ye are…" he gasped between coughing, "…the daughter of Duke William."

They both turned at the sound of raised voices and footsteps as a group of men arrived. Odo was about to stand when Sir Piers, and a noble he recognised as Duke William, flanked by men-at-arms, suddenly appeared. The *chevalier*, Sir Jean Courteney, appeared last, along with another *chevalier* he wasn't familiar with.

"Papa," greeted Josceline in surprise.

"Are ye unhurt, did he harm ye?" asked Duke William and gave Odo a look of contempt.

Sir Piers' face was scarlet in silent rage.

"Methinks the Templar has been in the Maghreb[9] with camels and the uncivilized savages for too long, his behaviour is disgusting," retorted Jean Courteney with a sneer.

Odo shot to his feet and grimaced at the effort and then quickly raised his staff to strike at the *chevalier* only to have it batted down by Sir Piers.

"It was nothing; I'm not hurt," Josceline quickly responded in puzzlement. She looked like she was about to question her father's appearance when Sir Piers spoke.

---

9 *Maghreb – the near east, or more commonly known as the far east.*

"Sir Odo, ye have shamed us all. I am truly dismayed."

"What is this? I have done nothing to be ashamed of!" Odo appealed. He looked past the Templar leader at the Frankian knight, who was still sneering at him.

Josceline placed her hand on Odo's arm. "Papa, I think ye misunderstand. This fine Templar knight came to my aid and prevented *Chevalier* Courteney from molesting me."

Sir Piers looked confused. "Does she speak the truth?" he asked.

Odo nodded. "I was standing by the tree, Sir Piers, and...."

"He lies," yelled Jean Courteney, "she and the Templar were together in embrace, *Mon Seigneur*[10], I saw them." He shook his head in disgust.

Duke William sat at a seat inside the *château*, Sir Piers stood at his side. Odo was also seated and faced both older men while *Chevalier* Courteney stood a short distance away near the room's rear with folded arms.

Odo could see that Sir Piers was absolutely livid, and while he expected the duke to be furious, he appeared somewhat calm and rational.

It was the duke who decided that further discussion should take place inside the *château*. He had spoken with his daughter, Josceline, for quite some time in private, while Odo, Sir Piers and the *chevalier* patiently waited in tense silence.

The duke had just returned to the room and taken his seat. He cleared his throat and paused until he held everyone's attention. "I am deeply distressed. What I have learned shocks me, fer I have placed trust in men and welcomed them into my home. In return, they have abused and

---

10 *Mon Seigneur – French – My lord.*

forsaken that trust." He turned slowly and made eye contact with everyone. "After intimidating and threatening her protector, the guard I assigned to watch over her, and by then sending him away, my youngest daughter fell victim to the unwelcome advances of *Chevalier* Jean Courteney."

"*Mon Seigneur*!" appealed Jean Courteney.

"Silence!" bellowed Duke William, his anger now palpable. He took a deep breath and paused again, this time to gather his thoughts and calm himself. "I spoke to the man-at-arms, and his account supports what my daughter told me." He turned to Sir Piers and nodded solemnly, then faced Odo. "Fergive me, and please accept my apologies and *merci*, yer gallant intrusion was, er, timely and appropriate. Ye, fine sir, have not offended me or dishonoured yer order."

Odo felt the relief. He looked at Sir Piers, who seemed to slump as his pent-up rage dissolved.

The duke wasn't finished yet. "*Chevalier* Jean Courteney, ye are no longer welcome at *Château de Caen* or ever to be again in the presence of my daughter. I will no longer offer ye cheer or haven. Ye are free to take yer leave."

The *chevalier* glared at the duke. "I must protest. This is most unjust; I have acted in accord; wait until my father learns of this."

The duke's face remained impassive. "I can have ye escorted…."

Jean Courtney glowered at the duke, then turned and gave Odo an equally disdainful look before acknowledging the duke's request. "*Mon Seigneur*," he said and appropriately dipped his head, then turned back to face Odo with his jaw tightly clenched.

Odo tensed and fully expected the *chevalier* to strike.

To everyone's relief, he abruptly spun and stalked angrily from the room.

When the reverberant sound of the heavy door slamming shut, faded. Sir Piers moved to stand in front of Duke William. "Why would he fabricate such a story? I confess to being puzzled, milord."

"*Chevalier* Jean Courteney has long sought the affection of my daughters. Initially, he had eyes for her older sister Eleanor, and when scorned by her, and against my wishes, he turned his attentions on Josceline." The duke looked thoughtful and paused briefly. "Sir Piers, far be it for me to dictate who should take the hand of my fine daughters in marriage. I believe, and against the fervent wishes of their mother, that they, only they should choose and decide fer themselves - I want nothing but happiness fer them. Both my daughters have expressed revulsion at the behaviour of Jean Courteney, and I believe he sought favour with me and incorrectly believed that I would accept *his* word over that of my daughter." He looked at Odo. "Thank ye again, I owe ye my gratitude. As promised, ye will remain here as my guest fer as long as needed."

Sir Piers looked like the weight of the world had been lifted from his shoulders. "Thank ye, milord."

Odo stood near the portcullis, the gated entrance to *Château de Caen,* and watched as his brother Templars departed with some sadness. Sir Piers and his sergeant stood at his side with their horses. All the knights looked impressive on their powerful destriers as they rode past. With their shiny armour and colourful pendants flying proudly, even townsfolk stopped to watch as the Templars slowly rode from the *château.* As each knight passed him by, they offered a friendly word of support and a smile. Even the sergeants and brothers who followed behind acknowledged him with a kindly word and a wave.

When the last man exited the *château*, Sir Piers turned to him. "Rest and recover, Odo, we will rejoice when we see ye within the year. Good health, and may the Lord watch over ye." With some difficulty, he mounted his horse, gave a wave, and rode to catch the column with his sergeant following on his left flank.

Odo stood unmoving long after the last man had ridden from sight. He felt saddened, yet at the same time believed that if Sir Piers had waited just a week longer, he would have been healthy enough to accompany them back to Jerusalem.

Did they abandon me? His mood turned reflective and soured as he considered his devotion and what he'd become.

He reasoned that he was a faceless knight who would fight without question for the Church and for what the Church believed. Certainly, he wasn't a man because he'd forsaken those liberties when he gave his vows. He was just a faceless, obedient, Christian warrior. "I am a faceless knight," he said quietly to himself. *What have I become?* He grimaced and decided to walk around the perimeter of the *château* again. He hoped that if he exercised over the next few days, he could ride a horse without pain and discomfort and catch up with Sir Piers.

He walked twice around and then stopped near the stand of trees where he'd first stood when the duke's daughter had been molested. After the exercise, his leg throbbed, and he sat gratefully beneath the tree to rest. He closed his eyes in despair as he realized his leg wouldn't heal sufficiently to permit him to ride anytime soon.

"I find this place my favourite, fer nowhere but here are quietness and peace to be found," said Josceline.

His eyes opened, then just as quickly snapped closed again as he saw her approach from the side. He should have moved, walked away, but he couldn't. He remained seated as his cheeks reddened. He heard her move to stand directly in front of him.

"Do ye prefer busy, noisy streets or the stillness of forested hills?" she asked.

He could tell she faced away from him because of her voice. Unbidden, his eyes opened on their own accord, and he stared and took in her form... her golden hair... even her smell. He breathed her in, ...her fragrance... she stood so close. It was an awakening, like waking from a troubled sleep to find it was only a dream – but this wasn't a dream. She must have had her hands clasped because slowly, they lowered. His eyes followed as her arms descended to her sides, hanging loosely and relaxed. Her fingers were long and slender... He felt his cheeks redden.

He wanted to tell her the view was spectacular from where he sat. But then felt the shame of his thoughts. But try as he may, he couldn't turn away or close his eyes.

Josceline may be beautiful, but a waif, she isn't, he reasoned. Behind her golden tresses and beautiful clothes, he sensed her inner strength. She was formidable, she would challenge, and above all, he sensed, she possessed a sharp wit. No wonder her father allows her such freedoms because if he didn't, she would wear him down and make his life miserable.

He smiled and felt an unfamiliar warmth descend over him.

He almost laughed aloud as he realized she deliberately stood with her back to him. She knew he stared at her. He was so absorbed; he never noticed her head had turned, and she, in turn, was studying him.

They burst out laughing together. At first, it was a simple short laugh, then expanded into a howl of merriment. The laughter was spontaneous and natural and erupted from deep within. It released anxiety, worry, pent up frustrations and even pain. He felt uplifted and light. His earlier feeling of disappointment melted away as they both laughed at the silliness.

Her laughter was musical and unforced, her eyes crinkled, and he saw deep into her soul and felt her warmth and energy. As the laughter subsided into chuckles and titters, he felt the connection; it was like magic, but not devilish, evil magic; it was a blessing, like an invocation, a gift of joy from the Almighty.

His hands began to tremble, and he moved them beneath his legs so she wouldn't see. From within his head, from his mind, the battle of internal conflict had already begun. Overshadowed by his Templar devotion, guilt, and shame imperilled his feelings of rapture and happiness. They pulled and thrust, speared and deflected. Such was his confusion he never noticed her expression.

She settled to her knees on the grass before him, smoothed her skirts and fully turned her attention onto him. She remained silent, her eyes bright, clear and focused, probed and searched. Captivated by her intensity, he could only stare helplessly at her; he couldn't look away; he didn't want to look away; he *wanted* to stare at her. He understood then that she could see into his conflicted and troubled mind.

"My dear gallant knight," she finally spoke. Her voice sounded so soft and melodic. "Fear not, fer I am not yer enemy. Don't challenge what yer heart tells ye, fer it will bring ye turmoil and worriment. Be yerself, fer I see yer goodness … can ye see it too?" She held his gaze a moment longer, then her expression dissolved into a smile. She stood and pointed with a finger skywards. "See the position of the sun? I will return at this time, here on the morrow." She smiled again, then turned and glided away.

He wanted to cry out and beg her to stay. Instead, he felt overwhelmed by guilt and numbed. Josceline was pure, naive and had no notion of the man he'd become or what he'd done. How he'd killed mothers' sons, slain brothers, and fathers. How many wives had despaired and wept because he had killed *their* loved one – their man? By his hand, he'd brought death on so many, committed and seen horrors, felt the unwashed pain and bathed in the blood of the vanquished and, in death, even celebrated in victory.

At this moment, at this very time, he understood completely. It was an awakening like a shroud had been lifted and revealed all. He felt it, like an exposed nerve.

His Templar vows and structured, devout existence prevented him from dwelling on his violent life. They were constructed like a shield to deflect truth, suppress feelings, and hide the reality of the pain and suffering he'd inflicted on others … and what he'd evolved into. He wanted to be sick and felt ashamed. He pulled his legs up and lay his face on his knees.

Near the *château* wall, Josceline stood and observed the Templar knight. She couldn't explain it; she didn't know or understand why she was drawn to this man. Her thoughts and feelings about him were so foreign and unfamiliar – but it felt right. She saw him lower his head to his knees and heard his muted cry of despair. She wanted to go to him and offer comfort and solace, but deep down, she knew he needed to be alone to face his demons. "Poor Odo," she said in a whisper.

CHAPTER SIX

Odo spent a troubled evening alone, tossing and turning as he recounted, over and over again, Josceline's words. He couldn't understand why, how in such a brief time, she had impacted and touched him like no one else he'd ever encountered. Perhaps he'd met her only a dozen times, yet she had connected with him more than any other. It was like they were familiar and could see deep into each other's souls. It was like she knew him. She had invited him to return to the rear of the *château* later, while his Templar vows and common sense told him he shouldn't, that it would be wrong. An inner voice said to him that if he met her later in the day, his life would never again be the same.

He rose from his chamber just as the darkness of evening gave way to the light of a new morn, and with the help of a groom, he set up some targets for archery practice. Odo felt the discipline of archery was invigorating. It required patience, strength, and mental fortitude, and after a restless night, he needed to regain rationality and objectivity. Part of him felt shame for his wayward thoughts about the Templars, and he wanted to re-examine and assess his reasonings. Archery gave him emotional balance and, most of all, allowed him to think.

He breathed in deeply, slowly exhaled and let the welcome calmness settle over him. He pulled an arrow from the ground, from where he'd placed it earlier, and carefully stroked the fletching's to ensure they were straight and undamaged. As his fingers slowly caressed the arrow's feathers, his mind focused on the target one-hundred paces distant. His eyes narrowed, and he removed all thoughts from his mind, and he concentrated on the arrow and its imminent flight. He gauged the strength of the breeze, which was negligible, and notched the ash wood shaft to the drawstring without taking his eyes from the target. He felt his heart rate slow to a measured comfortable cadence. With practised confidence, he slowly raised the large and powerful yew bow and drew the bowstring back. The muscles in his shoulders, back, chest, arms and legs responded accordingly and tightened. As the bow elevated to the correct position, he released the string without hesitation or pause. With a thwack, the arrow shot forward, and within a single heartbeat, it vibrated from a wooden plank resting against a bale of straw.

The groom was surprised, the arrow hit the plank's centre, and he gave a quiet, appreciative whistle.

Odo bent over and rubbed his thigh. It required enormous physical strength to pull the bowstring back and keep the bow steady. All parts of his body needed to work together in harmony, and he felt the discomfort from his injured leg. He increased the distance of the target. Again and again, arrows flew straight and true. After twenty arrows, he was spent. His thigh ached, and his shoulders and arms suffered from the exertions.

After careful instructions from the Templar on extracting the arrows without damaging them, the groom carefully dug the three-foot arrows from the targets with a knife. He'd witnessed archery before, but never had he seen such accuracy - and from a distance. At three hundred paces, the arrow groupings were all within three hand spans.

Odo looked skyward at the sun, it was still too early to meet with Josceline, and with his thigh painful after the archery, he decided to walk a little and hoped the exercise would relieve the discomfort. The groom had told him of a superb fletcher who made arrows in the village, and Odo decided to call on the man and, if his skills were adequate, then he would order more.

He hadn't long left the *château* when his progress was suddenly blocked by the *chevalier*, Jean Courteney. Either side of him, two more *chevaliers* stood; they scowled and offered no salutation. Odo made to walk around them when Jean Courteney reached out and placed a hand on his shoulder.

HeOdo stopped. "Without a friendly greeting, laying a hand on another is most unwelcome," Odo warned. Since that unpleasant afternoon, he'd not spared any thought to the disagreeable man or what he'd tried to do and was surprised to be waylaid by him. After the incident, Sir Piers had advised him to be armed. Since then, he'd strapped his sword to his belt, but he made no attempt to reach for it, not yet.

"I am aggrieved, Templar," spat *Chevalier* Jean, "Ye have offended my honour. And I must defend the good name of my family."

Odo inhaled deeply, then turned to walk back towards the *château*. Again, he felt a hand on his shoulder. He spun, jerking it free.

Jean Courtenay's hand dropped to grasp the hilt of his sword but did not unsheathe the weapon. "I have the right to defend my honour and respect."

"Then speak with the duke," Odo replied, "and allow me to pass." He knew he was in no condition to engage with the *chevalier* and his friends with swords. While all Templars were highly trained swordsmen, Odo was still weakened from his injury and would quickly succumb to even the most rudimentary of skilled opponents.

"But Templar," the *chevalier* sneered, "I have the right to demand that respect is returned to my family, an *affaire d'honneur*. I challenge ye, a duel."

Odo felt the chill. "Perhaps another day, *chevalier*. I am recovering from a wound. I know ye wish fer a fair contest, but alas, I am in no condition to fight." He went to turn away, but one of Jean Courtenay's friends blocked his path.

"I will not allow ye to be on yer way until an arrangement is made."

Odo shook his head. "Ye are foolish and beyond reason." Around them, villagers gathered to watch the disagreement. This added to his worry because now, Jean Courteney was playing to an audience, his confidence bolstered. He thought quickly, and coming to a decision, spoke loudly and clearly for everyone to hear. "Then, as ye challenge me, *Chevalier* Courteney, I have the right to choose the weapon!"

Odo saw the flash of annoyance cross the face of the Frankian knight.

His dark eyes narrowed. "What weapons, what do ye choose?"

"Bows!"

Those who stood listening gasped. The three *chevaliers* exchanged a look of surprise.

"Surely ye jest, Templar," exclaimed the *chevalier* with a nervous laugh.

Odo shook his head, "Nay, as ye can see, I am injured and cannot provide ye with a fair and equitable contest with swords or from the back of a horse. Archery serves us both well, is this not so, or are ye unnerved?"

Jean Courtenay stood straighter and puffed out his chest. "To what rules?"

"One arrow each of a bow of yer own choosing. We stand without armour at one hundred paces." Odo shrugged and tried to appear nonchalant. "But… if this is not to yer liking, then let me pass."

Jean Courteney chewed his bottom lip as he considered Odo's proposal. "Who shoots first?" he finally asked.

"We shoot any time after the signal."

Again, the Frankian knight gave the matter due thought. "One-hundred and fifty paces," he countered.

Odo could see the *chevalier* was unsettled. It suited him, and hopefully, he would change his mind about a contest. He turned and raised an arm and pointed to the grass expanse beside the *château*. "Very well. There, in three days when the sun is highest."

Jean Courtenay composed himself and nodded. "Aye, I accept, and I will restore dignity to my family name. Ensure Duke William is aware, fer he must witness yer death."

Disgusted by the man, Odo pushed past the *chevalier* and returned to the *château.*

William X, Duke of Aquitaine, Duke of Gascony, and the Count of Poitou, rubbed his chin in thought. "Sir Odo, it grieves me to find ye in this untenable position. I feel responsible." He removed his hand and stared at the young Templar with genuine concern. "The Courteney family of Burgundy is well-known, powerful and influential, while Jean Courteney is a despicable creature, nonetheless, this *affaire d'honneur,* yer duel is not with him, but with his family. I understand yer predicament, it is disturbing, and I should have had the man escorted from Caen so he wouldn't be bothersome." He sighed. "And now what? Ye must honour the Templars, yer good name, and chivalry. Ye have a duty to defend yerself and take his life."

"I have no desire to take his life or to lose my life to him. I think it best that a wound, er, a, painful wound, a troubling wound would suffice," Odo replied.

The duke laughed. "Here ye sit, casually discussing how ye will intentionally wound a knight, with an arrow, at one-hundred and fifty paces when most men would be nervous about their arrow reaching such a distance." He shook his head.

"I have faith in my abilities, milord; let's hope my decision is a wise one."

"Then I applaud your willingness to allow him to live, while I have no fondness fer his oldest son, I know his father well, and in his stead, offer ye my gratitude."

Odo dipped his head in acknowledgement.

"I wish ye well, Sir Odo." He rose from his seat. "I will avail myself to this contest as Jean Courteney requests. I just wish there was another way."

It had been quite a morning, and his leg continued to cause discomfort. The sun was high in the sky, and Odo limped towards the trees at the rear of the *château* and eased himself slowly to the ground. He leaned back against a tree trunk and tried to moderate his breathing, quell his thumping heart, and find composure.

He heard the sound of footsteps, and he turned to look behind and saw Josceline walking towards him. Behind her, a man-at-arms followed. He saw her pause and instruct the guard to remain where he was near the wall.

Odo turned away and faced forward as his face flushed. The familiar feeling of guilt washed over him, and again, questioned his decision to meet her. If he hurried, he could still leave; he had time… but his body refused to obey. He heard her soft footfall as she approached, and on its own volition, his mouth opened to speak, "I prefer the quietness of forested hills, meandering streams, and the sound of twittering, carefree birds to the congestion and filth of towns," he said as she came towards him.

The sound of her laughter filled his head with joy, and he marvelled how much he liked hearing the sound of her voice.

"Oh, gallant knight, that is only one question ye have answered fer me, but there are many, many more." She eased herself down to the thick carpet of grass and sat facing him.

One by one, he replied to all her unanswered questions while he lay bedridden. They lost track of time as the sun moved slowly overhead. The pain in his leg dissolved into nothingness and replaced by a warmth that filled a void in his lonely, empty heart. She amazed him. The sharpness of her mind, the force of her will, and her beauty left him breathless.

After a brief pause in their discussion, she looked up at him. The seriousness of her expression, a warning. "Papa told me of the contest with Jean Courteney. Odo, ye may be killed…."

He saw her look of worry. "Fear not, fer most knights know little of archery and even fewer have skills. At one-hundred and fifty paces, he will struggle unless God has gifted him with remarkable talent."

"And if he has…?" she asked.

Odo sighed. "Then it is God's will."

"I told papa I would be in attendance. Since this is all because of me, then I will observe." She looked down, plucked a green blade of grass from the ground, and began twirling it around her finger. "I will observe, not to see *Chevalier* Jean Courteney suffer, but see ye walk away." She raised her head and looked into his eyes.

If they sat closer, he would have leaned over and kissed her.

The sun was in its zenith, at its highest point in the sky, directly overhead. Neither contestant had an advantage over the other with shadows or glare. As far as archery conditions went, it was perfect, and the towering walls of the *château* provided shelter from the prevailing sea breeze that drifted inland. Word had quickly spread that two knights would contest on the lawn of the *château* and a substantial crowd gathered. Most were excited and anticipated the spectacle would provide adequate entertainment, and a welcome, although brief distraction from the humdrum of their daily routine.

One-hundred and fifty paces had been carefully marked out, and white wooden pegs hammered into the grass where each combatant would stand. From the perspective of the spectators who stood beneath the walls, *Chevalier* Jean Courteney stood at their left. The Templar knight, Sir Odo Brus, stood on the right. With him was the stable hand who'd previously been helping him with his archery practice. The young man felt honoured to have been asked to attend to the Templar knight as his second. He stood proudly holding Odo's large six-foot yew bow and a quiver with arrows.

It was previously decided that Jean Courteney's man, another *chevalier*, would stand in the middle as a referee but safely away from an errant arrow and release a white *foulard*[11] as a signal. The moment it fell from his hand, the contestants were free to launch one arrow each. Both men had readily reaffirmed, they were not to take a step or move; they agreed to stand fast until after their own, and their opponents' arrow had completed its flight.

Odo wasn't at all surprised to see that the Frankian knight had chosen to use a recurve bow. Much smaller than the yew bow he preferred, but nonetheless, it was an accurate and powerful weapon and a sensible choice. If the Frankian expressed any surprise at seeing Odo's yew bow, he didn't show it. But Odo knew the knight would be troubled. It was simple, an archer couldn't use a yew bow if he hadn't spent years training. Its mere presence would be disconcerting and cause the *chevalier* to rush, or so he hoped.

A handful of men-at-arms escorted Duke William and Josceline,

---

11 Foulard - Handkerchief

who securely clutched his arm, towards a roped-off area at the foot of the *château*'s wall, where they could safely observe. Odo felt his heart rate increase at the sight of her; she looked absolutely radiant. Her gaze upon him never faltered, and he felt her energy course through his veins.

It was time.

To gauge Jean Courteney's skill and follow through with his plan, Odo wanted to see the stance of the *chevalier* as he held his bow. As expected, the knight stepped to the marker peg, hoisted the bow, and briefly held it in position before stepping back. Jean Courteney was right-handed and, as he should, presented a narrow profile, standing side-on. Odo knew that the knight's body would briefly square up immediately after the arrow was released and offer a suitable target. At that exact moment, Odo would release his arrow, aiming for the right shoulder, which would be turning towards him. It was a risky undertaking because he would initially be aiming for where he expected the shoulder to be.

Odo knew that when struck from such a short distance by a three-foot arrow launched from a yew bow, the resulting injury would be severe and painful, and the knight would likely spend months in recovery. Of course, there was another complication. For his plan to work, the Frankian knight would have to launch his arrow first and miss.

"Sir Odo, are ye ready?" yelled the referee.

"I am!" Odo yelled in reply. He didn't step to the peg and assume a practice stance as Jean Courteney had done. He cleverly denied him that opportunity.

"*Chevalier* Jean, are ye ready?"

"*Oui*, I am!"

"Do ye agree to the rules? One arrow each, and remain standing, ye cannot move or take a step, ye must remain motionless until both arrows have completed their flight!"

Both contestants shouted their agreement.

Odo looked towards Josceline. To his astonishment, she blew him a kiss. He swallowed and turned away and tried to compose himself as his heart began to pound. He took a few steps away from the white wooden marker, looked up at the blue sky, and focused on the contest until he felt his heart and breathing slowly settle.

When again calm, he walked back to the white peg and held out his hand. The groomsman eagerly passed his bow and then an arrow. Odo shook his head, searched through the quiver, and selected another. He lightly stroked the feather's fletching's, notched the arrow, and held the bow and arrow pointing towards the ground between his feet. Odo closed his eyes and felt his heartbeat slow to its familiar tempo. Slowly he opened his eyes and raised the bow, gradually pulling back on the bowstring.

One hundred and fifty paces away, the Frankian knight, Jean Courteney, stood with his bow extended and aimed down the length of the arrow, intent on killing the Templar.

All chattering and laughter stopped; even the birds that flittered to and fro were silent. The referee stood near the midway point but safely out of harm's way with his arm extended. The *foulard* was easily visible, and everyone watched as he released it and saw it flutter towards the ground.

Odo's eyes narrowed, as he raised his bow.

CHAPTER SEVEN

Chevalier Jean Courteney had received extensive training in all aspects of warfare and weapons. By all accounts, he was very skilled. His family had ensured he was well prepared and conversant in all manner of martial skills, including the use of the recurve bow. However, he had not practised in quite some time. When he accepted the Templar challenge to use a bow, he felt confident of his abilities but feared the Templar reputation. He spent the next two days practising for hours and now suffered from some muscle discomfort for his efforts. When he saw the unmistakable and formidable yew bow the Templar would use against him, his fear turned to near panic.

When discussing tactics, his close friend *Chevalier* Jacque, who assisted him, strongly advised him to let loose his arrow first – before the Templar did. Jean readily agreed although he was sorely tempted to flee Caen and return to Burgundy. His decision to demand a duel was not the most sensible thing he'd done, and he now regretted it.

Jean spared a hurried glance over towards the spectators and saw Duke William and her... Josceline. He grimaced; the spoiled harlot had spurned his well-meaning advances and humiliated him. His breathing quickened as he slowly pulled the bowstring back. The white Templar mantle with the vivid red cross was a bold target. He couldn't miss.

The exertions from his training with the recurve bow had stressed his muscles. They weren't relaxed, they were tight, and he made a slight adjustment to counter the effects. Feeling his confidence return, he carefully aimed at the red cross, saw the *foulard* fall, and let the drawstring slip through his fingers – and then took a slight step towards his right and leaned away a little. It was only a tiny step, and he doubted anyone would notice. He watched as his arrow arced towards the Templar.

Odo anticipated the knight would quickly release his arrow, and when he saw the arrow leave the bow, he released his bowstring. The power of his bow was immense, and with unbelievable speed, his arrow streaked towards its target. However, to Odo's astonishment, the Frankian knight took a small step to the left. It wasn't a lot, but enough. Within the span of a heartbeat, Odo knew his arrow would miss.

The shorter Frankian arrow also flew true. It spiralled through the air, directly towards the centre of the red cross on his mantle. The missile reached the apex of its trajectory and dropped lower and lower, then skidded harmlessly along the grass and stopped harmlessly at Odo's feet. He didn't feel relieved at being unharmed; he was disgusted. The Frankian knight had spoken of honour, respect, and chivalry, yet, by intentionally moving, he had fouled, cheated, and declared to Odo, he was nothing but a guileful coward.

Jean Courteney heard the Templar arrow hiss past his ear, and in reflex, turned his head to see where it fell. It embedded in the grass another fifty paces distant. His relief was instantaneous, and with it, his fear turned to exuberance and bravado. He turned back toward his opponent. "Ye missed Templar!" he shouted and raised a defiant fist in the air. "Now ye are free to take yer vile whore, Josceline, into the stables and have sport with her, just like all the other *chevaliers* before ye. Ye live to fight another day!" Adding further insult, he spat in Josceline's direction.

Odo clearly heard the gross insult, as did everyone else. Already enraged from the *chevalier*'s illegal step, the slur directed to Josceline was nothing short of loathsome. He turned behind and stepped to the groom and snatched an arrow from the quiver. Without thought, he turned to face the Frankian, notched the three-foot shaft, and, as he'd done countless times in the past, pulled back on the drawstring as he raised his bow and, without hesitation, released the taut cord. Again, his arrow flew straight and true. It took only a moment to travel one-hundred and fifty paces and struck *Chevalier* Jean Courteney directly over his heart. The knight was sent sprawling. Such was the force of the missile; he was knocked backwards off his feet, with half the arrow protruding from his back. He was dead, long before his lifeless body fell to the ground, the head of the arrow impaling him to the earth.

The spectators were in an uproar. The beloved daughter of their patron and protector, Duke William, had been dishonoured, and they had witnessed instant retribution and deserved execution. Quickly, the duke was escorted to the sanctity of the *château* to fume.

"I will see ye and Josceline dead!" cried one of Jean Courteney's knights who came in support of his friend.

Another cried out. "We will avenge Jean Courteney's wrongful death!"

A couple of men-at-arms escorted Odo to safety in the event the Frankian knights turned even more hostile.

Duke William paced backwards and forwards inside the chamber where he'd spoken to Odo earlier. To Odo's surprise, Josceline sat in a chair and welcomed Odo with a smile when he cautiously entered. He expected the duke to show no restraint and unleash an angry tirade at him.

"Milord, please fergive me, I acted–"

The duke spun. "What ye did, was just! If I had a weapon in my hands, then I too would have killed the vermin."

Odo remained standing and watched as the duke continued his pacing.

"Papa, the Courteney family will not allow this to go unavenged. Can we explain to them...?"

The duke stopped, looked at his daughter, and his expression softened. He returned to his seat and reached over and grasped her hand. "Dearest Josceline, the Courteney's will not sit idly by. If I sent a missive and explained everything to them, they will see fault and will not accept that their son committed a foul, then offered insult and a slur of disrespect." He sighed heavily. "Sit, Sir Odo, I see yer leg ails ye still."

Duke William drummed his fingers on the wooden armrest on his chair and sighed loudly. "In a few days, I will depart fer northwestern Spain. I have a calling and will visit *Santiago de Compostela* to seek spiritual guidance. I cannot postpone this journey, and ye both must remain here in the protection of the *château*, fer I fear the Courteney's will come. I wish yer mother was here...." He sighed again and released Josceline's hand, and turned to Odo. "Ye are a good man, and it is unfortunate ye have been involved. This is not yer doing, but I feel, Sir Piers may see this differently. The Courteney family have considerable political influence; their allegiances will test Sir Piers, fer if he turns against them and advocates fer ye, he will lose much of the Frankian noble support from the Burgundians that he desperately needs. I will do all I can, but fer now, I ask ye, to please look after my Josceline in my absence." He turned briefly back to his daughter before focusing on Odo and smiled. "I see she is smitten with ye, and...." He twisted in his chair and leaned forward. "I know ye will do well by her. Heed caution, young man, danger lurks. I will send word to Sir Piers and detail how ye acted with honour and had little choice in the outcome. I will support ye with all I have." He eased himself upright, stepped towards Odo and placed a hand on his shoulder. "How you choose to live yer life and reconcile yer Templar vows is something ye and Josceline must determine. I will not interfere or make mention to Sir Piers."

Before Odo could speak, he walked from the room, leaving Odo and Josceline alone.

"Did he... did he just give us his blessing?" he felt his face flush and turned away, hoping she wouldn't see.

Josceline rose from her seat and stepped towards him. She bent down and took both his hands in her own. "My papa is a wonderful and dear man, a saint. Fer me, he is easy to talk with, and I share with him. He told me about ye when ye first arrived. Sir Piers informed papa about what happened in the holy lands and how ye unselfishly saved his life at risk of yer own. I wanted to see this man, the man who would do such a gallant thing. Fer men who think of others before themselves are not common. When I saw ye in pain, in that cot, I couldn't get ye out of my mind. Thereafter, I thought about ye every waking moment."

Odo stared at her in wonder. To him, this woman was truly exceptional. He breathed her in. It was intoxicating.

"I told papa about my feelings of ye. He expressed his joy and told me that I was fortunate; to find a man with virtue and honour is not easy." She looked down at her hands that still firmly held his. "He also said that I should be patient, fer such a man may not have the same feelings fer me and might not easily be won, especially since such a man gave vows to his order." She raised her head and met his eyes.

Odo swallowed and tried to calm his beating heart. Her eyes searched his - probing. Together, they both leaned forward, their lips met, and they kissed.

The following days passed in a blur for Odo. Josceline was constantly at his side. Her exuberance and energy were infectious, and he felt gladdened and full of joy. His current wellbeing and state of mind were in sharp contrast to the darkness that enveloped him when he first arrived.

They helped the duke prepare for his departure to northern Spain, and as he'd done a month before when his brother Templar's departed, Odo stood at the *château*'s portcullis and bid farewell to a most remarkable man. Duke William and his entourage rode from *Château de Caen* to the sound of fanfare and celebration in support of his pilgrimage. His presence would be missed, most of all, by Odo and Josceline.

However, all was not well. In five months, Templars would arrive at the *château* and Odo was expected to return with them to the holy lands. His desire and unfamiliar feelings for Josceline created guilt and went against his Templar vows. It was confounding, and he didn't know what to do. Increasingly, he sought solitude to resolve the internal conflict. His body was healing, his physical strength returned, and he worked hard to restore his skills and quickness. Odo practised with a sword against a wooden pell. He challenged all-comers to train with him and then, as he always did, found peace with his bow.

Josceline saw Odo's torment. She understood completely the discord and anguish he was experiencing. Rather than push him into making a decision, she did not broach the subject and gave him the respect and time to make up his own mind. He would tell her when he was ready, of that she had no doubt. But her resolve to remain silent became more difficult as her love for him strengthened. Between them, the conundrum was silently acknowledged, unspoken, but they both knew a reckoning was soon due.

Odo rode his large grey destrier in the countryside near Caen, where he had been hunting. He'd been unsuccessful and distracted; his mind was on other, more important matters. With heartbreaking realization, he knew the sensible option was to leave Caen without Josceline when the Templars came. Returning to the holy lands was the right choice to make. He'd made a sacrifice to his faith and forsaken his lands in Scotland and his wealth. Most everything had been endowed to the Church. He had virtually nothing but the Templars, they were his family, his calling, and without question or pause, he would also give them his life. He'd been trained to act with logic and considered thought, where emotions were cast aside and deemed a distraction and dangerous. 'Acting on emotion may see yer death,' Sir Piers had repeatedly told him. "Think, young man, always think it through," he emphasized time and time again. And Odo did.

He wandered around aimlessly as he thought of outcomes and repercussions. He considered his choices, his future and what was closest to his heart. Through it all, Josceline's face constantly appeared before him. He heard her voice and beautiful words of love and support… could he ever find another like her?

Either way, he knew his decision would cause anguish.

It was late when he swung his horse around and headed back to the *château*. He didn't doubt or question his resolve. Deep down, he knew what was right, although the despair and despondency he felt were almost unbearable. It would be difficult to break the news of his pronouncement, and he knew not how to do it; his concern and wellbeing was only for her. How would Sir Piers and other Templar friends react when they learned he'd repeatedly broken his vows because eventually, word would reach them of his indiscretions. No matter how he sought to soften the blow, it would cause grief. It was with a heavy heart when he rode through the gates of the *château*.

It wasn't the welcome he expected. As he entered through the portcullis and headed towards the stables, Josceline came running towards him. She wasn't smiling or laughing as she usually did when he returned after riding. Tears streamed down her face – something was horribly wrong.

He leapt from the saddle and stifled a cry of pain when his leg hit the ground. Without breaking step, Josceline flew into his arms, sobbing hysterically. Her chest heaved, as she held him tightly.

"What happened? Tell me?" he pleaded.

Around him, activity was not what he expected; men-at-arms, groomsmen, and servants stood in small groups talking. Something terrible had happened. Despite Josceline's arms around him, the hair on his neck rose. He held her tighter and lowered his head, burying his face in her hair. "Josceline, what upsets ye so?" his voice soft and caring.

She gasped, and it sounded like *papa*. "Josceline," he repeated, "What ails ye... what troubles ye?"

She pushed herself away so she could look up at him. Her eyes were red and swollen, and he could see she'd been weeping for some time. He looked down and stared at her in question and worry.

"Papa is dead, killed," she finally managed to speak before again succumbing to the protection and warmth of his embrace.

Odo shook his head in puzzlement. *The duke, William X, dead,* he thought, *how can this be*?

With his arm protectively over her shoulder, he led her inside the *château* where they could speak in private and where she could compose herself.

When somewhat composed and again able to talk, she explained that a rider had arrived at the *château* with a missive. It detailed how her much-beloved father, her saint, had been killed by an arrow launched by a renegade, an outlaw, his heart pierced. The arrow had entered from near his armpit, where armour could not protect.

Instinctively Odo knew it was not the action of an outlaw. Whoever had fired the arrow had done so with precision. All combatants knew that when facing an armoured opponent, the weak point was near the arm. A well-aimed arrow or thrust from a sword could easily slip between chainmail and pierce the heart.

"Who are his enemies?" he asked her. "Who wanted him dead?"

She shook her head. "He had no enemies; he wasn't that kind of man."

Odo wasn't so sure. "What of the Courteneys? Do ye think they would have done this?"

The fire in the hearth spat and crackled. Its reassuring warmth did little to appease their fears.

The question didn't need answering – they both knew. Despite the blazing fire, Odo felt the chill and believed the Courteney family had killed Duke William deliberately with an arrow, and now they would come for him and Josceline. It was revenge, and the Courteney family undoubtedly sought vengeance. Blinking away the tears, she looked at him as his mind considered all the facts and options.

He knelt on the floor in front of her and looked at her with intensity. He'd returned from his hunting trip with the resolve to tell her of his plans; however, the killing of the duke complicated matters. He had slain Jean Courteney in a weak moment of undisciplined rage, an action he must take responsibility for.

As if reading his mind, she spoke first. "We must leave here, fer we will never be safe. But where?"

Odo reached for her hands. "There are places, but we must hasten, fer I believe the Courteney's will rejoice in hearing of our fear and flight. They will plan and choose their moment. We must be clever and act quickly and with thought."

She pulled her hands from his clasp and wiped her eyes. "What of the Templars?" She asked the question both of them had not spoken aloud. This was the moment she'd feared, dreaded because she always believed Odo would return to them.

CHAPTER EIGHT

Josceline had previously explained to Odo that her sister Eleanor was in Paris with Louis, the son of Louis IV, the king of the Franks. Her mother accompanied Eleanor as a chaperone and preferred the excitement of the royal court to the boredom of Caen. However, with the death of their father, Eleanor would now inherit all his lands and titles.

"With papa gone, this grand place means nothing to me anymore. I care not fer fortune or nobility," she told him. "I seek only to raise a family with the man I love. Are ye this man, Odo Brus, or is your calling fer the Church and yer brothers with the red cross on their chests?" She lowered herself to her knees before him, wiped her eyes again and looked deeply into his. Despite her attempts to remain strong, her love for her father was profound, and she struggled for self-control. She gave up trying to wipe away the tears and allowed them to run freely down her face. She slipped her wet hands back into his warm and secure clasp and stared at him with sadness and a measure of hope.

"When I rode from here this morning, I sought answers, fer I have recently been troubled. At night, sleep did not welcome me, and food is bland and unpalatable. I struggled to make sense of my plight, and all that has happened between us."

Josceline didn't move.

"This afternoon, I made a decision." He suddenly shook his head to clear the confusion. "Nay, nay, I confirmed what I knew and believed. I wanted to ponder on this carefully so that nothing is left unanswered or ever in doubt. Do ye understand, Josceline?"

She remained motionless and wasn't sure the point he was trying to make.

He released her hands and stood. Her mouth dropped open as he unbuckled his sword and let it drop, clattering to the floor. He unfastened another, a smaller belt that held a knife and pouch. It, too, fell at his feet.

"Odo?" she questioned. Her voice was stressed and fearful – her bottom lip quivered.

Without hesitation, he raised the white Templar mantle and lifted it over his head and removed it completely. He balled the cloth in his hands and stepped towards the hearth, and threw it in. For an instant, he spared the flaming garment a brief thought, then turned back to Josceline with glistening eyes.

They stood in each other's embrace, the silence marked by the spitting fire. The warmth, their heat, fueled by their professed love and unspoken commitment. Josceline wept for her father, and she cried for the powerful declaration and very symbolic gesture Odo made to her. The white Templar mantle with the red cross transformed into ashes, and for Odo Brus – his past. Her future was in her arms, holding her tightly. Their hearts, in perfect synchronization, beat as one and affirmed their love but did not ease her despair. Her father was gone, slain to avenge the death of Jean Courteney, and now they lived in peril, but beyond the adversity, Odo was hers.

The following morning saw no respite from their pain and anguish when the unexpected appearance of a rider left no doubt in Odo's mind who was behind Josceline's father's death.

Odo was incensed and stood watching in seething anger as the messenger hurriedly departed. The hapless rider had delivered a verbal message to Odo and, in a voice that quavered in fear, spoke simply. "Ye and yer women are next, she first."

Perplexed and believing he'd misheard, Odo asked the rider to repeat it. Word for word, the messenger again said, "Ye and yer women are next, she first." Before Odo could question him further, the petrified rider dug his heels into his horse's flanks and galloped away.

"The Courteney's believe this is sport. They threaten and intimidate with merriment like this is – is, entertainment!" He shook his head in disbelief.

"As papa said, we should not underestimate them; he warned of their disposition," Josceline added.

Odo nodded and recalled her father's word all too well. "This leaves us with little choice."

Josceline waited.

"I can go to them and put an end to this...."

"Or we can both remain alive where they will not find us," she finished his sentence.

He looked at her, and his expression softened. "Aye, Josceline, I just want peace. But we cannot remain besieged inside these walls...."

Odo shook his head, "Nay, we must travel lightly and cannot take a wagon. We ride on horses and take two packhorses each to carry what we can. A wagon will slow us, and if people watch and follow, they will do so with ease. Can ye do this, fer this will not be easy?" he asked.

"If that is what I must do, then aye, I can, and without grievance. Servants will bring all that I need in a lengthy procession of wagons and horses after we arrive at yer castle," she smiled, one of the few she offered since learning of her father's death the day before.

Odo grinned at her humour and jest. Josceline fully understood the sacrifices they would both have to make. They'd decided to leave the *château* during darkness and immediately ride northwards to Calais. From there, they would take a ship to England and then travel overland, northwards to Scotland. They had to journey quickly and without encumbrance.

Templars swore an oath of poverty, chastity, and obedience, amongst others, and in observance, all lands and wealth were endowed to the Templar order. However, as quietly advised by other Templars in hushed, secretive voices, this practice only extended so far. Odo was told to withhold a hidden reserve of coin and a modest parcel of land. This would enable a knight to live quietly without want if he became crippled through injury or, if he survived, sought refuge away from the order in later years. Heedful of the advice, he'd done exactly that. It was to this land in Carrick, Scotland, where they were headed. No one knew of its existence and offered them the best opportunity to begin anew and share their lives together.

Odo was frantically sorting through his own meagre possessions and arranging Josceline's belongings. He'd carefully instructed her on what to bring and what to leave behind. Her beautiful dresses and jewellery would not be needed, he advised. To his astonishment, she did not complain, and with frankness told him, she was leaving her life as the daughter of Duke William behind. Her relationship with her mother and her older sister, Eleanor, was not close, and she knew she wouldn't be missed.

She would welcome hardship if it meant they could be happy, raise a family and experience old age together in peace. However, while Josceline readily accepted the possibility of a hard life, it did not prevent her from including a small chest filled with gold coin with her belongings. When he saw the chest, Odo grinned.

While he sorted and began packing the horses, Josceline was leaving instructions with the *sénéchal*[12]. Additionally, she and Odo composed two letters. Both missives were carefully crafted and detailed the events around the death of Jean Courteney and William X and how she and Odo were forced to flee. In the first letter to her mother and sister, Eleanor, Josceline added that once they were safe, they would send word. She also warned that they should be heedful of the Courteneys and exercise caution; they could also be in danger.

The second missive, which would be sent to the Templar leader, Sir

---

12 Steward

Piers, also contained Odo's reasonings and outlined his decision to forsake his vows and leave the order. He thanked Sir Piers for all he had done for him.

Both letters would be sent with riders after Odo and Josceline departed *Château de Caen* later that evening.

The *château* would be in safe hands. The *sénéchal* was a trusted and capable man, Josceline explained to Odo. He was frequently left alone to manage her father's affairs during lengthy family absences and would do so again. However, like everyone else, no one knew where they were going.

The moon shone brilliantly as Odo and Josceline quietly departed *Château de Caen*. The two packhorses were strung in a line and tied behind her horse. Odo told her that they would most likely encounter problems within the first two days, and he needed to respond to any threat quickly and without delay. Having a horse tied behind his would be a hindrance.

He was fully armed and wore chainmail, but not the familiar white mantle. His shield, bow and quiver were securely fastened to his horse, and his sword was strapped to his waist. Additionally, a smaller recurve bow and arrows were attached to one of the pack horses. Earlier, he told Josceline how he would teach her to use it. "No matter how proficient ye are with a sword, a hefty man with only moderate skills will easily overpower ye. But ye can, from a safe distance, launch arrows and make good yer escape," he advised with seriousness.

She willingly agreed and, with a twinkle in her eye, told him how she looked forward to his instructions. He blushed.

They avoided towns and villages and rode as fast as their pack horses could travel. It took them six gruelling days before they finally arrived at the small seaside port of Calais, where they quickly secured passage on a small ship to England. A fat purse easily convinced the ship's master to take two passengers and four horses to King's Lynn, another small but well-frequented coastal port, about a three-day horse ride north of Londinium.

The master of *Mary's Delight* was astute enough to not ask questions. He could easily see that the large, muscular, well-armed knight was not someone to double-cross or argue with. As long as he paid the tariff before they stepped foot aboard his beloved vessel, he would ensure they arrived safely at their destination. He informed the knight and his lady they would depart with the morning tide on the morrow after provisioning and loading the ship for the three or four-day voyage.

Again, Odo wanted to avoid significant ports where their presence might be noticed, which was why he chose King Lynn as their destination. However, his immediate worry was in Calais, where they both hoped no one paid them any undue attention. He would drop a false hint at the appropriate time and tell the ship's master that their final destination was somewhere near Wales. If anyone came asking after them, he hoped that little tidbit of misinformation may mislead any pursuers.

Over the past six days, Josceline grieved. Her father's death understandably affected her, and Odo continued to console her as best he could. During those times when she was overcome, he went to her, held her, and gave her comfort and support. She apologized for her weakness and promised him with a teary smile how her sadness would soon pass.

Between them, their bond strengthened, and during their journey Odo frequently found himself staring at Josceline and marvelled at how his life had changed for the better. Even though they fled from the Courteney family and slept outdoors in harsh conditions, he was happy, never had he felt so alive. However, tonight, they would sleep indoors at an inn and eat heartily.

However, their arrival in Calais did not go unnoticed. Unbeknown to them, a *pêcheur*[13] hurriedly left the docks and reported his sighting to a local merchant. The merchant quickly sent a missive to the reeve at the *manoir,* who in turn dutifully informed his master and lord. Five days later, word of Odo Brus and Josceline's sighting in Calais finally reached Count Courteney.

The weather was perfect, and the small coastal trader crossed from Frankia to England without mishap, then sailed slowly up the coast towards their destination. After three days, Odo was anxious and fidgety and couldn't wait to feel dry land beneath his feet again. Josceline didn't mind the voyage and enjoyed the rest and a chance to dwell on her past and future. Her grief subsided to an aching heart, but her future gave her hope. Odo Brus was more than she could ever have wished for. She acknowledged he was an earnest man and enjoyed teasing him in a good-natured way. Josceline also noticed how he always put her well-being before his own when he became anxious and worried. He was considerate to a fault and treated her with abundant love and always with respect, and other than dear

13 *Pêcheur – French, fisherman.*

papa, she'd never felt this way for any man; Odo was perfect.

They made landfall when the sun was highest and the tide favourable. The small port and town of King's Lynn was like many other coastal communities. It relied on fishing and coastal trading, and typically, many people were about the docks doing various tasks.

Once moored, Odo led the horses onto the dock and loaded the packhorses as quickly as possible. He didn't want to tarry, and to be journeying northwards without delay, Scotland was still some distance away.

Seated on a wooden bench outside a ship chandlery shoppe, Elis Rolfe watched with professional curiosity as the small coastal trader, *Mary's Delight*, arrived and berthed. While Elis appeared relaxed and uninterested, he was, in fact, moderately alert and attentive. With growing curiosity, he observed the ship's only two passengers unload their horses and begin loading and securing their possessions to their animals.

Elis Rolfe called himself a spotter. He was part of a well-organized band of outlaws who preyed on unwary travellers. His job was to identify potential victims and promptly notify the group's leader so that the outlaws could pursue and relieve them of valuables with intimidation and with a minimum of fuss.

From his slightly elevated position outside the shoppe and with feigned nonchalance, Elis's interest was piqued by several unusual but very acute observations. He quickly surmised the man was a knight, therefore probably a lord and landowner. The man was heavily armed, relatively tall, muscular, and had a slight limp. *A battle wound* surmised Elis. The knight's companion, a very comely lady, was actively helping to load the packhorses. *Why did they travel alone?* he wondered again. *Where were the servants and guards?*

While Elis had spent most of the evening at a local inn and suffered from the effects of too much mead, he was still cognizant that the knight and lady were the only passengers aboard the ship. They had coin and could afford such luxuries, and therefore, the likelihood they carried even more coin was more than a possibility; it was a certainty.

Already, Elis was envisioning how they would waylay the unsuspecting couple. The fact that the man was a knight and proficient with weapons meant they would need to be heedful. However, Elis' had at one time been a man-at-arms, as had most of the other outlaws in his band, and in his skewed opinion, believed he was very adept with a sword and perhaps even better with a crossbow. In his short career as a highwayman, his confidence was bolstered by the fact that he'd never actually had to use his weapons on a traveller; intimidation alone had proven to be enough, and, he hoped, do so again.

Elis continued to watch the knight and his companion and saw they were almost ready and packed. Casually, he rose from his seat and strolled away to inform the outlaw leader at the Inn.

He was not known by any other name other than Wolfe, simply Wolfe. He liked his name, it felt and sounded dangerous, and it added to the mysterious persona that he tried to cultivate. Wolfe listened attentively as Elis detailed the arrival of the ship and described its only passengers.

Wolfe nodded and scratched his scraggly beard. "Drink up, lads, we 'ave customers." He raised his tankard, drained its contents, slammed it down on the table and belched loudly.

His men, motivated by Elis's colourful description of the affluent couple and untold riches that were sure to come, needed no further urging. The group left the Inn and walked a short distance to a small farm where their horses and weapons were kept. Wolfe wasn't anxious about losing the travellers; he knew they wouldn't be moving quickly with packhorses. All Wolfes's five men each had lightweight crossbows, half-a-dozen bolts, and carried a sword. While the weapons were old and previously stolen, they were passably functional.

The road from King's Lynn wound through a shallow valley or two, but at one point, the road passed by a small ravine. It was at this location Wolfe would make his move. When accosted, their victims had two options only; they couldn't veer from the road because of the ravine that fell abruptly away to the right. On the other side, a steep hill prevented escape, so they could either remain and fight six armed men or abandon their packhorses and valuables and, in fear of their lives, flee to safety.

Wolfe and his men checked their weapons, saddled their horses and with an abundance of enthusiasm and self-assurance set out to catch up to the heedless wanderers. They'd been reasonably successful at robbing the unwary and never encountered any firm resistance. However, one rather distraught and obstinate merchant received a nasty beating when he chose to resist and refused to hand over his possessions.

Wolfe knew they had plenty of time to spare and was in no immediate hurry.

CHAPTER NINE

Odo double-checked each knot of the rope securing their belongings to the horses. He'd repositioned various items, ensured the load was balanced and sat perfectly to distribute the weight evenly over the horses' backs and flanks. He didn't want to impede the movement of the animal's legs to ensure they could travel at best possible speed.

Josceline watched. "I am sure, gallant knight, that if ye check the ropes one last time, ye may find they have come loose again," she teased.

Odo turned to her, but his expression held no mirth. Immediately she felt foolish as she sensed his disquiet.

"What ails, ye?" she asked.

"Methinks we may encounter highwaymen, vagabonds who will set upon us."

Her eyebrows furrowed.

"There was a fellow sitting outside the chandler's, and he spared us more than casual attention and then wandered to the Inn. I have been here before and in towns like this many a time. Why would a man be seated and observing as a ship entered port, then after a short time, return to the Inn?"

Josceline shook her head. "I know not."

"Because, shortly after, six men departed the Inn. As we speak, they are preparing to follow us. We must leave quickly and find a suitable place to defend ourselves."

Josceline looked frightened, and Odo's face relaxed, and he smiled at her. "Do ye think I am concerned? While six desperate men may cause ye worry, six men drinking at an Inn cause me no fear." He reached over and placed his hands gently on her shoulders. "Josceline, those men do not know that I see their intentions. The advantage lies with us." His unspoken thoughts were considerably different, but he didn't want to cause her unnecessary worry if he could help it.

Odo and Charlotte rode at a slow, unhurried walk as they departed King's Lynn. Once out of sight, they pushed their horses into an easy lope. A pace they could maintain for a considerable time, as long as the ropes binding their belongings didn't loosen and scatter possessions over the road behind them. All the while, he kept a careful watch for approaching riders but so far didn't see them. He'd travelled along this road a time or two before, and he recalled a portion of the road that wound alongside a narrow ravine. He believed that location would be the best place for outlaws to make their move. With renewed earnestness, he urged the packhorses to move faster.

If they could safely pass through the ravine, he could turn the confines of the narrow road against the outlaws and entrap them. He just hoped their speed would be enough.

He felt relief when he saw the road narrow and the ground beside fall away to a river below. To his left, the bank was steep, the incline too much for a horse to climb. Again, he risked a look behind. He could see some distance but no sign of any approaching riders.

"Could ye have been mistaken?" Josceline asked.

"I hope I am wrong," he replied.

They rounded a corner and entered the narrowest part of the ravine where the road snaked around the hill's contours, and this was the place where they were most vulnerable. He knew the packhorses were tired, and they'd need to slow down. He turned to look behind… still nothing. Ahead, he saw the track straighten and widen; trees cast lengthening shadows across the road and provided some shelter. He pointed. "There, there, we will wait."

He gave instructions to Josceline on where to position herself as he strung his bow and unpacked a bundle of arrows to replenish the quiver. She would be safe, behind the trees, well out of harm's way.

On the ocean voyage from Calais, he had begun teaching her how to use the recurve bow. While her practice had been limited and she lacked strength, she showed a natural ability and had a keen eye. If threatened, he knew she could defend herself. The horses were out of sight, and Josceline stood anxiously in the shadows behind a tree, armed with her bow.

On hands and knees, Odo scrambled a few yards up the hill to a fallen tree where he would have an unobstructed view that also provided him with suitable cover. He placed several arrows headfirst into the ground and waited.

Within a dozen heartbeats, he heard a sound. But it wasn't the sound of approaching riders. He was puzzled. The walls of the ravine deflected the sound, and he looked around uneasily for the source. He twisted to look behind as a cow appeared from around the bend in the road, then another, and finally a bullock pulling a small wagon. A man and a woman walked beside the bullock, and the small procession headed directly towards them.

Josceline heard the sound too, and in alarm, stepped from behind the tree to see better. She knew the couple were walking directly into danger. Without a thought, she ran down the road to warn them of trouble as the first highwaymen rode into view from the opposite direction.

Odo immediately saw the crossbows they carried, which confirmed that the group were outlaws, and within seconds he sighted on the first horse and hoped the rider was the group leader. If he could stop him, then the others may lose interest and flee. His breathing slowed, and with calmness, let loose his first arrow. Before it had completed its flight, he'd reached down for another. He briefly saw the arrow protruding from the man's upper chest before seeing him disappear over the rear of the horse.

More riders appeared and slowed as they witnessed their outlaw leader, Wolfe, struck by an arrow. The outlaws reacted quickly, and their horses skidded to a stop.

Odo took advantage of their error and let loose another arrow at the first inviting target. Just like the first man, another was flung violently from the saddle. *Two down, four two go*, he thought as he notched another arrow and sighted on the next outlaw.

Elis reacted first and ducked down, laying across his horse's neck. He yanked hard on the reins, and his horse squealed in pain as he cruelly wheeled the animal around. Elis hung on for dear life as the poor animal leapt away, heading back in the direction they rode from.

Odo's breathing was slow and measured. His focus was purely on the threat before him and the danger they represented. He trusted that Josceline had followed his instructions. He raised his bow and carefully sighted on the back of another rider who had turned his horse and tried retreat. He released the bowstring, and with the accomplished eye of a marksman, knew his arrow would fly straight and true. Another arrow was quickly pulled from the ground and the bow raised as the last horse turned the corner and disappeared. Three men lay unmoving on the ground.

He assessed the situation quickly. The outlaws had made a tactical error. They stopped and retreated when they should have ridden on and attacked him. These were not skilled fighters, but he felt no relief, the odds were still numerically in their favour.

Odo felt no satisfaction at seeing the carnage; he didn't enjoy killing, but what did concern him were the crossbows he saw. Each man carried a lightweight crossbow and sword. At short range, the crossbow was lethal, but over distance, they lacked accuracy and were slow to reload. Certainly, the crossbows were heavy and, on a moving horse, cumbersome. If they returned and managed to come within range of him, then the advantage turned even more in their favour.

He looked over his shoulder and saw the two cows and the bullock with the wagon. At least they had stopped. Josceline was with the couple, and he could see they were safely crouched down behind the wagon and peering above it. He felt relief seeing her there.

Quickly he removed the spare arrows from the ground, and with his injured thigh forgotten, slid down the bank and ran along the road towards the corner the outlaws had ridden around. They knew where he had been hiding and would not expect him to relocate to another offensive position even closer to them. Before reaching the bend, he picked up the discarded crossbows and tossed them into the river, then leapt from the track and slid out of sight down the bank. This was a tenuous position if the outlaws came within sword reach as he couldn't retreat, and he fervently hoped that wouldn't happen. He placed two arrows in the ground, and a third arrow was notched. He kept his body out of sight, and his eyes slightly raised, just above the level of the road and waited.

"He's one man!" Elis yelled. "We should'a kept riding and attacked." He shook his head in frustration and tried to control his horse which wouldn't keep still.

"Ye never said he had a bow? Whada we do now?" asked an outlaw. "Should we scarper while we can?"

"He's got valuables, lotsa coin, I expect," Elis answered. Naturally, he'd assumed the recently vacated role of outlaw leader. "I say we try again, this time, don't stop, ride directly fer him."

"I never seen a man shoot an arrow like that," stated the other outlaw. "He knew we were comin'."

"But he's only one man," implored Elis. "He and his woman have coin, and I'm gonna take it, ye want to ride away, go ahead, but three of us stands a good chance o'gettin' it."

The temptation was too great. The three outlaws prepared to attack again.

From his new position below the level of the road, Odo heard the horses approach before he saw them. First, one appeared, then the other two. He stood, swung the bow into position, and pulled back on the bowstring. It snapped.

Elis was surprised to see the knight's head, and then his shoulders appear from beside the road. His horse galloped past the knight, and he tried to slow and turn the animal around so he could use his crossbow. It was in his other hand, on the far side, and it was too cumbersome to reposition and let loose a bolt easily. More to his surprise, he didn't see the knight use his bow.

Odo didn't have time to restring his bow and dropped it before swinging himself up and onto the road before unsheathing his sword. Already, two of the three outlaws had ridden past him, and both were turning. One eager outlaw swung his crossbow around, and with a loud snap, sent a bolt in his direction. The errant missile disappeared skywards, then fell into the river below. The third horse and rider were a little slower. Grasping his long sword in both hands, Odo stepped quickly and lunged, spearing the unprotected side of the outlaw as he rode past. This was a tactic the Templars had practised repeatedly, and Odo executed it to perfection. The rider was mortally wounded; his horse slowed, and the outlaw clutching his side, slid painfully from the saddle.

Elis was frightened. The knight stood in the centre of the road without his bow, bravely wielding a longsword. Wisely he pulled his horse to a stop to reassess. He wasn't foolish enough to ride within striking distance of the sword; however, the crossbow would speak for him. As his horse settled, Elis awkwardly swung his crossbow into position. The other outlaw was a step behind him and pulled on the reins hard.

Odo knew he was in trouble. His leg was hurting, and he couldn't run as fast as he wanted. The only option was to charge at the two outlaws and hope he offered a difficult moving target.

With no other option, he ran at the outlaw. Calculating distance and time, Odo knew he wouldn't make it; he was too slow. In agonizing frustration, he saw the crossbow raise into position, waver a moment as the outlaw made an adjustment, and then inexplicably, before the rider could pull the trigger, he suddenly jerked and twisted in the saddle as his weapon slid from his hands.

Fearful of the approaching knight, the outlaw grimaced in pain, dug his heels into the side of the horse, veered from Odo's thrusting sword and rode away. Odo turned his attention on the remaining outlaw, but he wanted no further part of the skirmish. With a cry of fear, he threw his crossbow away and followed after the other. Odo bent down to rub his aching leg and saw Josceline standing in the middle of the road with her bow. He limped towards her and saw her body shaking.

They stood in a tight embrace in the middle of the road as the farmer and his woman walked tentatively towards them.

"What happened?" Josceline finally managed to ask.

"The bowstring snapped, weakened from moisture and damp while we were at sea," Odo replied. "That was a most timely and well-aimed arrow...."

"I knew not what to do, I, I thought I could help...."

Odo could see she was still troubled at having injured someone with an arrow. "I owe ye my life, fer had ye not let loose when ye did, then I fear, we may not be standing here chatting now." Odo smiled, then turned to face the farmer. "Ye couldn't have arrived at a worse time."

The farmer, a man of similar age to Odo, touched his hand to his forelock. Odo saw his hands tremble. The sight of death and killing unsettled the man. "Milord, I owe ye our thanks." He turned to Josceline, who was still distraught.

"Ye owe me nothing, I thank ye, fer keeping Josceline safe. Those outlaws were suitably armed, and yer wagon offered protection." Odo kept his arm around her shoulders and felt her beginning to relax. "Tell me, why is it ye travel alone? These roads are unsafe; highwaymen prey on the unwary."

The herdsman extended his arm and pulled his wife closer. "Milord, this is my wife, Hetti, and we are newly married." He looked at her, and both Odo and Josceline could see the strong bond of love between them. "We were travelling with others, but Hetti was stricken with a malady and could not travel; rather than wait, they moved on. We were hoping to meet with other travellers at King's Lynn."

Odo quickly scanned the area around them. He didn't want to be caught unaware if the outlaws returned. He saw the cows and bullocks foraging for grass on the side of the road. "Where are ye are headed?"

"There is a small hamlet, far south in Devonshire, called Mellester. Sir William, the lord of the manor, seeks freemen. My friend, Norman Bloxham, is reeve there and sent fer us. He told us the climate is agreeable for cows and grass, and we seek a home safe from strife and rancour, milord," the farmer explained enthusiastically. He turned and pointed to his two cows and bullock with evident pride. "They are our future, our nest egg. And with them, we will breed the best deierie[14] cows in all of England."

Odo and Josceline smiled at the enthusiasm of the herdsman. "God willing," he replied, "I believe ye." Odo looked up at the sky and saw it was growing late. "I must dispose of those bodies. And we should settle here fer the night. Ye are welcome to join us, together it will be safer, and Kings Lynn is too far to travel before nightfall."

"Aye, ye are most welcome, milord, we will do that, and let me help with the outlaws; I have a spade."

"My name is Odo Brus, and this is Josceline."

The farmer respectfully dipped his head. "I am Godwin Read."

---

14 Deierie - Dairy

CHAPTER TEN

Josceline and Hetti lit a fire and began preparing food as Odo and Godwin buried the bodies. It was difficult, hard work in the rocky soil, and when finished, Odo offered the dead men a brief prayer before they retrieved the horses, removed their saddle blankets, bridles, and turned them loose. As Odo expected, the outlaw weapons were old and had no value; he threw them into the ravine along with everything else before limping back towards the women with Godwin at his side.

"Did those outlaws hurt ye, milord?" asked Godwin with concern.

Odo walked on a few steps more and thought about his response. "Nay, I was wounded some time ago. It heals slowly, but not quick enough."

Godwin nodded and thought it best not to probe further. The smell of cooking food was a welcome distraction.

With food and wine, the two couples relaxed and as the sky darkened, their conversation became more open, and they spoke freely and with laughter. Odo liked the farmer and his wife. They were decent, honest people with values who dreamed of a bright new future in a small manor in southern England. In a way, he envied them; their lives were uncomplicated and full of hope and promise. He looked at Josceline, she laughed easily with Hetti, and the two women, with remarkably different lives, shared similar thoughts and beliefs. As women did, the conversation soon turned to babies and children, and Odo lost interest and focused on Godwin.

"What do ye know of this hamlet ye travel to?"

Godwin smiled. "The reeve, my friend, Norman, says Mellester manor prospers under an even-handed lord and that he seeks freemen and offers opportunities."

"Who is this lord?" Odo asked.

"Sir William Ainsley."

Odo hadn't heard of him, but then again, it wasn't unusual to never have heard of a lord from a small manor. "I wish ye both well."

"And where are ye, headed, milord?" Godwin asked.

Odo didn't want to deceive this man. He turned to look at him closely. His face was illuminated by the flickering flames of the fire. "I cannot speak untruths to ye, Godwin. But neither can I tell ye."

Godwin's eyebrows furrowed in puzzlement.

Odo turned and gave Josceline a quick glance before turning back. "Our lives are in danger, and it is best if ye do not know. If asked, it would serve ye well to not say ye met us."

Godwin nodded. He had little to do with nobility, and obviously, Odo was a knight, and from her mannerisms and deportment, guessed Josceline was also a high-born noble. He knew the complexities of a noble's life were considerably different than his own. Theirs was a life he didn't understand.

If Odo didn't want to share with them, then that was entirely his business. Godwin shrugged.

"Perhaps, one day I can explain, eh?" Odo said with a smile.

Godwin doubted he would ever see either of them again.

In the morning, they bade each other farewell and Godwin and Hetti watched as Odo and Josceline rode off.

"Who are they?" Godwin asked. "Did ye learn anything of them?"

Hetti shook her head. "She is Frankish, and he is a Scot, but she gave no clue."

"I wish them well," said Godwin. "Now, my queen, Mellester waits, shall we lead our loyal subjects to our fair lands?"

Hetti laughed. "All three of them?"

It took Odo and Josceline nearly three weeks to travel up through England before arriving in Glasgow, Scotland. It was a gruelling journey, and they were both exhausted and spent, and their horses weren't in better condition. Odo was constantly on guard, ever vigilant and ensured they were not followed or preyed upon by thieves or vagabonds. Not that they didn't encounter them, they did. However, the lone knight with a woman may have looked like easy pickings, but a closer inspection revealed the heavily armed knight wasn't to be taken lightly and wouldn't allow anyone to approach or come close without drawing his sword and warning them off.

On arrival in Glasgow, Odo purchased a wagon, a bullock, and a milking cow, along with provisions and some tools. With some difficulty, they set off towards Carrick about a day and a half journey away. Unfamiliar with handling a bullock and controlling a cow, Josceline was in hysterics as she watched Odo trying to keep the animals headed in the right direction. When the bullock became cooperative, the cow was intent on walking a different route. Odo had no patience, and his fretful demeanour did nothing more than agitate the animals.

"Perhaps ye could try singing a ballad!" yelled Josceline as Odo sprinted from the wagon to head the cow off and turn her back in the right direction. "Or rub her neck and whisper sweet words in her ear!"

"Perhaps I'll take to the cow with a switch, and to ye after!" he replied over his shoulder as the cow finally turned and began trotting back up the road. Odo bent over and rubbed his thigh. While the wound had completely healed, he still felt pain from overexertion.

People passed them by with curious stares and some mirth at seeing the knight with a sword bouncing from his waist trying to control a cow. No one said an unkind word and walked by with a smile and a laugh. Ahead, a man and a woman stopped to watch as Odo guided the cow back up the road and attempted to motivate the bullock to do the same.

"Hail, kind sir. I see yer cow and bullock are deaf to yer wishes," spoke the man.

Odo shook his head. "Aye, they must be foreign animals, fer neither understands English," he replied.

"Perhaps ye will allow me. We travel in the same direction, and I may be able to relieve the burden fer ye?"

Odo eyed the man and woman warily and was instantly suspicious.

Seeing the knight's intense scrutiny, the man spoke again. "Good sir,

I seek no coin or favour but offer only to help. My woman and I can just as easily be on our way.”

Josceline leaned down from her horse. “I think, gallant knight,” she whispered, “this generous man may yet be yer saviour.”

Odo smirked. “Thank ye, kindly. I welcome yer help. As ye can see, I cannot tie them together fer I also have packhorses, but these animals are in a foul disposition and only seek to torment me.”

Without another word, the woman slowly walked towards the cow, and instantly the animal stopped its foraging, turned, and began to walk in the right direction. The man went to the bullock, grabbed its halter, and within moments, plodded away without fuss.

Odo shook his head in amazement. Josceline was grinning but held her tongue as she handed him the reins to his horse. He saw her expression and muttered something under his breath before mounting and riding towards the man.

“How far do ye travel?” Odo asked.

The man shrugged his shoulders, “We go north and seek a laird[15] and manor fer work.”

“What are ye called?” Odo asked after a moment or two of silence.

“I am Inan Kelly, and my woman is Cannie, milord.”

Odo did not offer his name in return. “What is yer trade, Inan?”

“Oh, well ye see, milord, I can ‘bout do anything… whatever the work, I can do it.”

Odo believed him. He had an easy, confident manner and certainly could handle animals, as could his wife. “If ye both can help me fer the rest

---

15 *Laird – Scottish for landowner of large estate.*

of the day, I'll pay ye a tuppence[16]."

"So, it be, milord," Inan dipped his head in thanks and respect and said nothing more.

Inan and Cannie were still with them when they finally arrived at Odo's land four weeks later. Odo was impatient to show Josceline their new home, and after leaving the packhorses, cow, and bullock with Inan and Cannie, they impatiently cantered ahead, over a low rise and stopped.

Below them, surrounded by treeless, steep, and rugged hills lay a small peaceful and serene valley dissected by a small stream. To their left, and some distance away, but still visible from their elevated position, lay the Sound of Bute, fjords, where the ocean entered a series of bays and inlets.

Near the northernmost point of the valley, not far from the hills and surrounded by lush green grass, sat a stone building. Odo pointed, "That is our home, Josceline. It may not be *Château de Caen*, but it is ours."

Josceline, dismounted and took a step closer to look. A gentle northerly breeze disturbed a few strands of loose hair, and she stood unmoving, silent. Odo slid from his horse, and walked up behind her. She hadn't said anything, and he was fearful that she was disappointed. This place may not be what she hoped it to be.

Slowly she took a step to the side, turned, and enveloped him in a hug. He wasn't sure; was *this a hug of despair*?

"Josceline?" he asked, his voice squeaked. "Are ye disheartened?"

She pushed away and looked up at him. "Nay, Odo, this is more than

---

16 *Tuppence – The sum of two pennies.*

I ever dreamed it could be."

They stood together and took in the spectacular view beneath them as Inan and Cannie, along the wagon and animals, slowly plodded up the rise towards them.

Josceline was surprised when she saw the house close up. It was larger than it first appeared. Odo explained that it was a *bastle*[17] house and was constructed with defences in mind. Raiders would come from the south, and the houses were fortified with extra-thick walls to protect the inhabitants. Animals lived on the ground floor while the residents lived above them in safety. However, as Odo explained, this bastle had an attached byre for animals, leaving the ground floor available to them.

It was filthy inside, and immediately Josceline issued instructions for everyone to begin washing the walls, sweeping, and cleaning. Odo wasn't spared and worked tirelessly until she was satisfied.

Inan and Cannie were asked to remain, and Odo offered them both work and a roof. He showed Inan where he could build his own house, a short distance away, and imminently pleased, the quiet couple worked hard, kept to themselves, and proved loyal, hardworking, and invaluable.

With the bullock and wagon, Odo and Inan gathered sizeable rocks and began building stone walls. For Odo, security was paramount. In the back of his mind, he believed that the Courteneys would come one day, and he wanted to be prepared.

---

17 *Bastle, Bastel, or Bastille house, is a farmhouse found mostly around the Anglo-Scottish border in the region plagued by border raiders.*

The first few weeks passed quickly, there was so much to do, and Odo was impressed that Josceline had adapted so quickly to the harsh Scottish life. It was Cannie who taught her, and Josceline learned everything she could. There were tears and frustrations, but never did Josceline give up. Her fingers bled, she ached and suffered from minor cuts and abrasions. She helped where she could and hefted stones into the wagon to the best of her ability, she struggled and triumphed, and Odo's love and respect for her intensified. She was a remarkable woman and showed strength and resolve that astounded him. As a daughter of a prominent duke and unused to the rigours of farming, Josceline not only adapted, she thrived.

Odo heavily relied on Inan's knowledge of farming. Without him and Cannie, he and Josceline would have failed miserably and most likely starved.

Odo and Inan were unloading another wagon of stones for a wall they were building when Odo looked up and saw Josceline walking away from their home. It seemed aimless, and without purpose, and with curiosity, he kept watch. When the wagon was emptied, he slowly followed her. She'd climbed partly up the hill on the far side of the valley and stopped at a rocky outcrop, and sat down to look over their land.

"What took ye so long?" she asked when he finally sat down beside her.

"I wondered where ye were going?"

She looked away and studied the valley, and remained silent.

Odo couldn't help himself. "Is, is there something wrong, are ye ailing?"

Her hands lay in her lap, and he saw how she fidgeted. Something was wrong, and he felt his heartbeat quicken.

She turned to him. "Odo… I'm with child," she smiled.

CHAPTER ELEVEN

Once every fortnight, as he'd habitually done for the last two-and-a-half years since he and Josceline arrived in Carrick, Odo would mount his destrier and frequent his neighbours. It was an all-day trek, and he would visit with one, ride on and visit another. Eventually, he made a circuit of his property and usually returned home late in the day. He would discuss problems or difficulties his neighbours were having on his journey, and, if required, he and Inan would ride over a day or two later and help. In turn, and when needed, neighbours would lend a back and assist him. Although he was genuinely interested in the wellbeing of his neighbours, his visits also allowed him to learn about strangers or visitors who came to the area asking questions about him and Josceline.

As customary, when he returned home after making his rounds, he approached the valley, detoured from the path and rode a little way up a hill where he'd pause a moment and stare out across his land.

It was heartwarming to see a welcoming spiral of smoke drifting from the chimney, half a dozen cows grazed contentedly, and about two dozen sheep dotted the flat valley floor. In the absence of wood, he and Inan built sturdy stone wall fences. They kept the animals from wandering and were strategically placed to offer concealment for defensive purposes if they were ever attacked. Although, they weren't ideal and wouldn't prevent a determined well-structured force from overcoming them. However, if needed, the walls would slow an enemy advance and enable Odo and his family a chance to escape and seek shelter.

Odo leaned his arms across the pommel of his saddle and smiled. He felt contented, this valley was theirs, and together, he, Josceline and their three children were wonderfully happy. Inan and Cannie had two children, and their modest home was situated about a half furlong away from his, which ensured they both had privacy.

Already, the distant cry of a baby drifted up towards him. He recognised who it was immediately, and no doubt baby Odo needed feeding again. His eyes crinkled as his face broke into a broad smile. At times, the sound of children laughing or crying filled the valley, and it sounded more like a nursery than a simple farm. Odo didn't mind; he loved it. Eager to see joyful faces, he squeezed his legs, turned his horse, and rode down into the valley. His grin only widened when he saw his oldest, Katherin, stumble in the awkward gait of a two-and-half-year old from their home. Josceline, a step behind, carried Odo, their youngest, on her hip and welcomed him warmly as William slept.

In the typical Scottish tradition of handfasting[18], they both consented to marry not long after arriving. Josceline wanted Cannie and Inan to be with them, and the small betrothal ceremony, without a priest, took place at Castle Carrick on a beautiful summer day. Since then, life had been hard, the days long, but both were content and very much in love. Josceline blossomed, motherhood suited her, and she had indeed become a loving, supportive and hardworking wife.

It wasn't until later, when the children were asleep, that Josceline and Odo had time to talk. The fire spat in the hearth, its warmth comforting.

"The *cotters*[19] say this winter will be cold and wet, and already I saw deer trail again today. Their food is becoming scarce, and they're coming down from the hills to feed on our grass," said Odo once he'd told Josceline and updated her of the news from neighbours.

"We need meat, and we haven't had any for a week or so. Will you hunt soon?" she asked.

"Aye, I will. On the morrow, I will bring us venison, and we can feast."

"Inan and Cannie will be pleased."

Continuing the habit from when he was a Templar, Odo preferred to eat meat three or four times a week, while Inan and Cannie chose to eat meat more often. He avoided slaughtering their own animals, they were too valuable, and generally, he hunted only game to feed his family.

---

18 *Handfasting – A term for betrothal where both participants 'consent' and the ceremony is completed with a handshake, a pledge. Witnesses or a priest aren't required.*

19 *Cotter – Scottish medieval word for peasant farmer.*

Odo saddled his horse and prepared for the morning ahead. Before the sun had fully risen, he'd replaced his bowstring, selected half–a–dozen of his best-hunting arrows, and after saying farewell to the children and Josceline, departed with one of his pack horses in tow. Already, he could see Inan heading out to begin digging a new drainage ditch before the heavy rains came.

Hunting deer was difficult. They were always alert to danger, and the wind needed to cooperate so he could stalk and approach them undetected. Over the last couple of years, he'd learned their habits and knew from which direction they came and where they liked to forage on the best grass. To be able to stalk them, he'd need to take a circuitous route and then slowly approach them from downwind.

Because the prevailing wind came in from the sea, Odo needed to ride in a northerly direction, over the hills, circle around, dismount and creep back up to the summit, where hopefully he could select a suitable sized deer grazing on the other side. He never killed fawn's or the bigger harts or hinds; he always chose a smaller animal for the tenderest venison. On a larger animal, the meat would spoil and go to waste long before it could all be eaten, and managing a larger carcass was more difficult when hunting alone.

He knew where to find the deer, and if lucky, he'd make a quick kill. Once he'd bled the deer, he'd heave the carcass on his packhorse and be home well before the sun began its descent and then hang it, and preferably allow it to age for a day or two before butchering it.

With utmost care, he crept silently up the slope. In one hand, he carried his bow, while the other hand was used to help climb. The conditions were almost ideal. The sun was directly above, and the wind had settled to a light coastal onshore breeze which was practically perfect. As he approached the summit and headed towards a large boulder perched on top, he slowed. Cautiously, he crested the hill and stood with his back to the boulder to remain undetected. Earlier, and from a distance, he'd seen the deer but didn't know with certainty if they were still there, but if they were, and they sensed him, they would run. He needed to have his bow and an arrow ready and be quick.

Careful not to alert the deer, he notched an arrow, partially drew back on the bowstring, and pointed the arrow down between his feet. When his breathing slowed, he cautiously raised the bow and stepped out from behind the boulder.

In an instant, he scanned the terrain and saw the small herd of about a dozen red deer about forty paces away. Instinctively he selected a young buck who stood side on and presented a good target, quickly swinging the bow around as he pulled back on the drawstring. The deer saw him, and for the briefest moment, they raised their heads and froze. Odo released the arrow, and he knew he'd made a kill before the arrow struck the animal. The large head of the hunting arrow diagonally entered the buck just behind the front shoulder and pierced its heart and lungs. It was a perfect shot.

He would bleed and dress[20] the animal before retrieving his packhorse, and he set about his grisly task with a very sharp knife. Already the sun was

---

20 Dress – remove internal organs.

well past its zenith, and he knew he'd arrive home later than expected. With effort, he managed to hoist the carcass over the packhorse, and drenched in sweat, led the animal down the slope towards his hobbled horse and retraced his path towards home. He detoured slightly as he approached the valley, released the packhorse, which would begin to amble towards home on its own, and trotted to the summit to gaze out over his land as he always did.

Smoke did not drift from his chimney or even from Inan's home. Odo's eyes narrowed in puzzlement as he scanned the valley floor beneath him. Animals didn't graze; they were unmoving and were still. His chest tightened as the tendrils of fear crept up through his body. His heart began to beat furiously, and in desperation, he began searching for activity. Nothing moved, nothing stirred.

In growing panic, he searched the hills around him, looking for signs. He saw nothing untoward and, in consuming dread, spurred his horse and galloped down the hill towards home.

He took in the scene immediately. A pall of death hung over his land. Cows, sheep, and horses had been cruelly slaughtered and lay upon the grass with flies already buzzing and feasting on congealing blood. It was pure carnage. "Josceline! Josceline!" he yelled as his destrier thundered towards his home.

He leapt from the horse, sprinted through the open door, and again frantically yelled for her. There was no answering cry, no joyful shriek of a baby; there was only a stark, cold emptiness. He froze in horror. Inside was a shambles; their sparse furniture had been overturned and destroyed, and he could see the damage wasn't the result of a struggle; the destruction was deliberate and malicious, just like the death of his livestock. Worry and concern twisted painfully to a new, unwelcome feeling of sheer terror as he thought about the safety of his precious family.

Without hesitation, he ran back outside. "Josceline!" he cried with all his might and paused to listen for a reply. Other than his furiously beating heart, it was deathly quiet; nothing stirred.

He unsheathed his sword and tentatively walked around the perimeter of the house and immediately saw a body. He was relieved to see it was a stranger, and curiously he had an arrow embedded in his neck. Carefully be bent lower and recognised the arrow; it was one of Josceline's, but not the man; he'd never laid eyes on him before. *She'd killed him with her bow.* "Josceline!" he yelled again.

He ran around the corner and found another body, also killed by an arrow that protruded from the man's gut. He rushed past, sparing the man only a cursory glance.

In the event of an attack, he'd instructed Josceline and Inan to gather everyone and head to safety behind the boulders at the base of the hill.

It had taken them many days, but carefully, he and Inan had pried loose boulders and moved them to create a small hidden space. Only a careful inspection would reveal the area behind the rocks where two families could safely hide and defend themselves if needed. It was to this area that Odo ran.

He never made it. On seeing the heaped bodies in a bloodied tangle of arms and legs, he slowed in open-mouthed disbelief and fell to his knees as the hills reverberated with the cry of his painful lament. Thrown onto an untidy pile and discarded like unwanted garbage lay his dear family, and Odo wailed. His sorrow was encompassing and complete, like a spreading stain that indelibly marked his body. The tears that streamed from his filthy face instantly washed away the happiness of a joyful life and exposed the raw nerves of a tormented soul. His beloved Josceline ... their children, Katherin, William and baby Odo – dead.

He lay on the ground, curled into a ball, with his arms tightly wrapped around his heaving body, while his discarded sword lay forgotten at his side. As the late afternoon sun slowly traversed across a leaden sky, and oblivious of time, Odo lay alone, in total despair and misery. Spent of energy, he wept, and occasionally, a pitiful cry escaped his lips. Increasingly, his thoughts turned to his death; he wanted to die, here and now, and take his life to rejoin his family.

He had no desire to live, or even respond to the sound behind him. He was mindless and lost to the suffering, numb to everything except his loss ... but the noise continued and rudely persisted. At first, he ignored it. He didn't know for how long he lay on the ground, and he didn't care, but the incessant sound wouldn't stop. It was an intrusion, a disruption, and it trespassed on his grief. In anguish, he stirred, reached for his sword and rose unsteadily to his feet. With trembling hands, he held his weapon upright towards the sinking sun and stared at the cold steel blade - he knew then and understood that it would be the instrument of his death.

But the noise behind him was relentless, and with each passing moment, twisted his devastated mind into wretched fury. He stumbled towards the source of the obtrusive sound. It was the man with the arrow in his gut. He lived.

Odo coldly glared at the wounded man without sympathy or feeling. The fire in his belly rivalled the pain of the man who lay moaning at his feet. He tried to speak and couldn't; it was too much, and he heaved and retched. What flew from his mouth was the goodness from his body and the last remnants of a normal, happy life. He didn't bother wiping his face; he stared down at the man with vomit dripping from quivering lips.

"Who are ye, who did this!" he screamed. Sick and spittle flew from his mouth as his body shook uncontrollably in a virulent rage.

The injured man weakly looked up and grimaced, his torment not close to what Odo felt. Odo lifted his foot and stomped on the man's distended stomach. It was a hard, brutal thump and another tortured cry of pain filled the once peaceful valley.

"Who did this?" Odo repeated with clenched teeth.

The arrow moved in time to the man's laboured breathing, he looked up at Odo with a measure of hope, but his silent plea for help went unheeded. "C, Cour–" was all he managed.

Odo bent down. "The Courteneys?"

The man nodded, held Odo's savage, wide-eyed stare, and then closed his eyes.

Odo straightened and drove his sword down through the man's exposed neck.

The bloodied sword swung from his hand, and with tear-filled eyes, stared hopelessly at the pile of bodies that was his family. He couldn't bear to look and turned his head away. He felt paralysed. The grief was total and cruelly vivid; it was consuming and complete. There was nothing more to live for, and he accepted that only death would end it all. He reversed the sword and placed it vertically, hilt down, onto the stony ground and knew sanctity and peace were mere moments away. With an aching heart, he stared down at the blade that offered respite and salvation.

At first, he thought it was a bird, another untimely intrusion. Then he heard it again, but louder – a faint, delicate sound. It was a whimper, and he raised his head in growing awareness. With a tenuous thread of reason, he listened, and then his lips began moving in silent prayer.

He took a slow, tentative laboured step towards the sound, and the sword toppled onto rocks with a clatter; the sound was jarring and helped rouse his disordered mind back to the present. He took another step, and then he ran. He sprinted past lifeless heaped bodies and towards the boulders at the base of the hill. Just as he appeared to run into them, he veered and turned sharply to the left and disappeared behind a wall of stacked rocks and what he saw was a gift, a slender strand of hope that offered him life. Wrapped in a blanket between the boulders was his youngest son, baby Odo. Weeping for joy, he picked up the bundle and clutched it protectively to the warmth of his chest. *She saved Odo, she saved Odo,* he thought repeatedly. Overcome, he slid to the ground and tightly closed his eyes as his body began to shake.

Baby Odo cried and reminded his father he was hungry. Still numb, Odo knew he must find milk and feed him. Carrying his son, he reentered the bastle and searched for the bucket of milk that always sat in the corner with a cloth draped over it. Thankfully, it hadn't been overturned in the chaos. He found the cow horn nearby; it was perforated at the tip and allowed baby Odo to drink contentedly when filled with milk.

As he fed him, Odo wondered what to do. One thing was certain, and with thoughts of taking his own life cast aside, he knew that he needed to protect the boy and leave the valley as quickly as possible.

CHAPTER TWELVE

He dug into the ground with fierce determination. Oblivious to the time and with agonising slowness, the hole eventually deepened and widened. He barely had the strength, but his resolve was extreme; he fought through his torment and lovingly lay each body into the grave; Josceline in the middle, Katherin on her left and little William on her right. When finally buried, he held baby Odo in his arms and prayed for them all.

He discovered more bodies. Inan, Cannie and their two children were also brutally slain. He wearily dug another grave and also offered them a tearful prayer. Every living creature on his land, both man and beast, had been slaughtered; nothing survived; it was a complete massacre.

It was pitch black when Odo walked away. From this day on, he knew life would forever be different for baby Odo and himself. He spent a sleepless night enveloped in woeful despair while daybreak couldn't come quick enough.

With the buck he killed the previous day now discarded, he loaded the packhorse with essential supplies and prepared to leave, he knew he would never, ever return; he couldn't. Before riding away, and with one more thing to do, he clambered up into the upper level of his house, and with his sword, pried a brick loose from the wall. Hurriedly, he removed three more which revealed a large cavity. Inside was a wooden chest filled with gold coin. Most of it was what Josceline had brought with her almost three years ago, the remainder was his, and he had hidden it here, years earlier, before he gave his vows and joined the Templars. With the gold coins transferred to a couple of sacks and securely stowed on the packhorse, he set off as quickly as possible towards his closest neighbours. In the crook of his arm, baby Odo slept.

It was midday when he approached his nearest neighbour's home. Seeing the unexpected visitor, the widower, Alistair, greeted him politely, but his expression hardened when he saw the baby. His four children peeked out curiously from behind the door of their modest home.

"What happened, Odo?" Alistair asked without hesitation.

Odo swallowed. He had difficulty talking and shook his head before taking a deep breath. "I need yer help, Alistair. Jocel–, Jocel–" He coughed and cleared his throat. "They're all dead … killed by outlaws."

Instantly, Alistair was on guard. "Are they still here? Where are they?" His head swivelled from side to side as he scanned the distance for intruders. He didn't offer condolences or sympathy; it wasn't the way of the man.

Odo shrugged. "I think they've gone fer now. But, er, I need ye to take care of baby Odo, can ye do this fer me?"

The wiry man looked at Odo and shook his head. "I hardly have enough to feed the wee' uns as it is. I have not enough to feed another mouth. Sorry, Odo. T'is gonna be a hard winter."

Odo nodded. He didn't want to waste any more time with him. He jerked the reins, squeezed his legs, and his horse responded and began to walk off.

"I wish yer well!" shouted Alistair.

Odo didn't reply, and he headed for another neighbour.

It was late afternoon when Odo arrived at the bastle of Rob and Lili Mac a' Phì. He was exhausted, and baby Odo had been grizzling for some time. He carefully dismounted, and soon as Lili saw the bundle in Odo's arms, she grabbed the baby and whisked him inside, which allowed Odo and Rob to talk.

Rob and Lili had five children, three girls and two boys. They were a handful, and both Rob and Lili constantly struggled with their oldest, a sixteen-year-old and very obstinate daughter. Once her mind was made up, she was as stubborn as could be. Threats did little more than rile her, and no matter how much her parents pleaded, it did little good; she wouldn't relent or change her mind, which ultimately led to frequent conflict. Much to her parents' surprise and relief, she took baby Odo from her mother and immediately began to clean and then feed him without being asked.

"We feel fer ye, Odo," Rob shook his head in sympathy and disgust when he learned what had happened.

"Ye poor, man. What will ye do?" asked Lili. She kept an eye on her oldest daughter, who was still feeding baby Odo.

They sat inside the bastle near the hearth. Odo's head was in his hands, and he fought to keep his emotions in control.

"I, I don't know," he replied slowly. "I fear fer Odo's safety. When the outlaws find out he still lives, they'll come back."

"Then ye know who did this, and why?" Rob asked.

Odo removed his hands. "I think so. It's revenge fer something that happened some years ago. They want to see my death. So, I know they'll come again."

"Then we are in danger?" Rob looked worried.

"Nay, fer now ye are safe, whoever the men are, they've gone." He paused for a dozen heartbeats as he gathered his thoughts. "I can't take care of Odo… he needs a home, somewhere safe until I return." He glanced at Rob, then turned to Lili. "I was hoping that ye could look after him, er, fer a while at least?"

Rob and Lili exchanged a look. "Odo," began Rob, "Ye and the baby are welcome to stay the night, but… but we can't take care o'the wee lad. We want t'help ye, we really do. But times are hard. Ye will have to be on yer way in the morn."

Odo looked over at Rob and Lili's oldest daughter. She was quite large for her age, yet she showed extreme tenderness to the baby she coddled. He turned back to Rob and Lili. "Aye, I know its best."

"Where will ye go, Odo? Do ye have friends, family who can help ye?" Lili asked.

"I have a sister but know not where she lives. I have no one who I can trust. I, I uh don't know what to do." Again, he buried his face in his hands as he felt overcome.

Rob looked sympathetic. "Ye need a safe manor… perhaps in England, somewhere far from here might be best."

Odo yanked his hands away from his face and looked at Rob. "A manor…?"

"Aye, that's what I said."

An idea was forming in Odo's mind. He recalled the young couple he and Josceline encountered near Kings Lynn when set upon by outlaws. It was over two and a half years ago, and he was trying to remember their names and where they were going.

Lili saw his reaction. "Ye have a notion?"

"Aye, I do, but need to think on it more."

Odo was repositioning his belongings on the packhorse and was about to lead him outside into the morning's gloom when he heard an argument coming from inside the bastle. He knew better to involve himself in another man's family affairs and returned to thinking about his journey south. He vaguely remembered the manor the man had spoken of but couldn't recall its name. All he knew was that it was in Devonshire. That was far enough away to provide safety to baby Odo, and without an alternative, that was where he would go.

He retrieved his destrier, tightened the saddle and went back to the bastle to get baby Odo. The argument inside continued. When he entered, the yelling stopped.

"Uh, I'm sorry," he said, "I didn't mean to interrupt, but I must be on my way."

Rob stepped up to him. "Odo, can we chat a moment?"

Curious, Odo followed Rob outside.

"Odo, Rosa doesn't want to give baby Odo up. She refuses." He stood with his hands on hips and kicked at a rock in frustration.

"I can't stay here, Rob, ye and yer family won't be safe if Odo remains. Ye were right, is best we both leave."

"Aye, but… Rosa is adamant, she can be pig-headed, and this is one of these times. I swear that lass lives to torment me." He cursed. "She 'ought to be married and have her own wee 'uns by now and not living here." Rob kicked at another stone.

Odo turned his back on Rob and walked a few steps away to think. "Rob?" he said and turned back to his neighbour. "What if I took her with me? I'll give ye some coin, and perhaps I could buy a horse from ye, she could take care of Odo fer me, what say, ye?"

Rob took a deep breath and held Odo's expectant gaze. "Let me speak to Lili." He walked back inside the bastle, leaving Odo alone with his two horses.

Odo was becoming concerned with the lateness of his departure. He looked towards the bastle. At least the yelling and fighting had stopped. Finally, the door opened, and Rob and Lili appeared.

"Odo," began Rob. "We know ye will take care of Rosa, but what will ye do when ye arrive, will ye send her back?"

"Only if she wants to." Odo shrugged. "I will insist she returns here, but what if she doesn't?"

Rob and Lili nodded; they recognised the volatile nature of their daughter only too well.

"I will make sure Rosa comes back and that she is well-cared fer on her return, ye won't have a worry," Odo added with a measure of hope that they would allow her to go with him.

Rob stepped closer to Odo and lowered his voice. "Ah, Odo, it isn't that. Er, might be best if the lass, uh… didn't come back." He looked guilty. "Er, uh, she eats a lot, too."

Odo recoiled. *They don't want her to return home.* He thought quickly. "Uh, I understand." He scratched his chin as he considered the implications. He needed her to look after the baby, and what would he do with her once he arrived in Devonshire? He'd worry about that later. "Let me purchase a horse and pay ye. Have Rosa bring a few things; we travel quickly and lightly."

Rob and Lili almost looked relieved.

Rosa sat astride the horse Odo purchased from her father. Baby Odo was comfortably nestled in a sling that wrapped over her shoulders and seemed to be quite content. As they rode away, Odo saw Rob comfort Lili who looked distraught at seeing their daughter ride away. Rosa was unaffected. *Perhaps Lili's tears are joyous?* he wondered.

Odo's face tightened as he pointed his horse south. Despite lack of sleep and distress, he was reasonably focused, and his eyes scanned the countryside ahead, looking for threat and danger. He spared a quick glance behind. Rosa was singing to baby Odo, the packhorse plodded along and happily trailed behind.

Odo didn't want to talk or enter into any conversation with Rosa. He preferred to ride ahead in reflective solitude and think of Josceline, their children and the time they'd had together. It wasn't about planning for revenge, that would come later; for the present, his primary concern was only for Odo's safety. Once the boy was secure, he would concentrate his efforts on the Courteney family.

Seeking vengeance at any cost was not the solution. Odo knew he needed to put aside his anger and act with considered thought. He recalled Sir Piers' words, *'Acting on emotion may see yer death.'* That advice rang true, and first and foremost, he needed to protect baby Odo, and if he were dead, then he couldn't do that.

They'd crossed over into England without trouble. Occasionally Rosa would inform them they needed milk, or better yet, a wetnurse if one could be found. When baby Odo cried, Rosa would sing, it wasn't melodic or particularly delightful to listen to, but it seemed to help. Odo was genuinely surprised, Rosa was all he could have hoped for, and the baby was happy.

Late one afternoon, they approached a small hamlet, and a group of youths carrying farm tools were returning home, and they had to make way for Odo and Rosa by walking alongside the narrow path as they passed. Odo heard them yell a few unsavoury comments at her, but nothing malicious, just boys being boys who enjoyed teasing girls, he reasoned. He looked behind as she rode past them and saw her turn and wag a finger at them, "I'll see ye wee lads later," she said.

One youth, quick of mind, quipped in reply, "If mother don't fall from her 'orse."

Rosa gave them a withering look, but nothing more was said.

They entered the hamlet, and Odo sought an inn. Previously, he and Rosa had almost come to blows when he insisted they spend their nights outdoors. She stomped her foot, folded her arms, and told him they would sleep indoors, where it was warm, and baby Odo wouldn't become poorly. She wouldn't change her mind, no matter how he explained to her that it was dangerous and voiding towns and people would keep them safe. He didn't want to be recognised or remembered, he informed her. It made little difference. She adamantly refused to listen, and in reaching a peaceful compromise, and whenever the opportunity availed, they'd share a room with two beds.

Odo was tired, and after the horses were taken care of and stabled, he wanted to spend time with his son. Wearily, he lay down on his cot and began to play with baby Odo while Rosa searched for food and other necessities. He wasn't worried about her, as she could handle herself. In fact, he pitied anyone who tried accosting her. Not only was she a large young woman, but she was also unbelievably strong. However, this evening she was late returning, and he became more anxious and fearful. Much to his relief, he finally heard her heavy footfall outside the door and then she entered. She appeared flustered, and her face was flushed.

"Are ye troubled, Rosa? Did ye have bother?"

She turned to him, and he recognised her expression. She didn't want to be trifled with. "I have returned, have I not?" She leaned down and lifted baby Odo from his chest. "From now on, ye will call me, Mother Rosa," she exclaimed.

Odo raised an eyebrow at the unusual declaration. He wasn't going to argue. "Very well, em, er, Mother Rosa." She offered no explanation for her tardiness, and the subject was never spoken about again.

Two weeks into their journey, they were riding south when suddenly, and unbidden, he remembered. It came to him from nowhere. "Mellester Manor!" he said aloud.

Mother Rosa, as he'd now been calling her, queried him.

"Mellester Manor, that's where we are heading," he told her.

He looked behind, and she just smiled and said nothing.

He turned forward, surveyed the countryside, and rode on while baby Odo cooed happily in the sling. Odo began worrying about Rosa's willingness to hand baby Odo to the farmer and his wife in Mellester if they were willing to take the boy. He dreaded the thought and believed if she wanted to keep baby Odo, a physical confrontation would ensue… and then what would he do with her? He wouldn't be able to keep her anywhere near the boy.

Already there was a noticeable change in the weather. It was becoming colder and rained more frequently. He was becoming impatient and hoped to arrive In Mellester soon.

CHAPTER THIRTEEN

Mellester Manor was indeed a small hamlet, thought Odo as he glanced around. Above him, on a hill, sat a substantial stone manor house that overlooked the village and fields below. A main road dissected the village, and it looked peaceful and would have been serene if not for an argument someone was having not far away. He ignored the disturbance, surveyed the buildings around him, and wondered where the farmer and his wife lived. A small run-down church sat on the corner of the main road and the main village thoroughfare, but he saw no sign of a priest whom he could query. After a moment or two, he thought it best to find the manor's reeve. From memory, the farmer spoke about the reeve as a friend, and no doubt could point him in the right direction.

A woman approached and was about to walk past. "Fare thee well? he greeted.

She dipped her head in respect and averted her eyes. To her, it was apparent, the armed man astride the large horse was a knight. She was heedful and uncomfortable. "Aye, thank ye, kind, sir," she replied, eager to be on her way.

"I seek the reeve. Can ye tell me where I may find him?"

She stopped and pointed down the road. "That would be 'im, Reeve Norman, with the red beard."

Odo looked carefully and saw the man she pointed at was involved in the shouting match. "Thank ye."

The woman nodded and took a step to walk on, then paused and turned to stare back at the men whose shouting had just escalated. Other villagers also stopped what they were doing to gawk.

Odo looked back at Mother Rosa, "Remain here."

He spurred his horse and began to ride towards the small group of men. As he drew near, he could see two of the men were knights, and from their behaviour, they appeared to be drunk and were heckling another man, a serf. The reeve, as Odo observed, was trying desperately to diffuse the quarrel. He reined in near them and watched.

The two knights were determined and boisterously insisted that the peasant crawl on all fours along the ground. The reeve was doing his best to allow the peasant to walk away and spare him the humiliation. The knights thought otherwise. Odo was curious about how the reeve would deal with the drunken knights and allow them to maintain their dignity and that of the peasant. Suddenly, one of the knights drew a sword and went to poke the defenceless peasant in the chest.

The reeve responded by bravely stepping between the sword and the hapless serf. "Ye've had yer foolery, good sirs, allow this man to be on his way. He's done ye no harm," he said.

The knight withdrew the sword, then quickly struck the reeve with the flat of the blade across his upper arm. "Move aside, Reeve."

The strike didn't draw blood, but Odo could see the blow smarted. The unarmed reeve staggered, regained his footing, straightened, and with a grim expression, again appealed for the knights to stop. He turned to the peasant. "Off ye go, hasten home."

"Nay!" shouted one of the knights. "Ye will crawl like a dog!" He went to strike at the reeve again.

Odo had seen and heard enough. With a loud sigh, he dismounted and stepped towards the two knights. He saw they were young, inexperienced, and oozed cockiness and attitude. "Methinks, it's unsporting to pick on men who cannot defend themselves from such gallant knights as yerselves," he said, "perhaps ye should heed the advice of the reeve and allow this man to be on his way."

The reeve turned to the imposing stranger in surprise and with some relief.

The two grinning knights assessed him carefully. While their judgement was impaired, they were astute enough to see the stranger was armed, tall and muscular. Not a man to be taken lightly. Their smiles turned to nervous apprehension, and suddenly they weren't quite so sure of themselves.

Odo turned to the peasant. "Best ye go, as yer reeve suggests."

The visibly frightened peasant looked to the reeve for confirmation.

"On yer way, Peter," the reeve urged.

Needing no further encouragement, the peasant quickly ran off, and the reeve and the knights continued their appraisal of the armed stranger.

"Reeve Norman," Odo began while ignoring the two knights, "may I speak with ye?" he turned his back on the knights, placed an arm on the back of the reeve and encouraged him to move away. The knights watched and remained silent. After a few steps, he heard them laugh and thankfully, they turned away and headed towards the inn. Odo was relieved.

"Milord, thank ye fer yer assistance, but I know ye not."

"Reeve Norman, I seek a herdsman and his woman who brought cows to Mellester about two, or three years ago. Would ye know of them?"

The reeve was instantly wary. The man before him was heavily armed, his bright blue eyes were intense, and he sensed an experienced and dangerous warrior behind the easy smile. It was obvious he was a knight and needed to be treated with respect afforded to nobility. Yet the stranger had helpfully diffused the situation with the two drunken knights and tactfully avoided conflict. He gave the request some thought, then nodded. "Perhaps milord, but as reeve, it is my duty to ensure ye mean them no harm."

Odo understood the reeve's reticence. "I am known to them both, and I believe my presence here will not cause distress."

Reeve Norman saw the knight's destrier and the young woman sitting on the horse carrying a baby. "Then milord, ye won't mind if I accompany ye?"

"Nay."

"Take yer horses and follow me," suggested the reeve.

The reeve led Odo, Mother Rosa and the three horses up the road. Villagers stared as the small procession walked through the square and continued past. The reeve stopped at the very last home on the right-hand side, and Odo, along with the reeve's help, tied the horses to the fence beside a byre.

It was a typical cruck house built of daub, wattle, and mud. A single sturdy door provided the only access from the street.

"I expect Godwin and Hetti should be here," said the reeve and then knocked on the door as Odo helped Mother Rosa down from her horse.

The door opened, and Odo recognised her immediately.

Hetti looked bewildered, then broke into a broad smile, "Odo?" She turned back, "Godwin! Godwin! Come." Then she looked past Odo and onto the street. She saw Mother Rosa with the baby and, in puzzlement, looked back at Odo. "Where is Josceline?"

Hetti and Mother Rosa were cleaning the baby, and Odo, Reeve Norman and Godwin sat on benches in front of the hearth. They'd been talking for some time, and Odo had explained the tragedy that befell his family.

Hetti was wiping her eyes, and Godwin shook his head in disbelief. "Odo, I don't know what to say, I have no words...."

Reeve Norman watched and listened. While he didn't know this knight, the story he told was tragic and beyond belief. He had sympathy for him, the way he explained the death of his wife and children was heart-wrenching.

Odo took another deep breath. It helped to steady his emotions. He looked around the cruck and saw no evidence of children. "Have ye children?" he asked.

"Nay, God has not blessed us yet," Godwin replied.

"But we keep hoping," replied Hetti, still dabbing her eyes.

Odo raised his head and looked up towards the thatched roof. He needed a moment to compose himself. "I, uh, travelled here to Mellester to seek yer help. I can't take care of baby Odo, and I must leave alone. I have to end the killing, fer if I fail or do nothing, they will find and kill me, then Odo. He will never be safe unless I do this." He met the gaze of Godwin, then Hetti, and continued. "I do not know fer how long I will be gone, perhaps many, many months or longer. Can ye take care of Odo until I return? I will pay ye, I have coin," he appealed.

Hetti stepped up to stand beside her husband and placed her hand on his shoulder. Odo spared a quick look at Mother Rosa, who was cradling baby Odo and prayed she wouldn't cause a fuss. He again glanced at Godwin and Hetti. "Er, perhaps, I can allow ye some privacy to talk... I need to think a little too," Odo suggested and rose from his seat.

Seeking solitude and quietness, Odo walked away from the village and ambled towards a bridge that spanned a river. On his right, healthy cows grazed on lush, thick grass, and he presumed they were Godwin's. As he approached the river, he saw mist rising and could hear a waterfall. He crossed over the bridge, walked alongside a narrow riverwalk parallel to the river towards the falls, and looked down.

Stained brown by recent heavy rains, dark, silted water cascaded over sizeable boulders to begin its clamorous and chaotic plunge. Worn smooth from erosion, gleaming wet rocks embedded into both sides of the narrow chasm increased its force and funnelled the river, propelling the turbulent water forwards and down to collide on rocks in a continuous explosion of noise and spray. Caught by the prevailing breeze, even mild gusts whisked the spray up and back, where it fell like a gentle soft rain. It was invigorating, and with approaching darkness, he felt a calmness descend over him. He wasn't sure how long he stood watching... He pulled his gaze from the falls and looked up and saw Godwin leaning on the bridge handrail, watching him.

Odo walked from the falls towards him.

"T'is beautiful, is it not?" Godwin asked.

"Aye, it is. It brings me a calmness," Odo replied as he stepped up to him

"It is called Falls Ende."

"Falls Ende, eh," Odo repeated, then turned to look at the river one more time. "I hope I can visit here many more times."

Godwin saw the pain etched on the face of the weary knight and felt pity for him. "Come, let us return," he said.

Reeve Norman was still inside and welcomed Odo back with a smile.

"Milord, uh, Odo, we have thought carefully on this matter," said Godwin. Hetti stood smiling at his side, and Mother Rosa was gently rocking baby Odo backwards and forwards in her arms. "We will take care of baby Odo, we have no children of our own, and we can gladly do this for ye."

Odo felt the tension release and lowered his head. After a moment, he looked up and nodded. "Very well, thank ye, kindly." He took a big breath and prepared to battle with Mother Rosa, who had not commented or reacted to the decision. He rose from his seat and cautiously approached, with his arms extended to take baby Odo from her.

She looked up, met his gaze, then raised the baby and kissed him on the forehead and handed him over. He took Odo from her and spared her a look of puzzlement. She must have seen his expression. "Did ye think I wouldn't hand him back to ye?" she asked.

"Well, it had crossed my mind," he replied.

"I have no need fer baby Odo."

Odo's eyebrows furrowed, "Why is that?"

Godwin, Hetti and Reeve Norman listened keenly.

"Because I am with child," she said, then thrust her nose in the air.

Odo almost dropped the baby. "What is this? How is this possible!" he exclaimed.

She looked guiltily at him as he tried to remember back, along their journey… "Those lads, alongside the road, not long after we crossed over into England," he stated. "T'was them, wasn't it Rosa?" It was the evening when she had been late returning, he recalled that night all too well.

He saw her face colour.

Sensing his anger, she stood, placed both her hands on her expansive hips and glared at him. "I will not expect charity from anyone. I will have this baby, I will work and be a good mother and provide! Do ye not think I can't?" She inclined her head and waited. It was evident, she'd made a declaration and now waited to see if anyone was foolish enough to dispute her claim.

Of one thing Odo was sure of, Rosa, Mother Rosa would be a good mother. "But ye need work, a er, husband to earn coin and to provide."

"And I *can* milk cows, I'm a good milkmaid and have strong hands." She thrust a finger at him. "I will work longer and harder than most anyone, ye included, Odo Brus." She continued to glare at him and then clenched her fists.

Odo could see she was poised and ready for a fight that he wanted no part of.

"Can ye really milk cows?" Godwin asked.

"Aye, most better than anyone."

"Aye, strong she is," added Odo. "Of that, there is no doubt."

Reeve Norman shifted on his seat, then looked at her. "If Godwin takes ye on, ye'll need a place to live. I have a cruck, not four doors down that is empty, but ye'll need to pay rent to the lord of the manor."

All heads turned to Godwin. "Ye'll need to be here a'fore the sun rises. And if ye can prove ye can milk cows as ye say ye can, then I will take ye on."

Odo felt the relief. But he was still shaken with the revelation she was with child. A good thing her ma and pa, Rob and Lili weren't here, he thought.

"Good, that is settled then," said Mother Rosa with a satisfied smile ending the potential for any further discussion.

Odo thought carefully and decided he would pay her rent for a while, at least until she was settled. It was the least he could do. Thankfully, his dilemma of what to do with her had been solved. She wouldn't return to Scotland.

It was challenging and took some willpower, but eventually, he handed baby Odo to the eager arms of Hetti and then took a room at the inn. Reeve Norman showed Mother Rosa the cruck house he had for her and allowed her to spend the night there until she could prove she could work as a milkmaid.

He didn't sleep well, as his thoughts turned from his son to the Courteney family and all they'd done. Obviously, they were patient, and he knew they would continue their search for him. They had waited almost three years to exact revenge for the death of the eldest son, and no doubt they would eventually discover that they had failed in their quest for revenge. A baby boy survived, and he still lived, but would the small hamlet of Mellester in the south of England provide a haven for them both?

As long as the name Odo Brus was never again used, then he felt his son would be secure and protected here, but the name Odo Brus had to be forgotten. While he was relieved to be free of the burden of taking care of Mother Rosa, he felt quite good about the outcome. Godwin was thrilled with her milking abilities, and now she had work, a place to live, and to everyone's astonishment, she was with child. More importantly, baby Odo was with a good, honest couple who would take care of him until he returned. He liked Mellester Manor, and while small, it was perfect.

It was hard to leave baby Odo behind and much more difficult than he first believed. Hetti stood near his horse and cradled the baby as he stared down at his son. He swallowed his emotions and fought the need to leap from his horse and take the boy. He thought of Josceline, Katherin and William, and his expression hardened, and he knew if he didn't put an end to the Courteneys, they would undoubtedly kill the boy. Reluctantly he tore his gaze away from his son, nodded at Hetti, then turned to Godwin, who stood in the doorway. "Thank ye both." He swung his horse around and departed Mellester Manor before he changed his mind and snatched baby

Odo from Hetti.

CHAPTER FOURTEEN

The *Palais de la Cité* in Paris was positively enormous. If the grand *Château de Caen* owned by William X was huge, *Palais de la Cité* dwarfed it. Odo stared up at its towering walls and the spires that rose from the colossal building set behind and wondered how he would be granted an audience with Queen Eleanor.

She had a right to know what had happened to her younger sister, and before he continued with his quest to locate the Courteneys, he would face the unpleasant task of informing her. The fact that Eleanor, who he'd never met, was now Queen of Frankia only complicated things.

He rode towards one of the bridges that led to the sprawling palace, and immediately a lance wielding surly guard, stepped out and aggressively puffed out his chest in challenge. It was unlikely he could ride across without some sort of authorisation.

"Hale to ye! Er, I am Sir Odo Brus of Carrick and wish an appointment with Queen Eleanor!"

The guard laughed and brought his lance to bear. "*Fous le camp*[21]!" he spat and waved him away.

Odo wasn't surprised; he expected as much. He paused a moment as he thought of a suitable message to pass on to the queen.

Before he could speak and request a message be delivered, the guard took another step closer and raised his lance. Disheartened, Odo wheeled his horse around and left before the guard skewered him.

He rode to a nearby inn across the *Sequana*[22] river, where he stabled his horse. From a seat outside, he could easily observe the comings and goings from the palace. With hope and some divine intervention, he believed an opportunity would present itself sooner than later so he could send word to Queen Eleanor.

He waited a week before he saw an armed procession of *chevaliers* depart the palace and escort a carriage over one of the many bridges. The regal sight, along with the royal standard flying proudly, prompted locals to inform him that it was the queen. Another week passed, and again, at the same time, the procession left over the same bridge. Odo reasoned that in a week, she would again depart, and he prepared.

Odo ensured his impressive destrier was dressed in its finest livery, and he had made every attempt to clean his chainmail and wear his finest clothes. He sat a little way from the bridge astride his horse and waited. It wasn't long before *chevaliers* emerged and cleared the way for the queen's procession. He took a big breath; what he was going to do was foolish, and

____

21 *Fous le camp, French - Bugger off.*
22 *Sequana – Roman name for the Seine.*

he risked his life, but there were no other options.

The *Chevalier*s in front rode past and ignored him; a carriage appeared a moment later, and Odo timed his move perfectly. As the carriage pulled alongside, he spurred the horse and leapt forward and, within moments, was riding beside the quickly moving carriage. Drawn curtains prevented him from seeing inside. He bent low and yelled. "Queen Eleanor, I am Odo Brus and have tidings of Josceline!"

There was no response from inside, but there was from behind. He heard a cry of alarm and turned to see the *chevalier*s trailing, spur their chargers and ride towards him with lances extended.

"Queen Eleanor, I am Odo Brus and have tidings on Josceline!" he quickly repeated. The furious *chevalier*s were drawing closer, and there was still no response from inside the carriage. It was time to leave. He swung his horse away from the carriage and charged down a side street, scattering merchants and serfs. Behind, a handful of *chevalier*s followed, then reined in and quickly withdrew to rejoin the procession.

The following day Odo was back at the inn and again watching the entrance to the palace. He was frustrated. His plan had failed miserably, and now, after three weeks, he still had not spoken with Eleanor. Perhaps he shouldn't bother, he thought.

He observed a group of men-at-arms from the palace wandering around. They were spread out and casually strolled in his direction. Suspicious of their intentions, he looked around for the best way to leave unseen, but they had him surrounded; he was trapped. Before he knew it, six men-at-arms stood at his side, and there was nowhere to run.

He was grabbed by the arms, roughly hoisted to his feet, and promptly searched, and all his weapons were removed and confiscated. Without a word of explanation, he was marched towards the palace, and once inside, thrown into a cold, damp gaol. This wasn't what he had in mind when he wanted to enter *Palais de la Cité*. Indeed, it was his reckless antics the day before that brought him here. No doubt he'd have some explaining to do, he thought grimly. On the other hand, a sympathetic ear may yet help him obtain an audience with the queen. At least he was inside the palace. However, he explained to an easy-going guard the reason for his foolhardy actions and gave his name. He resigned himself to a long wait.

The following morn, two guards appeared, unlocked the door, and motioned him to follow. He was led through a labyrinth of corridors, dark passages and up narrow stairs and taken to an opulent well-furnished room where again he was searched.

Four men-at-arms entered, followed by a woman. He'd never met the Queen of Frankia, but he knew it was Eleanor, her resemblance to Josceline was obvious. He bowed deeply from the waist and remained silent as protocol dictated. He knew from past experiences that in the presence of royalty, you speak only when spoken to.

She took a seat and studied him silently. After a moment or two, she leaned forward. "Ye are most fortunate to be recognised. Yer face is well known, as are yer archery skills, Sir Odo. If not fer a man-at-arms or two who remembered ye from *Château de Caen,* you'd be spending considerable time in our dungeons. What ye did yesterday could have cost ye yer life," she coldly stated.

Odo nodded. "Yer Majesty, fergive my behaviour, but I had little choice. I apologise if I frightened ye, I mean ye no harm or ill will." Again, he bowed and hoped his explanation was enough. Her guards stood attentive and ready.

She studied him with intelligent eyes; she probed, and he saw how she was trying to read his thoughts and intentions. Coming to a decision, she relaxed and leaned back in her chair. "What is so important that ye seek an audience with me?"

Odo looked at her in amazement. She didn't know who he was and that he was the man who'd run away and then married her sister. She only gave him an audience because she believed he was just a knight that knew her father. He inhaled.

She must have sensed something, for she tensed, and her expression changed.

"Yer Majesty, I, er, I, bring news of Jos–" He cleared his throat. "I bring news of Josceline."

Eleanor saw his distress and reacted immediately. "Leave us," she instructed her guards.

"Yer Majesty?"

"Go, leave us!"

With reluctance, the four men-at-arms exited the room, leaving Eleanor and Odo alone.

Odo saw her extract a foulard from the sleeve of her dress. She knew he brought bad tidings. "Josceline and our two children, William and Katherin, were slain," he began. He told her everything as she listened patiently. When he was finished, he walked to a window and looked out as

Eleanor wiped her eyes and reflected.

"I was not aware it was ye she had run away with," she stated and then watched him closely. "Fergive me..." She looked down at her hands briefly, then looked at him with glistening eyes. "Ye loved her, did ye not?" she asked.

"Aye, with all my heart, and I still do, I will love her fer always," he replied. His voice was just above a whisper. He could see she was upset and struggled to maintain control.

"She always wanted children and a simple life," Eleanor sighed." I am pleased she was able to live that life with ye," she offered. "And a child lives...?"

"Aye, baby Odo. He is safe and away from danger.... fer now."

"How sure are ye that the Courteneys did this?"

"One of the killers lived, I questioned him," Yer Majesty."

She rose from her chair. "*Bâtards*!" She shook her head and walked towards the window where he stood. "What will ye do?"

Odo spun to face her. "My only son, yer nephew, is in danger. As long as the Courteneys live, they will seek to kill him and then me. I must put an end to this." His expression hardened, and his eyes blazed. "From this day forward, I will no longer be a knight, fer they will easily recognise me, and I *will* hunt fer them."

"I am rueful, Sir Odo. I am sorry fer my sister, fer her children, and fer ye. You must do what is right and what lays in yer heart. But know this, I cannot openly help. The Courteneys are powerful, influential, and the king and I rely on and need their continued support. ...As if we didn't have enough problems within the realm," she added as an afterthought.

She gave him a look of despair and then turned away. Odo silently watched her as she returned to her seat.

"What do ye know about the Courteneys?" she asked when again seated.

Odo shook his head. "I have not begun to learn about them yet."

Eleanor looked reflective and took her time before she spoke. "The man ye killed, Jean Courtney, *was* the eldest son of Count Albert Courteney. Three more brothers remain alive, and the oldest, and now the current heir, is Christophe Courtenay. He is no better than his elder brother, Jean."

Odo was surprised at how effortlessly she could recite the information about the family. He listened intently as she continued.

"However, Christophe has two other younger brothers, Édouard and Léon. The three are inseparable. It would have been the three of them, along with mercenaries, who killed our family." Eleanor dabbed at her eyes with her *foulard*.

"What type of man is Count Courteney?" Odo asked.

Queen Eleanor shook her head. "He is a vile, disgusting man. He is bitter, heartless and cruel."

Odo chewed his lip as he considered what she'd shared with him.

"I can tell ye this, Sir Odo, at this time of year, the Courteneys will be Toulouse, where it is warmer. Ye will find them there."

Odo controlled his pent-up rage. "Thank ye, yer majesty. And of the count?"

"*Non*, he will remain in Burgundy." She made eye contact with him. "Sir Odo, I can do little to help ye, and I hope this is enough. Is there anything else ye need?"

Odo nodded. "Aye, there is. I wish to travel quickly and unencumbered.

My horse is a young destrier. A wonderful, brave beast, but he is not suitable fer what I intend. I need a swift, strong horse. It must be fleet of foot. Have ye an animal I can trade or purchase?" From what Josceline told him of Eleanor, he knew she was an expert horsewoman. She had a keen eye and had a natural ability with horses.

Eleanor smiled for the first time. "I have such a horse fer ye. It will suit yer purpose well."

"Ye are most kind."

"It would serve ye well, Sir Odo, that my involvement in yer quest fer vengeance remains unknown. Do ye understand?" her eyes bored into his.

Odo held her gaze. "Ye have been most generous, Yer Highness, I need no further help, and I will not tell a soul of our meeting."

"Privately, ye have my blessing, and may ye strike fear into each of their hearts… long may they suffer." The *foulard* disappeared as quickly as it appeared. She put a hand to her chest, then stood and extended her other arm.

Odo bent down and pressed his lips to her hand, and straightened.

"I believe ye, Sir Odo." She sighed. "Now then, let us arrange fer ye to acquire this horse."

Odo knew that his quest to kill the three Courteney brothers was dangerous, and he was under no illusion that he could easily be maimed or die in the process. During his trek south from Carrick, he thought about what he could do to protect Odo in the event of his death. There was only one course of action and required an unpleasant task he was hesitant to do.

The order of The Poor Fellow-Soldiers of Christ and of the Temple of Solomon had a strong presence in Paris and had just completed construction of a temple in the area of Le Marais. He rode towards the temple on his new horse, a beautiful black stallion with exquisite fine lines that he traded with Queen Eleanor. The remaining gold coin he'd removed from his bastle in Carrick was secure in a large satchel attached to the saddle. With apprehension about how he would be received, he entered the building and sought the commander.

His unexpected visit caused no alarm, and he was quickly escorted to a chamber where he was brought before the Templar commander, Sir Godfrey de Lessassier.

Sir Godfrey warmly welcomed him with a hug and much backslapping. Once Odo had answered endless questions, the Templar leader looked at him and shook his head. "Sir Piers was devastated by yer decision, Odo, he thought of ye as his son... If only there had been another way...."

"Aye, and I will always have a fondness fer him, fer he is like a father to me, Sir Godfrey, but I also wish there had been another way, but I do not regret my decision."

The Templar commander's look softened. "What is it, young man, what ails ye, fer I see clearly ye are in pain?"

Odo turned away from the knight and collected himself before he spoke. "Sir Godfrey, I have an unusual request and want to ensure the wellbeing of my son in the event of my death."

Sir Godfrey nodded for him to continue. When Odo finished, the knight rubbed his chin and pondered the unusual demand. "I think it best if we transfer yer gold to Combe Templorium in England. I will provide ye with a document that will ensure that your son will understand what to do at the right time. Ye understand Odo, it will be ciphered; no man other than a Templar can read it."

"Aye, Sir Godfrey, it is best this way, but I do not want it known that this coin comes from me, and I want ye to manage this gift like an investment."

"Aye, I see yer point. I think there is a way we can help. Ye have given us so much, and all of us are grateful fer yer sacrifice and service. Is the least we can do, eh? Leave yer gold here, and someone will give it a reckoning and provide ye with the documents. Return on the morrow."

The next morning, Odo returned to the temple, was handed a couple of documents, and told to keep them secure. He looked at the documents and came to a decision. The coded documents would entitle the bearer to all the gold held by the Templars on his behalf.

"Sir Godfrey, may I leave these with ye? I will retrieve them when I return. If I do not return, please ensure they go to my son."

The elderly knight nodded. "As ye wish, Odo."

After saying farewell, Odo mounted his new horse and began preparing for his journey south to Toulouse.

He sold his packhorse and discarded nearly everything, even his chainmail, and kept only the barest of essentials. His sword was of the highest quality, balanced perfectly and expensive - he would need the razor-sharp weapon. He still retained a sizeable portion of gold coin for his needs and bought new breeches, a capuchin and cape, all in dark green or brown in colour. He sought a fletcher and purchased two bundles of the finest arrows for his bow.

Queen Eleanor's comment on how he had been recognised didn't sit well with him, and he acknowledged it was something he had not considered. He saw no reason to keep his face clean-shaven any longer, and he would allow his hair to grow. Along with the clothes he wore, he hoped his disguise would be sufficient.

He rode from Paris and, once in open country, put his new horse through its paces. It was impressive. He'd never ridden a horse that could put on such a turn of such speed. It was well trained and responded perfectly to his commands. While the horse was quite large, it wasn't a warhorse and wasn't trained to kill. He needed to be mindful of that limitation.

CHAPTER FIFTEEN

The sun had almost disappeared over the distant hills, and lengthening shadows expanded outwards, celebrating the end of a glorious day. However, Odo hadn't been contemplating the weather, he'd been thinking about the vile Courteney family and how he would put an end to it all. He'd hoped to reach Toulouse before nightfall, but it wasn't to be. His horse continued at an easy canter, more of a relaxed lope that allowed it to run for extended periods as he searched for a suitable place to settle for the night.

He was riding towards a cluster of trees a short distance ahead when he saw the telltale spiral of smoke, backlit against the setting sun and originating from within the stand of trees he rode towards.

He slowed the horse to a walk and changed direction. He wouldn't ride towards a camp without first scouting the area to determine who or what he was riding towards. Carefully, he circled and warily approached and saw four horses tied to a lengthy rope spanning two trees. The sound of voices and laughter drifted towards him, but he couldn't see anyone as yet. He paused and listened a moment before deciding he would proceed.

"Hail, friends!" he shouted and reined in his horse. It was dangerous to ride into a stranger's campsite without first alerting them of your presence.

The chatter and laughter immediately stopped, then two armed knights quickly appeared.

With a light squeeze of his thighs, he urged his horse to walk forward, and he kept his hands high and visible.

"Hail, stranger," came the reply.

"I was hoping ye would be willing to share the warmth of yer fire and some friendly banter," said Odo as he urged his horse to walk closer to them.

"Are ye alone?" asked the *chevalier*.

"Aye, just me," Odo replied.

The *chevalier*s conversed briefly and then turned back to him. "Aye, ye are welcome. Tie yer horse, yonder to the rope. A stream lies on the other side fer water."

Odo dismounted and led the horse to the stream that ran beside the camp. After the horse was watered and fed, he tethered his horse to the rope and gave the animal a quick rub down. He always took care of the horse's needs before his own. Once completed, he took his bow, quiver, and blanket, then stepped towards the fire and introduced himself. "I am Oswald, from Scotland and ride fer Toulouse."

"Ye are welcome to share our warm fire, Oswald, I am Émile, and this is Théo, we are from Bourges. Do ye come to Toulouse fer the tourney, the *hastilude*[23]?"

---

23 *Hastilude – Martial games. The word 'Jousting' was not used to describe a tournament until years later.*

Odo knew nothing of the tournament and thought quickly. "Aye, but er, only to watch, I am only an archer."

This seemed to satisfy the *chevaliers*, and soon the conversation turned to news and events of interest.

Odo learned that the Count of Toulouse, Raymond IV, held an annual competition. Many nobles travelled south to warmer climates during the winter months, and to break the boredom, the count hosted a tournament where *chevaliers* could challenge each other in a variety of martial disciplines. A reasonable purse was offered to winners of each event, and another sizeable prize was awarded to the *chevalier* who won the most contests. This made sense to Odo and explained why the Courteneys were here.

If he befriended these two *chevaliers*, they could help him blend in. One thing was in his favour, the three remaining Courteney brothers did not know what he looked like. However, as Queen Eleanor had stated, other, unknown men could recognise him, and he hoped his new appearance was enough to conceal his features.

The following morning, the *chevaliers* loaded their packhorses and invited Odo to ride with them into Toulouse.

A large open area had been designated on the outskirts of Toulouse to be used for the martial contests. Various camps had been erected, and pendants and banners flew boastfully from leather tents and heralded allegiances and alliances. It was a grand spectacle, and Odo could see groups of knights talking in various groups, bragging of their skills and prowess. He knew and recognised some of the pendants, but not all.

Sir Émile and Sir Théo invited Odo to camp with them. As he learned, his new friends were not wealthy and did not have the resources to have a bold and overstated presence like so many others. This suited him just fine; he wanted to blend in and be another faceless, unrecognisable man.

For two days, he wandered around and watched the spectacles. Knights contested with swords, and they competed in violent clashes on horseback where opponents attempted to unseat each other when struck by a lengthy blunted lance. He watched the archery competition with more than a casual interest and marvelled at the bowmens' skill and accuracy. He chose not to enter and preferred to remain anonymous. It was when he was observing a horse race that he overheard a conversation and identified Léon Courteney.

It took all his willpower to stop himself from unsheathing his sword and running the man through. Like his brother Jean, Léon was tall, had black hair and was loud, loathsome, and aggressive. He was vehemently berating another knight for a perceived indiscretion, and Odo could see how the young Courteney enjoyed belittling the knight in the presence of others. Even when the knight apologised, Léon continued to humiliate the man. It made Odo sick.

"I will find another *chevalier*, one more worthy of joining us on the *ferae*[24] hunt!" yelled Léon. "Begone, I tire of yer presence."

The aggrieved knight looked embarrassed and walked away to the sound of laughter at his back.

Odo loitered nearby a while longer and identified the Courteney coat-of-arms but learned nothing more. According to Eleanor, Léon's brothers would be close. But he saw no one else that looked like a Courteney.

---

24 Ferae – medieval expression for wild beast

Careful to not draw attention to himself, he wandered away to learn more about the hunt Léon spoke of.

He arrived back at his campsite to see his new friends, Émile and Théo, had returned. Émile had his arm wrapped in a bandage and had been lightly wounded in the sword fighting contest.

Seeing Odo's look of concern, Théo laughed. "But he is the victor, he won and will live to fight again."

Émile managed to shrug, "It is nothing, eh. On the morrow, I will contest another, and perhaps I will win."

"What do ye know of a hunt on the morrow?" Odo casually asked as he sat down on a tree stump beside them.

"Ah, the legendary hunt," Émile answered. "Will ye enter? Have ye been invited to join a team?"

Odo shook his head, "Nay, I heard someone speak of a hunt, and I was curious."

"Four teams made up of five *chevaliers* each will ride onto the hills," Émile pointed with his bandaged arm towards the distant forested hills and winced. "At nightfall, they return with their kill, and the team with the heaviest combined weight of their total kills wins."

Odo looked puzzled. "Four teams of five, that is too many men fer a hunt. It will be difficult."

Émile and Théo laughed. "Ah, *mon ami*, and that is the challenge," continued Théo, "As happens, a team will fiercely compete to outwit and take the prize of a kill from another team. This leads to some anger, and many are injured."

Odo couldn't see sense in it and shook his head.

"Ye do not wish to enter?" Émile asked.

Odo laughed. "Nay, I will rather watch ye fight and win."

"Then ye must wait, fer I fight last in the day."

"I will be there to offer support," Odo added.

Odo rose early, long before the sun had risen, and as quietly as possible left the camp and rode in the direction of the hills where he was told the hunt would take place. In the darkness, he located a tent and flags that identified the hunt-master's camp, and Odo determined, this would be the area where the teams would enter the forest.

The sun had only just begun to rise as he approached the still darkened forest and, with some apprehension, tried to reconnoitre the area and look for places where he could observe and remain unseen. More importantly, when he completed his task, he needed to find a way to leave the forest and return to camp without being identified.

He cautiously picked his way through narrow, darkened paths and climbed higher as sunlight began to seep through the forest's canopy. Eventually, he dismounted and led the horse over a low hill and up the other side towards a sheltered ridge that offered an almost unobstructed view of the valley below him. He hobbled his horse which allowed it to forage without wandering far and then erased the horses' hoofprints before exploring the area around him on foot. He also identified a route that would allow him to leave the forest quickly without becoming lost or seen.

Already he was beginning to regret his decision to come up here and felt the rage of seeing Leon Courteney at the horse race had affected his thinking. When he heard the distant baying of hounds, he knew the hunt had begun; it was too late to leave.

As with any hunt, a huntsman would enter the forest with his hounds and begin tracking game, either boar, bear or if nothing else, deer, if they hadn't fled. Once the hounds had scented an animal, the huntsman would signal with a horn, and the hunting party would set off in pursuit. Odo wasn't concerned about the hounds locating him; they were after beast, not man, and he only hoped the hounds wouldn't draw the huntsman to his position.

With care, he strung his bow and selected a few arrows. While the lengthy yew bow was a formidable weapon, an archer was disadvantaged in the close confines of trees and branches. A smaller bow was more ideal, however, the position he'd chosen offered a perfect vantage point on a rocky ledge that was free of foliage that wouldn't encumber his sizeable bow. He only hoped Léon Courteney would ride past and present himself as a target. He settled down to wait.

It was his horse that alerted him. Suddenly its ears rotated to a sound Odo didn't hear, and within moments a lone Greyhound, with a lolling tongue and long wagging tail, appeared, then moments later, another and finally two more. Greyhounds were the preferred breed for hunting, especially in more open, less dense forests, but they lacked stamina than other and more aggressive hounds. They ignored the horse, and with their tails swinging crazily from side to side, approached Odo. He gave them a friendly pat and tried to encourage them to move on with no success. He knew the huntsman wouldn't be far behind, and he didn't want to be discovered and have to explain his presence here. The hounds sniffed the ground around him but showed little interest in tracking game. A faint whistle drew their attention, and Odo tensed. With ears pricked, the hounds, with their long legs, finally loped away in the direction of the whistle. He breathed out a sigh of relief and relaxed; it was a close call.

His musings were interrupted by frantic barking, then he heard the huntsman yell encouragement, and below him on the path, he saw the hounds sprint past in a flash. The huntsman, gasping for breath, ran into view, paused a moment, and reached for his horn that was slung around his neck and gave two long blasts, then set off after his dogs. The hunt had begun.

Odo's plan was simple. From his elevated position, he could stand, notch an arrow, draw his bowstring, then step close to the edge of the ledge and have an unobstructed view of his target. Due to the six-foot length of his bow, laying down to launch an arrow wasn't feasible, he'd have to be upright. The moment he stepped close to the edge to release his arrow, he would also be visible to those below him if they looked up. Minimising his risk and ensuring he wasn't seen, he stepped away from the ledge to listen.

It wasn't long before he heard men on horses approaching. They were unbelievable loud and travelled quickly, forgoing stealth for speed. With other teams also seeking the game the hounds had identified, the team who arrived first stood a better chance of killing the beast. It was now a race to see which team would come first.

He eased himself closer to the edge so he could see and identify the knights. He knew the Courtenay colours and their coat-of-arms and hoped they would ride past. Suddenly he saw a group of five riders on his right, about one-hundred yards away, ride around a rocky outcrop. They were exposed briefly, then disappeared. Thankfully they weren't wearing the Courteney colours. From the opposite side, on his left, another group appeared. In single file, they rushed past and below him, following the same path as the huntsman. In the distance, the hounds still bayed, which added excitement to the hunt; their quarry was near.

Much further away, another group briefly rode into view. They travelled in a different direction and were moving too quickly to identify Léon Courtenay if he was part of that group.

Somewhere, another team was riding in his direction, and he hoped that Léon Courteney was one of the riders.

He heard the noise from above and behind. Quickly he stood back from the edge and pressed himself against the rock wall at his rear to hide. His horse was also close to the wall. Its black colour blended well into the shadows and would be difficult to see. The sound of knights on horses became louder, and he knew it had to be the Courteney team. They were above him and rode down the hill and would pass by his position on his left. Had they spared a look to their right, they would have clearly seen him. He felt his heart rate increase, and his loathing for Léon intensified. His knuckles were stark white as he gripped his bow. First, one rider rode by, then another. He identified the fourth rider as Leon, but no fifth rider.

At the bottom, they turned right and began to ride along the path, below the ledge the other team and huntsman had earlier taken. This was perfect, but where was the fifth rider? All the teams had five members, where was he?

Odo took a step forward and turned to listen and still couldn't hear the fifth rider. Perhaps he was injured, or his horse became lame. He couldn't dwell on it. In moments, the team would ride past, below him, and he had to launch an arrow or miss his opportunity.

With his arrow notched, he eased himself away from the wall and stepped towards the edge. Every footstep closer to the precipice gave him a better view.

The first horse sped by, then another closely followed. The third horse lagged by three horse lengths, and finally, he saw Léon Courteney's courser. The gap had widened, and Léon trailed by about five horse lengths. Odo turned quickly to listen and look. There was still no sign of the fifth knight.

Then he heard the sound, it was the fifth knight. His horse was moving fast, almost recklessly, and Odo hurriedly stepped back against the sheer rock face as the courser, with its rear legs locked, slid past him and down the hill. With one hand holding a lance and the other the reins, the knight showed remarkable skill and held on as the horse careened by. Odo knew he had but moments to launch his arrow at Leon, or he'd disappear around the far corner.

With the fifth knight safely past him, Odo stepped towards the edge of the ledge and raised his bow, Léon was almost at the corner and would soon be out of sight. He drew the bowstring back as hard as he could, breathed out, took aim, and let loose. The arrow only had to travel a relatively short distance, and Odo ensured the drawstring was taut. The arrow flew with incredible speed, and the impact was more than jarring. It struck Leon on his back, beside his shoulder blade and knocked him cleanly from his horse. Odo stepped back into the shadows before the fifth rider appeared below and saw him. He heard a loud yell from below and realised he might be too late.

Odo didn't savour the feeling of revenge; it wasn't about vengeance. The killing of Léon Courteney was about preserving the life of his son and his own. Nothing else mattered.

He knew the *chevalier* was dead. No one would or could have survived such a devastating injury. The arrow most likely pierced Léon's heart, continued through his body, and appeared through the other side. Strangely, he felt no satisfaction or elation at killing Léon Courteney, his only thought was to escape. With the bow secured, he unhobbled his horse and carefully led him from the ledge, mounted, and rode up the hill in the same direction the *chevalier*s had come. He knew the route he'd need to take that would lead him out from the forest and away from the hunt master's temporary camp where spectators gathered.

CHAPTER SIXTEEN

Chevalier Pierre Aubert barely managed to control his courser as he flung the animal to his right as he safely arrived at the turnoff that led beside a rocky cliff face. Earlier, he had inadvertently snagged his lance on a branch and dropped it. Annoyed at his fundamental error, he turned back, retrieved it, and then tried to catch up to the other members of his group before he lost his group.

As his horse skidded around the corner, he saw his charge, Léon Courteney, just ahead. He squeezed his legs, and his horse shot forward to close the distance. Without warning, he suddenly saw Léon flung from his horse with an arrow protruding from his back. In reflex, he screamed as loudly as possible to alert and warn the other members of his team. They were far ahead, and he only hoped they heard him.

In disbelief, he yanked his horse to a stop and leapt from the saddle to begin searching for Léon. He found the body down a bank laying beneath a bush with a three-foot arrow protruding from both his back and chest.

Pierre's expression hardened. Léon's father, Count Courteney, had tasked him to take care of his youngest son. Prone to fights, the cocky *chevalier* was always in trouble. His belligerent attitude and less than friendly demeanour towards others was a constant source of disquiet and frequently led to hostilities. Pierre's job was to ensure Léon didn't pick a fight he would lose and thus remain alive. Seeing the arrow in his back, Pierre knew he'd failed his liege lord, and Léon's older and equally heinous brothers would be outraged, distraught and more violence would likely ensue, and in all possibility, he would be blamed.

Pierre was an experienced knight, and automatically he turned around to gauge where the archer had been hiding. He calculated where Léon had been the moment he'd been struck by the missile and the best vantage point the archer would have had. He glanced into the trees and then turned to look back down the path; his eyes flicked up the rocky cliff to the ledge on top. He didn't expect to see the archer wave to him in greeting; by now, he'd be gone but guessed that's where the assassin hid. Already, other members of his team alerted by his cry were riding back.

Chevalier Christophe, the oldest of the Courtenay brothers, was genuinely distraught and paced backwards and forwards with his hands held to his face in despair. His younger brother Édouard was in no better state of mind and let loose a stream of profanity and curses. The other two *chevaliers* stood hopelessly nearby as the brothers seethed.

"It's not too late, we can find this assassin," *Chevalier* Pierre insisted. "But we must hasten, every moment we delay, he rides to safety."

"Who did this, why?" screamed Christophe. His face reddened from the exertion. "I will hunt him to the world's end and then dismember him, limb by limb!"

"Sir Christophe, we must ride. Let the others take Léon back to Toulouse, ye and Édouard, and I, the three of us, can find him, but we must leave now," implored Pierre.

Needing no further encouragement, the three *chevaliers* mounted and began searching for tracks. It wasn't long before they found the footprints of a horse and a single man who'd been hiding on the ledge above the path. In pursuit, they charged through the trees with branches whipping their bodies as they tried to make ground on the fleeing archer. While the Courtenay's were not gifted with an abundance of acumen, they were skilled horsemen and adept with weapons.

When Odo first heard the warning cry from the trailing *chevalier,* he knew the remainder of the team would come after him almost immediately, but as the Templars had instructed, he would act with consideration and thought. He didn't panic and rode quickly away over the summit by using the main trails and adhering to his escape plan. His horse left imprints on the soft soil of the paths, and he counted on the fact that they could follow him with ease. Each time a fork in the trail gave him a choice, he headed right, always towards the east.

When he judged he'd ridden far enough and left plenty of clues to show his pursuers the easterly direction he intended to travel, he dismounted at a turnoff and led his horse into the forest and tethered him to a tree. He found a leafy branch and walked back to the path, and began carefully removing hoofprints. He worked quickly and knew he didn't have much time. Satisfied, he returned to the forest and remained hidden beside his horse and waited. As a precaution, he had an arrow notched and was ready for them if they realized his deception and turned back and discovered him.

They came sooner than he expected and were bent low over their horses' necks to avoid low branches, and they rode hard and fast. When they reached the fork in the trail where the hoofprints disappeared, they slowed to a walk. Safely hidden behind a tree, Odo observed a *chevalier* point to the right and heard him shout "East!"

They spurred their horses and rode away. Odo waited a while, then by avoiding any paths, he led his horse through the forest in a northerly direction. After some time, he returned onto a trail, mounted, and with his horse well-rested, rode at best speed for a hill in the distance. Once he crossed over the summit, he knew the forest would end, and he could ride through open country, back to camp in Toulouse. If anyone saw him, he'd be riding in a southerly direction and not appear as if he'd come from the forest, or so he hoped.

The death of Léon Courteney caused some consternation back at the camp of the hunt-master. Not that anyone would grieve for the disagreeable young *chevalier*, the unspoken concern was over the unpredictable behaviour of his brothers.

Chevalier Pierre took charge and suggested that the team return to Toulouse with the body as quickly as possible while he would continue to search for the archer. In truth, Pierre was more worried about the repercussions and the admonishment he would receive from Count Courtney, the ageing and quick-tempered father. If he could locate the assassin, he could atone for his perceived failure in protecting Léon. As the remainder of the team rode away with Léon's body draped over his horse, *Chevalier* Pierre turned and studied the forested hills. He knew he'd been outsmarted. The archer had been clever and planned well. He squeezed his thighs, and his horse cantered northwards towards the far side of the hills.

After a while, he reined in, brought his horse to a stop and considered where to look for the assassin. He studied the terrain carefully and came to a decision. Before he could ride off, he saw a lone figure on horseback approach from the north. Pierre was instantly suspicious.

"Hail!" he yelled as the rider drew near. Pierre took in the horse. It wasn't a destrier, the pitch-black horse, while still a good-sized animal, was truly magnificent, it had a broad wide chest that tapered to a narrow waist. This expensive horse was built for speed and not the type of horse a *chevalier* would typically ride.

The rider did not wear armour or dress like a *chevalier*, although a sword hung from his belt, and a yew bow was strapped to the side. Pierre's stomach tightened as the rider pulled to a stop a short distance away.

"Hail, to ye, good sir," Odo replied. His hand casually eased down to the hilt of his sword. He knew this *chevalier* was part of the Courteney team and recognized him as the man leading the pursuit for him in the forest.

"I am *Chevalier* Pierre Aubert from the house of Courteney. What are ye called, yer name, and where have ye come from?" Pierre asked. His right hand firmly gripped his sheathed sword. He felt unnerved by the piercing, calculating eyes of the stranger. Sensing his anxiousness, his horse stamped a foot and wouldn't stand still.

Odo held the gaze of the *chevalier* a moment and considered his reply before speaking. "I have come from the forest where I slew Léon Courteney." He saw the reaction of the *chevalier*. Slowly, Odo lifted his leg, swung it over the saddle and dismounted. He began unfastening the leather thongs that held his bow. "Would ye care to know why?"

Pierre was caught off guard by the unexpected admission. The behaviour of the stranger was not what he envisaged, and the stark admission of killing Léon gave him a chill. "Do tell, stranger, fer I am here to bring ye back, and ye can tell yer tale to Count Courteney before he sees yer death." From his position, he couldn't see what the stranger was doing.

Odo was mostly screened by his horse, and the *chevalier* couldn't see him stringing his bow. "Were ye in Carrick, along with the other Courteney brothers?" He studied the *chevalier* carefully for his reaction and immediately saw the look of fear.

Chevalier Pierre wanted to turn and flee. He knew instantly who the archer was. It was the Templar, Odo Brus. His mouth went dry and felt the unwelcome tendrils of fear invade his belly. He was trapped and had no means of escape. His courage dissolved, and his countenance turned from confidence to near panic. He now saw what the Templar had been doing. His bow was untied, and he now had the drawstring attached. Pierre knew that he was too far away to charge towards the Templar, and if he did, he'd end up with an arrow in his chest.

"I, I was only following the command of my liege lord, I had no desire to kill defenceless women and children," he appealed. "I did not kill yer family, it wasn't me."

Odo fought to control himself. His rage simmered, and he took a deep breath to steady his emotions. "And ye didn't prevent it, either… tell me, who, who did the killing?" He pulled an arrow from the quiver.

"The Courteneys, it was them, good sir." Pierre tried to think of a way out. If he turned his horse and ran, he'd be caught with ease, or, if the Templar were a true marksman, he'd have an arrow in his back. If he fought the Templar with a sword, he'd be bested with ease. He knew the Templars were not just good swordsmen, they were unbeatable. He spared a quick look behind, back in the direction of the temporary camp of the hunt-master and safety. But here, he was alone with the Templar, Odo Brus; no one else was in sight.

"Then a valiant and honourable *chevalier* such as yer self would have prevented the brutality," Odo stated. His voice had hardened, and he barely managed to temper the fury that threatened to overcome him.

Chevalier Pierre Aubert considered himself a brave man, but he wasn't a halfwit. He had only one viable option, and he took the risk. He dug his heels aggressively into the side of his horse and leaned low over its neck as the animal obeyed the command. It was a sizeable powerful horse, and sensing its riders' nervousness, responded quickly. Pierre believed an erratic course would prevent an arrow from finding him.

Odo notched the arrow, pointed it at the ground between his feet and breathed out as his heart rate began to steady and slow. He unhurriedly drew back on the drawstring and raised the six-foot yew bow. The *chevalier* was laying across the horse's neck and offered only a small target. It mattered not. Odo automatically adjusted his aim to compensate for the breeze, the moving target and slightly elevated the bow before letting the string slip through his fingers. He took a step towards the fleeing *chevalier* before the arrow found its mark.

The arrow lay on the ground, and Odo casually strolled over, picked it up and studied it a moment before looking up. The *chevalier* lay on his back, gasping. Odo walked up to stand over him.

"My legs," Pierre cried, "I, I have no feeling in my legs,"

A vein throbbed on the side of Odo's neck, his expression stern and grim. His arrow had struck the *chevalier* directly on his spine and deflected; the force of the impact had most likely damaged his back. "Who, who gave the order to kill my family? Tell me, and I will end yer suffering!" Odo was enraged.

"I told ye, C-Count C-Courteney." Pierre replied through clenched teeth. He stared up at Templar with hope. "*Aide moi.*"

"Who else was there? Who did the killing?"

The *chevalier* was in severe pain. "Christophe, Léon and Édouard and three other mercenaries, two died from arrows," he gasped.

"And ye, ye were there!" Odo snapped back.

"Aye, but I did nothing, believe me."

Odo held Pierre's pleading gaze but felt no pity. He knew there was only one course of action for him as he'd witnessed similar injuries in the past and knew the man would never walk again; he'd have to take his own life. After a moment, he shook his head in disgust, turned, and walked away, deaf to the *chevalier's* desperate appeals.

He arrived back in Toulouse with time on his hands to watch his friend *Chevalier* Émile contest another *Chevalier* in a duel of swords. The fight was over quickly, and Émile had been forced to yield or lose his life. However, talk amongst the competitors had centred around the peculiar death of *Chevalier* Léon Courteney. A death or two during a tournament wasn't uncommon and, for most participants, hardly worth commenting on. Of interest was where and how Léon had been killed. Many believed it was purely retribution over the young man's penchant for creating enemies. Interestingly, Odo learned that all three brothers had been part of the hunt team. He'd had opportunity and chastised himself for his impatience and for not learning more before heading into the hills.

For the Courteneys, the tournament was over. Leon was buried, and the two remaining brothers, along with a contingent of *chevalier*s and servants, headed back to Burgundy to report the unfortunate death of Léon and *Chevalier* Pierre Aubert. Pierre's body had been discovered later in the day by a farmer. Curiously, he'd died through a self-inflicted wound; it appeared he'd pierced his own heart with a knife after suffering from a critical injury to his back, presumably from an arrow.

Odo said farewell to Émile and Théo not long after the Courteney's departed for Burgundy and proceeded to follow safely behind the slow-moving procession. He hoped an opportunity would present itself when they reached open country. However, the weather wasn't cooperative, it was torrid. An intense storm raged, and wind and rain swept down from the north, through the countryside, and the temperature fell. It was uncomfortable, and it came as no surprise that the Courteneys headed to the nearest hamlet for warmth and cheer.

Wrapped in his hooded cape and with only fond recollections of Josceline and his children for company, Odo endured the inclement weather and persisted on. He knew there would be little opportunity to seize any advantage over the Courteneys until they were again journeying. He sought another hamlet further along the road where he would spend the night.

CHAPTER SEVENTEEN

The following day saw no reprieve in the weather. It wasn't until the next day that the rain finally abated, and bright sunshine warmed many a damp traveller. Previously, the Courteneys had ridden in a tight group, which offered few choices in targeting them and not being killed in the process. He knew an opportunity would eventually present itself, and he needed to be heedful and patient. For two days, Odo had time to dwell on how to complete his task and slay the remaining two brothers

He departed the inn and rode easily over the soft ground ahead of the Courteney procession, which had still to appear. He didn't hurry as he knew the Courteneys group pulled wagons, which would slow their progress considerably. Nonetheless, he dawdled and hoped they would eventually catch up to him.

When his horse's ear twitched, Odo turned to look behind. Three *chevaliers* were riding toward him and slowed when they drew near. Their colours were evident to him; it was the Courteneys. He tensed and thought quickly. "A glorious day to be travelling," he greeted the first rider.

"Aye, to be sure," came the response.

Impatient to return home, the Courteneys had ridden ahead of their wagons which travelled more slowly behind. Left to their own devices, the wagons would eventually arrive.

Odo studied the three *chevaliers*, saw the *Courteney* likeness, and quickly identified the two remaining brothers, the third man who'd greeted him looked unfamiliar. They had yet to speak and only gave him the merest of a polite head-nod in salutation. "I head fer Paris, perhaps we ride together fer a while?"

He saw the *chevaliers* eyeing his horse.

"Ye have a fine horse," one of the Courtney's offered. "Ye may join us." He spurred his horse, and the trio cantered away.

Odo allowed his horse to catch up, and he fell in beside.

They travelled quickly and passed tiny villages and hamlets in a blur. They didn't give courtesy to peasants and arrogantly thundered past, spraying mud without slowing. They were in a hurry.

They stopped to water the horses late in the afternoon and allowed them to forage when the oldest Courteney brother, Christophe, approached him. "Ye are an archer?"

Odo shrugged, "I carry the bow but find it difficult to master."

The Courteney said nothing and gave the matter some thought. "Who is yer liege? Fer, a man with a sword, a bow and a beautiful horse, is not a peasant."

Odo found Christophe to be disagreeable and his mannerisms brusque. "I have no liege, and I lend my sword for coin only."

"Ahh, a *mercenaire*[25]," exclaimed Christophe. "A man with no country, allegiance... or guilt."

Odo shrugged. "A man does what he must. And guilt … do ye live with guilt?" he asked and tried to meet his gaze.

Christophe didn't reply and turned away to admire Odo's horse. "How did ye come by this horse, fer I have never seen such a fine animal with beautiful lines? Did ye kill someone fer it? To purchase such a beast would be beyond most men."

Odo sensed that the *chevalier* was deliberately trying to taunt him. *But to what end, why?* he wondered. He casually glanced around, the younger brother, Édouard and the other *chevalier* were some distance away, talking and not paying any attention to him or Christophe.

Odo laughed, "If I told ye how I came by this beautiful horse, ye would believe me not."

Christophe leaned forward, "Then spare me the angst, speak, archer."

Odo shook his head and lowered his voice. "I fear others will learn of my deception, and the honour and virtue of a, er... a certain lady is valued." Again, he spared a quick look at the other two men, they still chatted together and showed no interest in him or Christophe. "I cannot..." He took a step closer to where his horse grazed to increase the distance from the others.

Christophe laughed and followed Odo, clearly his appetite whetted, he was desirous to learn of this lady and how the archer obtained the horse.

"...Nay, I cannot fer my word was freely given," Odo affirmed.

Christophe looked disappointed and walked closer to Odo's horse. "A

---

25 Mercenaire – French, a mercenary.

horse such as this is a rare animal indeed, and I would care to own it." He stroked the back of Odo's horse. "I shall purchase this beast from ye," Christophe declared, then turned and squared his shoulders as he faced Odo. His hand hovered near the hilt of his sword.

Odo raised an eyebrow. *He's challenging me and is willing to kill me fer it.* He positioned himself so he could see Édouard and the other *chevalier* better. They were still in deep discussion and had their backs to him, and he judged the distance carefully. "*Chevalier* Christophe, I had no intention of selling this animal. But I am loathed to tell ye, this fine beast has a flaw."

Christophe looked puzzled, "A flaw?" His hand moved away from his sword.

"Aye, on the offside, front hoof, look, ye will see," Odo pointed to the horse's right front hoof.

Screened by the horse and out of sight from the others, Christophe bent down to look as Odo silently withdrew a knife from his belt and leaned over the *chevalier* to point. Quickly, he encircled his arm around Christophe's neck and drew the knife savagely across his throat. A stream of blood gushed from the fatal wound while the horse, unnerved from the smell of blood, quickly sidestepped. Odo released Christophe, who gurgled and slumped to the ground clutching his throat. Without sparing him another glance, he walked up to the agitated horse to calm it and quickly untied his bow. As yet, the other two had not seen what had happened.

He notched an arrow, closed his eyes briefly and allowed his thumping heart and breathing to settle, then looked up towards Édouard, he was only thirty paces away… He raised the bow and carefully sighted. Édouard was unaware that he was only moments from death and stood unmoving while he talked. It was now or never...

Édouard jerked violently as an arrow struck his shoulder. The impact knocked him forward, and with a painful cry, he was flung hard to the ground.

The surviving *chevalier* reacted quickly and spun, at the same time, he drew his sword, only to see Odo notch another arrow and aim it directly at him.

"What have ye done?" he cried. His eyes flicked to the younger Courteney writhing on the ground.

"Lower yer sword!" Odo yelled, "Lower it, and I may yet spare ye!"

The *chevalier* was astute enough to know there was little he could do. He couldn't run, and he was too far away to attack the archer. Again, he looked down at Édouard, who was thrashing in agony.

"Throw it towards me," Odo yelled. Slowly he stepped closer towards the *chevalier* with his bow still raised.

In helplessness, the *chevalier* tossed the sword away and shook his head. "I had my feelings about ye."

"Sit," commanded Odo and kicked the sword away, out of reach before lowering the bow and extracting his own sword.

Odo ignored Édouard, who continued to moan and clutch his shoulder in pain. "Do ye know who I am?" he asked the *chevalier*.

The *chevalier* shook his head and then looked in puzzlement for Christophe.

"I am Odo Brus, and Christophe is dead."

Édouard may have been in agony, but Odo's declaration only worsened his condition, and he wailed. The *chevalier* gave no response and shrugged after nervously sparing Édouard another quick glance.

"Did ye go to Carrick in Scotland?"

The *chevalier* looked puzzled. "Nay, I have never been to Scotland, and I know not of what ye speak. Where is Christophe? Why gave ye done this terrible thing?" He turned to look at Édouard in sympathy then searched for his brother.

"As I said, he is dead, and he," Odo pointed to the Courtenay struggling with the arrow, "will soon be."

The *chevalier* still looked puzzled. "Why did ye do this horrible thing?"

"What is yer name?"

The *chevalier* stood with his mouth open and clearly looked distressed. "I am René, from the house of De Villiers," he spluttered.

Odo took a step closer to Édouard and prodded him in the back with his foot.

He screamed.

"Did *Chevalier* René go with ye to Carrick?"

"I, I, did nothing, I, I did not kill them!" Édouard managed to yell.

Odo kicked him again. "Did *Chevalier* René go with ye?"

"Nay, nay, he did not. Please help me… remove the arrow!" he pleaded. His cries became more desperate.

René was becoming more flustered. "This is bestial, why do ye do this?" he appealed.

Odo took a breath. "He will tell ye." Again, he brutally kicked Édouard in the back with his foot.

The jarring kick elicited another painful yelp.

"Tell, René what happened in Carrick, or I will strike ye again."

"Nay, please, Sir Odo, I will tell."

René's mouth fell open, and he looked at Odo. "Sir Odo?"

"My brothers, they slew yer woman and yer servants. But I did not. Nay, I didn't want to," he implored.

Odo drew back his foot and again struck him even harder. Édouard screamed and squirmed in agony. "Tell René everything," Odo hissed.

"It was them; it wasn't me, Sir Odo, my brothers, they killed yer woman, and yer servants, another man and woman."

Odo had heard enough and pulled his leg back.

"Nay, nay, uh, and the children, they killed the children too."

"Children?" René asked incredulously, his voice just above a whisper. He shook his head in disbelief as his face contorted into a mask of horror at the revelation. "What is this ye speak of?"

"It was them, they did it, they killed all the children." Hoping for a reprieve, Édouard pushed his good arm onto the ground and managed to partially sit up.

Odo felt sick and turned away.

"Who, who does he speak of?" René asked.

"The Courteney brothers," Odo replied. "Their father ordered the death of my wife, my three children and me."

René De Villiers bent over with his hands resting on his thighs and shook his head. "Fergive me, Sir Odo, I did not know of this. I, I am deeply hurt, and by association, my honour is aggrieved. How... how, could anyone do such a thing?"

"Who went with ye to Carrick? Give me names?"

Édouard was whimpering loudly and tried to remove the arrow.

"Names, give me names."

"My brothers, the three of us and Chevalier Pierre, we hired three men in Scotland, two were killed by yer woman. No one else… Please help me!" he cried.

What Édouard said supported what he'd learned earlier from *Chevalier* Pierre. Odo was disgusted. "Where is yer father, in Burgundy?" he asked while ignoring *Chevalier* René.

"Aye, aye, he is," nodded Édouard enthusiastically. He stared up at Odo with a measure of hope.

"Now ye will join yer brothers." Odo tensed and spun. With both hands firmly grasping his sword, and with all the power he could muster, the razor-sharp weapon arced parallel over the grass in a blur. It struck Édouard's exposed neck perfectly, and in a gush of crimson, his head cleanly separated and fell to the grass as the body slumped forward onto the ground.

Odo was exhausted. Not physically but emotionally. He leaned on his sword as he tried to collect himself. He thought of Josceline, Katherin and William… He mouthed a silent prayer.

René studied him carefully and saw the pain and torment etched on his face. He couldn't bear to look at him and, in respect, turned away to allow the knight his privacy and solitude to reflect.

After a while, Odo exhaled a long, drawn-out breath. René turned back to him. "Why did they do this to ye?"

Odo took a deep breath to steady himself. "Because I slew their brother, Jean."

René gasped. "That was ye? I'd heard the tale. Some said his death was unjust, others said it was fair and deserved."

Odo shrugged, "It matters not."

"And Sir Knight, what will ye do with me?"

"Ye are free to ride away, but I ask fer yer word ye will not journey to Burgundy, fer then, ye may warn Count Courteney."

René nodded and then looked thoughtful. "Sir Odo, I knew nothing of what the Courteney brothers did. I rode with them to the tournament in Toulouse because it was convenient. But what I have learned is obscene." His face contorted to disgust. "I have a family, children, and my heart is with ye... but I cannot forget or let this go. I ask ye a question, a simple question, why did ye slay Jean Courteney?"

Odo swallowed. "Because he tried to force his will and have his way with a young woman... my Josceline, I saw this and prevented him from harming her. He insisted and felt his honour had been grieved and demanded a duel. I was never going to kill him in that duel, I was against it. Then he fouled in the duel - he moved, then offered public insult to the woman I loved." Odo realized he'd raised his voice and took another calming breath to steady himself, then spoke more quietly. "If I could relive that day, I would have, should have walked away... and Josceline would have lived."

René nodded. "Sir Odo, I think ye acted with honour and agree with ye, fer I would have done much the same." He met Odo's gaze. "Walking away may have changed everything, perhaps a lesson fer us both. However, what is done, is done. Now, I ask ye a boon, let me ride with ye to Burgundy. I will not warn the count."

Odo considered the request, "I think it best you keep yer distance from me and not involve yerself."

"But I have family…" *Chevalier* René appealed.

Odo shook his head. "If I see ye in Burgundy before one month, ye may not have family. A month is all I need."

"But Sir Odo, my family, they will wonder where I am, what am I to do?"

"In a month, you can go to yer home, think yerself fortunate ye will have family to return too, fer I do not."

René looked at Odo a moment longer and remained silent.

"I have no quarrel with ye, *Chevalier* René. Ye live because ye were not part of the execution of my wife and innocent children. If ye are seen with me, then ye and yer family might be in danger." Odo stepped towards the *chevalier*'s sword and kicked it towards him. "Pick it up. If ye choose, ye can kill me now and end it here."

Chevalier René looked at the sword briefly, then reached down, retrieved it, and stood silently facing him.

Odo tensed and waited.

Slowly, René raised his sword, held it aloft, then sheathed it. "I will give ye a month, then I will return to my family. What ye have done to the Courteneys is no less than what I would do."

Odo nodded his head. "If I succeed and survive, then I will head to Paris. Wait fer me on the main road. If I see ye on my return, then my task is done, and ye may go to yer family sooner."

René nodded. "So it shall be, ye have my word of honour."

"Honour?" Odo inclined his head in question.

"Aye, honour," replied *Chevalier* René De Villiers.

Slowly, Odo sheathed his sword.

It was growing late, and René wanted to bury the brothers. Odo helped him to dig a shallow grave but offered the Courteney brothers no prayer or forgiveness. Afterwards, beside a roaring fire, they talked long into the evening.

CHAPTER EIGHTEEN

A cold wind raced along damp, darkened passages, through rooms and disturbed tapestries and banners that hung in forgotten and dusty splendour. The fire that roared in the hearth muted the incessant howling wind, but not its effect. Flames responded, danced, and conformed to the draught, their protestations unheeded, as did the chamber's only occupant who sat quiet and desolate. Draped in a blanket, the old man clutched a goblet of mulled wine with arthritic fingers and stared in reflection at the stone wall directly in front of where he sat. Beneath the cloth cap he wore, wisps of grey hair poked out, his bottom lip trembled, and his pale, sunken cheeks gave a hint to his age but not his countenance or conscience. Count Courteney was mourning or, better described, contemplating the loss of his four sons and typically was in a foul, morose mood.

The solitude afforded him was not out of respect. His servants and vassals found him to be controlling, disagreeable, and quick to anger. His volatility was unpredictable, his words frequently harsh and cruel, did little to encourage sympathy or compassion from others in his time of need.

Being in his presence was challenging and nearly always because there was no other alternative. Count Courteney was simply a repugnant man, a terrible father, and a worse lord.

Since he'd received word that his two surviving sons had simply vanished, he knew they were dead, and he knew who had killed them. He had only one surviving heir, his daughter. A pitiful wretch who'd married into a wealthy local family. He'd never spent much time with her and found her vacillating behaviour irksome, and her presence did little more than evoke hostility and more harsh words. However, now she was heir to his dominion and titles, and he needed to consider the implications and his legacy.

Count Courtney had no regrets ordering his sons to go to Scotland and kill the Templar knight's family. While the decision had cost him three sons, he felt their deaths were avoidable due only to their lack of commonsense and martial skills. They'd erred and failed to kill the Templar. They were fools, and now they were dead. It was their own fault, and he took no responsibility.

The Templar knight would come for him; of this he was certain. Twenty years ago, he would have stood at the *château*'s gates and challenged the knight with bravado and taunts, and when he did come, he would have beaten the man mercilessly and then killed him with nary a thought.

Four sons... *Odo Brus killed my four sons.* Unbidden, he felt his chest tighten and his eyes well. It was an unexpected and unfamiliar sensation, *perhaps it's the draught*, he thought. He lowered his head, the goblet and wine spilt to the floor, and he sobbed.

It had been over a week and Odo was no closer to determining how he could meet Count Courteney. The elderly count never left the confines of the *château,* and no one he'd spoken to in casual conversation knew anything. As far as they knew, the man could even be dead.

On the ninth day, when casually strolling by the gates of the *château,* he saw a carriage appear and enter. A vendor nearby hawking trinkets informed him it was the count's daughter, Gisela. This was news to Odo. He didn't know he had a daughter and immediately chastised himself for not finding this out earlier. This gave him an idea, and he decided to follow the carriage when it departed and see where she lived.

Later in the day, the carriage departed through the gates of the Courteney stronghold, *Château de Brancion,* and Odo mounted his horse and followed. Thankfully, it wasn't a long ride, and after observing where the carriage went, he decided to learn all he could about the count's daughter Gisela. The local inn was the best place to gather information, and that was where he headed.

The locals didn't disappoint, and without appearing too curious, Odo discovered the Gisela had won the affections of *Seigneur* Fabian Chastain, a minor lord, who came from a wealthy family, and they had married almost two summers ago. They had no children, which became a robust, healthy topic for locals to discuss, but other than that, he learned little else of value. He retired to the room he rented and tried desperately to think of a solution.

The following day, he walked through the village when he observed a young woman leave the Chastain manor house carrying a bundle of cloth. Perplexed, he followed. To his disappointment, the young lass was only a *fabrician*[26], and she was making an alteration to a dress belonging to Gisela.

An idea began to form, and the more he thought about it, the more he realized his audacious plan could work. He needed that dress.

Nightfall couldn't come quick enough, and he soon as it was dark, he returned to the home of the seamstress and knocked on the door.

A man appeared with a spluttering candle. "*Mon Seigneur?*" he inquired, looking perplexed. Seeing a large armed man at his door was not expected by any means, and he was becoming increasingly anxious.

"Best we go inside, eh." Odo firmly pushed the man back into his home and shut the door behind him.

The front part of the house was dedicated to the woman's trade. Clothes were hanging in racks, and a large table stood in the middle of the floor. The *fabrician*, clutching a baby, backed into a corner and was visibly frightened.

The man opened his mouth to protest.

"I have not come to hurt you," Odo began.

"We have no coin, we are poor..." the man quickly added and slowly withdrew to stand fearfully near his wife.

Odo was looking around the room. Where is Gisela's dress, the one you brought here earlier?" he asked.

The seamstress and her husband didn't respond.

"Where is it?" Odo asked, his voice hardened.

"It is there, the red one," she pointed. "*Mon Seigneur*, why do ye have

---

26 *Fabrician – A dressmaker or seamstress.*

interest in this dress?"

Odo saw the dress and immediately reached for it.

"*Non!*"

Ignoring her cry, he grabbed the dress, opened his purse, extracted a gold coin, and placed it on the table. To the seamstress and her husband, this was a small fortune. "Tell Gisela ye damaged the dress and make her a new one." To the consternation of the couple, he gathered the dress and hurriedly departed their home.

Once outside, he packed the garment into a leather satchel affixed to his saddle, mounted, and quickly rode away.

The following day, Odo rode towards *Château de Brancion.* As he approached, and as expected, a man-at-arms prevented him from entering.

"What is yer business, *Mon Seigneur?*"

"I wish to see, Count Courteney."

The man-at-arms shook his head, "It is not possible, go away."

Odo didn't move. Instead, he reached behind and opened the satchel's flap and retrieved a bundle of red cloth. He handed it to the guard. "Do ye know what this is?"

"*Oui, Mon Seigneur,* it is a kirtle[27]," simply stated the guard.

"It belongs to Gisela. I have her, and this is proof. Inform the count, if he doesn't see me, he will forsake his last living child. Give this to him. I will wait here fer his answer."

The guard studied Odo a moment in uncertainty, then turned away and spoke to another man-at-arms. With the kirtle in his arms, he jogged

---

27 Kirtle – Medieval type of dress.

away.

Odo was searched and his weapons removed. A door was opened, and he was led into a room containing a sole ageing man. The guard remained standing just inside the door.

Count Courteney stood with unsteadiness on senescent legs. His frailty, compounded by a crevassed face and watery eyes, showed no curiosity or concern, only a profusion of hostility and hate. His expression was cold, pitiless, and hard. His eyes challenged the stranger. "Have ye killed her too?" he asked in a phlegmy voice and forgoing a greeting. "And have ye come here to gloat – to rejoice?" He spat at Odo's feet. The kirtle lay heaped on the floor near the hearth.

Odo met the gaze of the despicable creature in front of him. A thousand words came to mind, yet none of them seemed fitting. He wanted to reach out and grab the spindly neck and throttle the evilness from the depths of his soul. He controlled his aching heart and allowed his breathing to settle. "Tell the guard to leave," he instructed

The old man didn't move.

"Now!" Odo yelled.

The guard shuffled his feet nervously.

Odo turned and faced the guard. "Leave us!"

The man-at-arms wanted no part in whatever was happening and quickly left the room. The old man remained silent. Like a serpent, his tongue snaked out and licked dry lips. Odo was repulsed.

"I could have ye killed," the count finally spoke.

"Aye, and yer daughter's body will be hung from yer gate if I do not return - that is what will happen."

"*Dégénéré*[28]!" Count Courteney spat again and unleashed another profanity-laced tirade.

Odo was pleased, the count believed his deception. "I have not come here to kill ye, although that is what ye deserve. Nay, fer I will allow ye to live. Ye will spend the remainder of yer sorrowful life in grief. Every day ye will rise and know yer sons are gone, never to return. The torment serves ye well, fer it will never come close to the pain ye have caused me. What man, what real man kills women and children?" Odo took a step closer. "Ye are like yer sons, cowardly, weak and Godless." He thrust out his hand and poked Count Courteney in the chest. "Every morn when ye rise to face a new day, think on yer vileness and may ye suffer endlessly, long into the coldness and desolation of each day and every lonely night."

The old man's lips trembled.

"If ye come fer me, either today or on the morrow, next summer or thereafter, I will return and cruelly slay every last one of yer family. Do ye hear me!"

The count looked frightened, and his eyes turned away, and for the briefest of moments, Odo saw the shame. It made him sick.

"I cannot hear ye!" Odo shouted. Again, he resisted the urge to take the old man and drive his head into the hearth.

"Aye ... I hear ye," the count replied. Spittle seeped from the corners of his mouth.

Odo was enraged, his chest rose and swelled as he fought his fury. Never had he felt such consuming madness. He spun and stormed from

---

28 *Dégénéré – French for inbred.*

the room in revulsion and encountered the man-at-arms who arrogantly blocked his path.

Years of practice with his yew bow and sword had given him incredible upper-body strength. When the guard brazenly prevented him from leaving, Odo reached out, grabbed the man's leather vest, and, consumed by rage, hauled him from his feet and flung him with force against the stone wall of the corridor. His unprotected head impacted the wall with a sickening crunch. Odo didn't pause to reflect, stepped around the body, retrieved his weapons from the gatehouse and stormed from *Château de Brancion* feeling queasy and disgusted.

Odo didn't feel avenged and didn't feel better, but now, and perhaps with some certainty, he knew his son wouldn't be killed. He wouldn't seek out Gisela, her father would warn her of his threats, and that would be enough.

He headed for Paris to the Templar's in Le Marais, where he would retrieve the documents he left with Sir Godfrey, return to Mellester Manor, be reunited with his son, and then finally allow time to reflect and mourn.

A day's ride from *Château de Brancion,* he was finally overcome by sorrow and despair. It crept upon him like a thief in the night. Like a rising spring tide, creeping higher and higher and caught him unaware. For months, he'd pushed his thoughts and emotions aside. First, to ensure that baby Odo was safe and cared for, and then to search and deal with the vileness of the Courteney family.

Such was his emotional state, he couldn't continue. He found an inn and remained indoors for three nights while he grieved for Josceline, Katherin, William, and even for Inan and Cannie. He felt guilt and shame for the death he'd brought on others. He wept for Josceline and his children, and finally, he thought of his only surviving son, Odo.

The pain was consuming, the feeling of loss and helplessness was debilitating, and his despair and heartbreak were beyond what any man should ever experience. The solitude of the room at the inn was the catalyst, the breakdown was complete, and he bared his soul in a shameless outpouring of emotion and pain. He loved Josceline with his entire being, and he missed her so much.

But through the bleakness of loss, a glimmer of light hinted at hope and salvation. There was life beyond the wretchedness of desolation and sorrow, and by grasping at the fragments, he re-opened his eyes.

Baby Odo gave him belief in a future and pulled him from the consuming dark depths of seclusion and loneliness. After four days, his wits returned, and with his misery temporarily purged and once again in control, he rose from his cot with resolve and renewed purpose to return to his journey.

After the Templar knight departed, Count Courtney sent for Gisela. She arrived flustered soon after and entered the room where her father sat wrapped in a blanket. She'd seen him only a day or so before, yet the transformation was shocking to her.

"Father?" she asked in concern, "What has happened."

"Yer brothers are dead, killed by that heathen," the old man hawked into the fire.

"No, no, this cannot be so!" she exclaimed and immediately sunk to her knees and covered her face with her hands.

"That whoreson Templar killed them all," the Count affirmed. He didn't spare his daughter a look, nor did he consider consoling her.

Gisela wept. While not particularly close to her brothers, their deaths stuck her hard.

"Stand up," the Count ordered. "Show some courage, and weep not like a dotty crone," he snarled.

Slowly Gisela stood and wiped her eyes.

The count turned and faced her for the first time. "This heathen Templar, Odo Brus killed them, and he must *aby*[29] fer what he did. Do ye hear me?" he screamed at her. Slaver flew from his mouth.

"Aye, aye, father,' she blubbered.

The old man's tongue darted out, and he licked his dry lips. "He will disappear, no matter how hard we look, we will not find him. He is too clever." He removed a gnarled hand from beneath the blanket's folds and repeatedly thrust a finger at her. "I will have ye do one thing fer me. And ye *will* do this." He coughed and held her gaze. "One day, word will come, and ye will learn of the name Odo Brus. Hear me!" he cried in rage. "When this happens, ye will see his death and that of his family and end this. It may not be fer years, but be patient, he will err, when he does, ye will have vengeance in my name. In the Courteney name!" he screamed at her. The cords on his thin neck were tight with tension and hate.

Gisela pulled her hands away from her face. "I will do this, father," she replied, trying to sound strong.

29 *Aby - Atone*

"Ye *will* do this!" Again, he stabbed his finger at her. "Now be gone, wench, and leave me." He turned away and stared into the fire and thought, *there is still a chance….*

It came as no surprise to see *Chevalier* René De Villiers sitting astride his horse, waiting for him on the road to Paris.

"Hail, to ye. It gladdens my heart to see ye, fer now I can return to my family," offered René in the way of a greeting.

"Travel safe, my friend. Ye have endured much, and yer family waits," Odo replied.

"Aye, but it is now late in the day, and we need a room each," suggested René

They both sat in an inn with a mug of mead.

"I trust yer visit with Count Courtney went as planned?" René asked.

Odo took a deep breath and sighed. "I did not kill him as I intended. I left him to ponder the deaths of his children and hope that is penance enough."

René's eyebrows furrowed. "Then ye have not heard?" he asked.

Odo shook his head. "I have heard no news since I left. What news do ye speak of?"

René leaned closer to Odo. "Count Courteney is dead. It appears he took his own life and leapt to his death from the *château*'s ramparts."

Odo leaned back against the wall and thought about it. He wasn't shocked; his visit must have impacted the despicable man after all. Strangely he felt no satisfaction. But… *what would Countess Gisela*

Chastain-Courteney do now? She would inherit title, lands, and power.

Along with her husband's wealth, Gisela would be in a good position to send men after him. *Would she seek retribution?* He doubted it. Most likely, she would enjoy her new status and wealth and leave him alone. At least no one knows baby Odo lives. "Then we have cause to rejoice," said Odo and raised his mug.

Countess Gisela Chastain-Courteney had always lived in the shadow of her brothers. She was a girl and only tolerated. Emotionally and physically abused by her father and brothers, she grew into subservient adulthood without discernment and always in fear. Her father's death came as no surprise; when she saw him last, she knew he would end his life, and she didn't shed a tear or mourn his passing. In fact, she privately welcomed it. Now she was spared the endless humiliation and endless tirades of his volatile and unpredictable temperament. If the deaths of her brothers did anything, it made her acutely aware of her new position and status. She inherited everything, land, wealth and most importantly, authority. The feeling of power was exhilarating, liberating, and for the first time in her life, she could make her own decisions and control her own destiny, she felt empowered and free.

Her husband, Fabian, was weak, unstable and a coward. She immediately left him, moved from his modest uninspiring manor, and took residence in *Château de Brancion,* her family home. She took charge and made the *château* her own, and she transformed from a diminutive passive young woman into a forceful, outspoken, and cruel countess. She adapted quickly, she'd had good teachers, and she continued her father's pitiless legacy with vigour.

As she came to understand, she didn't care less about the death of her brothers and father, but she was offended by the man who had so brazenly taken their lives. Her father had made her promise to seek vengeance on the family of Odo Brus, and she intended to do precisely that. Not to honour her father but to satisfy her desire to be in control. This renegade, Odo Brus, whomever he was, had disrespected the Courteney name, and for Countess Gisela Chastain-Courteney, that was reason enough – Odo Brus gave her a cause.

She thought about her father's last words to her, and she agreed with him. The name Odo Brus would resurface, and when it did, she'd descend on him with everything and anything at her disposal.

Since his death, she'd learned her father had ignored the Templar warning and sent men out in the countryside in search of him. At first, she was horrified and believed that he would come for her when the Templar learned of this. But with the confidence of newfound power and wealth and an expanding sense of invulnerability, she soon changed her mind and now thought there was little hope of finding him anytime soon. She was patient and could wait, she no longer had encumbrances.

CHAPTER NINETEEN

Sir Godfrey de Lessassier welcomed Odo with open arms and a warm embrace. They sat together in the private quarters of the Templar commander in in Le Marais, Paris and talked candidly.

"What will ye do, now Odo? Have ye plans?" asked the Templar commander with genuine interest and concern.

Odo held the document that would ensure his son would be taken care of in the event of his death. He trusted the knight commander and knew he would go to his grave and never utter a word of what he divulged to anyone. "I will take Odo and together, find somewhere safe to live without fear. What else can I do?" he shrugged.

"Do ye have a place to go?"

Odo thought carefully and decided he would speak truthfully to Templar commander. "There is a small hamlet in southern England called Mellester, that is where I shall first go."

Sir Godfrey stroked his beard. "And what shall ye do?"

Odo fidgeted with the document seal, "I know not, I have not thought that far ahead. Mellester Manor is safe, and together we will begin anew."

"And may God go with ye." Sir Godfrey looked thoughtful. "Odo, my brother could assist ye in the event ye need help–"

"Thank ye, Sir Godfrey, but I will overcome–"

"Nay, ye don't understand, Odo. My brother is Archbishop of Kent, Roger de Lessassier."

Odo raised his eyebrows at the revelation. "I had no knowledge of this."

Sir Godfrey laughed. "It seems our family was always destined to serve the Church." His expression turned serious. "I will give ye a letter of introduction in the event ye need help, please use it."

A scribe was called for and a letter was composed. Once the ink had dried, it was sealed and placed in a small waterproof leather tube for safekeeping. Odo thanked Sir Godfrey, and departed Paris, for England. By his reckoning, and by the time he arrived back in Mellester, he would have been gone almost a year, he couldn't wait to see baby Odo.

He rode through the filthy streets of Paris and finally reached open countryside where he could relax and think. Now that he'd dealt with the Courteney's he could focus on baby Odo and their new life together. His thoughts became increasingly melancholy when he thought of Josceline and their children. The ache in his heart was absolute and he knew it would never go away; it was a matter of learning to live and adjust to it. He couldn't forget her, he couldn't, he loved her so much.

Shouts from ahead broke his reverie, and he pulled his horse to a stop as he recognized the approaching rider, it was *Chevalier* René De Villiers. Odo's eyebrows knitted together and immediately he began scanning the countryside for anything untoward. *He should be with his family*, he thought, *why is he here?*

"Odo, I have been searching fer ye everywhere, ye are a difficult man to find," said the *chevalier* when he pulled alongside.

"I prefer it that way, René, but ye should be home with yer family…"

"Aye, I should, but after I left ye to return home, I encountered six *chevaliers*. They travel lightly and are well armed. These men are familiar to me, and they asked me about Odo Brus."

Odo's expression hardened.

"These men seek ye, Odo. They have been sent to kill ye."

"Where are they?"

"I told them I had not seen ye and that I had ridden from Paris. They changed direction and then headed towards the coast, but fer how long before they turn back this way, I do not know."

"Who sent them, who is their liege?" Odo shook his head. "Count Courteney is dead, so who do these men ride fer, Gisela?"

René shook his head. "She is weak, I think not. They spoke of the count, and I thought it best that I should warn ye before ye ride into strife."

Again, Odo searched for men on horseback. "Ye should have ridden to yer family, ye are not beholden to me."

"Odo, ye told me that I have a family waiting fer me, but ye do not. What the Courteney's did to ye is wrong. Ye suffer alone while my family is unharmed. I will help ye find safe passage to England."

Odo sighed. "Thank ye, kindly, René, but where I ride, then trouble is sure to follow, ye should leave, go home."

René was steadfast and shook his head. "Where shall we go, fer we cannot ride to the coast?"

Odo looked thoughtful. "Six *chevaliers*… how were they armed?"

"Lightly, swords, chainmail, but no lances or shields."

"Do they carry bows?"

René shook his head. "Nay, I saw none."

"How far behind are they?"

"Two days past," replied René.

Odo seethed. "If these men ride fer the count's daughter Gisela, then I will see her death."

"Gisela? She is weak," exclaimed René. "Nay, she has not the nous. As I said, the *chevaliers* spoke of the count, I am sure they do his bidding."

"Someone sent these men … But methinks you are correct, the count talked to others before his death," Odo stated.

René shrugged.

Odo looked skyward, "The day is still young, is best we do not remain here in the open. Let us head towards the safety of the forest."

Both men swung their horses around and headed west towards the low rolling forested hills.

Their horses were watered and rubbed down and Odo walked a short distance away to a gap in the trees and looked out across the landscape. René stepped up. "We can ride north where ye can find a ship to take you to England."

"Aye, I thought of that, but fleeing does not solve the problem. Will these men stop looking, or will they cross to England if they do not find me?" Odo asked.

René didn't reply.

"Perhaps the hunted should become the hunter," Odo stated. He turned and studied the Frankian *chevalier*. He was taller than most with a similar physique to himself. His hair was black, but then again, the men who came for him had never seen him before. If anyone gave a description, then they would have said he wore dark green clothes and rode a beautiful large black horse. An idea began to form.

"But I look nothing like ye," René protested after Odo explained his plan.

Odo grinned. "These men do not know how I look; they seek a man on a large black stallion. If ye ride my horse and wear my clothes, it will match what they know. Their eagerness to find me will overcome caution. That is the way of a hunter."

"Ye have confidence," René asserted.

Odo smiled. "Aye, and that is why I still live. René, we need to find an elevated piece of ground where I can lay in wait. When they see ye, ye will run and head fer me at best speed and I will use my bow against them, one-by-one. I will get two of them, possibly three if they are slow to respond. It evens the odds somewhat," Odo explained.

"And then what?"

"Ye are a *chevalier* and can use a sword, or is it a decoration?"

René looked indignant. "I will have ye know, I am still alive, which proves I can fight *and* be victorious."

Odo laughed.

With the horses safely tethered, Odo and René decided to spend the night on the edge of the forest, and the next day René would dress in Odo's clothes and ride his horse back on to the main road from Paris while Odo would lay concealed and wait. If the *Chevaliers* were identified, René, would immediately flee and head towards and then ride past Odo's hidden position. As he explained to René, the *chevaliers* would be so consumed with catching him, they would ride directly into his trap, or so he hoped.

Without a fire, both men lay down to sleep. Odo lay wrapped in his cape with a blanket over him. As he always did when sleeping in the open, he unsheathed his sword and lay with it alongside his body. Its hilt was always near his head and within easy reach.

Sleep didn't come easy these days. Most frequently, his thoughts turned to Josceline, and he imagined her fear and panic before being slaughtered. The thoughts haunted him and more often he began to be consumed with guilt. He should have been there, he should have protected his family and not left them alone. If he had not gone hunting that day, then his family would still be alive.

The forest was quiet, the breeze had eased, and nothing stirred. Usually, he heard one of the horses move or the sound of a scurrying small nocturnal animal as it ran past or up a tree, but now it was deathly still. Unnaturally silent. His eyes snapped open.

Instantly alert, he reached out and prodded René, grasped his sword, rolled away, and rose silently to his feet. Above them, through the sparse forest canopy, stars twinkled, the waning moon provided a little light, but only enough for him to see the dark outline of René as he rose in uncertainty and stood listening. Neither man spoke, but each was acutely aware danger lurked. Odo raised his arm and pointed to a large tree, its massive trunk large enough to offer concealment. Thankfully René saw the signal and silently stepped towards the tree.

Another similar tree behind him offered Odo the same protection and with infinite care he inched quietly towards it. With his back against its trunk, he listened. He opened his mouth, which helped to hear better, steadied his breathing and patiently waited.

It seemed like an eternity, and he wasn't sure for how long, and most likely it may only have been a short while, but one of their horses snickered softly. Odo's eyes opened wider and the hair on his neck rose. Someone or something was stealthily approaching.

It could be a bear, but Odo discarded that thought immediately, a bear would make noise and the horses would become agitated. It was human. Slowly he raised his sword and held it defensively upright, protecting his face and neck. He tightly closed his eyes and focused on his listening... then he heard it. It was the sound of metal on metal, a muted 'tink'. A sword touching armour... a greave... He opened his eyes.

Slowly he eased down into a crouch and turned his head to look around the base of the tree and stared into the blackness. Then he saw them, or rather he saw blackened movement. One man behind the other, following in single file. To ensure quietness, each man closely followed in the steps of the man in front.

His bow lay beside where he'd been sleeping, and anyway, it was too dark to use it effectively. For now, it would be swords. Through experience, Odo weighed the odds. The men who approached may not know two armed men were alert and in wait for them. From their mannerisms, they appeared to be skilled, and they certainly were confident. While the intruders were armoured, he wasn't. This gave Odo the edge with mobility and speed, but the advantage turned back to the aggressors with their protection and numbers. A long, drawn-out skirmish with swords favoured them. Odo needed to strike first and move quickly. He wished he could somehow signal René, instead he'd have to trust his experience and hoped he would be ready when he made his move.

Odo kept his head as low to the ground as possible and continued to watch. From their path, Odo believed they would pass by the tree he hid behind. The danger of following, one man behind the other was, the men in front could not protect the last man.

If these men were the same men that René had spoken of, then there were six of them. Six against two were uneven odds.

The first man passed Odo's tree, then barely a half step behind, another followed, then another, finally six men closely packed together passed. At this point they should have spread out, Odo reasoned. Their error.

As the last man cautiously stepped by, Odo eased around the tree, drew his sword back and thrust it forward with all his might. It entered the exposed side of the *chevalier*'s neck, and he gave a short cry before falling to the ground. Odo had planned his moves carefully and dropped down onto his knees and ducked in preparation for his next strike. He felt a sword blade swish past, directly above him as the next *chevalier* turned with a warning cry of alarm. He swung his blade parallel to the ground and struck him across the back of the legs at the same time René launched his attack at the man in front who had turned to face the threat from behind.

Three men had fallen and the other three quickly separated and ran in panic. In the darkness they couldn't regroup and counterattack without risking injury to themselves. Their plan had been to stealthily approach and slay Odo and René while they slept, and they almost succeeded.

There was no point in pursuing the three *chevaliers* as they crashed through the forest and Odo called René back.

"Are ye hurt?" Odo asked.

"Nay, and ye?" René asked.

"Fortune smiles upon us, but not him." Odo referred to the wounded attacker who lay groaning in pain with bloodied legs on the ground. The other two were dead.

In the distance they heard horses galloping away.

"We should build a fire. They won't return this evening."

CHAPTER TWENTY

"Were ye in Carrick, Scotland?" Odo asked for the umpteenth time.

"Nay, nay, what is this ye speak of?" the *chevalier* gasped. His face contorted in pain.

A fire had been lit, and René was wandering around in the darkness, keeping watch in the unlikely event the others returned. Odo bent down and studied the man's face in the firelight.

"Why did ye come fer me, who sent ye?"

"My legs! Help me!" cried the *chevalier*.

"I will ask ye, once more." Odo took a deep breath, closed his eyes momentarily, and then placed his sword on the chest of the wounded *chevalier* and applied some pressure. "Who sent ye?"

The man stared up at Odo helplessly and told him what little information he knew. "It was Count Courteney, he sent us."

"He is dead."

"He gave us instruction before he passed."

"And did ye go to Carrick?"

"Nay, nay, I did not."

Odo paused a moment and studied the *chevalier* closely. Finally, he lowered his sword and walked away to find René.

"Did ye learn anything," René asked when Odo approached.

"Aye, and ye were correct, it was Count Courtney who sent those men."

"And what do we do now?"

Odo looked into the darkness and considered his options.

"The other three won't have travelled far. They will come again. We should leave here now," René suggested. "And what about the wounded man… or is he dead?"

"He lives, and his friends can help him. But we should load the horses and move them. I believe that this time they will prefer to catch us in the open. Three against two in daylight favours them, so we should remain here in the forest, and they can come to us where we have cover and protection.

A pink dawn greeted Odo and René as they began moving their horses and camp.

"Those *chevalier*s… they will expect us to ride away, and methinks they will return to find their friends."

"An ambuscade?"

"Aye, in the trees suits us better. We should hide the horses and find a suitable place to wait."

René grinned.

"With my bow, I can hit one, perhaps two," Odo said.

"That is unfair and leaves me only one," René laughed.

They could hear the cries of the wounded *chevalier* in the distance, his pitiful pleas for help went unheeded, but as Odo hoped, his cries would draw his friends to come to his aid. René found suitable cover near the summit of a rise that afforded him a spectacular view, while Odo climbed a nearby tree and kept watch in a different direction. They couldn't see the entire area, but it was the best they could do. It was just a matter of watching and waiting.

Odo saw him first, a lone rider approached from the north trailing three horses. He scampered down from the branches, grabbed his bow, and ran for a fallen tree that was perfect for his needs. René followed.

"Where are the others? René asked.

Odo shook his head. "I don't know, but I am concerned." Ahead they could hear the yells of the approaching *chevalier* as he called for his friends. The painful howls from the wounded *chevalier* intensified as he heard the shouts from his friend calling to him. "Somewhere, there are two more."

An arrow was notched, and Odo tried to settle his breathing. Something didn't feel right. He shrugged and focused on the approaching rider and calculated the distance at a little over two-hundred paces. A lengthy and difficult shot.

The *chevalier* made no attempt at stealth as he rode towards the forest and his injured friend. But he never came any closer and maintained a respectful and safe distance. Then he continued past, and obviously wary of arrows, still did not venture any nearer. His head swivelled nervously from side to side as he surveyed the area around him. Odo saw he was heavily armoured, and this presented a more challenging target. If his aim was slightly off, the arrow would glance off the armour, he needed to be precise.

Odo kept his head lowered and waited patiently. *Of course, the chevalier is bait, the other two are near.* With eyes narrowed and breathing calmly, he quickly rose to his full height, drew back on the bowstring to its fullest extent, sighted carefully, elevated the bow slightly, and released the bowstring. At the same time, a sound behind alerted him to danger, he dropped the bow and dove for the ground as a sword blade hissed past his ear.

Odo rolled along the ground and sprung to his feet, his sword already in his hands as he faced his adversary. The *chevalier* was unknown to him, but he was skilled and very quick. René caught unaware, had also rolled away, and stood crouched with his sword held defensively. Another *chevalier* stood poised, ready to engage with him.

"*Chevalier* René, this is not yer fight, lower yer sword and walk away," stated one of the attackers.

The *chevalier* challenging Odo lunged, and his sword swiped dangerously close to his stomach. Odo was driven back as the sword slashed, probed, and thrust. The man was strong and quick. It took all Odo's skill to keep the *chevalier* from skewering him. He could hear René engaged in a similar contest but couldn't spare a moment to look as he fought for his life.

Odo forgot about Rene and focused on remaining alive as he began to react defensively to his opponent's relentless attack. The *chevalier* was good and forced him to step backwards.

The change was minuscule, but his retreat slowed, then stopped. In a flurry of quick counterstrikes, Odo began to slowly pressure the *chevalier* to retreat as their swords clanged and struck. At first, the *chevalier* withdrew only a single step, then another. Now the tables had turned, and the *chevalier* was compelled to defend for his life as Odo bore down on him with speed and superior skill.

Odo knew he needed to end this fight quickly as he felt himself beginning to tire. The *chevalier* facing him was strong and appeared to have more stamina. Then he heard René yell in a cry of pain. He couldn't look but from the noise, guessed he still fought furiously.

Blood ran down René's arm, and he instinctively knew he needed to end this fight soon, or he would weaken through blood loss. He quickened his strokes and changed his foot position, and counter attacked with fury. His opponent wasn't prepared for the change of tactic and stumbled backwards. It was all René needed. Despite his wound, he increased his speed, defended a wild slash, and saw the opening. He sprung forward off his rear foot and lunged. His sword pierced through chainmail, easily penetrated clothing, and entered the doomed *chevalier*'s midriff.

His friend fighting Odo heard the painful cry. In reflex, he flicked his eyes to spare a look and immediately felt the coldness of a sword blade pressing up against his chin. For the briefest instant, he froze, in less than a single heartbeat, he considered his options, and instead of yielding, began to raise his sword.

Without hesitation, Odo elbowed away the *chevalier*'s arm and thrust upwards. The *chevalier* crumpled to the ground.

Odo spared a quick glance at René, who was looking at his arm, then ran down the hill in the direction of the heavily armoured *chevalier* who had first approached trailing the horses. The horses were standing motionless, but of the rider, there was no sign. René followed.

They began a search and quickly found the man. An arrow was deeply embedded in his side and had cleanly pierced through his armour, chainmail, and lungs. He was dead.

Odo breathed out a sigh of relief and looked in concern at his friend. "Yer arm!"

René looked at the dead rider and shook his head. "I have never seen such accuracy with a bow. Such power... ye have a wonderful gift, *mon ami*." He looked at his arm. "It is nothing and looks worse than it is. But we must stop the bleeding."

The *chevalier* wounded during the previous evening had finally succumbed to blood loss, and so weakened, lost consciousness and passed away. After Odo had bandaged René's arm, they dragged all the bodies into a natural depression in the ground and covered them with a pile of rocks and stones as the ground was too hard to dig a deep grave. It took an age, and both men were exhausted by the time they were finished. Odo gave a brief prayer, and then both exhausted men walked to a stream to slake their thirst and recover.

Odo sat on the bank and threw pebbles into the water. "Despite my warning, Count Courteney still sent men fer me, what instructions did he leave Gisela?"

René was lying on his back. "I think not, it is not her way. She is not a leader or quick-witted." He shrugged, "I do not know."

Odo was considering riding back and slaying the count's daughter, Gisela, but he had no appetite for more killing, and according to what the dead *chevalier* had said, they were following the orders of the count before he took his life.

He'd killed enough, and already there would be many women grieving the loss of their men. He couldn't continue to kill. *Not any more ... when would it stop?* "I think ye can safely return to yer family, René. I owe ye my gratitude, without yer help, it would be me laying back up there."

"Will ye return to England?"

Odo wasn't sure if he could fully trust René. Yet the man had fought alongside him and been a friend and offered his help when he needed it the most. "Aye, I will disappear in England."

René looked thoughtful. "Odo, if I hear that the Courteney family will continue to seek vengeance, can I send word to ye?"

Odo threw the last of the pebbles into the stream and looked at his friend.

"I will make a promise," continued René, "If I hear that Gisela will come after ye, then I will send someone to warn ye. Is the least I can do to atone fer what my liege lord has done."

Odo rose to his feet. "It is time fer me to leave."

René stood.

"Thank ye, my dear friend. Ye will find me in Mellester, in Devonshire southern England."

Odo waved farewell to *Chevalier* René De Villiers and rode towards the coast at a brisk canter. He'd lost his family but gained a friend and fervently hoped they would meet again. For now, he was impatient to see his son.

CHAPTER TWENTY–ONE

Mellester Manor hadn't changed much during his absence. It was still peaceful, and this time, there was no argument in the main street as he rode along its length. He received curious stares, but thankfully not of hostility or resentment, and with impatience, he headed towards Godwin and Hetti's cruck house.

He reined in outside the byre and, when he dismounted, heard the delightful squeal of baby's laughter. He peeked around the side of the byre and saw Hetti playing with baby Odo in the field a short distance away. She never saw him, and his heart melted. Baby Odo's joyous and playful cries were in sharp contrast to what he experienced over the past year, and he watched the interaction between Hetti and Odo closely. He felt his face crease into a broad smile. Hetti was giving the boy all the love and attention he needed. Baby Odo had grown and was trying to walk. It was comical to observe, and he laughed at the antics and uncoordinated attempts. Hetti had yet to see him.

"I trust yer journey was successful?"

Odo's head whipped around. He'd been so engrossed in watching Hetti and Odo he never heard the footfall. "Reeve Norman, good tidings. I never heard ye."

The reeve laughed. "Yer lad is healthy and grows fast. Hetti is a good mother and has grown to love him." He looked intently at Odo. "Ye have come to take him?"

Odo stepped around his horse to stand beside the reeve. "Aye, I have been gone nigh on a year. Ye ask if my journey successful?" He leaned over and risked another peek around the byre to look at his son. "Reeve, I took no pleasure in what I have done. But I know that Odo can live a normal life, and I no longer need to fear someone will come fer him."

The reeve remained silent as he considered his words. "I hardly recognized ye. This horse is indeed a handsome beast, the finest horse I have ever seen in these parts. And yer hair and beard, ye look like a vagabond." He laughed. "Care to join me fer a mead. I think we should talk, eh. What say ye?"

Odo turned back and looked again at baby Odo. As yet, Hetti was still unaware he'd been watching.

"Aye, ye want to see yer lad, he'll still be here, but we do need to talk," said Reeve Norman. His voice had taken on a serious tone.

Odo didn't know the reeve well, but he knew the man was agreeable, fair, and had people's genuine interests at heart. He nodded. "Aye, let me take the horse to the inn and have him stabled, I will meet ye inside."

They sat in the gloom of the inn, each with a tankard of mead. Other men left the reeve and the stranger alone and allowed them space to talk in privacy.

Odo gave a brief account of his travels but did not go into details of the horrors he'd committed. Reeve Norman understood and didn't press him. After a brief pause in their conversation, the reeve leaned forward. "Where will ye and baby Odo go, do ye know?"

Odo shook his head. "I have thought on this, and nay, I know not. Perhaps I should remain here."

"Aye, that ye could… Ye know Hetti and Godwin will be heartbroken to see baby Odo taken from them." Reeve Norman observed Odo. "They could give the lad a normal life. And ye could remain here, in Mellester, if ye could find a craft, a calling, and still see yer son."

Odo looked down into his tankard and saw no answers, no easy solutions.

"Godwin and Hetti will give Odo everything the boy needs," continued the reeve, "he needs a good mother and father; can ye give him that?"

Odo was confused, he hadn't expected this.

"Odo will always be yer son. That will never change; perhaps there is a way where they could raise him, and ye could still be part of his life?"

Odo raised his head and turned to the reeve. "Why are ye doing this? Why do ye involve yerself in Godwin and Hetti's life?"

Reeve Norman's expression hardened. "Because I care fer them. They are like family, and if ye take baby Odo from them, they will be heartbroken, and the poor lad will again be torn from a woman who could be his mother."

"I, I, need to think on this."

"When ye knock on Godwin and Hetti's door, she will know ye have come to take him and has come to dread that moment. It is yer right to take the boy, and ye are his father, but be aware, think carefully of the boy's future. What will ye do? Ye cannot farm, ye ain't a tanner or cooper, and ye certainly ain't a fisherman."

Odo stared at him with his mouth open.

"What can ye do? I know ye can fight and are a knight, who was yer liege lord?"

"It isn't that simple, Reeve."

The reeve waited and lifted his tankard to his mouth.

"I am, er… I was a Templar."

The reeve spluttered. "What say ye? A Templar!" He looked surprised and shook his head at the revelation.

Odo nodded. "Aye, a Templar."

Reeve Norman leaned closer to Odo. "Milord, how can a knight, a Templar knight, take care of a boy?"

Odo shrugged. "I know not, but I will make do. I must."

The reeve looked thoughtful. "Odo, Ridgley Manor is half a day's ride from here. The priest there, Priest Kirby, is a good pious man, and his counsel is wise. I suggest ye pay him a visit and talk with him. Considering ye were a Templar, I think he can help or offer words of wisdom."

Odo was silent and looked despondently down at the table.

"I know ye want yer boy, but before ye break Hetti and Godwin's heart and take yer son, talk to the priest. Ye'll only be gone a day or two."

Odo felt the wisdom in the reeve's words. Since leaving Frankia, he'd repeatedly asked himself the very same questions, and no answers came to mind. He stared down at the scarred wood benchtop a moment longer, then looked up at the reeve and nodded. "Aye, methinks I should."

Ridgley Manor was larger than Mellester Manor and flourished under the firm hand of its lord, Sir Hyde Fortescue. Odo quickly found the church but could not locate the priest. It was Kirby who found him. He was not dressed as a priest and looked more like a farmer than a holy man.

Odo had stabled his horse and was aimlessly wandering through the village when a tall man with a craggy face stepped up to him. "Fare thee well, stranger. I hear ye seek someone?"

Odo studied the man carefully. He had a deeply lined face and open, expressive eyes. "I am seeking Priest Kirby, I know not where he'd be," Odo replied.

"Ah, well ye see, Priest Kirby is indeed a busy man and has been in the fields helping with the crops. It serves a parish priest well to assist villagers from time to time. Remaining cloistered inside a church doesn't fare them well, or does it?" He raised an eyebrow. "Er, unless ye seek spiritual guidance?"

Odo smiled. "Then ye are Kirby?"

"I am, but I know not who ye are, milord. Fer a peasant, ye are not, and I see a sword at yer hip, and I see yer eyes, they have seen battle and death. I can only ask myself, what does a man such as yerself want with a simple parish priest?"

It became apparent to Odo why Reeve Norman suggested he talk to Priest Kirby. He was a delightful man. "Priest Kirby, is there somewhere, er, private where we may speak?"

"Would ye prefer to go to the fields and help with the crops? We can talk there." smiled the priest with a twinkle in his eye.

"In this instance, methinks the church is more suitable." Odo returned the smile.

"Ah, spiritual guidance…." Priest Kirby placed a hand on his shoulder and guided him towards Ridgley Manor's modest church.

"Reeve Norman from Mellester Manor urged me to talk with ye. I am in need of counsel, and I have a quandary."

"Reeve Norman is a good man, if he suggested that ye talk with me, then it must be important. I have time, what ails ye, milord?"

Odo spoke at length and held nothing back. The priest was astute and asked probing questions, and lying to him was out of the question. Priest Kirby was quick of wit and could sense any deception with ease.

Priest Kirby rose from his seat and began pacing. After a short while, he stopped and faced Odo. "Reeve Norman is correct, and ye must consider the boy. Taking him away from a woman who could be his mother is not good fer her or the wee lad. Can a man such as yerself provide everything the boy needs?"

"Methinks I can."

Priest Kirby stood with hands on his hips and faced Odo. "I think yer relationship with the Knights Templar may serve ye well. Why not become a priest, and ask that ye be given Mellester parish? There is always a chance the bishop may agree, although he may need convincing…." He stepped up to Odo. "And then ye can keep an eye on yer son, help the village and provide spiritual and moral guidance, what say ye?"

"I, I... I have not the makings of a priest!" Odo was flabbergasted.

"Nay? Yet ye took Templar vows, ye know Latin and were a monk. I think ye would make a fine priest," smiled Priest Kirby. "Most priests cannot even read, and many are nothing more than.... Well, better left unsaid, eh?" He paused to allow Odo time to think. "Our bishop is, er ... somewhat... uh, challenging. I warn ye, this presents ye with some difficulties, as the decision lays with him. If he does not give his consent, then there is little ye can do."

The more Odo thought about it, the more he liked Priest Kirby's suggestion. It made sense. However, it all hinged on becoming the Mellester parish priest, but first, the bishop needed to grant his blessing. "Who is this bishop, and where is the cathedra[30]?"

Priest Kirby scratched his face. "His Grace, Bishop Barden Clarke, and his seat is in Exeter...."

"Ye care fer him not?"

Priest Kirby looked around the church to ensure no one was nearby. He stepped closer to Odo. "Nay, he is senile and deranged," he whispered.

"If I wanted to pursue this notion of becoming Mellester's priest, then it is to him I must speak to?"

"Aye, and the man is most responsive to fawning and flattery, and then he may still turn on ye." He scratched his head. "Perhaps my idea was ill-thought, and I spoke hastily, fer I do not see him being easily agreeable to yer request."

Odo recalled his conversation with Sir Godfrey in Paris. He'd almost forgotten. "Uh, Priest Kirby, are ye familiar with Roger de Lessassier?"

---

30 Cathedra – The bishops seat.

He nodded enthusiastically. "But of course, he is our archbishop. But ye cannot approach him, for selecting a priest is the onus of the bishop. Such inconsequential matters fall only to the bishop, and the archbishop is a busy and powerful man. It would be a gift from heaven for a simple parish priest or a layman to receive an unannounced audience with him."

"And this Bishop Clarke… if he granted my request, then could he change his mind after?"

Priest Kirby nodded. "Aye, if it suited him. As I have come to learn, he is not a reliable man of his word."

Odo nodded. The more he thought about Priest Kirby's suggestion, the more he liked it. But the bishop… Being a parish priest could enable him to be near his son. He could teach, guide, and advise and still play an active part of his life without interfering with Godwin and Hetti's role. "Where would I find, the archbishop?"

"Have ye lost yer senses?" exclaimed Priest Kirby as he raised both arms to the heavens and appealed for divine intervention.

"Aye, in the hills of Scotland," Odo stated. "But I have one thing in my favour, I have a letter of introduction to Archbishop of Kent, Roger de Lessassier."

Priest Kirby's mouth fell open, and he slowly lowered his arms. "A letter, ye say… then Odo, ye have been blessed."

Odo looked reflective. "Also, from this day forward, I will only be known as Oswald, not Odo Brus."

Priest Kirby returned to his seat. "Why Oswald?"

"He was my mother's father, my grandsire. He taught me much and influenced my life. This is why I shall take his name. If I retain the name

Odo Brus, then people will learn of me, and young Odo's life could be in danger."

Priest Kirby patted Odo on his back. "I wish ye good fortune, Oswald. I see goodness in yer soul, and ye are welcome to come visit me anytime."

Odo stood. "Thank ye, Priest Kirby."

"The door to my humble church will always be open, and may God be with ye, Oswald."

CHAPTER TWENTY–TWO

The following two days and evenings were spent in solitude at a nearby inn, considering his own and baby Odo's future. Reeve Norman was correct, it wasn't possible to take care of the boy and provide him with what he needed. As the reeve clearly pointed out, he had no skills, he wasn't a farmer, that was obvious. In Carrick, it had been Inan who had done all the farming and made all the decisions around breeding, taking care of the animals, and planting and harvesting what few crops they'd grown. He'd devoted his entire adult life to the Church as a Templar Knight. Under strict vows and discipline, he'd trained as an armed monk to defend Christian pilgrims who ventured to Jerusalem. He knew how to kill, nothing more, nothing less.

According to the reeve, Hetti and Godwin had grown to love the baby. If there was one thing he was sure of, if baby Odo were to grow into a decent Christian man with goodness and virtue, then he needed the foundation of structured familial love. Godwin and Hetti could provide that to him, and he, as a priest, could help with education and prepare him for his journey into manhood and raise his own family.

Odo acknowledged that Priest Kirby and Reeve Norman spoke rationally; their advice was sound; the tricky part was accepting that he would not be Odo's accepted father. His grief resurfaced, and overcome in emotions, he remained in his room. He prayed and found spiritual guidance, strength, and the resolve to continue with Priest Kirby's suggestion.

When the inn's landlord saw the stranger reemerge from his room, he saw a change. The distracted and distant warrior with a severe expression who rented a room was gone, replaced by a determined and focused young man with an easy smile.

Feeling refreshed and empowered, Odo ordered a meal, ate quickly and departed with a kindly word of thanks.

Odo rode for Kent and Canterbury Cathedral. Six days later, he arrived to stare in wonder at the grand structure. Its immense spire rose majestically to reach the heavens and, in its shadow, felt a closeness that reaffirmed his faith. It was calming, reassuring, and absolute, and he only hoped the archbishop was supportive and could help as Sir Godfrey believed.

He found an inn, stabled his horse, and obtained presentable clothes and cleaned himself before approaching the archbishop.

A passing monk informed Odo that The Most Reverend, Roger de Lessassier, Archbishop of Canterbury, resided in the Archbishop's Palace, beside the cathedral. Curiously, Odo wandered around the cathedral until he found the grandiose home of the archbishop. Guards prevented him from entering, and on showing them the missive written by Sir Godfrey, they reluctantly allowed him to enter after removing his weapons.

An inquisitive cleric met him inside, and again, Odo was required to present the letter of introduction. Told to wait, the cleric scurried away only to return moments later.

"Milord," the cleric respectively dipped his head, "Regrettably, His Excellency, is journeying on some urgent matters and will return later this evening. I have scheduled an appointment fer ye in three days hence. If ye return then, at midday, then ye may see him briefly." The cleric offered a smile exposing rotting teeth.

"I offer my gratitude and will return in three days. May I have the letter returned to me?"

The cleric retrieved the letter, handed it over, and Odo left the building and returned to the guardhouse for his weapons.

Three days was an eternity, and during that time, Odo rehearsed how he would appeal for favour and the words he would use to convince the archbishop to assist him. Privately, he felt the clergyman would be lukewarm to his request and need some convincing. It was with some nerves and trepidation that he returned to the guardhouse, surrendered his weapons, and again met with the cleric with rotting teeth and foul breath.

"Please, be seated." The cleric waved to a bench and asked for the letter, which was promptly handed over.

Prepared for a long wait, Odo took the proffered seat and steeled himself for an afternoon of boredom.

In only a matter of moments, the cleric returned and gestured for him to follow and was led into a luxuriously furnished room. Tapestries and paintings graced the walls, and beautifully carved furniture filled all available space. A fire blazed in a large, oversized hearth, and behind a large table sat the archbishop, hunched over and reading his letter. Another man, a scribe, sat at another raised desk to the side and ignored him. Odo nervously entered.

"Yer Excellency, my I present Sir Odo Brus, of Carrick."

Odo heard the heavy sound of the door closing behind him, and the archbishop stood. The resemblance was uncanny, the likeness of Sir Godfrey's features evident.

The archbishop stepped from behind the table and extended a hand. As protocol dictated, Odo dropped to a knee and pressed his lips to the episcopal ring.

"Yer Grace, thank ye fer taking the time to talk with me," Odo said in the way of a greeting.

"Welcome to Kent, Sir Odo, please be seated." The archbishop sat on a padded chair positioned in front of his table, and Odo eased himself onto another. The cleric moved to stand near the door in the event he was needed.

"And how fairs Godfrey?"

"Paris keeps him busy, there is always much to do. The Templars are recruiting, and Sir Godfrey commands fairly and with purpose, Yer Grace," Odo politely replied.

"Aye, I expect he does. I wish I could see more of him," Roger de Lessassier said wistfully. "Now then, his letter simply states that I should afford ye the courtesy of providing ye with assistance if and when in need. I admit, Sir Odo, this is a most unusual request, and I am quite perplexed. Why is it ye have journeyed all this way to see me?" Archbishop de Lessassier adjusted the pectoral cross that hung around his neck and crossed his legs.

"Yer Excellency, I find myself in a difficult situation and need some guidance on how to proceed. It is rather personal and requires that I speak to ye in, er, uh, confidence."

The archbishop raised a single eyebrow, held Odo's gaze a moment and remained silent for a dozen heartbeats. "Very well." He turned his head. "Please, allow us privacy."

The scribe stood with a peeved expression, gathered an armful of scrolls, and shuffled towards the door. "Yer Grace," replied the cleric, waited for the scribe to leave, and then stepped through and closed the door quietly behind him. With the door closed, the cleric pressed his ear to the door to eavesdrop.

Now alone, Odo recounted his experiences, beginning with the battle where he was injured and ending with his discussion with Priest Kirby.

Archbishop de Lessassier rubbed his chin as Odo finished his harrowing tale. He exhaled loudly. "I, er, offer ye my condolences fer yer loss," he shook his head in sympathy. "Most unfortunate."

"Yer Grace, I want to become Mellester Manor's parish priest. I am fearful of approaching the bishop, as I am told he is likely to refuse me."

"Then ye want me to influence his decision?"

"Aye, Yer Grace, I beseech ye. Grant me this request as I have nowhere else to turn."

The archbishop looked appropriately serious. "But there is more if I understand ye?"

Odo nodded. "I need the assurance my position as Mellester's priest will never be taken away as long as I meet the tenets of the Church and obey my vows." He looked at the archbishop with intensity. "And, Yer Grace, I enter the priesthood as Oswald Carrick, as I explained. No one must know of my real name."

"Aye, I understand the need fer yer concern." The archbishop looked puzzled. "I cannot recall, uh, who is the bishop?"

"I believe it is Bishop Barden Clarke, Yer Grace."

"Ah, yes, Barden, he is quite hoary these days." The archbishop stared at a tapestry on the wall and gave the matter due heed. After a moment, he turned his head. "Francis!"

Almost instantly, the door opened, and the cleric, Friar Francis, with rotting teeth reappeared and bowed at the waist. "Yer Grace?"

"How fares Bishop Clarke?"

"I fear he is not long fer this world, Yer Grace, his time is almost upon us."

"Oh, uh, who is undertaking his duties in the meantime?"

"Ah, that would be Deacon Ulmer Immers, Yer Grace."

"Immers … Immers. I do not recall him."

"Yer Grace, he brought the Church that derelict land in Rodenbury a short time past."

"Aye, of course, an ambitious young man," smiled the archbishop in approval.

Odo watched and listened with interest.

"Bring in the scribe, I want a missive sent to Bishop Clarke and Deacon Immers."

The cleric bowed subserviently. "As ye command, Yer Grace," and backed out of the room.

Within moments he reappeared with the scribe still carrying an armful of scrolls. The scribe sat and prepared his desk to write a letter. With his quill at the ready, he looked expectingly at the archbishop.

"To His Grace, Bishop Clarke, and Deacon Immers, Exeter Diocese," began Archbishop de Lessassier. He turned to Odo and smiled. "Uh, please accept this missive as er, confirmation of my recommendation that the bearer, uh... Oswald Carrick, be accepted and enter the common priesthood, *sacerdos,* in the diocese of Exeter, and on completion of his learning and Sacrament of Holy Orders, be assigned to the parish of Mellester where he will remain at his choosing. Uh, The Most Reverend, Archbishop of Kent, Roger *Cantaur*[31]"

"Er, and a duplicate fer His Grace, Bishop Clarke?" confirmed Friar Francis.

"Aye, and when is the next messenger due to leave fer Exeter?"

"At the week's end, Yer Grace."

"Ensure both missives are sent with him most soonest."

"As ye command, Yer Grace."

"Now then, Oswald, let us break our fast and eat, eh, and ye can expound to me in more detail of how Godfrey fairs in Paris," insisted

---

31 Cantaur – Latin for Canterbury. Archbishops of Kent are permitted to sign their name with Cantaur. While Anglo-Saxons referred to Canterbury as Kent, Cent, Lond or Centrice. Initially, the diocese was first referenced as 'Kent' and later became 'Canterbury'.

Archbishop de Lessassier with a clap of his hands.

Odo departed the archbishop's palace with a full stomach and feeling the effects of too much wine. While he found the archbishop to be agreeable, something was lacking in him. Perhaps he expected him to be more pious and devoted like the Templars who sacrificed so much for their faith. Regardless of Roger de Lessassier's disposition, he had been most helpful and endorsed his request to enter the priesthood. He felt better, but his stomach felt queasy.

The following day, he returned to the inn and prepared for his journey to Exeter and towards a new future and a new life as Oswald of Carrick. To ensure baby Odo's survival, the name Odo Brus would vanish, just disappear, and with a bowed head and a prayer, he hoped, be forgotten.

As explained to him, Bishop Clarke was of ill-health, and his deacon, Ulmer Immers, was administrating the diocese while the ageing bishop was ailing. The archbishop believed that Bishop Clarke was too old and unlikely to rise from his cot ever again. However, while the man lived, he was still a bishop and must be afforded the respect of his office and *see*, and it was the deacon's responsibility to ensure the bishop was apprised of developments. A new priest, informed the archbishop, was of little consequence and a mere formality as long as the deacon took the missive of recommendation seriously.

CHAPTER TWENTY–THREE

Deacon Ulmer Immers sat in his officium at Exeter's cathedral and sorted through the various items of official Church correspondence he received from the Archbishop of Kent via messenger. There were the routine updates and directives, nothing of importance, and all would be dealt with appropriately. Two additional missives were most unusual. The first, written in the untidy scrawl of Friar Francis, the archbishop's steward, piqued his curiosity, and he re-read the letter a couple of times.

While Deacon Immers considered himself pious and devout, he was also quite zealous. Not satisfied at having risen to the office of deacon, Immers' goals were much loftier and had his sights firmly set on becoming a cardinal, and God willing, perhaps even one day, the Pope. To ensure he was kept updated and enlightened of unusual goings-on that he could use to his advantage and leverage to seek favour and praise, he paid Archbishop de Lessassier's steward, Friar Francis, an unpleasant and odious man, a generous reward for any information that would be useful. The amount of the stipend was in direct proportion to the value of the information he provided.

As Immers re-read the missive, he was perplexed. Why would a Templar knight seek to become a common priest in a small manor of no apparent consequence? Mellester Manor held no importance… was there something about this hamlet of which he was unaware? He shrugged, put aside the letter and broke the seal to read the other missive.

Immers tossed the scroll aside, leaned back in his chair and thought about it. As expected, and forewarned by Francis, the missive just detailed how the archbishop requested that Oswald Carrick become a priest... There was nothing to lose by agreeing to the request and potentially much to gain. Interviewing Oswald Carrick would be interesting and could prove helpful in determining why Mellester was so important to him. After all, reasoned Deacon Immers, knowledge was truly power.

A week after leaving Canterbury Cathedral, Odo arrived in Exeter and stared at the building, which was the seat of Exeter's bishop. It was less than impressive, while moderately large, or certainly and considerably more prominent than a typical church, it wasn't grand, not like the other cathedral's he'd seen. It mattered not; what was important was seeking the deacon's blessing and becoming a priest.

After stabling his horse, he announced himself to a priest and politely requested an audience with the deacon. Again, and most unusually, he was not told to wait but led to a vestibule and was told the deacon was expecting him, and he would be seen momentarily.

Odo still felt nauseous, his stomach was in knots as he was led into the deacon's officium. Before him, a fleshy, rotund man of about his own age rose and greeted him warmly. Odo was instantly on guard, while the deacon was genial and smiled easily, the friendliness did not extend to his eyes.

"Hail to ye, The Reverend, Deacon Immers," Odo formally greeted him.

Immer's eyes flicked over Odo and assessed him. In that briefest instant, he took an immediate dislike to the man. He recognized the knight was physically intimidating with well-developed shoulders and arms and clear, blue, inquisitive eyes. Immers felt vulnerable, a feeling he did not enjoy. He forced a practised smile. "Greetings Oswald, fare thee well?

"Aye, weary from travel, and thank ye fer asking, Deacon Immers," Odo politely replied.

"Please be seated," invited Immers and then eagerly settled back on his cushioned chair behind the table where he felt safe.

Odo sat as requested and waited.

"I have several matters that require my attention, so we shall keep this brief." He smiled again and reached for the missive he'd been sent and held it up. "Archbishop de Lessassier informs me ye wish to become a priest."

"Aye, the archbishop was most gracious," Odo replied. "I have devoted my life to the Church, and I received a painful injury which troubles me greatly, and it makes travelling and, er, fulfilling my vows and duties as a Templar, most difficult."

Immers nodded. "And ye wish to serve in Mellester when you've received yer Holy Orders."

"Aye, Deacon Immers," Odo confirmed but didn't elaborate further.

Immers' eyes flashed annoyance. "Why is that? If ye wish to become a priest, well, that is one thing... but ye chose Mellester, it is a small hamlet...."

"Deacon Immers, ye are correct and astute," Odo offered. He instinctively knew that the deacon was a type of man who responded to flattery. "I have made the acquaintance of Reeve Norman, and he suggested that Mellester held promise and that its good folk could benefit from guidance and spiritual counselling."

Deacon Immers couldn't hold the gaze of the knight and looked away. He chewed on his bottom lip thoughtfully. "Normally, a son is presented to the Church, and his father offers a modest dowry. After all, it is costly for the Church to feed, clothe and enlighten a man who intends to dedicate his life to God. Are ye capable and have the means to provide a modest gratuity?" enquired Immers. If the man before him was indeed a lord and knight, then he must have coin.

Odo had prepared for this, and in the event it came down to coin to secure his position, then he was willing. He reached under his tunic and untied a purse. Once in his hand, he ensured the deacon saw it. "Of course, Deacon Immers, it is only fair that costs are reckoned. I do wish to become a priest, and in doing so, I wish to be Mellester's parish priest. As Archbishop de Lessassier detailed, the position is for as long as my choosing. I cannot be re-assigned."

Immers saw the bulging purse and could only dream of how much coin it contained. He licked his lips. Oswald's mention of the archbishop was a reminder that once he became Mellester's priest, then he would always remain so. If he, as deacon, or hopefully, soon as bishop, re-assigned Oswald, then it would reflect poorly on his obedience and future. He had no choice but to agree. "Yer calling to serve God and the Church is admirable, Oswald. Are ye capable of learning Latin?"

Odo nodded enthusiastically, "Aye, I can already read and write some Latin."

Immers raised an eyebrow and smiled. Most priests couldn't read or write and learned the sacraments by memory. "And ye need to be able to recite liturgy, and when ye can do this to my satisfaction, then ye will be ordained," Immers informed him.

"Then I will do my utmost, Deacon Immers," Odo affirmed.

"Aye, I think ye will. Very well, Oswald, then ye have my full support and blessing. Ye may present yerself to the abbey and Abbot Andrew at yer soonest," smiled Immers while his gaze was affixed on the purse in Oswald's hand.

Odo felt the relief wash over him. "I have some matters to attend to first and will return to Exeter within a few days, if, uh, that is acceptable, Deacon Immers?" He reached over and placed the purse on the table. "Please accept this modest dowry in recognition of yer investment."

Deacon Immers fought the impulse to snatch the purse from the table. He licked his lips again. "That is admissible, Oswald, but I need to remind ye, once ye begin, yer obedience and service cannot be questioned, if found to be lacking, then we will have no hesitation of releasing ye of the bond. "Do ye understand?"

Odo tried to look into the deacon's eyes, but the man was fixated on the purse. "Ye will never have cause to question me, Deacon Immers."

Reluctantly, Immers tore his gaze from the purse. "As his proxy, I will inform Bishop Clarke of our arrangement." In truth of fact, Immers fervently believed the Templar wouldn't last as a *novitiate*[32] and would walk away. That would be a most equitable outcome, he decided.

Odo walked from the Cathedral Church of Saint Peter in Exeter in a daze. His heart pounded, and he felt ill. While the outcome of his meeting had been positive, he found the deacon to be disgusting, repugnant and far removed from the piety and devoutness he expected. He only hoped that he wouldn't have much interaction with the man. He found an inn and sat in solitude with a tankard of mead as he considered his new future.

Deacon Immers ensured his goblet was refilled, and he sat back in his chair and thought about the peculiar and earnest man who'd just departed. The purse contained not silver as he expected, but gold coin. It was a small fortune, and Immers gave thanks to God with a brief prayer. Feeling the pleasant warm effects of the unwatered wine and the weight of gold, he wondered again what interest did Oswald have in Mellester, what was there that was so important to him, and to hand over a fortune in gold?

Mellester's current parish priest was an unkempt, uneducated, and childless man who performed only the essential and most basic tasks required of him. The tithes he received were well below what they should be, and it was only through the good graces of villagers that the man was able to feed and clothe himself. Replacing him with Oswald might be

---

32 *Novitiate – Is a novice who is undergoing training and preparation prior to taking his vows for priesthood.*

another gift from God. Immers raised the goblet in a gesture of thanks and downed the contents. He was scheduled to visit some parishes soon. *Perhaps it would be an excellent time to visit Mellester,* he thought.

He called for his cleric, and when the man entered his officium, he issued instructions for Abbot Andrew to prepare for a new *novitiate* and commence induction at the week's end. "And it is time I paid a visit to Mellester Manor," stated the deacon, "Uh, perhaps in a day or two, eh, and I will spend the evening in Ridgley." Immers rubbed his hands as he thought of the comely maiden he liked to spend time with at Ridgley Manor when visiting that fool, Priest Kirby.

The next morning, Odo departed Exeter and headed for Mellester Manor. Firstly, he would find the reeve and inform him of the developments and then hopefully see baby Odo and tell Hetti and Godwin of his plans and how they could raise the boy as their own. His involvement would need to be agreed upon because he had every intention to prepare the boy for his life ahead.

It felt strange to be walking through the village unarmed. His sword lay on the cot at the inn along with his bow. The feeling of vulnerability was discomforting, but he knew it was something he'd have to adjust to. The sword represented a part of his life he wanted to forget. In his hands, it was a harbinger of death, yet at the same time, it offered security and comfort. His desire to feel its closeness conflicted strongly with his emotions and the endless killing that he wanted to come to an end. The cold, sharp blade had been a part of his entire life, and he needed to rid himself of the hold it had over him. Leaving it at the inn had been challenging but also, to a certain extent, liberating. Most presently, and for defence, he had only his wit – something he'd have to adjust to.

He'd been told that the reeve was in the fields supervising the lord's winter wheat planting.

"And what a sight to behold, milord," exclaimed the reeve when Odo walked up.

"And ye can forget the milord, for I am to become a priest. Now, I am Oswald Carrick," smiled Odo.

The reeve grinned and clapped him on the back. "Well done, Oswald, well done. Have ye seen Godwin and Hetti?"

"Nay, I thought we could go together so I can explain to them. I imagine they will be aggrieved when they see me, er, ye can help keep things calm."

"Aye, let's go and find them, eh?"

Reeve Norman and Odo walked towards the fields that Godwin rented from Mellester's lord. Ahead, Odo saw Godwin and Hetti toiling hard on building a new fence while baby Odo played on the grass at their side. When Hetti saw Odo, her hand flew to her mouth, and she protectively picked up the baby and held him on her hip as they approached. Godwin smiled in greeting. If he felt uncomfortable, it didn't show. "Milord, it is good to see ye again."

"And it warms my heart to see ye all," Odo replied and then looked at his son. The boy had grown so much, and he saw the resemblance of Josceline. His voice caught in his throat. "I, uh," he coughed, "I have looked forward to this day fer a long time."

"I'm sure ye have Odo," Godwin replied. "Would ye like to hold him?"

Odo nodded, and Hetti reluctantly handed him his son. It felt wonderful to have him in his arms and feel him. He'd dreamed of this day...

"Perhaps we could talk?" interjected the reeve.

"Baby Odo needs feeding, we can go inside," replied Hetti.

To Odo, she was a little cool towards him. But then he understood why and didn't blame her. He awkwardly handed Odo back.

Once inside, Odo came directly to the point. He didn't want to delay Godwin and Hetti's agony any longer than necessary. "I have not come to take Odo away," he shook his head. "If ye are willing to keep him, then I think it best fer Odo, ye both are good people and can give him the life he needs, I... er, I cannot." His voice faltered again, and he looked away briefly.

Hetti looked incredulous. "Odo!" she exclaimed, "What is this ye speak of?"

"Hetti, Odo is, er, no longer Odo, he is Oswald, Oswald Carrick, and soon to be Priest Oswald," Reeve Norman added.

Both Hetti and Godwin's mouths opened.

"I have approval from the Church and will become Mellester's priest," he raised a hand to prevent any interruption. "I do not want anyone, no one, including baby Odo, to know I am his father fer as long as I live. Ye both are his mother and father, do ye understand?"

Hetti began weeping.

"But I want to contribute to baby Odo's life and can do this as a priest.

Will ye allow me to do this?"

Godwin stepped up and placed a hand on Hetti's shoulder as she clutched baby Odo to her chest. Od– Oswald, I don't know what to say, I uh…."

"Why, why are ye doing this?" Hetti gasped between sobs.

Odo could see she was overcome, and he found himself struggling for composure. "Because Odo and yer lives may be in danger if people know his real name is Odo Brus," Odo looked down at his son and took a breath. "He must take yer name and be known as Odo Read." He swallowed and continued to fight the upwelling of emotions. "And I am now Oswald Carrick, and soon, God willing, Priest Oswald." He wiped his eyes with a sleeve.

"And ye will be here in Mellester?" Godwin asked.

"Aye, I will."

Hetti stood and wrapped an arm around Odo and gave him a tight squeeze as the baby cooed on her hip. "I don't know what to say, I; we were worried what would happen when ye returned and were fearful ye would take him from us." She looked at the baby and smiled proudly. "He is such a good wee boy, and we love him so."

"Aye, he takes after his father," Odo added with a laugh. "But I must know that ye will allow me to see the boy, and as he grows, I want to teach him, make sure he has learning and to prepare him for the future. While I may not be acknowledged as his father, ye must allow me to do this."

Godwin looked at Hetti, then turned back to Odo. "We are joyous, and of course we agree, our home will always be open to ye, Od– Oswald. But ye spoke of danger…?"

Odo's expression changed. "Aye, there are those who seek my death and his," he pointed to baby Odo. "I will always ensure he and ye are kept safe, but fer now, I believe there is no need fer worry."

"Are ye sure?" the reeve asked.

Odo nodded. "Aye, fer now." He could see that Godwin and Hetti were happier with the knowledge they could keep the baby rather than being informed of a distant threat. He turned to look at his son and felt his love for the boy well up again.

From deep within his soul, he fought the urge to grab the baby, hold him close and take, and raise him by himself to become a decent man, someone whom he could be proud of. His chest rose and swelled as his conflicting emotions settled. He wiped his eyes again, and Hetti raised the baby for him to hold. Gratefully, he took Odo from her and sat down on a bench near the hearth.

"Come, let us give Oswald some time alone," suggested the reeve. The three of them exited the cruck house and stepped outside.

Odo cradled his son in his arms and spoke to him from his heart. He told him of his pain and suffering, he spoke of Josceline and his brother and sister. He made promises to the boy and declared to him that he would never desert or leave him, that he would always be there, somewhere, watching closely. He prayed that one day when baby Odo was old enough, he could share with him and tell him of his love and all that happened. "One day, ye shall know," he declared to his son, then leaned down and kissed him on his forehead as Hetti and Godwin returned.

"How fairs Rosa?" Odo asked.

Godwin gave Hetti a quick look and then laughed. "That woman is remarkable. She works harder than anyone else, and she has taken charge of the milkmaids. She bothers no one and is a pure delight, and we have come to depend on her. A couple of times, she took to some youths and hurt them badly, but they deserved a good beating."

"I had to have a stern word with her and felt frightened she would attack me," laughed Reeve Norman with a shake of his head.

"But the lass means well," Hetti added, "We are truly blessed. "She has a healthy baby girl, and she is a hardworking and wonderful mother."

Odo grinned, *if her parents only knew.* "I look forward to seeing her."

Part Two
Sacerdos

CHAPTER TWENTY–FOUR

Fields of wheat swayed rhythmically in the gentle afternoon breeze, although the wind did little to provide any respite from the heat as the sun beat down on those who toiled and harvested Exeter abbey's ripe wheat crop. It was hot, unbearably so, yet the temperature did not deter all the monks from the gruelling task of reaping and threshing.

It was only natural that Odo would be assigned to scythe. He was tall, muscular, and more than capable of performing the back-breaking work, and better suited than most other monks who were either lazy, unfit, or just unwilling to bend a back and complete the arduous labour.

Beneath the wide-brimmed straw hat he wore, sweat dripped from his nose, his tunic was soaked from perspiration, and he'd already been hard at work from the moment it was light enough to see.

He paused a moment, raised his hat, and wiped his brow, and immediately felt the willow switch strike his back. He grimaced.

Monk Grimwald was a merciless, cruel, sadist. He took great delight in inflicting pain and humiliation on the *novitiates*, especially on Oswald.

Grimwald struck him again. "Whatever ye do, work heartily, as fer the Lord and not fer men, knowing that from the Lord ye will receive the inheritance as yer reward. Ye are serving the Lord Christ," he said, and the pliant willow switch descended and slashed across his back one more time. "Ye lazy heathen! Ye have no time to dilly-dally, work damn ye!"

Before the switch descended on his back again, Odo grasped the scythe's wooden handles and returned to cutting the wheat. His back stung from the repeated beating, but he held his tongue and ignored the cruelty.

His life at Exeter's abbey was far removed from the structured life of a normal *novitiate*. Since the day he arrived at the abbey, he'd been targeted, abused, insulted, beaten and humiliated. Primarily by Monk Grimwald and supported by many others.

Reeve Norman had kindly allowed Odo to leave his sword, bow and other valuables with him in Mellester, including his coin. Although Odo had taken a little coin with him to the abbey, and it had been pilfered within days.

Odo believed the torment and the punishment inflicted on him was deliberate and encouraged him to forswear and walk away from his desire to become a priest. A test. He'd lain on his wooden plank bed and schemed on how to exact revenge on Grimwald, but so far, he had resisted the temptation and managed to demonstrate obedience, discipline, and resolve. How easy it would be to turn and challenge Grimwald... but he didn't; he continued to ignore the abuse because one day soon, he'd be free of this hell.

From his first day at the abbey, he'd been assigned to work in the kitchens, clean and maintain the *necessarium*[33], work in the fields, tend to the animals and whatever tasks the monks decreed he must attend to. However, each day, time was allocated in the afternoons and early evenings for more non-secular studies. The time he spent with the ageing monk Pepin was what he enjoyed the most.

Monk Pepin was a true scholar, a man who loved words and written text regardless of language. Cursed with failing eyesight, Pepin taught Odo with enthusiasm and zeal. He challenged Odo to think, interpret scripture and even ask questions, he told him one day in a hushed whisper. While Odo was no stranger to Latin, Pepin brought him a new level of understanding, and he listened and learned. Pepin was a true master, and Odo was a perfect pupil.

Early evenings were spent with Priest Oliver. A droll, uninspired man who was lazy and uninterested. His dreary monotoned voice intoned lesson after lesson on rites, observance, and sacraments. "The liturgy of the Church is the foundation of its practice," he emphasized. Unlike his tuition with Monk Pepin, which was one-on-one, his classes with Priest Oliver were with the other four *novitiates*. This way, they could recite and practice with each other as Priest Oliver fought to remain awake.

In total, Exeter's abbey had five *novitiates*. Originally there had been seven, but unable to adjust to the hard monastic life, two had runoff. Odo was by far the oldest and was treated more harshly and brutally than the others. Why? Odo couldn't fathom, but he believed Bishop Immers was somehow behind it.

---

33 *Necessarium – Communal latrines found in medieval monasteries.*

As predicted, Bishop Clarke passed away, and Deacon Immers was the natural choice to assume the vacant seat, and with zeal, Immers embraced his newfound power and status.

Since his induction almost two years ago, Odo hadn't spoken to the bishop. He'd seen him frequently, mostly when attending church services in the cathedral or when he came to visit Abbott Andrew. He'd overheard monks or priests talking about him many a time, and his opinion of the man lessened.

Monk Grimwald wandered away to seek shelter in the shade of a tree, leaving Odo alone to continue his work. His sharp scythe swished backwards and forwards in an efficient tempo, and wheat stalks fell in orderly alignment. *Novitiates* behind picked up the wheat stalks and hoisted them onto a wagon, and under the sweltering sun, Odo laboured. His thoughts were always on his family, it gave him the strength to continue.

He hadn't returned to Mellester since he stepped foot in the abbey, but Reeve Norman had come to visit him many times and kept him updated on news and developments. Baby Odo was a true delight and growing into a healthy boy, the reeve informed. Odo longed for the day he could return, hold the boy in his arms again, and hear his gleeful cries. Mother Rosa, he added, was again with child. But despite her increasing weight and girth, she continued to work hard for Godwin and Hetti. She'd made herself indispensable and become a part of Mellester Manor.

It was almost time for Odo to hand the scythe to a monk who would continue while he went to see Monk Pepin for his Latin tuition. Monk

Grimwald swaggered towards him, and Odo tensed.

"Before ye leave, I'll have ye do another task fer me," he demanded.

"As ye wish," replied Odo respectfully and then handed the scythe to a waiting monk who'd just stepped up.

"This way."

He followed Grimwald to the south end of the dorter[34] and immediately sensed the monk had a most unpleasant undertaking for him.

Monk Grimwald stopped at the corner of the dorter and pointed with his switch. "The channel is blocked, clear it," he simply stated and then turned to him and grinned.

The *necessarium* was always situated as far from the chapel as possible and was accessed through the dorter. Holes were inset through the floor, and a rudimentary plank with a slotted hole allowed the user to sit on the plank and defecate. Waste fell into a channel where water, diverted from a stream, would eventually carry the excrement into the river. Because it was summer, the stream had not been providing enough water to clear the channel and heaps of stinking faeces lay beneath each of the openings beneath the dorter's floor.

Odo swallowed and rubbed his nose. "Ye want me to clear it?" The stench was overpowering.

Without pause, Monk Grimwald struck him across the shoulder with his switch. "Are ye deaf as well as witless? Ye can see it needs clearing, get on yer belly, make yer away along the channel and push the scumber[35] through to the river." He shook his head in mock disbelief at Odo's absurd

---

34 Dorter - Dormitory
35 Scumber - Excrement

question.

The sharp, vile, foul odour was already assaulting the back of Odo's throat. To block the thoughts of his noxious task, he thought of his son and what his assured safety meant to him. His face hardened. "I will need a rake to push it." Without waiting for a response and another wallop from Monk Grimwald's switch, Odo hurried to the building where tools were kept.

"Don't dilly-dally, ye lazy philistine!" came Grimwald's shout from behind.

He returned moments later with a rake, then removed his hat and the cloth rag tied around his head and began to place it across his nose.

"What ye be needin' that a'fore?" Grimwald reached over and snatched the rag from Odo's face and threw it on the ground. "That'll be holy ordure, softling!"

Odo fought the temptation to strike out at the sneering monk. He allowed his breathing to settle and knew this torment would soon be over… it must…. it couldn't go on.

"Don't have all day, be at it, quickly now." Grimwald raised his switch, but Odo had already moved away.

It was truly vile, the heaped excrement reeked of foulness, and the thought of lowering himself into the channel and crawling beneath the floor of the dorter was revolting. His insides remonstrated, and he wanted to be sick. Slowly he eased himself onto his stomach and slid into the fetid channel. With the rake extended in his hand, he began to slither beneath the building, through excrement, and towards multiple heaped mounds of faeces that blocked the ditch. He turned his head and saw Grimwald walk away. Already muck ran down his face and over his eyes, and he had to constantly wipe the odorous sludge away.

His stomach protested at the vileness as he continued to slither in the channel and through the excrement. He dry-retched. The piles of faeces were quite large, and it took some effort to move them, but eventually, he began to make progress. Again, his stomach spasmed as he pushed and shoved the putrid filth along the channel to unblock it.

He was covered in excrement; it was all over him like a coating, a blanket of nauseating putrescence. But now, the urge to vomit was too strong; his stomach convulsed, and he heaved, adding to the stench and accumulated filth. He pushed on, slowly clearing the heaped dung. The end was in sight, and only one last pile remained. The rake did its job, and what little flow of water there was, helped. He was beneath the last hole in the dorter when he felt something splatter on his neck. His empty stomach convulsed again, and his stomach heaved. Someone was defecating above him. He recognized the unmistakable laugh, it was Monk Grimwald.

Odo fought the impulse to crawl out from beneath the dorter and run. With teeth tightly clenched, he knew that in a short time, he'd be finished and could leap in the river to wash away the vileness, and he could forget about the sadistic monk until tomorrow when the torture would likely begin anew. Most importantly, he needed to make it through the day.

When he emerged from the channel dripping waste, Monk Grimwald appeared with a wide grin and walked up to him with his switch raised. "What took ye so long?" He waved his hand in front of his face and crinkled his nose. "Ye stink, ye filthy, good fer nothing skellum."

"Monk Grimwald, I am tardy fer my sitting with Monk Pepin, may I be permitted to cleanse?"

The monk glared at him. "Ye disgust me," he spat. "Ye will never wash away the corruptness of being a Templar and killer of women and children." He raised his switch and tensed to lash Odo across his shoulder.

Odo's vision exploded into a kaleidoscope of colour. Reason, logic and commonsense vanished. Consumed in a blind rage, he reached out and grabbed Grimwald's extended arm before he could strike at him. With superior strength and agility, he harshly twisted Grimwald's arm behind his back and felt the joint give. He didn't care. In a frenzy of madness, he shoved Grimwald towards the channel. The monk was not a slight man, he was, as were most others in Exeter's abbey, considerably overweight, but to Odo, he was as light as a feather. Fueled by anger, he threw the squealing monk down into the waste where the channel appeared from beneath the dorter, and with his foot, thrust the monk's face, down and into the excrement. Grimwald spluttered and writhed, but he lacked the strength to free himself. Unable to breathe, he opened his mouth, and it immediately filled with putrid foulness.

A vein pulsed erratically on Odo's neck as he watched the monk's weak attempts to free himself; his legs and an uninjured arm flapped uselessly in the sewage.

Odo's chest rose and fell through exertion and emotion, and then slowly, he calmed. After a dozen more heartbeats, he removed his foot, turned, and walked slowly towards the river.

"Fergive me, Odo," he said quietly.

Behind, he heard Monk Grimwald's weak appeals for help as he tried to crawl from the ditch.

He'd not been allowed to finish washing. Unbelievably, a monk yelled at him to come out of the river, put away the rake, and help him with another chore. "Ye can finish cleaning on the morrow," the monk had coldly stated.

Odo didn't see Monk Grimwald, and no one spoke to him about the incident. However, he knew a reckoning was due.

It was too late to attend to Monk Pepin's Latin tuition. He sat alone during his evening meal and expected to be called upon to account for his reprehensible behaviour. Still, surprisingly, nothing was said, although he received some strange looks, probably because he reeked. When he arrived for his class with Priest Oliver, he was admonished for being unclean, however, and other than that, everything appeared normal, and this only added to his distress and anxiety.

CHAPTER TWENTY–FIVE

Bishop Immers sat behind his oversized table and scratched at something on his scalp while he considered his current quandary. Approximately a day-and-a-half ride from Exeter lay the small parish of Harford. Leofric, Harford's parish priest, was without mettle and weak. Although grudgingly admitted the bishop to himself, he was usually quite proficient and reliable at collecting tithes. However, a freeman shepherd landowner named Robert had been negligent and not paid his tithes. Every time Priest Leofric approached Shepherd Robert, he was threatened and chased away. The amount of coin the shepherd owed was now substantial and, in Bishop Immers opinion, a determination was long overdue. But how to collect? Priest Leofric was genuinely fearful of his life and believed that Shepherd Robert was quite capable of following through with his violent threats.

What Immers really coveted was the shepherd's land, and according to Priest Leofric, the man owned an unusually sizeable piece of arable acreage that could be immensely profitable – although not from farming. Leofric believed that Shepherd Robert had discovered traces of black tin in a valley on his holding. Having a tin mine on Church-owned land would be a Godsend, and already Immers was dreaming of the wealth it would provide his diocese. While he had the power to excommunicate Shepherd Robert for his failings, in the long-term, it was unwise, as doing so wouldn't solve his immediate problem.

Bishop Immers kept secret how he had solicited the help of a merchant who had allowed Shepherd Robert to accumulate debt with him. On his urging, the merchant had unexpectedly called in that debt and, as the bishop fully expected and hoped, Shepherd Robert had been unable to pay. The merchant had taken the shepherd's flock of sheep in lieu of that debt, which now meant he could not earn money or pay his tithes to the lord of the manor and the Church. Bishop Immers was pleased with his plan, it was quite clever, and all he now needed was to force Shepherd Robert to admit he couldn't pay his mounting tithes and then the Church could seize his land. However, Priest Leofric was now fearful of his life and wouldn't go near the man.

His musings were interrupted when a cleric entered his officium.

"What is it?" barked Immers, unhappy at the intrusion.

"Yer Grace," bowed the cleric. "Abbot Andrew wishes to see ye about an important matter."

"What is it this time?"

The cleric shook his head. "I know not, he, uh, he said it was of some urgency, Yer Grace."

Immers tapped his fingers on his desk. "Very well, see him in."

Moments later, led by the cleric, Abbot Andrew entered. "Yer Grace," began the abbot, "We, er, I have a problem and believe it best that this issue is best dealt with by ye."

"What problem, Andrew, tell me."

"Er, is the *novitiate* Oswald, he attacked and threatened one of my monks. The man is a burden and become increasingly violent."

A look of concern flashed across Immers face. "Oh, what happened?"

"*Novitiate* Oswald was asked to perform some basic housekeeping duties; he refused, then threw a monk to the ground and broke his arm."

Bishop Immers raised his eyebrows in surprise. "That is indeed unfortunate and totally unacceptable," he tut-tutted. While he had no genuine concern for the well-being of the injured monk, an idea began to form. "Uh, Andrew, how long has Oswald been a *novitiate*? Surely, he must be ready to receive his Holy Orders. How does he fare?"

"Yer Grace, do ye recall how I asked that his ordainment be postponed until after the harvest. He is, er," Andrew coughed. "He was a valuable worker, and we needed his labour."

Immers nodded and repeated his question. "Then he is ready to receive his Holy Orders?"

"Yer Grace, I came here to seek yer support fer his expulsion, I cannot have my people threatened and living in fear," appealed the abbot. "T'is unchristian."

"Who was the monk that was attacked ... would it be Grimwald?" Immers inclined his head as he waited. Bishop Immers had instructed the abbot to be firm with *Novitiate* Oswald and privately hoped he wouldn't be able to cope with life in the abbey as a *novitiate* and walk away. Much to his surprise, Oswald had endured, not only that, but his tutors also informed him that the man had a quick mind and the capacity to learn.

"Well, aye, Yer Grace, but it was an unprovoked attack."

Immers knew of Grimwald's reputation all too well and doubted the abbot's assertion. "Enough, Andrew. Bring Oswald to me, here, after morning mass."

Abbot Andrew looked flustered and looked like he wanted to say more. Instead, he bent at the waist and bowed. "As ye wish, Yer Grace."

"Now leave me, I have much to do."

Abbot Andrew backed out of the room and left the bishop to ponder his dilemma.

Perhaps, thought Immers, *Oswald may indeed be the answer to my problems, a gift from God.* He raised his head and gave thanks, then crossed himself.

Bishop Immers called for his cleric, and when the man appeared, he issued some detailed instructions and informed him to prepare for the morrow. When again alone, Immers smiled. *It has been a glorious day.*

"Ye stink!" exclaimed Bishop Immers when Odo was brought before him.

Abbot Andrew tactfully stood a couple of paces away from Odo, who was standing before the bishop, while Cleric Peter stood near the door.

"Why in God's name would ye bring this disgusting man here, like this?" appealed the bishop as he retreated to the far side of his table. "Well?"

Odo remained stoic as he waited for the abbot to answer.

Abbot Andrew wasn't sure how to respond.

Bishop Immers turned to Odo in question.

"Yer Grace, I was clearing the channel," Odo replied. "I wasn't permitted to fully clean afterwards."

Bishop Immers looked incredulous. "The channel? Ye mean ye were *in* the channel?"

Odo nodded.

Immers crinkled his nose. "Was this where ye took to Monk Grimwald?"

Odo looked contrite. "Fer give me, Yer Grace, it was a moment of weakness, and I regret my actions."

The bishop turned from Odo to look at the abbot, then back again. "And why did ye attack him?"

Odo wasn't sure what to say. "Yer Grace, Monk Grimwald defecated on me when I was beneath the *necessarium*."

Bishop Immers mouth opened; he felt his stomach tighten and wanted to be sick. He looked for a goblet of wine, but it was a little early... He swallowed, deeply inhaled and paused a moment to settle his queasy stomach. "Ye disappoint me, Oswald. I thought ye a better person than that." He shook his head to emphasize his point and paused momentarily to refocus. "*Quis non ulciscetur iniuriis uestris. Quod si quis te percusserit in dextera maxilla tua praebe illi et alteram.*"

Odo nodded and, without hesitation, translated into English the bishop's flawed Latin interpretation. "Do not take revenge on someone who wrongs ye. If someone strikes ye on the right cheek, turn to him the other also."

"Aye, a good lesson fer ye." Immers was pleased with Odo's quickness to translate. It served his purpose, and he reasoned, *Oswald may yet be the man for the task.* He made eye contact with his cleric. "*Novitiate* Oswald, go with Peter, clean yerself, and return here at yer soonest. That will be all." He waved an arm in dismissal.

Cleric Peter waited for Abbot Andrew to leave, then led Odo away.

Odo was puzzled as to why Bishop Immers had not immediately expelled him. Although, the look on his face was entertaining at best when he informed him of what that snake Grimwald made him do. It was apparent, Grimwald had also lied to the abbot. But what now? The bishop had requested that he return to see him once he was clean, perhaps then he'd receive penance and be sent on his way.

Odo scrubbed away the last remnants of filth and faeces that had not washed away when he leapt into the river yesterday. Finally, he was clean and realized his clothes were still filthy and foul, he had nothing to wear. Before stepping back into his soiled garments, Cleric Peter reappeared and handed him a black robe. Odo was dumbstruck, he stood facing the cleric with his mouth open. "What is this? Must I return this robe when my clothes have been washed?" he asked.

The cleric smiled, "Nay, methinks not. Put it on, we must hasten to the bishop."

Again, Odo stood before the bishop, except, this time he was clean and wearing a simple black robe normally worn by priests.

Bishop Immers expression was cold and unfeeling. He looked at

Novitiate Oswald and frowned. "It saddens me to learn of yer weakness, yer tendency fer violence unsettles me and I must question yer ability to receive yer Holy Orders. What am I to do?" He sighed loudly and looked down at his table. He still found it difficult to hold Odo's gaze.

Odo felt deflated and disappointed. He could have resisted the urge to fall victim to the goading of Monk Grimwald, and now he stood before the bishop to atone for his behaviour.

Immers allowed silence to impart the seriousness of Oswald's misdeed. He knew he had him right where he wanted him, Oswald *would* do his bidding, of that there was no doubt what-so-ever.

"Common sense tells me that I must release ye, Oswald, but I am fond of ye and see a goodness in yer heart." Immers looked up at Odo, then turned away as he leaned back in his chair. His fingers interlaced across his slightly bulging belly. "However, the good Lord has provided me with guidance, and there may be a way I can help ye."

Odo's curiosity was piqued. His eyes opened wider, and he looked expectingly at the bishop.

"I, er ... have a problem, and ye might be able to assist the Church. If ye can do this simple task, a, er, a test, then I think we can put this unpleasant experience behind us, eh?"

Odo knew the nature of the bishop and wasn't fooled by his silky words. "Yer Grace, ye are most compassionate," he replied and subserviently dipped his head.

"I want ye to journey to the hamlet of Harford," Immers began. "There ye will find Priest Leofric, and he will assist ye. A parishioner there, Shepherd Robert, has been remiss in paying his tithes. Ye will collect the coin owed to the Church. If he is unable to pay ye, then, by the *Magisterium*[36] of the Church, ye will inform him that his lands are being confiscated. Do ye understand?”

“As ye wish, Yer Grace. Why can’t Priest Leofric collect the tithes, why do ye need me, a *novitiate*, to do this? I have no authority.”

“Ah yes, Shepherd Robert has threatened Leofric numerous times, and he feels the man is capable of following through. As ye have a, uh, familiarity and a predisposition with violence, then, ye are well suited to, er, overcome the threat and, er, evict the man–”

“Only if he is unable to pay his tithes?” Odo clarified.

“Of course,” quickly responded the bishop. “Now, concerning yer authority.” Immers reached for his goblet and took a healthy pull before setting it carefully back on the table. “I am satisfied ye have learned enough and can receive yer Holy Orders. Ye will go to Harford as a priest.”

Odo was stunned. His legs weakened, and he almost fell. With his heart pounding, he looked down at the floor and collected himself. After a moment, he looked up at the bishop. “Thank ye, Yer Grace.”

Bishop Immers rose from his seat and made his way around the table to stand before him. “Are ye willing to do this task in Harford fer me, Oswald?”

“And then I become Mellester’s priest?”

Bishop Immers nodded, “As we agreed. I have already recalled the priest from Mellester.” He turned to Cleric Peter fer confirmation.

“Yer Grace, as ye requested, Mellester’s priest will return here in a

---

36 *Magisterium - Is the Church’s authority or office to give authentic interpretation of the Word of God*

fortnight."

The bishop turned back to Odo for his answer.

"Aye, aye, I will, Yer Grace."

Bishop Immers sighed, "Let us go to the Cathedral."

Odo couldn't remember much of the brief service. His mind was numbed as the realization that finally, after almost two years of torment and beatings that he was finally receiving his Holy Orders.

He'd suffered, wept, and felt the loneliness of his ordeal at the abbey. In a way, he felt he'd sacrificed himself so that he could protect his son and keep him safe. He had no regrets; it was never an option to dwell on his decision to become a priest. Instead of feeling sorry for himself, and with determination and resolve, he'd endured and also learned. The scholarly monk, Pepin, had been his only friend, and with an almost fatherly bond, the monk had taken him under his wing and taught him. More than was required, beyond what was expected, and through his guidance and teachings, he came to glean more about his faith and role as a priest. He came to comprehend more about the people that dwelled in the shadow and pretence of Christianity who served only themselves and their perverted needs. While Monk Grimwald was such a man, Monk Pepin was, in contrast, the opposite. One lived in selfish greed, the other in selfless need – to study, interpret, and teach, all in the name of God.

He barely remembered Cleric Peter shaving part of his head or the baptism that followed.

The sacrament was short and powerful. In conclusion, Bishop Immers placed his hand on Odo's newly tonsured head. "Lord, Holy Father," he said, "when ye had appointed high priests to rule yer people, Ye chose other men next to them in rank and dignity to be with them and to help them in their task … You extended the spirit of Moses to seventy wise men … Ye shared among the sons of Aaron the fullness of their father's power." The bishop removed his hand, and he and Odo each crossed themselves.

Immers raised his head and looked at the newly ordained priest. "Ye now have the power to change bread and wine into the body of Christ and to fergive sins."

Odo slowly stood; it was over. He thought of Katherin, William, and of course, Josceline and smiled at their memory. *I will keep Odo Brus safe*, he silently vowed.

Immers saw the smile and knew he would have to keep a wary eye on the man.

CHAPTER TWENTY–SIX

For the first time in his life, Odo walked through the countryside as a priest. He'd passed by solitary priest's countless times, always alone, lost in thought and meandering to where? He never knew or cared. Now he was such a man. He wore a straw hat to protect his newly tonsured head from the sun, his robe flapped against his exposed legs, a simple bag with a few meagre possessions was slung over his shoulder, and in his hand, he carried a staff. It was liberating to be away from the vileness of the abbey; he felt free, unencumbered and to a certain extent, empowered. If one thing was certain, he carried with him more questions and doubts about the men who administered God's faith than when he first entered Exeter's abbey. But in accompaniment, he had the belief that good men, pious men, also accurately interpreted and administered God's word. Men like Monk Pepin and Priest Kirby.

Monk Pepin had wisely instructed him not to judge those men who claimed to serve the Church and yet served only themselves. Instead, serve the Church as ye would expect a pious and devout priest should. Do not protect the backs of those who hide in the shadow of the Church or even the self-proclaimed false prophets; instead, guard and preserve the institution. Spread the gospel of Jesus Christ, administer the sacraments and exercise charity because the Church needs good men of faith.

Odo took his vows seriously and would follow Monk Pepin's advice to the best of his ability.

His departure from the abbey had not gone entirely as planned. After receiving his Holy Orders and final instructions from Bishop Immers, he returned to the dorter to retrieve a few possessions when he encountered Monk Pepin. The ageing monk had taken him aside and offered him heartfelt congratulations and a few words of encouragement. Then, he leaned towards him and lowered his voice. "I know ye were robbed and coin stolen from ye when ye first arrived here," he said in a hushed whisper. "My eyesight is failing, but God has not taken my hearing. If ye want yer coin, look beneath Grimwald's cot, there ye will find yer coin in a small box. God be with ye, Oswald." He patted him on the shoulder and shuffled away.

Odo felt his cheeks immediately flush in anger. He quickly retrieved his things and paused outside the dorter, where he knew Monk Grimwald was recuperating.

He entered the room to find the monk alone and propped up on his cot with his arm bandaged and in a sling. Grimwald's mouth opened when he saw the newly ordained priest appear, and Odo saw the fear in his eyes.

"I have come to take back what is mine," Odo simply stated. He stepped up to the cot, bent down and looked underneath and saw the box that Pepin described. It had no lock, only a rudimentary latch. He slid the box out and opened it. Inside were some sundry items. A few folded pieces of parchment, a cross carved from bone, and Odo's purse.

"Ye heathen dross!" spat Grimwald. "Ye cannot come in here and thieve from me."

Odo took the purse and returned the box, back beneath the bed. He untied the leather thong, opened the purse, and turned it inside out. He held it out for Grimwald to see. The letters 'O. B' were embroidered on the inside and clearly visible. Josceline had insisted on doing it for him.

Monk Grimwald stared incomprehensibly at the purse. "Judas! Thief!" he cried. No one could hear him as all the monks were out in the fields.

Odo knew the monk was illiterate and couldn't distinguish the letters 'B' for Brus and a 'C' for Carrick. "As ye cannot read… this embroidery is my name." He replaced the coins, retied the thong, and turned to leave.

Monk Grimwald may have been injured, but nonetheless, he still knew how to inflict pain. He used his weapon to its fullest extent. "Women and baby killer!"

He froze when he heard Grimwald's obscene utterance. As the hateful and spiteful words sunk in, and to the sound of the monk's mocking laughter, Odo turned. The sound of the monk's cackling filled the room, his ears, his head, and deafened him to reason and commonsense.

The impact of Grimwald's accusation descended over him. Through the red haze of fury, he recalled Monk Pepin's words of wisdom, "…serve the Church as ye would expect a pious and devout priest should. Do not protect the backs of those who hide in the shadow of the Church or even the self-proclaimed false prophets; instead, guard and preserve the institution. Spread the gospel of Jesus Christ, administer the sacraments and exercise charity because the Church needs good men of faith...."

Monk Grimwald was genuinely evil. He thought that God's earth and the Church would be better off without the stain of men like Grimwald.

He stepped quickly towards the cot, reached down, and yanked the soiled pillow from behind the monk's greasy head. Grimwald yelled in pain as the sudden movement caused his broken arm to jolt. He thrust the pillow onto Grimwald's hideous face and pushed hard.

The monk writhed and twisted to no avail. He fought Odo with all the strength he had, but he was soon overcome. Slowly, his movements lessened and eventually stopped, and his chest no longer rose and fell. Odo held the pillow to his face a little longer, then removed it, placed it back where it had been and leaned the monk's lifeless body against it. He recited a quick prayer and crossed himself.

He walked from the room without remorse or contrition, and as far as he was concerned, he just did humanity and the Church a kindness; after all, he just did his first good deed as a priest. Abbott Andrew would likely be told that Monk Grimwald had passed in his sleep, and God had taken the poor, pious monk to heaven. Odo hoped it was to the fiery depths of hell.

Odo slept outside in the open, and when possible, he stayed overnight in small churches and was fed by welcoming priests. Although some were less than kindly, unwilling to share their food, and were only too happy to see him on his way.

Before leaving Exeter's abbey, he'd asked the bishop if he had a horse to ride. "If ye need a horse, then purchase one," laughed the bishop.

As his horse was in the care of Reeve Norman in Mellester, Odo walked and planned for his future as Mellester's new priest.

After five days and nights, he arrived in Harford and found the hamlet was small and poor. No wonder the bishop was keen to increase the tithes he received from here, Odo thought. He found Priest Leofric at the church, repairing wooden benches.

Odo explained the reason for his visit and found Harford's unfriendly priest, less than eager to assist.

"Ye don't understand, Priest Oswald," said Priest Leofric with a head shake, "I have to endure long after ye have gone. As I told Bishop Immers, Shepherd Robert is unable to pay his tithes, and I will have to suffer his tongue and threats. Nay," he shook his head. "Best ye do this alone, ye look capable."

Leofric stood near the church doorway and pointed, "That be his cruck. Ye'll find him there."

"May I leave my things here in yer care, Priest Leofric?"

"Aye, they'll be safe," replied the priest. "I wish yer good luck."

Odo left his bag and staff in Leofric's care. "Aye, methinks I will need it," he replied and walked towards the shepherd's home.

As he approached Shepherd Robert's cruck house, the curtain covering the entrance parted, and a man stepped out wielding an old, rust-pitted sword. He saw the tall priest walking towards him and waved the sword threateningly. "Be off with ye, priest, bugger off, I tell yer," he exclaimed, then took an aggressive step nearer.

Undeterred, Odo kept walking towards him.

"Away with ye priest!" the rusty blade hissed past Odo's face.

"Shepherd Robert?" Odo asked.

"Begone!" again, the sword swished.

Odo took another step closer, then as the sword began to descend in another uncoordinated and savage wild slash, he leaned to the side, dodged the blade, grabbed the shepherd's arm, and twisted. The sword clattered to the ground.

"Might be a good time to talk, eh?" suggested Odo. "If ye have water, my throat is parched," he asked casually.

Shepherd Robert squealed and rose onto his tiptoes. While in some mild pain, he looked shocked, and his countenance deflated. "Who, who, are ye?" His voice rose in pitch as he tried to ease the discomfort from his arm.

"I am Priest Oswald, and I am here to talk with ye." Odo smiled. "I have no need to be disembowelled by a rusty sword, so if ye give me yer word that ye won't try to hurt me, then let's go inside, out of the sun."

He reluctantly nodded, and Odo released his arm. With a toe hooked beneath the sword, he expertly flicked the blade up, caught it easily by the hilt, and handed it back. Astonished, Shepherd Robert shook his head and led him inside while rubbing his arm.

Shepherd Robert was a thin, wiry man with a long unkempt beard. His woman was also lean with a leathery face, and she looked at him like she wanted to attack and beat him senseless with a wooden ladle she grasped. Her knuckles were white as she pondered how to inflict mortal damage to the priest that just disarmed her husband with ease and invaded her home.

"I mean ye no harm," Odo appealed with his hands raised, "I wish to talk with ye, just talk."

Shepherd Robert sat on a bench. "Best ye sit then. Ye can tell me what ye want, then be on yer way."

The woman stared a moment. "Thieve'n bastards," she said, then turned to the pot on the hearth.

Odo sat as invited and looked at Shepherd Robert. "Are ye saying the Church are thieves? I have been told ye are behind in yer tithes, and I have come to ask ye about this and what can be done."

Robert laughed and shook his head. "That rotter Leofric..." he pointed in the direction of the church down the road. "...is because o'him this all happened."

"Perhaps ye can tell me then, what did Leofric do to upset ye so?" Odo asked.

Shepherd Robert exhaled loudly. "Get the priest some water," he grumbled to his woman. "A while ago now, I found some strange rocks in a valley in the hills where my sheep graze. I took one of them to Priest Leofric and asked him if he knew what it were. And blow me down, he told me it was black tin. Well, I never... black tin on my land? This was a surprise to me, I tell yer. I later found out this tin can be mined and that it is worth something, valuable it is, to be sure."

Odo nodded, said nothing, and allowed him to talk. A mug of water was thrust in front of him.

"Well then, shortly afterwards is when the trouble began. Next thing I knows, I have a merchant from Ridgley manor telling me I can buy a mule and cart to help me to dig out the tin, and I can pays 'im later."

"And ye accepted his offer?" Odo asked.

"Aye, wouldn't ye? But then, nigh on a month, the mule and wagon are gone. Someone stole em. If I catch them bastards, I'll run em through, I will," the shepherd exclaimed. "Then from outa the blue, the merchant appears and says he wants to be paid his coin or I gotta return the mule and wagon. I don't have his coin or his mule and wagon. And that's what I told him to his fat face!"

Odo could see the shepherd was becoming worked up. "Then what happened?"

"Next day, armed men arrived and said if I didn't pay up, they'd take my flock of sheep. And the sods did; took the lot of em. The sods threatened me and her they did."

Odo looked with a measure of sympathy at Robert. "Let me guess; then Priest Leofric knocks on yer door and wants ye to pay yer tithes?"

"Aye, but more than once. Each time I chased him away and told 'im I had no coin, and if he kept comin' back, I'd run 'im through."

Odo sighed. *Poor Robert.* He felt sympathy for the man and his wife. No wonder he showed such hostility. "I need to explain to ye, Robert. I was sent here by Bishop Immers to get ye to pay yer tithes if ye are unable to pay, then in the name of the Church, I am to evict ye and yer woman, and the Church will take title on yer land."

"But ye can't!" Shepherd Robert shot to his feet and knocked over his seat in the process. "That land has been in my family since King William[37] came…!"

---

37 *King William – William I, or more commonly known as William the Conqueror.*

Shepherd Robert's woman turned from the hearth and her cooking to stand supportively beside him. She continued to wield the ladle like a weapon, and to Odo, it looked like she still wanted to pound him with it.

He raised his hands. "Easy. I will try to help ye, but first, let me talk to Priest Leofric. He may have more to tell me, and I will do my best to ensure ye can keep yer land, Robert. Allow me this."

Shepherd Robert's chest heaved as he tried to quell his anger and pent-up frustration. After a moment or two, he nodded, turned his seat upright and sat down.

"Who is this merchant ye speak of?"

"The fat sod, Finnian from Ridgley Manor," spat the shepherd.

Odo stood. "Thank ye, I will do all I can, and I will return."

Priest Leofric looked uncomfortable when pressed by Odo to recount the details about Shepherd Robert's discovery of black tin. Undeterred, Odo asked him again. "Tell me, Leofric, what did ye tell Bishop Immers?"

"Priest Oswald, since Immers became bishop, he wants to know everything that goes on in his diocese. He pushes and pushes, I had no choice." He paced backwards and forwards inside the small church. "I told him that the shepherd had found black tin, that is all."

"Did he ask ye to do anything else?" Odo asked.

"Nay, except to bring him a sample rock and to collect tithes, he wanted Shepherd Robert to pay his tithes and told me to keep returning to his cruck and demand them."

Odo scratched his chin. The more he thought about it, the more he was convinced Bishop Immers was behind the theft of Robert's wagon and mule. "Are ye familiar with Merchant Finnian from Ridgley Manor?"

Priest Leofric shook his head. "Nay."

Odo took a deep breath. "Then I will visit Ridgley Manor and speak with this man. Ah, Leofric, do ye have a horse?"

The priest shook his head.

CHAPTER TWENTY–SEVEN

Priest Kirby's smile was huge. He spread his arms wide and warmly greeted Odo. "When I last saw ye, ye were a lost wandering soul; now look at ye, a priest!" he laughed.

"And now I am a lost wandering priest," Odo replied. His broad smile rivalled that of Kirby's.

They sat beneath the shade of a tree outside the inn, and each sipped from a mug of mead. Odo finished detailing all that happened to him during his tenure at the abbey and concluded with his tale of Shepherd Robert and why he was in Ridgley Manor.

"Merchant Finnian is well known to me, I find him to be odious at best, and ye are correct, Oswald, he is well acquainted with Bishop Immers.

"Then I need to speak with him. Where is best? Where can I find him?" Odo asked.

"He lives in a large home on the outskirts of Ridgley. Methinks, his house is more suitable and private fer ye than his shoppe. Do ye need me to come with ye and offer an introduction?" he offered.

Odo shook his head. "Nay, is better ye do not become involved, if I am unsuccessful, then word will reach the bishop of yer connection. I will do this alone." He smiled at Kirby. "I want to do what is right. Shepherd Robert has done no wrong, and he is being targeted and taken advantage of..."

"Ye are a good man, Oswald. I would do the same and have done similar. Call on me if ye need my help, I will always support ye."

After receiving instructions on how to find the merchant's home, Odo made his way to the large estate. Being a priest had its advantages, and a guard allowed him access to the secure property. After knocking, he stood patiently waiting at the door.

Eventually, a rather hefty man opened the door with a quizzical expression, and Odo introduced himself after guessing he must be the merchant.

"Fergive the intrusion Merchant Finnian, it is important that I ask ye a few questions to clear up a matter of some confusion, do ye have time fer me?" Odo politely asked.

Finnian was a short, extremely overweight man with no teeth and no chin. His eyes flicked here and there and were constantly moving.

Odo assessed he was a nervous man, consumed by guilt and inherently suspicious by nature.

"Have ye journeyed far?"

"Aye," Odo replied, "from Exeter."

Finnian's eyes darted around, then settled briefly on his unexpected caller. "We can talk inside, come."

Once seated, the merchant came directly to the point. "What is it ye need, Priest Oswald? Why is it ye have come to my home?"

Odo considered the information he needed to obtain from the man and believed it best to be forthright. "Merchant Finnian, why did ye allow Shepherd Robert from Harford Manor to buy from ye a mule and wagon when he had no coin to pay ye? Surely ye knew there was risk?"

The merchant's outward demeanour didn't change, but Odo saw the reaction in his eyes.

Finnian sucked his gums briefly as he pondered his reply. "Is His Grace, Bishop Immers, aware of yer visit here?"

"Indeed, he is." Odo smiled.

Finnian grunted. "Why is this important?"

Odo didn't want to spar any longer with the man. "Merchant Finnian, did ye knowingly allow Shepherd Robert to purchase the mule and cart and expect him not to pay so ye could seize his animals? Was that part of a plan?"

The merchant's face glowed red in anger. He hefted his bulk from the seat and stood. "It is time ye were on yer way, I will have words with the bishop about yer discourtesy." He pointed to the door. "Be off!"

Odo remained seated. "I think yer honesty would be most welcome."

"Thomas!" yelled Finnian. Immediately a rough, tousled man entered the room and strode with purpose towards Odo.

Unconcerned with the visitor, Odo continued. "Was this part of a plan conspired by Bishop Immers?"

The minder reached fer Odo to haul him to his feet. Before he could grab his robe. Odo's hand snaked out, grasped Thomas's outreached wrist, and twisted. Immediately Thomas yelped in pain and sunk to his knees. His arm, held firmly by Odo, was angled straight, and his wrist was painfully bent back. Thomas wrapped his other arm around his chest and grasped his shoulder to ease the pain. He was completely immobilised while Odo remained seated and composed.

"Merchant Finnian, is best if ye speak plainly with me. Fer a man who relies on the parish fer customers, it would be a shame if the parish were, er, forewarned of yer unchristian like behaviour towards a poor village shepherd. Is this not so?"

Merchant Finnian didn't know what to do and took a step back and away. He shook his head. "The bishop will hear of this... he'll hear of this." Again, he shook his head and folds of fat around his neck rippled.

"I suggest that ye kindly answer my questions, or yer business will suffer greatly." Odo slowly rose to his feet while still firmly holding Thomas's outstretched hand.

"Tell, 'im, please," cried Thomas as Odo added more pressure to his wrist.

Odo could still see the merchant was conflicted. "Sit," he demanded. "Answer my questions, and I will be on my way."

Merchant Finnian reluctantly returned to his chair. "If the bishop learns I spoke of...."

"If ye do as I ask, then there is no reason fer the bishop to know anything," Odo appealed. He turned to Thomas. "If I release yer arm, ye will leave the room and not bother me, do ye agree?"

"Aye, aye," Thomas readily agreed and nodded his head enthusiastically.

Odo released the man's arm and expected him to try to attack him, he tensed, but wisely, Thomas stood and slowly walked away, rubbing his shoulder and flexing his wrist and hand.

"Who are ye, fer methinks ye are not just a priest?" stated Finnian.

Odo ignored the question. "Merchant Finnian, I am short on patience."

"I am beholden to Bishop Immers," began the merchant. 'He came to me and suggested I sell the wagon and mule to the shepherd with only a promise of payment. I was to wait one month and then return to the shepherd and demand full payment." He shrugged as if it was nothing. "And I did only what was tasked of me."

"But then, when he couldn't pay ye, ye had his sheep seized."

"Aye, and unbeknown to me, because the wagon and horse had been stolen. And the shepherd had no coin... that was what the bishop demanded from me to do."

Odo was furious. "And ye are telling me that ye did not take the wagon and mule?"

"Aye, I did not take them." He shook his head to support his denial, and again, jowls quivered long after his head stopped moving.

"And where are the sheep?"

"Aye, the sheep, they're safe and not far from Harford and well-cared fer."

"And what of the wagon and mule, who has them?"

Finnian's face crinkled as folds of flesh resettled. "I know not," he shrugged. "Methinks the bishop arranged for them to be, er, taken. But as I am out of pocket, then I would like them back. What use do I have for sheep? I am a merchant and sell wool and hides, not live animals."

Odo studied Finnian a moment and decided the man was being truthful. "Do ye have any notions?"

"Thomas?" yelled the merchant.

The minder re-entered the room and warily kept his distance from Odo.

"Ye asked around about the mule and wagon, who was it ye thought may have taken them?"

"I, uh, believed it may have been old man Brooker and his lads. I ain't sure, though. I heard from someone at the inn that he was trying to sell a wagon." He kept an eye on Odo.

"Who is old man Brooker?" Odo asked.

"He's a slacker, a petty lag, and a thief, who passes by here from time to time with his three boys."

Odo thought quickly. He needed to resolve this issue and couldn't do it alone, he needed help. "Merchant Finnian, here is what ye can do." He exhaled. "Ye will return Shepherd Robert's animals to him immediately, then–"

"–But I'm out of pocket!" Finnian shook his head vigorously, and jowls and numerous creases of flesh quivered.

"Return the animals, and find out where I can find this thief, Brooker. I will speak to him and have the wagon and mule or coin returned. If he took the wagon and mule and has neither the coin nor the goods, ye can arrange with him to pay it back. Fer yer sake, I hope he still has them," Odo added.

"The bishop!" exclaimed Finnian, "What am I to do when he asks? He will be riled, and I do not wish to be the cause of his wrath."

"Worry not, fer as long as ye keep yer mouth shut about our arrangement, he will never find out. If ye do tell him, then not only will ye suffer from his anger, but from the parish. I do not believe either suit ye, is this not so?"

Finnian looked despondent, then grimaced; one of his chins briefly appeared before receding again. "Aye, perhaps this is fer the better. I will do as ye ask." He turned to look at his minder. "Thomas, find old-man Brooker, tell him of an undertaking that could be of, er, profitable interest to him..." Finnian looked puzzled and turned to Odo. "Where would ye like to meet him?"

"At the edge of town, near the big oak by the road, just after sunset when it is dark. I will be there each night waiting fer him until he arrives. If ye need to get word to me, I shall be at the church."

Merchant Finnian sighed. "Very well, I will do this and prefer to do what is right. I have no wish to cause grief within the parish."

For the next two nights, Odo waited near the Oaktree for Brooker to arrive and began to doubt he would come. On the third night, when he arrived at the tree, a man and three young boys stood waiting for him. Aided by a rising moon, Odo approached, and he could see the look of puzzlement on the man's face. "Brooker?" he asked.

"Who are ye? I was told to meet someone here, I didn't expect a priest." Old man Brooker cautiously looked around, clearly, he was suspicious. His boys fidgeted with surly expressions but remained silent.

"I asked to meet ye and hope ye can help."

Brooker's eyebrows furrowed. "Help a priest? In what way?"

"I've been told ye have a wagon and mule, stolen from a shepherd in Harford."

"Nay," Brooker shook his head in denial, "Methinks ye have the wrong man, I will be off, then. Be at it, lads." He turned to walk away.

"Bishop Immers had ye steal the mule and wagon, did he not?"

Brooker froze, then turned back to Odo.

Even in the moonlight, Odo could see the man's eyes had turned to slits, and a hand eased to his hip. His three sons had moved away and began to step around and surround him. Odo tensed, he knew the boys would cause a distraction while Brooker pulled a knife or another weapon. This move was clearly rehearsed, and the boys knew exactly what to do. Odo took a step away, swung his staff to the side and gently prodded the oldest and largest boy who was closest, forcing him back to stand beside his father. "I will not have ye attack me, hear me well and clearly." Odo's voice was measured yet firm. Quickly, he repositioned the staff and, before Brooker could react, placed the tip beneath his chin. He stepped up beside him and lifted his tunic, and pulled a large knife from a sheath attached to a belt.

"Pa?" the oldest boy questioned. The other two boys looked at their father, querying what to do.

Brooker's eyes darted from side to side as he considered his options. The staff was still pressing up from beneath his chin. Brooker was sly, and Odo didn't trust the man for a moment.

"I want the mule and wagon returned to Merchant Finnian, if ye don't do this, then the Lord of the manor will hear of it, and ye will be brought before him. Then, when he is done with yer, then I will have a go." Odo leaned forward to emphasise his point, then felt the searing pain shoot up his leg as a knife impacted into his thigh. He leapt back, swung the staff, and knocked one of the boys to the ground, the other two now held small knives and, with wavering confidence, brandished them.

Ignoring the burning pain in his leg, Odo dropped to a knee and swept the staff in an arc parallel to the ground and into the legs of the two nearest boys. With a squeal of pain, they fell to the ground. Before anyone could react, Odo snatched the small knives away and threw them into the darkness. "Sit," Odo commanded the oldest boy.

Reluctantly the older boy sat down near his father.

Old Man Brooker looked like he was about to flee. Odo reacted first. Again the staff swung with speed and struck him hard across the back of his knees; like his sons, he collapsed with a cry. The Brookers, apart from the oldest son, were rubbing their legs where the staff had struck them, and none were happy.

The knife was still embedded in his thigh and was extremely painful. Carefully he removed it and expected a gush of blood as the blade came free. To his astonishment, it was only a relatively small knife but had entered his thigh, deep enough to be quite painful. He was thankful it didn't bleed much.

Odo was furious at himself for not expecting the boys to be armed and dangerous. A valuable lesson that could have cost him his life. He calmed himself as old man Brooker and his three sons watched. To Odo, they were like serpents, waiting for the right opportunity to strike.

"I want the wagon and mule returned to Merchant Finnian, if ye do not do this, then the lord of the manor and Bishop Immers will be told." Odo shook his head, "I expect the bishop will not take to yer disobedience very kindly and will excommunicate ye." Odo bent lower, closer to old man

Brooker. "Do ye know what that means?"

Brooker nodded slowly. "Take them to Merchant Finnian?" he asked.

"Aye, to Merchant Finnian, they belong to him. If ye are excommunicated, no one will talk to ye, give ye work, or do business with ye fer the rest of yer life, ye will be outcast, shunned and laughed at."

"Pa, does he fib?" The oldest boy asked in fear.

Old man Brooker reached out and clipped the boy across the back of his head. "Shut it."

"Is that what ye want?" Odo asked.

Brooker shrugged. "I will return the wagon and mule as ye ask," he finally conceded.

"On the morrow, not thereafter, do ye hear me, Brooker? If ye don't, then ye will be excommunicated."

"Aye, worry not, priest."

"It would serve ye all well to attend mass from time to time," Odo advised, then turned, and with the aid of his staff, limped away.

CHAPTER TWENTY–EIGHT

Priest Kirby cleaned and dressed the wound in Odo's thigh. It wasn't a broad cut, but it was deep, and the blade had mainly cut through muscle. Odo knew he'd hobble for a few days; he'd suffered worse and wasn't overly worried.

"Ye are playing a dangerous game, Oswald," advised Priest Kirby, "Merchant Finnian and Brooker should not be trifled with, ye were blessed to not be more seriously hurt."

"Aye, Brooker is bad man, and his boys are no better. As fer Merchant Finnian, I think I can trust him. However, I still have a problem."

Priest Kirby looked at Odo.

"According to Bishop Immers, I am to seek coin from Shepherd Robert for his tithes, and when I return to Harford, I will find out if his sheep have returned—"

"And if Brooker returned the wagon and mule," added Priest Kirby.

"Aye, I know the bishop covets the land, but my instructions were clear, have the shepherd pay the arrears in tithes, if he cannot, then evict him and seize the land. The black tin is what the bishop really wants."

"Ah, yes, I see," said Priest Kirby.

"And I do not believe he has any coin to pay his tithes."

"Oswald, Shepherd Robert could sell his flock at market or even slaughter them." Priest Kirby suggested.

"That may be his only solution. I will give my leg a day of rest, then visit the merchant and see if Brooker brought him the wagon and mule, then leave fer Harford."

"And I'm coming with ye," stated Priest Kirby emphatically. "This time, ye won't go alone."

Much to Odo's surprise, Merchant Finnian greeted them warmly, and with a smile, explained how Brooker and his morose sons had returned the mule and wagon.

"Shepherd Robert's debt is settled, and I'm satisfied," Merchant Finnian said while rubbing his hands together. "But I am still somewhat alarmed," He leaned forward and whispered, "The, uh, the bishop...."

Odo nodded, "I don't see any reason for Bishop Immers to know about our arrangement."

"I fear I have no choice but to place my faith in you, Priest Oswald," stated Finnian. He turned to give Priest Kirby a look, who nodded to confirm what Odo had told him.

"And were the shepherd's sheep returned?" Odo asked.

Fleshy folds of skin quivered and shook as Merchant Finnian nodded vigorously. "As we agreed."

Odo looked thoughtful.

"Is there a problem?" asked Finnian, looking perplexed.

"Aye, there is, Shepherd Robert needs to still pay his tithes, and he has no coin."

Finnian scratched his balding pate. "Uh, I may be able to, uh assist."

"And how might that be," Odo asked warily.

"I'm told his sheep need to be shorn. I might not be a shepherd, but I knows long wool isn't the best at this time of the year – his sheep need shearing."

Odo was puzzled.

"I am in need of wool, it is my trade," Finnian explained. "Wool fetches a good price; if the shepherd brings me his wool, then I will pay him handsomely."

Odo's mind was working furiously, er, perhaps what Finnian offered was a way out for Shepherd Robert. "Aye, I will speak to him about this, thank ye."

"I think ye are a good man, Priest Oswald. Methinks fer a priest ye are different but honourable, I wish ye well."

Priest Kirby and Odo departed Ridgley manor and set out for Harford and enjoyed each other's company. They talked together and shared experiences and stories, and one thing was sure, they shared a similar outlook on life and their faith. When they arrived at Harford's church, Leofric was somewhat confounded. The arrival of both Priest Oswald and Priest Kirby was most unusual. He did confirm that the shepherd's flock had been returned, however, when he approached the shepherd for tithes, he was still greeted with a rusty sword and then some unsavoury and less than kind words from his woman.

"I think it is time we paid Shepherd Robert a visit," said Odo.

"I will leave ye to it, I have other things to attend to and have no desire to be attacked or to receive a tongue lashing," Priest Leofric added.

As Kirby and Odo approached the shepherd's cruck, the curtain parted, and Robert stepped out into the sunshine waving his sword. When he saw Odo, he immediately relaxed and lowered the weapon. "I thought ye were that no-good lazy priest, Leofric, come beggin' fer coin," he told them both.

"I heard ye now have yer flock," Odo stated, "and also, so ye know, the mule and wagon have been returned to the merchant. Ye are no longer in debt to him."

"Aye, and if ye did this, then I am happy, thank ye, Priest Oswald, but I still have my tithes to pay."

"Aye, ye do, but perhaps there is a solution," Odo offered.

After explaining to the shepherd, he stood shaking his head. "It ain't so easy… it takes people to help. Shearing is a big job…" he stood with both hands on his hips and continued to vigorously shake his head from side to side. "I can't pay anyone, if I could, then I wouldn't have the coin to pay the church."

"Merchant Finnian will give ye a good price fer yer wool, and, er, what if we were to help ye, Shepherd Robert?" asked Priest Kirby. "If myself, Priests Oswald and Leofric helped ye, what then?"

"Well now…" Shepherd Robert's face contorted as he thought it through. "Perhaps…"

"I have shorn sheep a'fore," volunteered Priest Kirby. He turned to Odo. "And ye?"

"Uh, no, never, I have helped sort fleece but know nothing about the shears," Odo replied.

"What say ye, Robert?" asked Priest Kirby.

Robert took a deep breath and slowly exhaled. "We begin at dawn; the sheep will be in the byre overnight, and in the morn, we start."

"I will do no such thing!" exclaimed Priest Leofric. "Have ye lost yer mind?" he harrumphed.

"Well now, if ye do not wish to help a parishioner, that is up to ye," Odo said. "I will let Bishop Immers know... after all, the coin from the wool will pay tithes, if ye cant help, then it does look bad."

"I'm a priest, not a shepherd."

"Are ye not?" questioned Priest Kirby with a grin.

They laboured in Shepherd Robert's byre. It was hard, back-breaking work, and everyone, including Priest Leofric and Shepherd Robert's woman, pitched in and helped. Shearing forty sheep wasn't an easy task. Early on, Leofric complained bitterly, but after his protestations went unheeded, he gave up his whining and lent his back and helped. Odo worked through the pain in his leg and was exhausted by the day's end. It was nightfall when the last sheep was shorn and scampered away to join the others.

Shepherd Robert straightened and rubbed his aching back and grinned. "We did well this day, thank ye all."

"I hopes the merchant pays ye as he promised," added Priest Leofric grumpily.

"Tomorrow, we can take the wool to Merchant Finnian, and God willing, he will give ye enough to satisfy the bishop," Odo added.

Robert's woman had not spoken much throughout the day, mostly she instructed Odo on how to sort and arrange the fleece, other than that, she remained quiet and worked hard. Later, and shortly before finishing the shearing, she prepared a hearty meal, and they sat down to eat and satisfy their ravenous appetites. She coughed and cleared her throat. "I, uh…"

All heads turned to her in surprise.

"It might not be my place to speak, but it needs to be said. What ye have done here… uh, helped Robert and me… is a blessing. We are simple poor folk; we work hard to better ourselves, and ye made a difference." She lowered her head, and it appeared that she was thinking before speaking again. "Uh, that be all."

Priest Kirby looked at Odo and smiled.

"I think we did make a difference," said Odo.

"If I may," said Priest Kirby. He raised his head to look at the shepherd. "Priest Oswald had an idea, and I think it may be worth looking into. Let me speak with Ridgley Manor's lord, Sir Hyde Fortescue, he may have an honest solution over this black tin. Will ye allow me to do this?"

Shepherd Robert looked over the top of the bowl from which he was eating. "I heard he's even-handed and fair, is he?"

"Aye, he is," replied the priest. "He is a good man, and if something can be done with the tin, then he will know."

Robert looked at his wife, who nodded in agreement. "Aye, thank ye."

Shepherd Robert owned only a large handcart. It was lightweight and similar to a wagon but pushed by a man and not pulled by a beast. All the wool was carefully and tightly bound and stacked precariously atop the cart, and the small procession departed for Ridgley Manor and Merchant Finnian. Priest Leofric didn't go with them, claiming he had more important things to attend to. Everyone, even Odo with his sore leg, took turns pushing and pulling and finally, late afternoon, they arrived in Ridgley manor. Merchant Finnian stood rubbing his hands together as his wool grader carefully inspected the fleece as it was offloaded. After a brief discussion with the grader, Finnian turned to Shepherd Robert. "Yer wool is of good quality, I'll give ye two shillings and tuppence fer the lot."

Shepherd Robert smiled; it was better than he'd hoped. "Thank ye, Merchant Finnian, I will–"

"Two shillings and sixpence," interrupted Odo.

Merchant Finnian's head whipped around to stare at Odo in surprise. Fleshy folds of skin around his neck wobbled in protest at the unexpected movement.

"Two shillings and sixpence," Odo repeated. He met the challenging stare of the merchant and didn't turn away. He raised an eyebrow and waited.

Merchant Finnian's fingers tapped against his extended belly. With considerable effort, he nodded and then sighed loudly. "Perhaps if ye seek to leave the Church ye can work fer me, ye drive a hard bargain Priest Oswald. So, it be, two shillings and sixpence it is."

Odo had yet to see Shepherd Robert's woman smile, but he saw her beaming when he looked over towards Robert.

Priest Kirby couldn't help himself and grinned.

Shepherd Robert counted out the money he owed to the Church in tithes, it was just over half the amount of coin he received. Nonetheless, he did so; happily, the extra coin he received from Priest Oswald's haggling would make a difference. "Thank ye, Priest Oswald," he turned to Priest Kirby and dipped his head in respect. "And I thank ye both fer all ye have done."

Odo was pleased that everything had worked out. The knife wound in his leg continued to cause discomfort, and he was anxious to return to Exeter as soon as possible and inform the bishop how Shepherd Robert had miraculously found the coin and paid his arrears without implicating anyone.

CHAPTER TWENTY–NINE

Sir Hyde Fortescue warmly received Bishop Immers in his day chamber at the manor. After the formalities of kissing the episcopal ring, both men sat down and raised a goblet of wine.

"I offer my heartfelt congratulations on yer new appointment," began Sir Hyde, "This is the first time I have welcomed ye to Ridgley Manor as bishop."

Bishop Immers dipped his head in acknowledgement of his recent appointment to bishop. He chose not to mention his last visit here, when he'd stayed at the inn in the village with the woman he had a fondness for. He pushed his lurid thoughts of her aside. "Aye, and I see the manor prospers and thrives," he cordially responded. "The Church is pleased, and I, uh, we, hope all the manors in the diocese flourish like Ridgley." He smiled at Sir Hyde and then took another sip of the fine wine but wished the lord had not diluted it with water. "Although, I am uh, a little perplexed … Priest Kirby did not greet me…."

Sir Hyde looked over the rim of his goblet at the bishop.

"Is he unwell?" asked Immers.

Sir Hyde didn't know where his priest was. "I expect he may be calling on parishioners, he tends to involve himself in the parish, and he is always doing what he can to help. I'm sure he will learn of your arrival and make an appearance soon," remarked Sir Hyde, curious to the reason for the bishop's visit.

Bishop Immers nodded, crossed his legs, and adjusted his robe. "Sir Hyde," began Immers, "I understand ye have a mine or two."

Sir Hyde was instantly on guard. He didn't trust or like the bishop and was trying to fathom why he was interested in his mines. "Aye, I have a small iron mine, and another will begin producing soon. But nothing of real importance."

"Then ye are familiar with the intricacies of extracting ore?"

Sir Hyde laughed. "Fergive me, Yer Grace, I am a knight and know not about digging in the ground fer valuable ore. I leave that to others."

"Aye, I understand." Bishop Immers rubbed his chin. "The Church has er, recently obtained a portion of land not far from here that contains black tin. I think this discovery could benefit us both, is this not so?"

Sir Hyde resisted the temptation to react outwardly to this news. He thought quickly and knew if tin was discovered nearby, it could offer significant economic benefits. However, if the Church were involved, the bishop would undoubtedly want recompense and possibly offer the land to be leased. He shrugged. "It is doubtful this finding would amount to much, and the cost of developing the land fer mining may not be viable. Is this discovery in Ridgley manor, fer I would need to discuss this with my experts?"

"Indeed, of course," Immers leaned forward and reached for a small box that sat at his feet and extracted a rock from inside. He handed it to Sir Hyde. "Black tin lies in Harford. However, there are other interested parties, and yer commitment to this venture would prevent them from taking this, uh, opportunity away from ye."

Sir Hyde turned the rock over and examined it carefully. At first glance it appeared similar to coal with black shiny surfaces. "And the Church has possession of this land?

"Uh, in a manner, aye."

Sir Hyde turned his attention back to the bishop. "And what are ye suggesting, Yer Grace?"

Bishop Immers leaned back in his seat. "Oh, I don't know, I have not pondered this at all, really."

In fact, Sir Hyde knew the bishop had given this a lot of thought and was probably the reason for his visit. He handed the rock back to the bishop.

"Keep it, a memento." Bishop Immers placed the rock on a small table and wiped his hands on his robe, and shrugged, "A simple lease and a portion of the, er, profits." He looked up at Sir Hyde briefly before readjusting the pectoral cross that hung from around his neck. "I have heard that mining such valuable resources can return a substantial income. As ye are an honourable lord and Ridgley Manor thrives under yer firm guidance and hand, then this arrangement would suit ye well, does it not?"

Sir Hyde chewed his bottom lip and considered his response. "Most certainly, Yer Grace, A productive mine can be profitable, but as I've been advised, yield and cost must be reckoned carefully. Thank ye kindly, Yer Eminence, I am honoured that ye thought of me, however, I am not in a position to undertake a new risk at this time," he smiled. "I think the other lords ye have spoken to might be more worthy."

Bishop Immers had not spoken to anyone else about the black tin and believed Sir Hyde would grovel for an opportunity to obtain the lease on the land. He hid his surprise and disappointment. "Perhaps if ye leased the land, er, then at the appropriate time, then when ready, ye could begin to mine the black tin? Of course, er... fer a very moderate tariff," he added as an afterthought.

"Once this land is owned by the Church," clarified Sir Hyde.

Bishop Immers was not known for his patience and determined that Priest Oswald had dutifully evicted the farmer from his land as instructed and intended. While he had not spoken to him yet, he believed the young priest would not experience any difficulties.

After all, concluded Immers, the shepherd was debt-ridden and had no choice but to give up his land to satisfy the holy demands of the Church. Finding enough coin to meet his overdue tithes was beyond all possibility and reason. Had the bishop known that the young priest had just received payment from the shepherd and settled his debt with the church, he may have thought differently.

Bishop Immers nodded his head vigorously. "Indeed, we have just taken possession through unpaid tithes," he looked appropriately sympathetic and sorrowful. "Very unfortunate."

Sir Hyde was perplexed. Typically Priest Kirby was very forthcoming with sharing information regarding the Church and the manor, but he had not mentioned this development to him. Priest Kirby would have told him if a landowner had his land confiscated due to unpaid tithes. What the bishop had explained was unfamiliar to him, and what he offered was indeed worthy of consideration. Mining ore was profitable and a valuable resource the king desperately sought. "Yer Grace, what would this *fair* tariff be?"

Bishop Immers sipped from his goblet. After a moment, he lowered the vessel. "Two pounds!"

"Two-pounds? spluttered Sir Hyde. Fergive me, Yer Grace, two Stirling pounds is a great deal fer a lease on unproductive land, is it not?"

"Nay, Sir Hyde, not at all, it offers encouragement to begin mining soonest," smiled the bishop. "Uh, but that is two-pound per year," he explained.

Sir Hyde rose from his seat, walked towards the hearth, and pondered the bishop's offer. "Let me discuss this with my steward. I will send word to ye. Is that acceptable?"

Bishop Immers smiled again, "I will await yer answer, Sir Hyde, and God bless ye. But I will not avail myself to yer hospitality fer the night as I have made alternative arrangements." Again, he cast aside the thoughts of the buxom woman in the village he would visit later and met the gaze of Sir Hyde, "Then, and before my departure, ye can inform me of yer decision and secure your lease with payment."

"Before I have assessed the land?"

Bishop Immers pointed to the rock on the table. "Black tin is to be found on that land, as I said. And while I am here, it would be best to secure payment before I leave, keeps it simple, eh?"

"And If I make payment, and the land can't produce, or the Church has no rights, then that tariff is refundable?"

"Sir Hyde, ye have no need fer worry," responded Bishop Immers with a wave of his hand.

Sir Hyde's steward was an ageing, droll, and unimaginative man with pasty skin and little patience. He stood before his lord with hands clasped and explained what he'd learned. "Milord, metallurgists claim black tin needs to be smelted at the mine and then sold as ingots. So, there is expense."

Sir Hyde shook his head, "And what is tin used fer, will it fetch coin, has it value?"

"I believe the tin is used to create bronze and pewter, amongst other things, aye, it has value, but is the land capable of producing sufficient quantities to make it profitable?"

"Well, that is why I'm asking ye," exclaimed Sir Hyde in growing frustration. "Bishop Immers requires a decision from me, and I need give him an answer."

"Milord," the steward responded, "Perhaps I can send a metallurgist to this mine and have him look it over?"

"It isn't a mine, not yet it's only a parcel of land where black tin has been found! I need to know if it is worthy of investing in," repeated the lord in growing exasperation.

"I see," replied the steward.

"More importantly, Bishop Immers requires that I pay him two pounds fer the lease before he departs. So, I will ask ye again, can the manor spare the coin?"

"The coffers are all but full milord, and the question remains if it is a worthy investment? But two pounds, milord, that is significant."

Sir Hyde kicked at a log in the hearth, and a shower of sparks and ashes flew into the room. "I will take the risk. Bring me two pounds. I will see the bishop receives it, then, hopefully, we can learn the potential value of the land." He spun and faced the steward. "I will ask the bishop where this land is, and meanwhile, call fer a metallurgist and a miner. I will have them visit this farm and report to me their findings. I will insist the coin is returned if the land cannot produce."

"As ye wish milord."

Sir Hyde was in his day chamber reflecting on his meeting with Bishop Immers the previous day. Against better judgement, he'd acquiesced and given him the two pounds for the lease as asked, and he was waiting on the results from the miner and metallurgist who went to the farm to investigate the claim. His musings were interrupted by a knock on the door.

"Enter!"

"Milord, Priest Kirby is here to see ye," informed a scullery maid.

"Good, and about time, send him in."

"Where have ye been, Kirby? I had need of ye, and ye deserted me and left me all alone to deal with that confounded bishop."

"Milord," smiled Priest Kirby, "I know yer fondness fer him and thought it best ye could chat in private and enjoy each other's company."

"And I'll see ye swing by a rope," laughed the lord.

Priest Kirby smiled. "Milord, I had a matter to attend to in Harford, it was of no consequence, and all was dealt with, although it took a little longer than expected, but there is a matter I wish to discuss with ye about my visit there.”

“It will have to wait, Kirby. I have a more pressing concern.”

Priest Kirby took a seat and waited for Sir Hyde to continue.

When the lord finished detailing the reason for Bishop Immers visit, the priest was unusually quiet.

“Has the cat got yer tongue?” Sir Hyde asked.

Priest Kirby looked at the floor and then mouthed a silent prayer. When finished, he looked up and met the inquisitive gaze of his friend and lord. “I confess, milord, yer ears may not take kindly to hearing.”

Sir Hyde’s eyebrows furrowed.

Priest Kirby explained the reason for his absence and how he and two other priests assisted the shepherd in helping him pay his tithes. He included how Merchant Finnian had taken the shepherds flock and then returned them on the urging of this new priest.

Instead of being angry, as Kirby fully expected, Sir Hyde bent over in hysterics and laughter. He laughed so hard his face turned red, and tears streamed down his face and into his beard. He clutched his stomach and howled in pure delight. Priest Kirby could only helplessly watch, and eventually, he too joined in but wasn’t sure why?

“I wish,” gasped Sir Hyde between fits of merriment, “I could see the bishop’s face when he learns how that land is not his.” He shook his head. “This new priest, he is a clever one, eh? Watch yerself Kirby, or I shall request Immers send him here to replace ye.”

“I welcome that milord, fer then I may receive a parish where the lord of the manor has his full wits about him.”

This declaration only set Sir Hyde off again. When he finally calmed down, he looked at Priest Kirby. "But with all jests aside, I am out of pocket two pounds, and Bishop Immers is now obliged to return it."

"And milord… er, give it to Shepherd Robert – if he agrees," suggested Priest Kirby. "Because there is black tin on the land, and I have seen it."

Sir Hyde pointed a finger at the priest. "Ah, now that is worthy of consideration. However, first, we must learn if the black tin on Shepherd Robert's land is worth mining. I expect the miner and metallurgist will return soon, then we will know if it is worth investing in, eh."

"I agree, milord."

"Now tell me, Kirby," Sir Hyde smiled, "How will this new priest go about telling Bishop Immers how his plan failed, and the shepherd miraculously found the coin to pay his tithes? Fer, I would pay another two pounds to hear that conversation."

The miner and metallurgist returned to Ridgley Manor two days later and stood before Sir Hyde, Priest Kirby, and the steward.

"Well, I keenly await yer findings, what news do ye have fer me?" began Ridgley's lord.

The miner and metallurgist exchanged a look, then as previously agreed, the miner spoke first. "Milord, we think the land belonging to Shepherd Robert contains sufficient quantities of black tin to warrant a mine."

"Ye think?" Sir Hyde turned from one man to the next. "I need more than thoughts."

The metallurgist coughed. "Um, sire, the quality of the tin is excellent and deposits substantial. We dug some shafts and found enough black tin to keep Tinners busy for quite some time. That's why we were delayed, milord."

"I see, and in yer opinion, is there enough tin to employ Tinners and will the quality be good enough to fetch a good price?"

The metallurgist and miner exchanged another look and then faced their lord and simultaneously nodded. "Aye, milord," said the metallurgist.

"How was the shepherd, er, was he welcoming to ye poking around his land?" asked Priest Kirby.

"At first, he was wary, but when he learned we came from Ridgley Manor at the request of its lord, then he was, uh more than familiar."

Priest Kirby smiled.

"I thank ye fer yer efforts; that will be all fer now," concluded Sir Hyde.

As the two men departed, Sir Hyde turned to the steward. "What say ye, do we have the coin to pursue this?"

"If I may suggest to ye, milord, the coffers are full, but ye have reckonings due. Er, my advice is, er, that it may be in yer interest to negotiate an agreement with the landowner soonest."

"Kirby?" questioned Sir Hyde.

"I'm no Tinner, milord, but I agree."

Sir Hyde stroked his beard and stared at a colourful hanging tapestry depicting a battle. After a few moments, he pointed to the steward. "Ye will go with Priest Kirby and visit the shepherd and negotiate with him an equitable tariff to lease his land fer mining black tin." His expression hardened. "In my name, ye will be fair. Is this understood?"

"Aye, milord," nodded the Steward.

"Now, ye can both help me with a missive I need to send to Bishop Immers and request the return of two pounds." He grinned.

"Milord? Perhaps we should wait a few days before ye send the missive," Priest Kirby suggested.

Sir Hyde raised an eyebrow in question.

"Uh, it would be most unfortunate if Bishop Immers received the missive before his priest returned to Exeter and explained what happened. If it weren't fer him, then it would be a different situation fer ye, is that not so?"

Sir Hyde looked reflective and finally nodded. "Aye, it would be fair to him. Perhaps the following week is best."

CHAPTER THIRTY

Usually, the walk from Ridgley Manor to Exeter was not a great chore and would take about three to three and half days, but as Odo departed Ridgley manor, the pain in his leg from the knife wound became more acute. By the time the sun had fully risen, he had to stop. About a furlong from the road, a stream ran beside a stand of trees, and he diverted from the road and limped slowly and painfully towards them.

On arriving at the stream, he immediately removed the bandage Priest Kirby wrapped around his thigh and washed and cleaned it thoroughly. Although small, the wound seeped foulness, and the surrounding area was red and inflamed. When finished, he lay back against a tree and thought he'd rest a while, gather his strength, and continue onwards in due course. He closed his eyes for a moment or two.

He woke in a sweat sometime later. The sun was low on the horizon, and he surmised he must have slept for most of the afternoon. His thigh throbbed and felt hot to the touch. Again, he cleansed the wound, rewound the cloth around his thigh and pondered what to do.

Ultimately, he knew he needed help. The wound festered and needed medical care and potions to treat it. Where he lay was beyond the road and visible only to someone attentive and looking. In his current state, he was weak and had not the strength nor stamina to walk unaided, even with the help of his staff. As night fell, he succumbed to a troubled sleep and disturbing horror-filled dreams.

As the grey of dawn peeked above the distant hills, Odo stirred. His mouth was dry, and he suffered from ague. He was so thirsty, but the stream, only an arm's length away, may have been a distant furlong. He had no strength to crawl or move towards it. His throat was parched, his tongue thick, and the gentle gurgling sound of water trickling over small stones cruelly increased his need to drink the cool refreshing liquid.

It was pure agony, but slowly, he crawled and slithered the short distance to the water and lowered his head into the stream. It was absolute ecstasy, and he swallowed mouthful after mouthful. Satisfied and with no energy to move away, he lay his head down and closed his eyes to briefly rest.

He saw evil creatures that dwelled in the fiery abyss of hell. They called to him, taunting, teasing and wagged long knurled fingers, enticing and beckoning him to come. Then they came for him. He fought them off; he writhed, reached out and struck them, resisting their feigned charms, temptations, and mock solicitations. He felt the heat of searing flames, saw enormous snakes, and felt them crawl over his body. He lashed out, again and again, he kicked and punched, but they came for him, always smiling and calling his name. He heard them, "Odo," they reviled, "Odo," they whispered. He had to escape from the evil, or they would take him. "Odo!" they slathered from above. The cool wetness dripped over his face, and he resisted with all his might. Despite his frantic efforts, they grabbed and held him down.

"Odo!" they yelled.

He wasn't Odo, he was Oswald. He was trapped and held firmly. He had no strength, and despite his weakness, tried to fight his tormentors. "Odo," he cried to his son, "Save me!" It sounded like a croak.

He was beaten. In trembling fear, he reluctantly succumbed and allowed his eyelids to flicker open to confront the horrors. Harsh daylight caused him to blink, and he shivered with cold. As his eyes adjusted to the brightness, a form loomed threateningly over him. He tried to rise and run but couldn't. He tried to strike at them but couldn't find his sword… *Where are my sword and bow*? The blackness slowly dissolved into familiar shapes, and he saw and recognized her immediately. It was the woman from the abbey in Frankia, and she held his arms and spoke his name.

"Odo, all is well," she said calmly. The sound of her words … reassuring and soothing.

His chest rose and fell in desperation and his heart raced.

"Odo, we are here to help ye," she said.

He saw her smile and then felt a weight on his good leg. He looked down, and it was the boy, her son lay over him.

He stopped struggling. "I, I," was all he could manage.

He felt the lightness as the boy moved and the woman released his arms. Slowly his breathing settled, and he swallowed thickly, his throat parched and dry.

She held a clay bottle to his lips, and he drank greedily. The cool water helped, and slowly his mind returned to lucidity, and he could focus on the present. "My leg, I suffer greatly," he managed to croak.

"We will help ye and are not here to cause ye harm," she comforted. "Yer mind had taken ye to dark places, but everything is as it should be, fear not."

Odo looked at the boy, who stared innocently back. Suddenly his face creased into a friendly boyish smile, and he immediately relaxed and felt the tension ease. But the pain in his leg didn't. "My leg," he cried.

Odo watched as the woman removed the soiled cloth from around his leg, cleaned the wound and then gave instructions to the boy who ran off. Within a short time, he'd returned with an armload of greenery. What they were, he couldn't fathom. The boy collected plants, leaves, even roots. He didn't care, he felt ill and shivered uncontrollably.

The woman was pleased with what her son brought her, and she took time to instruct and point out various things of regard to him. The boy listened with interest and occasionally nodded as she sorted through the items he brought. Eventually, the boy reached into a leather bag and produced a mortar and pestle, and she began rhythmically crushing the plants and roots into a paste.

She hummed as she ground and fused the substances together. The melody and sound of her voice was uplifting and put him at ease. The previous torment of his nightmare was still raw and unsettling. *How is it possible she is here ... and then to find me?* he wondered.

When the wound had been attended to and a clean cloth strip wrapped around his leg, she sat back against the tree and closed her eyes.

"How is it ye come to be here?" Odo asked.

"We head fer Ireland, …to home," she simply stated.

"But I last saw ye in Frankia, at the abbey that was, uh, years ago." Odo turned to look at the boy. He'd grown since he saw him last.

"Aye, we go where needed, and we do what we can to help." She paused a moment, then opened her eyes and studied him closely. "When we saw ye in the abbey, ye wouldn't speak to me."

Odo felt reflective, "Aye, a lifetime ago." His leg throbbed, and his teeth chattered.

"And ye still live."

"Aye, thanks to ye and Cot… Cet…"

"Cathal," the boy replied.

"Aye, Cathal. I owe ye my gratitude, and ye too. What are ye called?"

"I am Macha," she dipped her head. "And now ye are a priest."

"I am, but ye know me as Odo, and I am known here as Oswald. Please, I ask ye–"

"We will call ye Oswald, as ye ask," she suddenly said as if anticipating his request.

Odo was exhausted, his leg was painful, and he shivered. He closed his eyes. *This woman and boy were confounding.*

They built a fire and set traps for food. There were instances where the fire wasn't enough to keep warm, at other times, he was hot and broke into a sweat. Macha and her son, Cathal, remained at his side and tended to him. She used the stream to wash his robe that he'd soiled and cleaned the dirty bandages while the boy hunted for food and wild vegetables. He lay beneath a blanket that kept him warm and felt immense relief that Macha and Cathal had heard him and come to his aid.

After two days of torrid nightmares and discomfort, he began to feel better. On the second night, he slept soundly and woke feeling refreshed and stronger. The throbbing from the wound in his thigh had gone, and his mind was again alert.

"The poison has mostly gone," Macha told him. "But ye need to eat and regain yer strength. If ye must, then tomorrow ye can be on yer journey if ye travel slowly."

Odo nodded reflectively. "Aye, I will heed yer advice and wisdom. How was it that ye found me here, fer the road is some distance away?"

She held his gaze a moment. "Methinks, Oswald, that ye found us. We were travelling, and yer cries and torment alerted us to yer need."

"Is this what ye do, help the sick and ailing?" Odo asked.

Cathal sat back against a tree and was cleaning a rabbit skin, he looked towards his mother and listened to her response.

"Is it not our duty to help those in need? We could have passed ye by when we heard ye cry out," she shrugged. "But methinks ye are a good man and would do the same fer anyone – fer a peasant or noble." Her head turned and followed the flight of a murder of crows as they flew past. "We do what is right, not because we must."

Odo thought back to the words and advice of Monk Pepin at Exeter's abbey when he said, 'God needs good men of faith.' "Then ye follow yer faith?" he asked.

"Of course, but not as ye do. Yer faith is decided by men; my faith is determined by the world around me and the laws of nature." She saw the look of puzzlement on his face. "Who created this?" She spread her arms wide. "Our God did. Not mortal men with their judgements, prejudices and greed."

Odo thought of Bishop Immers and his privileged lifestyle and his desire for riches and power. He grimaced.

"Use the world around ye, Oswald," she added. "Did ye see the crows that flew past here moments ago?"

He did see them and thought nothing of it, they were birds, just birds flying away to feed. "Aye, I saw them."

"They flew from south to north silently. That means all is well. They were not alarmed or frightened. Does that mean I am a witch?"

Odo was shocked, no one openly spoke of witches. His mouth opened, and he stared at her.

She smiled at his reaction. "I am not a witch, but I use what God created – the birds, trees and animals to help me, and then I help others."

Odo relaxed as he understood her point. "Ye had me fearful."

She laughed, then her expression turned serious. "Why is it ye have become a priest?"

Cathal paused from his task with the skin and looked at him with curiosity.

He thought carefully. "Because, Macha, I have dedicated my life to protect someone." He saw the corners of her mouth twitch.

"I see ye have suffered greatly. Yer eyes tell a story of pain and suffering, not through a wound from a sword or lance. The hate within ye festers like the poison in yer leg, allow it to pass, if ye don't, it will destroy ye," she advised.

"That pain and my memories keep me alive and remind me of why I do what I must." Odo turned away and couldn't look at her.

"Acting on emotion may see yer death," she simply said.

Odo's head spun. "What did ye say?"

"Ye heard me, Oswald, and ye know what I mean. Protect yer son as best ye can. But do not do so at the risk of yer own life, fer ye have much to give him. If ye die, he has nothing."

Odo's eyebrows knitted together. She spoke the same words as Sir Geoffrey, she knew of Odo. *How is this possible*? It must have been his incoherent ramblings when struck with ague. She'd heard him. He exhaled slowly. "I try hard not to make decisions based on my past and anger," he said. "But it is not always easy."

Slowly she raised a hand and pointed a finger at him. "Be warned, yer greatest enemy is the bishop. He will seek yer death and that of yer son. It matters not where ye go or travel too; his shadow is long, and the darkness will follow. He will not rest."

Odo felt his heart begin to race. How does this woman know these things? He felt the fear, her words rung true.

"In the morn, we will leave," she suddenly said. "We will not see ye again, but God will be at yer side. With yer help, yer son will survive and leave his mark on the world, fer he is special."

"What do ye speak of?" Odo shook his head.

"I tell ye these things because the knowledge is plain fer all to see. But ye cannot see the stories nature has to tell." She spread her arms wide to encompass the area around them.

"Cathal, do ye see what yer ma sees?"

He nodded emphatically. "She teaches me."

"Then my son will live, and I have no reason to fear?" Odo asked Macha.

She shook her head and laughed. "Nay, Oswald, I do not predict the future. I said, if ye help yer son, then he will survive."

"But you predicted ye would never see me again, ye can't possibly know that."

"Aye, except, we journey to Ireland, and ye will remain near yer son. It isn't likely I will see ye again, she laughed.

This conversation was all too much for Odo. He wanted to rest and think. *This woman was an enigma, a contradiction...*

The next morning, Macha and Cathal inspected the wound and repacked it with a fresh layer of herbs, and small crushed leaves, then rewrapped his leg. He didn't know what the herbs and plants were that she placed over the gash in his leg, however, whatever they were, they had helped. When finished, Macha told him he could safely continue his journey as long as he didn't overdo it, rested frequently and tended to his leg.

"Only clean cloth, do not use soiled rags," Macha insisted. "Wash the wound with fresh water twice a day, just as we have done. Ye will heal quickly now."

After giving his thanks and saying farewell, he watched mother and son walk away. They were peculiar, and yet… He shook his head. There was still so much to learn about people.

He retrieved his staff and satchel and tenderly walked towards Exeter. He didn't rush, he couldn't and did precisely as Macha told him and cleaned and dressed his injury just as she and Cathal had done.

He felt weak and travelled slowly with the aid of his staff and encountered no difficulties. By the day's end, he was exhausted and slept soundly; thankfully, his nightmares didn't return. She had given him plenty of food, and after two days, he was beginning to feel close to normal as he approached Exeter.

One of the things he enjoyed about walking was how it gave him time to think. On a horse with a weapon on his hip, he was focused on danger and staying alive. As a poor, solitary priest, he was left alone with his thoughts and distractions, and the closer he came to Exeter, the more Bishop Immers dominated his musings.

It took him longer than expected to reach Exeter, and it was already nightfall when he arrived feeling tired and hungry. He returned to the abbey and immediately felt his stomach tie up in knots when he was told that Monk Grimwald had passed. According to Abbott Andrew, Grimwald's heart had finally stopped, and much to his relief, no one gave any hint or suggestion that he was involved or suspected in the monk's untimely death.

To Odo, it appeared that Grimwald's passing caused no real grief, and if anything, the only sadness felt at the abbey was through a restructuring of duties and responsibilities where the lazy monks now had the burden of undertaking more individual tasks.

He couldn't wait to meet Bishop Immers and then head to Mellester Manor and be done with this place.

CHAPTER THIRTY-ONE

Bishop Immers hands were steepled beneath his chin as he appraised the young priest. The man was haggard, filthy, and unkempt. Interestingly, he walked with a limp, and no doubt had encountered some difficulties along the way. He removed his hands and placed them flat down on the table before him. He was keen to learn if the shepherd had been evicted without unpleasantries. "What kept ye, ye have been gone for nigh on four weeks?"

"Aye, Yer Grace, fergive me fer my lateness. It was most unavoidable," Odo replied and respectfully dipped his head.

"Then I trust ye were successful?"

"Indeed. I did as ye askcd, and I am pleased with the outcome as ye must be."

"Well done, Priest Oswald, I knew my faith in ye was just. Did the shepherd cause any mischief when ye evicted him?" Immers smiled and rubbed his hands together.

Odo steeled himself for what was to come. He kept his face devoid of expression and prayed his version of the events would stand up to the bishop's tirade and subsequent reckoning. He leaned over and dropped the purse on the bishop's table. "As ye requested, Yer Grace, one shilling and sixpence."

Bishop Immers mouth opened, and he stared at the purse in incredulity, then up at Odo. "What is this? Dear God, what have ye brought me?"

"Shepherd Robert's tithes Yer Grace." Odo could see the bishop's face turning crimson.

Bishop Immers didn't know what to say or how to respond. He leaned back in his chair, trying to calm his seething anger. Finally able to speak, he swallowed. "What happened, spare me no details, fer my understanding was that the shepherd was heavily indebted, and ye, ye bring me this…?" He waved his arm at the purse.

"Aye, Yer Grace, it was most fortunate, and God smiled upon him."

"I seriously doubt whether God had time to smile upon anyone in Harford, let alone a shepherd." He crossed himself. "Well, out with it, what happened?"

"It was quite curious, Yer Grace, Shepherd Robert's sheep, his flock was taken from him, stolen they were, and shortly before I arrived, his sheep managed to escape the pen or byre they were in and returned to the shepherd's farm. And, Yer Grace, of their own accord." Odo nodded his head enthusiastically in support of his account and good turn of events.

Immers eyebrows furrowed. "That doesn't explain from where the shepherd received the coin to pay his tithes!" he exclaimed.

"He had his sheep shorn and sold the fleece."

"To whom?" spluttered the bishop.

"I believe it was to a merchant in Ridgley manor, Yer Grace."

"That fat sod Finnian?"

"Why I believe so, Yer Grace, is he known to ye?" Odo innocently asked.

Bishop Immers looked sceptical. "How is it that Finnian paid the shepherd for his fleece when the man owes him coin. He was in debt to him!" Immers thumped his hand on the table.

Odo remained impassive. "Yer Grace, I learned that the shepherd had purchased a wagon and mule from the merchant, and again, it was stolen from him."

Bishop Immers nodded.

"The man who stole the wagon and mule tried to sell it to Merchant Finnian, and he recognized it as the same wagon and mule he sold to the shepherd."

The bishop placed his hands over his face. "Dear God," came the muffled response. He removed his hands. "And let me guess, Merchant Finnian possessed the wagon and mule and then fergave the debt to the shepherd and purchased the fleece?"

"Aye, yer Grace, that's where the coin came from, from Merchant Finnian. I knew ye'd be pleased," Odo added.

Bishop Immers rose from his chair and paced backwards and forwards behind the table. After a few dozen heartbeats, he paused and turned to Odo. "How is it yer leg worries ye?"

Odo's expression turned appropriately serious. "Yer Grace, as ye warned me about Shepherd Robert, he was most violent, and when I first approached him, he didn't take kindly to my visit. He had a rusty sword and poked it into my thigh. It was most unexpected and caught me unaware, and the wound corrupted and became festered a day or two later, which caused my delay."

Something wasn't right, and the bishop believed that the priest's account of what happened in Harford was a little too convenient. Whatever shenanigans happened at the shepherd's farm… the deception, Oswald was behind it, of that there was no doubt.

Suddenly Bishop Immers raised his hand to his forehead, he'd forgotten. Sir Hyde paid him two pounds for the lease on the shepherd's land. The lord would be furious when he learned the shepherd still owned it and demand a return of is his coin. *Two pounds*! *It was a king's ransom*! "Get out of my sight, begone with ye!" he yelled at Odo. "Go to ye sorry little hamlet and rot, fer I care less."

"Yer Grace." Odo respectfully lowered his head, spun, and grinned as he stepped from the bishop's *officium*. Finally, he was going to Mellester.

Behind the closed door, he heard the bishop yell in anger.

Odo spent another evening in the abbey and tended to the wound in his leg, which continued to improve and early the next day, he departed for Mellester Manor. Two days later, he arrived. It had been two gruelling years since he was last here, and nothing had changed. He made his way to the church, then to the rectory beside, which was nothing more than a simple cruck and found it devoid of any personal items, only some furniture. The previous priest, as Bishop Immers had explained, had been recalled back to Exeter and reassigned. The parish was his. He left his few possessions inside and walked outside, towards Godwin and Hetti's cruck at the far end of the village. It was already growing dark, and he knew they'd be home. With a smile spreading from ear to ear, he knocked on the door and waited.

When Hetti opened the door and saw him, she smiled and stepped forward and embraced him warmly. "Godwin! Godwin! she cried.

"It gladdens my heart to see ye, Oswald," said Godwin. "Ye have changed, ye look older, thinner, ye need a good hearty meal or two," he grinned, then turned and yelled over his shoulder. "Odo?"

Odo's heart beat furiously when he saw young Odo scamper to the open door and stare curiously at the unknown visitor.

He was speechless, the boy had grown so much… his eyes, hair and the quizzical expression… just like his mother. He could easily see her resemblance in him. His eyes welled as he fought for the right words to speak. Godwin and Hetti thoughtfully stood aside and allowed him to interact with his son.

He crouched down. "My name is Oswald, what is yer name?"

The boy looked at him with a questioning look, then up at Godwin.

"Ye can speak to him, Odo, Priest Oswald is a friend," Godwin encouraged.

"Now he knows my name, I wanted to tell him," young Odo exclaimed.

Everyone laughed, except the young boy who looked angry.

"Come inside, Priest Oswald, we have food and ye can eat with us and tell us all how ye have been," Hetti offered.

The days turned into weeks and the weeks into months, and Odo lost track of time. He immersed himself into village life and contributed where and how he could. The church was a mess, filthy and in need of repair.

With help from villagers and with no funds, they made improvements and patched holes in the walls and mended a leaky roof. They were all proud of their efforts and combined achievements, but the repairs were only temporary at best.

The people of Mellester Manor warmed to the serious young priest who offered himself for work when someone took ill or when they became busy and needed an extra hand. He helped in the fields and did more than was expected. In return, he was given enough coin to feed and clothe himself and even had a little leftover. More importantly, he spent time with young Odo, and for the first time in years, he was essentially free of worry and felt peace.

He wanted to begin teaching young Odo but was reluctant to do so without other children participating, or his singular efforts at helping Godwin and Hetti's son would cause others to question his unusual interest in the boy.

The problem was solved when Cheeseman Gerald and his wife Agnes agreed to allow their oldest daughter, Charlotte, who was around the same age as Odo, to join them. Huntsman Edgar and Mother Rosa readily agreed soon after and allowed Priest Oswald to teach their children as well. Having a priest provide learning to village children was most unorthodox. Others weren't so eager and believed their children were better spent helping in the fields where they could be productive and contribute.

It became apparent to Oswald that two children from his small group showed unusual aptitude. While he admitted to himself his viewpoint was somewhat biased, none-the-less, he explained to Godwin and Hetti, and

Cheeseman Gerald and Agnes that young Odo and Charlotte had learning capabilities, and with their permission, would begin to teach them in earnest how to understand words so they could read when they were old enough to learn. Initially, they were hesitant, reading words was a privilege afforded to a few, but in the end, they reluctantly agreed.

Reeve Norman had kept Odo's horse safe while at the abbey, but since he had no need for such a fine animal anymore, he sold it to Sir William Ainsley, Lord of Mellester Manor. With the coin, he purchased a wagon and a hackney that was more suited to a priest. His sword and bow, along with a cache of his last remaining coin, were hidden securely in the church.

Plentiful rain and subsequent warm summers produced bountiful crops. The granaries were full, abundant grass fattened animals, and the people of Mellester were mostly content and happy. Mellester's lord, Sir William Ainsley, was equally satisfied and immensely proud of his small manor and what his villagers had accomplished. In response, he called his key people to attend to him inside Mellester's hall.

"I have some tidings of importance," began Sir William, with a broad smile. "We have had another prosperous harvest, and the manor fares well." He cast his gaze over the small group of people who sat before him.

Odo sat on a bench seat beside Reeve Norman. On the other side sat the lord's steward, and Sir Dain, a competent knight who was Sir William's marshal.

Sir William enjoyed the moment and kept everyone in suspense to the 'tidings of importance' he spoke of.

"Lady Constance and I have decided that Mellester Manor will host a *vigilia*[38]."

Reeve Norman stirred at the revelation and grinned in appreciation of the announcement.

Sir Dain stood. "Well done, milord. It has been some time, and I'm sure everyone will be thrilled."

"Priest Oswald?" Sir William looked at Odo. "As customary, the churchyard can be used for stalls and fer merchants?"

Odo nodded.

"Reeve Noman, we'll use the common for other activities, and we will discuss those details later."

"As ye wish milord," replied the reeve who dug his elbow into Odo's side in excitement.

"Sire, when do ye intend to host the *vigilia*?" asked the steward.

"We will honour and celebrate *St. Edmund the King and Martyr* on the twentieth day of November." Again, Sir William smiled as he surveyed the four men before him.

No one was averse to Sir William's announcement, and most were roused. Odo was unsure and not entirely comfortable with the planned festival. Of course, his misgivings were privately compounded by his fear of the Courtneys. Later, he acceded, his reaction may have been premature. Mellester Manor was small, and of no consequence, Gisela Chastain-Courteney had no reason to send men to southern England because a minor lord was hosting a *vigilia*. It might even be an enjoyable occasion, he reasoned. Regardless, he couldn't affect the lord's decision and had to

---

38 *Vigilia – An early medieval word for a fair, or faire.*

accept that.

The village was abuzz when news of the announcement spread. Merchants had the opportunity to display and peddle their wares. Farmers could show off prized animals, and food stalls would ensure everyone was fed and catered to.

As Odo knew, the reality was far different. Merchants overpriced their goods, food was unaffordable for most, and the *vigilia* essentially catered to noblemen with coin. Nobles would arrive in droves, they'd come from everywhere, and someone outlandishly suggested they'd even arrive from Frankia. Festivals were always a great source of entertainment and provided the perfect opportunity to gossip and catch up with old friends. Nonetheless, preparations had to be made, and the good folk of Mellester Manor set about the task with enthusiastic high spirits.

CHAPTER THIRTY-TWO

Château de Brancion was still draughty, which irked Gisela Chastain-Courteney to no end. She'd spoken to masons and asked, then insisted, and finally, at her wit's end, she'd screamed at them to repair whatever it was that caused the wind to race through the *château* and howl. The incessant noise grated on her nerves and was an unkind reminder of her father. It was like the voice of his lament and pain that ghosted through dank passageways and corridors and into the furthest rooms to seek her out. The masons had partially succeeded, but only after threats and eventually with a measure of punishment.

As she'd discovered about herself, there was an element of perverse pleasure that she derived from seeing someone face cruelty in the form of pain. She'd tried to analyze her sadistic fondness and failed. She loved the feeling of power and just learned to accept it; it was who she was and whom she'd become. Another part of the inheritance she received from her father.

Inside her mind, she'd reserved a special place for Odo Brus. She'd not forgotten him and probably never would. What he had done to her family was unforgivable, and with resolve, she'd decided that Odo Brus would spend his last days in the dungeon of *Château de Brancion,* at her pleasure and succumb to her will.

When word reached Gisela of another *vigilia* to be held in southern England, she didn't overreact. Over the last few years, she'd sent men to many festivals, and they scoured the locale and enquired after Odo Brus to no avail. Not even an intimation. The man had vanished, disappeared, and receded like a puff of smoke. As always, the results of returning *chevaliers* were disheartening, but her determination intensified. The harder Odo Brus tried to remain hidden, the more scared she knew he was of her. And as she since learned, he had a son who still lived. Her brothers had failed in their duty to kill his entire family in Scotland, and now the burden of vengeance sat on her lap. The warnings Odo Brus had imparted on her father were laughable, the man had neither the heart nor will to honour his own portent. Gisela didn't fear Odo Brus; he was nothing more than an obstacle and merely a pest that needed eradicating.

By mere coincidence, she'd learned another manor, not far from Londinium, was also holding a *vigilia* about a month before the one in Devonshire. Having two festivals within a short time made her decision easier. She selected and called for three *chevaliers* to attend to her so she could inform them of their unusual mission.

The knights finally arrived at the *château,* where Countess Gisela Chastain-Courteney informed *Chevaliers,* Jacque, Émile and Théo what she wanted them to do. Find the renegade knight, Odo Brus and his son, and return them both to Frankia, and if that wasn't possible, then kill them both.

The *Chevalier*s were noticeably stunned when they learned of their undertakings. While seeking a wayward knight was one thing, killing children was unheard of. Their reticence did not go unobserved, and Gisela increased the stakes. The *Chevalier*s stood apprehensively in front of her and could not hold her piercing gaze. "Odo Brus killed my brothers and my father," she stated coldly. "He hides like a coward from me, and he will suffer for his crimes. His son, his heir, will also die for the misdeeds of his father. Fer yer sake, I hope ye can bring them both to me, if not, then see they are savagely killed."

"Milady?" cautiously questioned, *Chevalier* Émile, "I understand what ye want, yer orders are clear, but it is not the way of a *chevalier* to slaughter children."

"Perhaps the three of ye can be motivated by the safety of yer own families and children." Her voice hardened. "It would be most unfortunate if they came to harm in yer absence."

Chevalier Émile's chest rose and fell as he fought to control his fear and anger. "Aye, milady, it is our duty to serve ye." He bowed, low and deep from the waist.

"Arrange fer yer departure, and it would not be wise to have yer families leave, fer I will be watching them," she added.

The three *chevalier*s again dipped their heads in reluctant subservience. "At yer command, milady,' said *Chevalier* Émile then turned and exited the room, the other two followed.

The three *chevalier*s she'd selected for this task were minor, unimportant lords. They would not be missed in the event of their failure or death. Privately Gisela believed nothing would come from this journey and most likely be a waste of coin and time. However, she had made a promise to herself to investigate at every opportunity and discover the whereabouts of Odo Brus and his son, and with commitment, she would follow through – even for a thread, a mere snippet of information that would lead to his eventual capture.

Gisela had no knowledge or understanding of martial skills. Her approach and thought process was quite simple. Because of a numerical advantage, two *chevaliers* were better than one knight, therefore, three *chevaliers* must be three times better. There was no need to send more men, three was sufficient and even allowed for an injury – a spare. In her mind, she had planned well, and if they discovered Odo Brus, her three *chevaliers* were undoubtedly motivated to bring him and his son to her.

Odo had just finished Sunday morning Mass and stood near the church doorway as his parishioners thanked him and departed. Some stopped to chat briefly, others walked past and dipped their heads in respect and thanks. Lastly, Godwin and Hetti stepped up, and young Odo stood at their side, picking his nose. Odo looked down at his son and gently pulled his arm away, only to receive a scowl.

"Odo!" Hetti warned, "Show respect."

The young boy looked contrite and then turned away to look at his friend Charlotte as her parents and sister stepped up beside them.

"Are ye ready fer the *vigilia*, Priest Oswald?" asked Cheesemaker Gerald.

"As well as I can be," Odo replied. "I never thought I would be so busy, there is so much to do, and aye, as ye asked, I have the tables ye need."

"I knew ye would find something fer me," replied the cheesemaker with a smile.

"I'm sure everything will go as planned," offered Godwin.

All heads turned to Reeve Norman as he clomped onto the church step and caught Odo's attention.

"Uh, I have work to do," said Godwin, realizing the reeve wanted to speak to Odo, he grabbed young Odo's arm, and Hetti followed as he began to walk away.

"Aye, work awaits," replied Gerald, and he, Agnes, Charlotte, and their youngest daughter, Odilia, stepped from the church, leaving Odo alone with the reeve.

Both men watched silently as the two families ambled away.

Soon as they could talk without being overheard, the reeve turned to Odo. His expression serious. "I need speak with ye, somewhere private."

Odo was instantly on guard, his eyes narrowed, and he immediately scanned the village for anything untoward. "This way." He led the reeve to the rear of the church and then looked expectingly at him.

"Oswald, there is a knight at the inn, he seeks ye and is asking questions."

Odo's stomach tightened. "Did he ask fer me?"

The reeve shook his head. "Nay, but I knew it could only be ye he sought."

"And did he offer his name?"

The reeve nodded, "Aye, a Frank, he says he is called *Chevalier* René De Villiers."

Odo's hands flew to his face, and he shook his head. He felt his heart begin to pound and his face flush as he recalled René's promise to him.

Seeing Odo's reaction, Reeve Norman was equally fearful. "Should I alert Sir William, we could chase the knight away?"

Odo removed his hands from his face. "Nay, he is not to be feared."

Reeve Norman looked puzzled.

"I suspect he brings tidings and unlikely to be welcomed ones."

"What can I do?" asked the reeve.

Odo tried to quell his racing heart. "I need to speak with him most soonest. But not where anyone can see us talk. Have him meet me at Falls Ende, on the other side by the riverwalk, it is not uncommon fer travellers to look at the falls when they visit and won't be unusual if he is there. I will go there now and wait fer him."

Reeve Norman reached out and grasped Odo's sleeve. "Oswald, is Mellester in danger?"

Odo returned the reeve's stare. "Best if ye sharpened yer sword."

Odo stood on the far side of Falls Ende in the shadows beneath a tree, waiting for René. He saw the knight slowly walk from the village towards Falls Ende, then cross the footbridge and walk down the path. As yet, he'd not seen him.

When Odo stepped out, René jumped. "Odo, ye startled me!" He held his arms wide to embrace his friend. "But *mon ami*, ye have changed, a priest?" he laughed. "A good disguise, *non*?"

Despite the anxiety, Odo felt good to see his friend. "I am sorry, René, people here know me as Priest Oswald. It is not a disguise, fer I am a priest now."

René nodded. "I understand." He turned his head and looked over Falls Ende. "I wish I could have come here to visit and share a mead and recall the time we spent together with laughter...."

He turned from the tumult of cascading water back to Odo. "I made a promise to ye, and I am here to honour that promise. Ye deserve that ... and more, my friend."

Odo took a step closer to René. "But not all is well?"

"I came as soon as I learned... Odo, Gisela has sent three *chevaliers* here to Mellester. As we speak, they travel from Londinium, and I know not when they will arrive."

Odo grimaced and nodded. It was as he initially feared. "They come because of the *vigilia*, and that does not begin for six more days." Immediately he began to think of all he could do, the preparations he could make, where he could hide young Odo...

"Odo, I came as soon as I could, but I cannot remain to help, I must return home."

"Ye are a dear friend, and I thank ye. God bless ye, René. I will make do. Yer warning is enough and will suffice. I am forever in yer debt."

Reeve Norman leaned on the bridge handrail and watched with growing concern. While the *chevalier* and the priest were well acquainted, he could see Oswald's expression, and it appeared that the tidings the *chevalier* brought were not good.

He saw the *chevalier* hug Odo one last time and walk away towards him. When he drew near, he went to walk past then stopped. "He is a good man, help him if ye can."

"Aye, that he is. Whatever ye did fer him, thank ye, milord."

Chevalier René De Villiers smiled and continued on.

Odo was lost in thought and stared out over Falls Ende and never saw the brief exchange between both men and was surprised when the reeve slowly ambled towards him. He contemplated on how to answer the questions that he knew would come. No matter how unpleasant, the truth is always best, he reasoned and then exhaled. "Reeve Norman, I fear fer the life of young Odo. Three *chevaliers* will come here to Mellester; they seek my death and that of young Odo." He met the reeve's stern look. "They want to kill us."

"Because of the *vigilia*, is this why they come to Mellester?"

"Aye, that is the reason they come, and when they do, they will ask questions about me, someone may say something, or they may see and recognize me, I know not, but nothing good will come of this. A celebration like this brings many people, it is the perfect place to ask about someone in the guise of friendship."

The reeve looked pensive. "We cannot tell Sir William… and ye can't hide, ye are needed here, Oswald. Yer absence will only draw notice to ye." He shook his head.

"I cannot bring any attention to this, reeve, the villagers must not know of my past. The more people know, then the risk increases fer Odo."

Reeve Norman turned away and watched the swiftly moving water. "The safest place is the manor house; someone could take him there fer safety."

Odo nodded. "Aye, if the boy were at the manor, then that would be best."

A mother duck quacked and called to her young as they drifted on the river towards the falls. Odo turned his head to watch. With the mother duck's vocal warning, her ducklings paddled quickly upriver to safety before the current took them over the edge. The danger was averted.

"Ye say three *chevaliers*? Surely ye can't fight three skilled knights?" The reeve asked. "Ye need help."

Odo turned from the ducks and looked at the reeve. His expression hardened, and his piercing blue eyes were cold. "I fear not three *chevaliers*, Reeve Norman. My quandary is how to solve this problem without alerting the manor, Sir William and the person who sent them."

"And after... will they come again, will others arrive here to Mellester and seek ye and Odo?"

The sound of water tumbling over the falls never changed; it was constant, reliable, and present. It was reassuring because it was always there. To Odo, it offered a form of peacefulness and provided clarity when needed. Slowly he shook his head. "Nay, fer these men have travelled from Londinium, and their disappearance could have happened anywhere along their journey. Yes, they will be missed when they do not return, but Mellester is a small manor of no importance. She will believe Londinium is the area where the *chevaliers* went missing."

"Only if *all* three men do not return," stated the reeve.

"Aye."

"Ye said she?"

Odo raised an eyebrow. "Best ye didn't know, reeve."

The reeve's face soured. "What can I do?"

Odo rubbed his chin. "If ye can speak to Godwin and have Odo taken to the manor stables to look at the horses, he likes horses and will be distracted by them. Perhaps have Mother Rosa look after him, she has nothing to do at the fair, and I trust her. And reeve, wear yer sword. Keep an eye out fer three *chevaliers* asking questions, and if ye see them inform me."

"I am tasked by Sir William to keep order at the *vigilia* and will have opportunity to watch fer three *chevaliers*, but, Oswald, there will be many knights at the vigilia, they come from afar, and it will be difficult. I can do my best... nothing more."

Odo patted the reeve on the shoulder. "As ye will be mingling and keeping the peace, then it is only natural that ye be looking vigilant. I will have to remain near the church but will be ready to make my move once they have been identified."

"I can't have any trouble, Oswald. Sir William will want answers if something happens. His honour and reputation are at risk." The reeve's expression turned serious.

Odo nodded. "Aye, Sir William will never learn of this."

"Then ye have a plan?"

Odo hadn't yet thought of a plan. "Aye, all will be well."

CHAPTER THIRTY-THREE

Merchants, bards, and hawkers began arriving and preparing for the *vigilia* that honoured England's patron Saint, King Edmond, the martyr. The weather remained sunny and pleasant, although locals expected it would rain in a day or so, but they were thrilled that the sun shone and was near perfect conditions for Sir William's festival. Flags in abundance, mostly displaying a dragon, King Edmond's banner, flapped from buildings and trees in the mild breeze, and there was a good feeling of cheer and carefree spirits.

Amongst the throngs who began arriving, petty thieves, rovers and outcasts were drawn to Mellester like moths to a flame. With furtive glances and shifty eyes, they surveyed the stalls, eyed prosperous vendors, and dreamt of liberating bulging purses and stealing untold riches. In reality, they'd pilfer from the unwary, a penny here or there, a pie from a distracted baker, or a trinket that took their fancy. Like any experienced artificer, they were adept and skilled and minimized their risk with deviousness and sly cunning, and they were fully aware their shady presence would be carefully watched.

Old man Brooker and his three sons, Bert, Samuel and Tedric, had only just arrived in Mellester, but rather than walk through the centre of Mellester and draw undue attention to themselves, Brooker and his boys kept to the peripheries where he knew opportunities existed to observe and steal. To anyone watching, the boys appeared to be playing, but they were scouting and carefully looking for anything worthy of being nicked. They warily approached the churchyard and the stalls, where they calculated the pickings would be easy. Rather than advertise their presence by wandering around, they maintained a low profile and didn't stray too close to busy merchants who were readying their wares for the big day on the morrow. As was their nature, they carefully observed until occasion presented itself.

There was still much to do, and Odo had been busy organizing space and stalls specially allocated for vendors near the church. The more successful merchants had set up tents or were selling from wagons in more open spaces around the village. Entertainers would perform in the common, and attractions and games for children or adults were spread out, filling all available spaces along Mellester's main thoroughfare.

However, Odo had lost interest in the festivities and been preoccupied. Earlier, when he had time, he sharpened his sword, oiled his bow, and checked his dwindling supply of arrows. Then, he ventured into the forest, and away from prying eyes, practised with his sword. He never slept, and consumed by dread, spent a listless night trying to calculate how best to deal with the *chevalier*s. He'd been thinking about his conversation with

René when he recalled watching the mother duck warn her young of the danger of the falls. He then remembered how a duck will feign an injury and appear wounded and then make a half-hearted attempt to escape a predator and flee. To the hunter, the wounded duck was a better and easier proposition, and so tempted, the predator would chase the adult duck while the ducklings hid in safety.

To Odo, this presented a viable solution. He could offer himself as bait and entice the three *chevaliers* to come after him. He would flee to the forest near Falls Ende, where he would use his bow and pick them off, one at a time. Further, Sir William had decreed that Falls Ende was too dangerous for people to visit and prohibited anyone from approaching by blocking access. By luring the three *chevaliers* away, no one in the village would be aware of what was happening, and he could dispose of the bodies later. However, afterwards, he would need the reeves help to identify their horses and be rid of them. He couldn't leave any trace of the *chevaliers* of having ever been at Mellester Manor.

As soon as he had a spare moment, Odo returned inside the church rectory, retrieved his bow and quiver, wrapped them in a blanket and by using a circuitous route, behind the stalls, headed for the bridge that would take him to the forest. He looked towards the merchants and activity, and thankfully, no one paid him any attention.

Brooker and his sons were loitering near the rear of the church when Samuel alerted his father with eye contact and a subtle head movement to something most curious. Brooker shifted his gaze to where his boy indicated and immediately saw a priest hurrying away carrying a lengthy bundle in his arms.

Brooker had taught his sons well. They never drew attention to themselves by pointing or loudly exclaiming, all instructions were through eye contact and slight head movements. He held Samuel's gaze and gave an imperceptible head nod. Immediately the boy ran off to follow the priest as his father wanted. Of his three sons, the oldest, Bert, was the most aggressive and largest and fancied himself as the leader. The middle son, Samuel, a quick thinker, was by far the smartest with nous. Tedric, the youngest, was strong and, unfortunately for his father, had the kindest and gentlest nature of the boys.

Brooker watched Samuel bound away in silent approval. The boy was adept enough not to directly follow the priest but keep close and only observe.

Odo hurried as quickly as he could, and of most concern to him was that his presence at the stalls wasn't missed. Rather than look nervously around to see if anyone noticed him, he kept his attention on the bridge and forest beyond and didn't see or hear the boy following.

Once he rounded the barrier that kept people from Falls Ende, he crossed over the bridge, entered the forest, and then thought about a vantage point from where he could lay in wait for the *chevaliers*. He needed somewhere high, not far away, that offered concealment and an escape route if needed.

The forest offered plenty of choices, and when possible, Odo had previously walked through the meandering paths and explored all he could. During the previous winter, a severe storm had blown a diseased tree over, and it fell onto a small ridge. It was the perfect location and ideally suited his needs for concealment and escape.

Soon as he arrived at the fallen tree, he began to remove soil and small branches from beneath the trunk until he had a space large enough to hide his bow and quiver. It didn't take long in the soft soil, but he had no time to double-check and had to return quickly. He knew that no one would discover his bow before tomorrow if and when he needed it. He wiped away most of the dirt and leaves from his robe and hurriedly left the forest to return to the stalls. He passed by young Samuel, who lay hidden beneath a small leafy bush.

When he reappeared in the village, he found Godwin waiting for him.

"Priest Oswald, may I have a word?" he asked.

Odo knew what it was about, Godwin's face betrayed his emotions. "Perhaps inside, Herdsman Godwin, I have a little time, eh," he smiled. "Come, what ails ye?"

Once inside the church, Odo turned to Godwin. He saw the look of worry.

"Priest Oswald, the reeve told me…" he looked around for anyone close who could overhear. "…Is Odo truly in danger?"

Odo decided to be forthcoming. "Godwin, three *chevaliers*, are coming here to Mellester, and they wish to see my death and that of young Odo. As the reeve told ye, the safest place for him to be is at the manor house. If ye cannot be there with him, have Mother Rosa look after him." He took a step closer to Godwin and placed a hand on his shoulder. "If something happens to me, then tell Sir William, tell him everything, but do not let those men come near Odo. Can ye do this?"

"Hetti and I are frightened fer Odo," Godwin replied. "But I will do as ye ask. I know ye will do what is best fer him, I just hope it is enough."

"Aye, I hope so too, Godwin."

Knights and lords, including Sir Hyde Fortescue, of Ridgely Manor, began arriving in Mellester and immediately began setting up camps on the manor's outskirts. Sir Hyde was a high-ranking lord and a good friend of Sir William and would reside as an invited guest at the manor.

The *vigilia* had not yet begun, and already Mellester was bulging at the seams. People were everywhere, and for many, the festivities were already well underway. Odo was kept busy at the church and was in regular contact with Reeve Norman, who prowled through the village with a few of Sir William's men-at-arms maintaining order.

As late and lengthening afternoon shadows began dissolving into darkness, old man Brooker and his middle son, Samuel, casually strolled towards Falls Ende and the forest while Burt and Tedric kept watch over their meagre possessions in a hand cart near the church.

Earlier, and much to Brooker's surprise, Samuel told him that the priest who hid a cloth-wrapped bundle in the forest was the same priest he'd stabbed in the leg near Ridgley Manor some time ago. With his curiosity piqued, old man Brooker was keen to learn more about the enigmatic priest and what he'd hidden in the forest and why.

Samuel retraced his steps and showed his father the area where the priest had been. With darkness settling over the forest, they searched for the bundle around the fallen tree, and in frustration, found nothing. Samuel recalled seeing the priest wiping dirt from his robe. 'He buried it pa, I knows he did."

Again, they looked and soon discovered the cloth-wrapped bundle.

"Well, I never," said Brooker in a low voice. "What would a priest want with a bow? Look, it's a beauty, it is." He held it up and examined its fine woodwork in the diminishing light. "It'll fetch a bit too." He paused, looked around and spoke quietly. "Grab everything, let's scarper, be at it, quickly now."

Old man Brooker and his son left the forest with Odo's bow, and quiver rewrapped in the blanket. He would hide it in his handcart and take it with him when the *vigilia* had ended.

Odo finished resharpening his sword. He'd gone over his plan, again and again, it wasn't the best, but it was all he had. It hinged on one crucial factor, he needed to identify the *chevaliers* before they saw him. He hoped the reeve was attentive and alert him when they arrived. When he knew where the *chevaliers* were, he would carefully entice them away from the village and then run into the forest, and, God willing, they'd follow. In case things didn't turn out as he expected, he'd leave his sword here in his home, then he'd have something to defend himself with. It had been over two years since he felt the reassuring weight of a sword on his hip, and he wished he could belt it to his waist, but that would create another series of problems he didn't want to face.

He lay down to sleep on the floor, as far from his bed as possible, with his sword at his There was always the possibility the *chevaliers* had learned where he lived and crash through the door to surprise him. He took no chances. It mattered not, he didn't sleep, and no one entered the rectory during the night, and he was already up and ready for the day, long before the sun peeked above forest-clad hills.

Odo stepped outside and walked through the village. People were already up and about preparing for the day ahead. There wasn't much for him to do today, most of his tasks had been organizing and preparing for the *vigilia,* and that work had all been completed.

Disturbing the early morning's tranquillity, he turned to the sound of baying hounds. The lord's huntsman, Edgar, appeared with three *Alaunt*[39] hunting hounds. Good-sized, aggressive animals that Sir William preferred to use on bear or boar instead of greyhounds.

"Hail, Priest Oswald, and a fine day it is," warmly greeted Edgar.

"Aye, and ye are about early," Odo commented.

"Sir William and his guests are hunting on the morrow, and this morn, we will drive game into the area where they will hunt."

"Indeed," Odo replied. He remembered with fondness the thrill of a hunt. He looked at the dogs and wanted to bend down to give them attention. Edgar was reticent about people coming near his precious and fearsome beasts and had warned him of the hounds unpredictable and aggressive nature. "Don't look 'em in th' eyes," he constantly advised.

Forewarned, Odo kept his distance and ignored them. "I wish ye well, Edgar."

"Good day to ye, Priest Oswald." With quiet whispered commands, the

---

39   *Alaunt – Medieval hunting dogs, now extinct, were used for hunting large animals.*

dogs instantly obeyed and withdrew to stand eagerly at their master's side. With a wave, Edgar set out for the forest.

Odo walked on and paused outside the door of Mother Rosa's cruck and knocked. It was very early, but he knew she'd already be awake. Within moments the door opened, and she filled the space with a baby on her hip. "Priest Oswald, fare thee well? I don't have time to natter; I need to begin milking."

It never ceased to amaze him how much Rosa had changed. She'd become a good woman, a wonderful mother and a nurturing and kind person. Oh yes, she had grown, her weight increased, and without question, she was someone to be reckoned with, but to Godwin and Hetti, she was a Godsend. She worked hard, more so than anyone else they had hired, and without her, their milk production and costs would escalate. Rosa thrived in Mellester, she was popular, goodhearted, and quite frequently, she looked after young Odo when Hetti was busy elsewhere. If Rosa's parents could only see her now.

"Good tidings to ye, and are ye ready fer today?" Odo asked.

"Aye, best ye come inside," she suggested and stepped aside to allow Odo in.

With the door closed, she turned to him with a grim expression. "How serious is it? Is Odo truly in danger?"

"I believe so, but… Mother Rosa, if I fail, then ye must turn to Sir William, he will be the only one who can help ye and keep Odo safe. Godwin and Hetti have much to do, and they cannot leave their stall."

She nodded. "We have spoken, and once I have finished milking, then I will look after him. Fear not, fer if anyone comes near that boy to harm him, I swear on the Lord's name, I will cause them misery." She raised a meaty clenched fist.

Odo couldn't disagree. He knew she meant every word. "Thank ye, it means a lot to me." Without another word, he exited her cruck and walked towards Godwin and Hetti's home. Before he could knock, Godwin stepped outside and saw him.

"Is all well, Priest Oswald?"

Odo looked at Godwin in the darkness and shook his head. "Truth be told, I am fearful, Godwin. I have done all I can, and now I must wait. Nothing more...' He sighed and turned to look down the street at the activity as dawn's greyness seeped over the village.

"I feel it too," replied Godwin. "But I am not a knight, I am a herdsman and know nothing of swords and fighting. I have placed my faith in ye."

Odo looked away from the street and back at Godwin and smiled. "I will give my life to see him safe."

"Aye, I know ye will. Is there anything I can do?"

"If ye see or hear three *chevaliers* asking fer me, then send word. I will not stray far from the churchyards."

Godwin nodded and then turned to greet Mother Rosa, who arrived with her two daughters. "Well, Priest Oswald, we cannot tarry, there is much work to be done." He paused as if to speak more, then thought better of it and disappeared inside his cruck with Mother Rosa and her brood following.

CHAPTER THIRTY-FOUR

One thing Odo was pleased about was where Mellester's church was situated. It was the very first structure on Mellester's main thoroughfare. When a traveller turned into Mellester from the road headed south towards Exeter, a half day's ride away, the church was on a slight rise on the left-hand corner. Its prime location enabled anyone standing near the church to see who entered Mellester village, and he ensured he would stand close to the church to carefully observe comings and goings.

A stream of people came. Peasants, nobility, the wealthy and even the unwelcome. Word had spread far-and-wide of Sir William's *vigilia,* and after a productive harvest, it also offered respite to peasants from their daily mundane routines with entertainment and opportunities to renew acquaintances with old friends or to just have a good time.

Odo stood at the near corner of the church, beneath the shade of a tree, where he could see who was arriving, and if he turned his head slightly, he could observe activities at the churchyard stalls. Seeing him standing there, Reeve Norman, with two men-at-arms for company, walked over to stand beside him and folded his arms, and quietly surveyed the activity. After a few moments, he lowered his arms and faced Odo. "I know ye worry, so do I Oswald, but we will overcome this, eh?" He reached out and gently clapped Odo on the shoulder, then motioned to the men-at-arms and wandered off.

Odo noticed the sword that swung from the reeve's hip. *I hope he can use it*, he thought.

Mellester's vendors were making a brisk trade. There was laughter, haggling and the usual groups of children gleefully running around, causing havoc. When needed, he gave them a stern look or a scowl, and once or twice, threatened to inform their parents if they didn't settle down and behave. Admonitions from Mellester's priest were taken seriously, and in fear of incurring his wrath, they adjusted their manner accordingly.

Raised voices caught Odo's attention, and he turned towards the churchyard's stalls. In response to the yelling, a small crowd began to watch, and curious to the reason, he ambled over.

Lothar, the cooper, was loudly arguing with the tanner. Lothar was an aggressive man and easily provoked to anger. His woman could attest to that and frequently suffered because of his violent temperament. Odo stepped up and stood between both men, and just in time as the cooper raised his fists in anger.

"Cooper Lothar," Odo said, his voice calm, "What ails ye?"

"He keeps puttin' his bleedin' barrels into my space," exclaimed the tanner in frustration. "I tells 'im not too, and he won't be a listen'n."

"He," Cooper Lothar reached around Odo and pointed at the tanner, "ain't tell'in th'truth."

"Perhaps we can make an arrangement," Odo suggested and turned to look at the space behind each of the men's adjacent stalls. He saw the problem immediately. He leaned his staff against the table and stepped over, and began moving the cooper's barrels to create a symmetrical line to form a divider between both spaces. "Will that work?"

Lothar looked over and nodded. "I suppose," he said petulantly.

"I told 'im to do that," replied the tanner, who shook his head in frustration.

"Good, then if ye are happy, then ye can return to selling wares, eh?" Odo suggested.

Lothar grunted and turned away.

The situation had been resolved quickly and thankfully hadn't escalated. Odo stepped from behind Lothar's stall, retrieved his staff, gave the cooper's woman a warm smile and began to walk back to the church to resume his vigil when he saw Reeve Norman hurrying over.

Odo felt his chest tighten; this didn't bode well at all. He looked at the reeve in question as he stepped up, breathing hard.

"Tis, them … they came … and asking fer ye," the reeve explained between breaths.

Odo looked around and couldn't see who the reeve was talking about. "Who, how many?"

"There'd be four o'them, and not three as ye said," the reeve leaned towards Odo so no-one could overhear. "They were asking after Odo Brus."

He thought quickly as his heart began pounding in his chest. He knew he needed to gain their attention and lead them away from the village towards Falls Ende and the forest. "Where are they?"

"Come, I'll show ye," Reeve Norman replied and began to walk from the churchyard and onto Mellester's thoroughfare. "There, do ye see 'em?" He was astute enough not to point, and Odo followed his gaze.

Odo's heart was beating furiously. Ahead, and blocking the street, he saw four horsemen, two of them were distinctive and wore the familiar white surcoat emblazoned with the red cross over chainmail armour, the other two were sergeants and wore black surcoats. They were Templars. Already people stared curiously at the legendary knights, this was a most unexpected visit and didn't portend well. Odo was anxious.

"What shall we do?" asked Reeve Norman.

Odo stepped back, out of sight from the Templars and thought quickly. He knew they weren't here to cause him harm, or so he hoped, however their presence and reason for their visit could cause many questions. "There is no room fer them to stable their horses at the inn." Most horses were secured in a field near the common on the far side of the village. But the church had a small area behind the rectory where Odo kept his horse and wagon. "Go to them and suggest they can tie their horses safely behind the church where there is water."

The reeve's mouth opened to protest.

"Reeve, these men are not the ones who have come to kill me. But I cannot have them speak of the name Odo Brus." He shook his head. "They mustn't."

Odo saw the reeve immediately relax. "Aye, there is nothing amiss about using the church to tether their horses." He exhaled and then smiled. "We are fortunate, eh?"

"Aye, fer the moment reeve, but hasten, these men must not be allowed to talk to villagers and inform them of who they seek."

The reeve quickly strode off, and Odo, with hands on his hips, returned to the church and questioned why the Templars had to come this day.

"Hale to ye priest," greeted one of the Templars as he dismounted. "I'm told ye can help us, fer we seek someone."

"Good tidings, and may God watch over ye," Odo returned the salutation. "Who sent ye?"

The Templar paused from tethering his horse while the other knight dismounted. The two sergeants were filling a trough with buckets of water and ignored him. If anything, the knight looked surprised at Odo's question. A simple parish priest did not question Templar knights.

Odo needed to know why the Templar's came to Mellester and was reluctant to divulge his identity to these men who he'd never seen before.

"As I told ye, we seek–"

"I know who ye seek," Odo interrupted before the Templar spoke his name again. "I ask ye, most kindly, sir, who sent ye?"

The knight's annoyance was evident as he stepped confidently up to him, but if he intended to intimidate, he failed. The priest didn't back away and was equally as tall. More so, the priest looked at him as if expecting an answer.

"We came at the bequest of Sir Godfrey," replied the other knight as he removed his gauntlets and tucked them into his belt as he walked over. "I am Sir Brian, and this is Sir Drogo."

Odo felt immediate relief. The first knight still looked a little peeved at the perceived disrespect he'd been shown. He glanced around, but no one else was near them. "I am he, the man ye seek, but it is best that my real name is not known here. Please, the people of Mellester know me as Oswald, and I wish to keep it that way," he told them in a low voice.

The first knight, Sir Drogo, looked disbelievingly at Odo, then looked him up and down and shook his head. "We came to find a brother, a Templar, and ye... ye are–"

"A parish priest?" Odo completed his sentence. He admitted to himself that his clothes were soiled and stained. His old straw hat... and his beard was a little straggly and unkempt. Certainly, far removed from the discipline and order of the Templars. "I fought in Jerusalem, Montgisard, Acre, Ascalon and most recently, I served under Sir Piers. Would ye care to know more?"

Both knights exchanged a look. "Nay, Priest Oswald," said Sir Brian. "But we are puzzled."

"Aye, I expect ye would. But here in Mellester, my previous life is unknown, and it is important to me it remains so and, having Templars here asking questions and talking with me is most unusual and draws unwelcome attention I do not seek."

The knights both looked awkward.

"How fares Sir Godfrey, is he hale and hearty?"

"Aye, he is growing old, but a capable man and Sir Piers has also aged," answered Sir Brian. "Sir Godfrey asked that if we had reason, then we should visit Mellester Manor and enquire on his behalf of yer wellbeing. We were journeying from our lands in the south to Combe Templorium and heard of the *faire*, we thought it opportune to visit."

"I thank ye and also pass on my tidings to Sir Godfrey, and tell him I fare well. Will ye stay long?"

"Nay, we must soon be away again," said Sir Brian.

"Why is it ye seek to remain unknown here?" Sir Drogo asked.

Odo sighed and looked at the ground by his feet before answering. "I encountered some hostilities, and Mellester offers safe refuge … I hope."

"Then ye are expecting trouble?" continued Sir Drogo with another question Odo didn't want to answer.

In reflex, Odo cast a quick eye around him; since the Templars arrived, he hadn't been keeping vigil. "Aye, perhaps. That is why ye received a less than hearty welcome from the reeve."

Both knights laughed. "May we ask, what trouble?"

"It is nothing that I cannot solve. Thank ye kindly." Odo was growing more uncomfortable. While the young Templar knights were agreeable, their continued presence was a distraction, and the longer they spoke to him, the more likely people would begin to notice. He wanted them to leave.

Sensing his disquiet, Sir Brian spoke. "We will depart soon. First, we will look around while the horses rest. Is this acceptable, Priest Oswald?"

"Aye, enjoy yerselves. There is excellent milk and cheese yonder," he pointed in the direction of Godwin and Cheesemaker Gerald's stalls.

"Good cheer to ye, Priest Oswald," Sir Brian said, then called for the sergeants to join them and began walking in the direction Odo pointed.

Sir Drogo paused, then looked at Odo. "Fergive me fer my rudeness," he dipped his head in respect and followed the others.

Seeing the Templars walk away, Reeve Norman approached. "Is all well, Oswald?"

"Aye, I believe so. No harm done, I hope." Odo exhaled and felt the tension ease slightly.

Reeve Norman readjusted the belt that his sword was attached to. "Do ye think they'll still come?"

Odo surveyed the churchyard and the road. "I know not, Reeve. I have prayed that I was told wrong."

"Then fer now, all will be well, eh," said the reeve and ambled off to rejoin the men-at-arms who were eating pies at a stall.

Old man Brooker was lying against a tree a short distance away from the festivities, near the main road guarding his hand cart while his three boys were scavenging. He'd given them instructions to bring food, preferably a pie or bread, or better - both.

To Brooker, it was simple. If one of his boys was caught nicking, and an irate vendor approached him with the guilty boy in tow, he'd apologise to the vendor, wallop the lad and admonish him loudly. No, not for pilfering, but for being caught. To the vendor, the verbal rebuke was usually enough. If not, the guilty boy would receive another blow across the back of his head which generally satisfied the aggrieved merchant. Brooker may not have been gifted with intelligence, but he was, if nothing more, a logical and practical thinker.

When Brooker heard horses approaching, he half opened his eyes to observe and immediately tensed as the three knights paused near him. He gave no outward reaction to their unwelcome attention upon him and continued with the pretence that he was napping.

"Hale, to ye," greeted one of the knights.

Brooker heard the unmistakable Frankish accent, and he quickly sat up, feigning surprise. As he always did, Brooker pretended to be a halfwit. People treated fools differently and would disclose and say far more if they believed he was nothing more than an idiot. He rose to his feet and stood, slack-jawed, and blinked his eyes, then stared uncomprehendingly at the three knights.

"Ye may be able to help us," one of the knights said.

Brooker moved his head slightly and listened. *This could be an opportunity*, he surmised.

"We seek a man and his son, he is called Odo Brus. Do ye know of him or the name?"

The name Odo Brus meant nothing to Brooker. He shook his head, which he would have done anyway, even if he had heard of the man.

The knight paused a moment, then, as an afterthought, continued. "He is an archer."

An archer? thought Brooker. His logic and practical thought process kicked in. He knew of no archers, but then he'd taken the bow from that peculiar priest... *An archer*, he reaffirmed to himself. Again, he shook his head. "Uh, his son's name?" he spoke for the first time.

"We know not," the knight shrugged. "But there is a reward."

Old man Brooker fought to remain composed. *A reward!* "A reward, mil, milord?" he asked, feeling quite motivated.

"Aye, a shilling fer ye if ye can tell us where he may be," confirmed the knight.

Old man Brooker gave a big, stupid grin. "And if I bring the archer and his boy to ye?"

All three knights burst out laughing. "Then ye can have the entire purse." The knight reached beneath his tunic, extracted a small bulging pouch, and waved it. "Ye will find us at the *faire*." With that, he squeezed his legs, and his horse responded. All three knights rode on towards Mellester. Brooker touched his hand to his forelock as they passed and then sat back down to think.

The name Odo Brus was unfamiliar, while the name Odo was common, he reasoned, there weren't that many archers around here that were distinctive enough to garner the attention of three knights. The only man who may be of interest was the priest. He thought of the bow they'd taken from him and determined he must be an archer, but a priest and an archer? He remembered his meeting with the priest at Ridgley manor and the unusual way he'd conducted himself. An ordinary priest, he wasn't. *Quite odd*, he thought, and then tried to recall the priest's name.

His three sons returned, and Samuel, it was always Samuel, handed over a pie he'd pilfered. Wordlessly, Brooker began to devour the delectable pastry. He and his sons hadn't eaten today, and he was ravenous. He gave no thought to his boys about food, nor did he offer to share the pie. If the boys were hungry, they could forage and take care of themselves. "What else have ye brought me?" he growled as the last remnants of the treat disappeared.

The oldest, Bert, shook his head. "Nothin' pa."

Old man Brooker grunted in disappointment. He wiped his mouth with his sleeve and then stood, stretched his back, and stepped from behind the tree and turned to gaze out across Mellester Manor. He was still musing over the reward offered to him for information about the man Odo Brus. "I think we shall make our way to the other side of the common and have a nosey." He offered no reason or explanation. However, earlier, he'd seen the priest walk from the church and believed he was heading to the common. Keeping an eye on him could prove valuable.

"Now?" asked Bert.

"Nay, in a while, go back and bring me another pie," he ordered.

Odo decided to check that young Odo was safely in the stables of the manor house. There were many visiting knights, and their horses were all being cared for by Sir William. Ostlers, groomsmen and squires would be wandering around, and under the protective and watchful eye of Mother Rosa, he knew the boy should be out of danger.

He waited until the Templars were finished their business at Godwin and Hetti's stall and then walked over.

They were both busy, and Godwin spared a quick look at Odo.

"Where is Mother Rosa?" Odo casually asked.

"Priest Oswald, care fer some milk?" Without waiting, he handed Odo a clay mug. "She is with Odo," he whispered with a wink.

Odo downed the fresh milk and wiped his mouth with his sleeve. Godwin's answer was what he wanted to hear. They were at the manor's stables. He nodded his thanks, placed the empty mug on the table and decided to return to the church. He turned around, and what he saw caused his mouth to instantly dry, his face reddened, and his heart began its familiar pounding when alerted to danger. Immediately he dipped his head to hide his face. He needed to think and plan with some urgency.

CHAPTER THIRTY-FIVE

To return to the church, he needed to walk past the three *chevaliers* who had just entered Mellester. What bothered him the most was that he recognised the faces of two of them, the third was unknown. He took a deep breath, pulled his hat lower over his face and went to walk past them.

"Priest!" shouted one of the *chevaliers*.

Odo didn't react and walked on.

"Priest!" the *chevalier* yelled again.

Reeve Norman was walking quickly towards Odo. They made brief eye contact, and the reeve continued past him and towards the Frankian knights. He heard the reeve question the *chevaliers* but nothing more. As quickly as possible, he hurried to the church where he could prepare himself and wait for the reeve to return. The Templar horses were still tethered to the rail, but where Sir Drogo and Sir Brian were, he had no notion.

Once out of sight from the street, he paced backwards and forwards as he considered how to affect his plan.

The dilemma was, who were the two *chevaliers* he recognised? He knew their faces but could not recall their names or where he'd met them. With his hands behind his head, he walked to and fro in growing anguish.

"Oswald?" suddenly came the voice.

Odo spun and faced the man and immediately recalled his name. He'd met them at the *hastilude* in Toulouse.

"Er, *Chevalier*... uh, Émile, it is a pleasure to see ye again," Odo replied, feigning surprise.

"*Mon ami*, what is it ye are doing here? ...and a priest?"

Odo forced himself to act naturally. "And I could ask the same of ye, what brings ye to Mellester?" There was no sign of the other two *chevaliers*, and Émile stood alone at the rear of the church. "I last saw ye in Toulouse at the *hastilude*."

"Aye, and I had injured my arm in the contest." He flexed his arm as if the memory caused him pain. "It is healed now, but this year I won and did not become injured," he grinned, then shook his head. "But, er, a priest?"

"Aye, I had a calling to serve our Lord, and God brought me here to Mellester," Odo added. "But what brings ye here?"

Émile's expression hardened. "We come here to search fer someone, a man and boy. Perhaps ye may know of them?"

Odo looked over Émile's shoulder and saw the two Templars and their sergeants approach. They slowed and appraised the *chevalier*, then looked questioningly at Odo; they felt the tension.

Sir Drogo's hand lowered to grasp the hilt of his sword. "Are ye well, Priest?" he asked and gave the *chevalier* another look.

This was the time. It was now or never. He could solve his problem this instant. Two Templar knights and sergeants would easily overcome three *chevaliers* of that Odo had no doubt. But the resulting action would create issues that would draw the curiosity of Sir William, and he would forever become associated with the name Odo Brus. Young Odo would never again be safe in Mellester.

"Aye, all is well, thank ye, milord," he forced himself to reply with a smile.

Sir Drogo nodded and walked past. Within moments, the Templars untethered their horses, mounted, and with a wave, departed Mellester and cantered away.

"What were they doing here?" asked Émile.

"They ride fer Combe Templorium and were just passing by. There is no room at the stables at the inn fer their horses, and I allowed them to water them here."

Émile nodded.

As yet, there was no sign of Émile's two friends. "Ye said ye were looking fer someone?" Odo reminded him.

"Aye, a man and a boy. Ye might know of them or heard their names," Émile stated.

Odo kept his expression neutral. "Who?" his voice took an edge.

"He is called Odo Brus, he was a…" he paused and turned to look down the road at the Templars who'd just ridden away. "…a Templar knight."

Odo saw Émile's demeanour change at the coincidence. Inside the rectory, only a dozen steps away, his sword lay hidden beneath the mattress of his cot. He considered all his options, and his mind worked furiously to weigh the odds of survival. He sighed heavily and stood a little straighter. "Were ye sent by Gisela?"

Chevalier Émile's head jerked back in surprise. "What say ye?" he exclaimed.

"I am he, Odo Brus, the man ye seek."

Émile shook his head and laughed, "Nay, ye are Oswald."

Odo inclined his head and waited for him to make sense of it all.

"Ah, my friend," Émile looked over his shoulder, "The other knight with Théo, he can identify Odo Brus, fer he was there in Caen, at *Château de Caen* when Jean Courteney was slain in the archery..." he let the last word trail off. Again, he paused as the revelation dawned on him. "... ye are an archer, I remember now." His puzzlement changed to a look of apprehension, and then he swallowed in fear.

Odo tensed and waited. For defence, he had only his staff, while Émile was fully armed. Was Émile brave enough to take him on, or would he fetch his friends? His entire plan hinged on what Émile did next. He moved his staff a little, and the *chevalier*'s eyes followed the movement.

Coming to a decision, Émile squared his shoulders and placed his hand on the hilt of his sword. "Priest, or Oswald, or Odo Brus, I know not, but if ye are he, then ye must come back to Frankia with us. It is our duty to bring ye and yer son back."

Odo shook his head and moved the staff again, another reminder to Émile he wasn't totally defenceless. The *chevalier* also knew he was once a Templar, and the reputation of the Templar's fighting ability was not to be underestimated.

Suddenly, Émile turned and began to jog away to retrieve his friends.

He wouldn't fight the priest by himself. This was what Odo hoped, and without pause, he turned and began to walk quickly away from the church towards Falls Ende. He fought the urge to run. By doing so would only draw attention to himself. He saw the *chevalier* look over his shoulder at him before disappearing around the corner.

The *chevaliers* had only just arrived in Mellester and had yet to tether their horses. The only place available to them without riding to the common, some distance away, was behind the church where the Templars had been. Odo knew this would give him the time he needed. From the church, the *chevaliers* would easily see him walking behind the village buildings towards the footbridge near Falls Ende; it was crucial that they see him and follow. Just like the mother duck offering a tempting target to her hunter.

Reeve Norman was fraught with worry and was trying to keep the two *chevaliers* occupied and distracted. So far, there wasn't any commotion coming from the church, and he trusted that Odo had everything well in hand. When he saw the Templar knights walking in the direction of the church to retrieve their horses, he felt relief. He knew Odo would call on them to help. But when he saw the Templars ride away, he felt a knot of fear in his stomach. That feeling turned to pure despair when he saw the *chevalier* appear moments later from behind the church and jog towards him, waving desperately to gain his friends attention.

To make the situation even worse, he saw Sir William, Sir Hyde, and a handful of other lords and knights walking down the carriageway from the manor. He was to escort them through the village while they did a social tour to greet everyone. He didn't know what to do.

"T's him, I found him," cried *Chevalier* Émile as he quickly approached.

"Where?" asked one of the *chevalier*s in total surprise.

Émile pointed, "He is trying to run away, we must hasten."

One of the *chevalier*s turned his head to look where Émile indicated. "Our horses…"

"The church, we can tie them at the church; quickly, we mustn't tarry." Already, he began to swing his horse around to lead it away. People were everywhere, and managing the horses without hurting someone was difficult.

"Ye go, keep an eye on him, we'll catch up," Théo suggested. He knew one person couldn't manage three spirited destriers by himself within the close confines of the village.

"Reeve Norman, Sir William has called fer ye," said a man-at-arms who quickly approached, ignoring the *chevalier*s.

Reeve Norman turned back to the *chevalier*s, but already, one had run back towards the church while the other two were trying to turn three horses.

"Reeve!" the man-at-arms appealed.

The reeve knew Odo had a plan, he'd told him so and insisted he could deal with the *chevalier*s by himself. He had to trust that Odo knew what he was doing. "Stop yer grizzling, I'm coming damn ye," he snapped to the man-at-arms. Reluctantly he walked towards the Lord of Mellester Manor and his esteemed guests. The *chevalier* on foot was already nearing the church. Behind him, the two *chevalier*s now had control of their horses and were trying to manoeuvre them towards the rectory.

"What was all the bruhaha about?" questioned Sir William as the reeve approached.

"Milord, it was nothing, the knights were confused and upset they couldn't find anywhere to tether their horses."

"Nonsense, there is plenty of space near the common where other horses are," Sir William suggested. "Young fools."

"Aye, milord."

"Now then, where is best to begin?" Sir William asked. His interest in the *chevaliers* was quickly forgotten.

Sir Hyde kept his head turned in the direction of the church and watched the *chevaliers* hurrying to manage their horses. He stepped forward away from Sir William and the other lords and up to the reeve and lowered his head slightly. "Seems to my eye, ye have a problem, Reeve."

Reeve Norman looked at the Lord of Ridgley Manor. He knew Sir Hyde was a powerful and respected lord, and word was, he even had the ear of the king. He swallowed away his fear. "Sir Hyde, is best ye not ask any more questions." He bravely held the lord's gaze and didn't flinch.

Sir Hyde's steel grey eyes bored into the reeve. After a moment, he relaxed. "If ye need my help, ye know where to find me," he whispered. "Good luck."

Reeve Norman exhaled in relief. "Milords, may I suggest we begin at the churchyard stalls."

Mother Rosa was battling boredom in the Marshalsea[40], at the manor atop the hill that overlooked Mellester Village. Her two daughters and Odo had lost interest in watching the horses, and her oldest daughter and Odo now squabbled with each other. The reeve had arranged with the ostler that she and the children could visit and spend time in the stables, but already they'd outstayed their welcome. The children were weary of watching the horses and wanted to return to the village where they knew there were fun things to do. Only a short while ago, a bad-tempered young groomsman had demonstrated his lack of patience at the children and challenged Mother Rosa, telling her in less than polite terms, "To be off."

Had it been any other day, she may have responded in a more civilised manner, but this day her patience was worn thin, and she had little tolerance for the little man who spoke so unkindly. It was the ostler who may have saved the groomsman's life. He knew Mother Rosa and her reputation all too well and prevented an incident that would have blemished Mellester Manor and caused a scene that would have been spoken about for years to come. When the ostler finally pried her fingers from around the groomsman's throat and lowered the man to the ground, the young man wheezed apologetically and became aware of how close he'd come to death. Meanwhile, the children played in the straw, unaware of what had just transpired.

"Mother Rosa, it, er, may be fer the better if ye took the wee 'uns elsewhere," he bravely suggested.

She looked at him and briefly considered another admonishment, but

---

40 *Marshalsea – The domain of the marshal where the lord's animals are housed.*

reason prevailed, and she agreed. With the children following, she moved from the stables to find somewhere else to while away the time. The sun was shining, it was warm, and a nearby grassy bank beside the carriageway presented a perfect place to rest her aching feet.

When she arrived, she was surprised to find another person, a young woman about her own age already there enjoying the sunshine.

"Do ye mind if I join ye, fer my feet ache, and the children are churlish?"

"The young woman turned and smiled. "Of course, I'd enjoy the company, fer I have only just arrived here in Mellester and know not a soul, neither friend nor foe."

Mother Rosa was an honest judge of character and immediately had a liking for the young woman and sat wearily down beside her. The children, content to play in the grass, ignored the adults.

"My name is Grace."

Mother Rosa smiled, "It's a pleasure to meet ye Grace, I'm Mother Rosa."

CHAPTER THIRTY-SIX

Odo approached the small bridge that spanned the river Eks, near Falls Ende and looked over his shoulder. Behind him, but still, a safe distance away, he saw *Chevalier* Émile hurrying towards him as best he could. Running with a sword belted to your waist and slapping against your leg was never easy and prevented him from moving at anything faster than just a quick jog.

He rounded the temporary barrier and crossed the bridge. In the pretence of adjusting his sandals, he gave the *chevalier* a little more time to draw nearer before leading him into the forest. Odo didn't want Emile to lose sight of him.

He looked behind one last time and saw the other two *chevalier*s, some distance behind, turn the corner near the church and also begin making their way towards the bridge.

Judging his timing carefully, Odo disappeared into the forest and headed directly for the fallen tree where he'd hidden his bow yesterday. Soon as Émile appeared, he would launch an arrow and kill him, reposition, and wait for the other two. Émile was crashing through the bush behind him as he leapt over the fallen tree. He discarded his staff, dropped to his knees, and frantically began scrambling in the soil for his bow and quiver. They weren't there.

In near panic, Odo searched again for his trusted weapon but couldn't find it; it was gone. He looked up in dismay as Émile appeared. In growing realisation, he knew he was in genuine danger.

Odo reached for his staff and slowly rose, and resolutely faced the *chevalier* who stood ten paces from him. As yet, he hadn't reached for his sword, but with a sinking heart, knew he soon would. His thoughts turned to Josceline, Katherin, and baby William, up in heaven looking down on him. Before the sun set, he and young Odo would probably join them.

"Ye deceived us," yelled Émile, "Yet ye are a killer with no conscience or honour. Ye killed Jean Courteney unjustly in a fair duel." Émile shook his head. "Then his entire family. What kind of man are ye?"

The *chevalier*'s claim of conscience and honour felt hollow to Odo, and he remained silent, allowing him to talk.

"Look at ye, ye disgust me and hide behind yer faith and the guise of a priest. Have ye no shame!" he yelled.

Odo heard a sound from the forest and calculated that the other two *chevaliers* were almost upon them. Émile heard the noise too and relaxed. "We are to take ye back to Frankia, but methinks it will give me gladness to end this here." He raised an arm and jabbed his finger multiple times at Odo. "I will take pleasure in yer death."

At first, only one broad, flat-headed face appeared from behind a leafy bush, then two more moments later. With raised hackles, the three *Alaunt* hounds began to growl aggressively and took a tentative step forward.

The *Alaunt* dog breed had a broad, wide head, similar to a mastiff and had a reverse scissor bite, where the teeth on the lower jaw protrude beyond the teeth of the upper jaw. These animals were strong, fearsome, possessed a mean disposition, and were renowned for their aggression and unprovoked attacks on their handlers. These hounds belonged to Sir William and were trained by his huntsman, but where Huntsman Edgar was, Odo didn't know.

The sound of three growling *Alaunt* hounds was a foreboding sign that gave Odo a chill. The lead dog lowered its chest slightly as it tensed to lunge. He held his breath and didn't move.

Émile was equally surprised to see the three animals appear. He turned his head and inadvertently stared at the lead dog, and made unwelcome eye contact. The second error he made was suddenly lowering his arm, which had been raised and pointing at Odo, to unsheathe his sword.

The unexpected and sudden movement caused the lead dog to leap forward. With a savage snarl, it clamped firmly onto Émile's lower arm, sunk its teeth in and shook it vigorously. Émile cried out in pain and tried desperately to strike at the dog's head with his other hand. The other two hounds reacted instantly and attacked. The combined weight of three large dogs knocked Émile to the ground; one dog went for his neck, while the other, for the *chevalier*'s exposed crotch.

Émile screamed in pain and terror. It sounded inhuman and only further enraged the assailing dogs. He writhed and kicked to no avail, and the more he fought them, the more savage their frenzied assault. The hounds were merciless, and Odo could only watch in horror as the *chevalier* was literarily torn apart. The *Alaunt* were bred as war dogs and to hunt powerful beasts. As trained and with savage efficiency, they mutilated Émile.

Suddenly Huntsman Edgar appeared; out of breath and winded, he saw the carnage and looked horrified. He reacted quickly and immediately gave a low whistle, a command for the hounds to stop. Odo knew it was too late. The dogs, in a primal madness and intent on destroying their quarry, ignored him. He repeated the whistle, this time louder, and bravely struck the lead dog lightly on its snout with a stick he carried as it continued to thrash at what remained of the *chevalier*'s mangled arm. The impact of the stick on its nose broke the dog's focus, and it released Émile and moved obediently away to stand beside its master only to begin hungrily licking the *chevalier*'s blood from its nose. Again, Edgar whistled, and with the help from his stick, one by one, the other two hounds reluctantly disengaged. Émile lay unmoving; both the huntsman and Odo stared in disbelief at the shredded corpse.

In shock, Edgar looked towards Odo; his expression conveyed the ghastliness of what he witnessed. "Dear God," was all he managed to croak and then crossed himself.

Odo thought quickly. "Edgar, ye must go from here. Leave quickly, return to Mellester and find Mother Rosa at the lord's stables, she has young Odo, take the boy and hide him." Odo knew there wasn't another person in Mellester who knew the land, the forest, and paths around the village like Huntsman Edgar. If anyone could hide his son, Edgar could. "Please," he appealed.

The huntsman stood paralysed and stared at the still form of the *chevalier* as blood oozed from multiple places and collected beneath the body. The consequences of what his hounds had done would be catastrophic and his punishment severe.

"Edgar!" Odo shouted. "Edgar."

Huntsman Edgar's head turned to look at Odo, and slowly his eyes refocused, and he nodded, "Aye... I will find her ... and take Odo fer ye," he spoke haltingly. "But why ... what is happening? Why are ye and this man–"

"I can explain later, Edgar. Speak to no one about this but the reeve. Do ye understand? Not a soul, not even Sir William. No one will ever know what happened here."

Edgar nodded again but didn't move.

"Hasten, more *chevaliers* come, do not let them see ye as yer own life may be in danger. Go, go," he encouraged.

Feeling the urgency, Edgar attached leads to the dogs and, without another word, turned and silently melded back into the forest. Feeling some morbid relief, Odo stepped over the fallen tree and approached what was left of Émile. The man was surely dead, he didn't move, and what little remained of his mangled neck was a lurid bloodied mess. He heard the cry from the other *chevaliers* as they called for their friend. But they had yet to enter the forest; this gave him time.

Odo crossed himself and spoke a few words of prayer, then, with a tightly clenched jaw, carefully rolled the *chevaliers* body over and unclasped his belt and sword. He stood and belted the weapon to his waist. It felt strange, but the familiar feeling of a sword on his hip gave him a measure of hope. *This day isn't over yet,* he thought as he crept silently down towards the forests' fringe.

Chevaliers Théo and Jacque hurried across the footbridge and paused momentarily as they tried to determine where Émile had gone. They turned to each other with mouths agape when they heard the blood-curdling cry emanate from the forest. Instinctively they knew it was Émile. As one, they unsheathed their swords. They listened carefully, and what indistinct sounds they heard gave no clue as to what was happening.

"Émile!" shouted Jacque. "Émile!"

There was no answering reply, and both *chevaliers* stood in uncertainty near the bridge, wondering what to do. Neither was keen to enter the forest and face whatever it was that caused the inhuman scream.

With swords defensively raised and offering scant protection, they began to tentatively walk along the riverwalk, their pace measured and slow. Their heads swivelled from side to side as they sought a clue, a sign, or anything that could help them discover what was occurring. From what? Neither knew.

The sound of water cascading over boulders grew louder as they approached the falls. The ever-present mist caught in the mild afternoon breeze drifted up and away. Like every visitor who approached Falls Ende for the first time, the *chevaliers* turned in curiosity and looked down at the tumult of water as it crashed onto the exposed rocks at the base of the falls.

They were distracted for only a moment as they took a step closer to peer down. But a moment was enough and all that Odo needed. With the roar of rushing water masking any sounds he made, he sprung from concealment across the path and launched himself at both chevaliers.

Sensing danger, one man moved and quickly sidestepped, only to fall on the dampness. His sword clattered away.

Odo had to quickly adjust and also lost his footing on the wet slippery ground and fell. His momentum carried him into the back of the remaining *chevalier's* legs, and he teetered. With a cry, the *chevalier* tried desperately to regain his balance; his flailing arms waved like windmills as he staggered momentarily at the precipice, then unable to regain his balance or purchase on the wet moss, he toppled over.

Chevalier Théo bounced from one protruding boulder to another, the sickening sound of each impact muted by the constant roar of water. After his erratic plunge, his misshapen body landed on one of the largest rocks that ringed the pool at the base of the falls. Legs and arms lay in unnatural positions, his head unrecognisable. However, Odo never saw the *chevalier* fall or land, he was scrambling to find a handhold to prevent himself from sliding into the falls and following the *chevalier* down.

The quick move by the Frankian knight caused Odo to change direction slightly, and as his weight shifted, his feet slid out from beneath him. Initially, he intended to push both men together simultaneously, but one of the *chevaliers* had sensed danger and moved aside before falling and losing his weapon. Odo knew he had only a heartbeat or two before the other *chevalier* regained his wits, his sword and attacked.

With both arms fully extended, Odo clawed frantically at the ground, searching for a rock or handhold… anything to slow and stop his slide. Already his legs began to slither over the edge when his fingers found an exposed protruding tree root.

He glanced over at the *chevalier* who was scrambling to retrieve his sword. Odo hoped the root would hold his weight as he pulled on it and cautiously eased his legs back over onto the bank. Quickly he leapt to his feet and tried to create some distance from the edge and the *chevalier* as he unsheathed his own sword. He was breathing hard, the frightening thought of going over the falls were pushed aside as he faced the lone *chevalier* who now stood aggressively facing him.

"Where is Émile?"

"He is dead," Odo replied and took a step closer.

The *chevalier* lost some of his confidence and appeared hesitant. "Now I see ye close, I recognise yer face. When I saw ye last, ye were clean-shaven and wore the clothes of a Templar. Now ye wear a robe, a beard and hide as a priest," *Chevalier* Jacque said as he shifted position to meet the threat. His sword arced threateningly from side to side.

Odo believed he'd never laid eyes on the man before.

The *chevalier* laughed. "Ye don't recognise me, do ye. I was Jean Courtenay's second[41] at *Château de Caen*. He was a loyal friend… and then ye slew him."

Odo was secretly pleased the *chevalier* wished to delay fighting and talk. He needed to regain his breath and wits. The longer he spoke, the better. "Then ye saw Jean Courteney move, he fouled. Had he not moved, I would have hit him with my arrow. It flew straight and true."

Chevalier Jacque shrugged. "It was and always will be the way of the Courteney's… seek advantage from a fool and win. Ye were a fool to duel with a Courteney."

---

41 Second – In a duel, the second is the duellist's helper, normally a trusted close friend who assists in preparation and offers moral support and advice.

"And now Jean Courteney is dead," Odo replied. He could feel his anger rising.

Again, the *chevalier*'s sword scythed through the air. Odo wasn't impressed with the *chevalier*'s bravado, he knew each unnecessary sword swing was wasted energy and one less the man could do in battle.

"And, so ye will be too," *Chevalier* Jacque stated.

It occurred to him at that moment that *Chevalier* Jacque was not bound by chivalry and honour. Instead, the man believed that winning and success was achieved at any cost. Just like the Courteney's, they thought cheating in a duel was acceptable, that it wasn't shameful to foul or disregard rules or honour if you were victorious. Dishonouring your own word was justified if you won. This is why Jean Courtney tried to molest Josceline; this is why they killed his family; this is why they could not accept they had done wrong. He knew then that the man before him wouldn't fight with honour, he would use underhanded tactics to win this contest at any cost. He felt the rage swell from within.

Odo took a deep breath and faced his adversary with renewed purpose. He stood before this ungodly sword-wielding man who did not understand the basic tenets of morality and integrity, and he would kill him. To Odo, the man who stood aggressively before him represented the entire Courteney family, the count, his sons, and daughter, Gisela.

Behind him, he knew Josceline, William, and Katherin stood. He fought for them, for young Odo and goodness.

He heard another swish of a sword as Jacque stepped closer.

CHAPTER THIRTY-SEVEN

Reeve Norman had been guiding Mellester's lord, Sir William, and his entourage from stall to stall, where he was greeting everyone. The lord's buoyant and friendly disposition was welcoming, but for the reeve, his thoughts lay elsewhere, and he was increasingly concerned for Odo.

While Sir William may have been enjoying his stroll through the village, not all his guests felt the same. Sir Hyde Fortescue, lord of Ridgley Manor, was not as enthused as his host. Still, he respected and honoured his friend and pretended to be equally interested as they strolled and greeted merchants and attendees.

Sir Hyde was astute and observant and quickly surmised something was happening in Mellester that involved the reeve. He's seen the man's demeanour, the furtive looks, and the look of worry. In his exuberance as the *vigilia*'s host, Sir William was oblivious to the reeve's disquiet, and Sir Hyde was becoming more perplexed as the reeve's anxiousness increased.

Reeve Norman couldn't wait any longer, he stepped up to Sir William.

"Milord, I have a small matter to attend to, if, er, may I seek yer leave?"

Sir William, who'd been in deep discussion about the finer points of hunting boar with a local knight, looked at his reeve with some annoyance. "I dare say, reeve, I'd prefer your presence here, after all, ye know these people and can–"

Sir Hyde overheard the reeve's request, leaned towards Sir William. "Aye, let him go," he interrupted, "he has a most difficult job to do this day, and the responsibility for order falls on his shoulders. We can manage fer a while, eh?"

Sir William looked at his friend, then turned back to his reeve and sighed. "Very well, be off with ye. Return soonest."

Reeve Norman respectfully dipped his head. "Thank ye, milord." And quickly retreated and turned towards the churchyard.

Sir Hyde watched him walk away, then turned over his shoulder and made eye contact with a knight, part of the group that followed them a step behind.

The young knight, eager to please his liege lord, walked up.

"Something is amiss here," whispered Sir Hyde, "follow the reeve. Ye know what to do."

"Milord," the knight nodded in acknowledgement. Then stepped back and away.

Reeve Norman rounded the church as quickly as he could and immediately made his way behind the village buildings and down towards the bridge where he knew Odo had gone. What he didn't realise was that at that same time, Huntsman Edgar was just crossing the river Eks, at the shallows, downstream from Falls Ende, to find him and Mother Rosa as Priest Oswald had instructed.

Huntsman Edgar was beside himself with worry. The hounds, his responsibility, had killed a visiting knight, and when the lord learned of it, he would be held to account and punished. He didn't know what to do, but the intensity of Priest Oswald request gave urgency to his instructions and would do as asked. He only prayed his questions would be answered and hopefully absolve him of any wrongdoing. With the hounds securely leashed, he forded the river and made his way up the far side of the common and fields towards the road and manor house beyond.

Reeve Norman approached the bridge and looked down towards Falls Ende, and was just in time to see Odo scrambling to his feet. Near him, six paces away, a *chevalier* stood in anger, waving a sword at him. He was too far away to overhear what was said, but what he saw next gave him pause. He stopped as he saw Priest Oswald wield a sword and stand defensively.

Cautiously, the reeve continued, crossed over the bridge, and began to make his way towards them. The *chevalier* faced away and had yet to see him approach. One hand behind his back held a vicious looking knife with a curved blade that Odo had probably not yet seen.

At one time, the reeve aspired to become a man-at-arms and been taught elementary martial skills, and he knew what the *chevalier* intended to do was unorthodox and gave him an unfair, underhanded advantage.

"Priest Oswald?" the reeve yelled. "Be warned, the *chevalier* has a knife!"

Odo looked over the *chevalier*'s shoulder at the reeve. He hadn't seen him come. *A knife?* It made sense, the *chevalier*s posturing was to distract him and designed to keep his attention on the sword blade, which never remained still. When they fought, the knife would suddenly appear and slice him open. Without armour, he was most vulnerable.

Chevalier Jacque's head spun as he heard the warning. Now there was a man behind him with a sword on his hip. He knew safety was back at the *vigilia*, the village, and around people. Without further thought, he turned and ran at the reeve with his sword extended, and in his other hand, the lethal *Karambit*[42] knife with its curved blade glinted in the sunlight.

Reeve Norman was frozen in indecision. The *chevalier* bore down on him quickly, and in each hand, he held a weapon. The reeve fumbled for his sword and finally managed to unsheathe it. He took a step backwards and to the side, away from the falls' precipice and prepared to defend himself. He wasn't a swordsman; the sword he carried, when occasion required, was used to deal with unruly peasants or drunkards. Not knights, let alone an angered *chevalier* charging for him wielding a sword and a lethal knife.

Odo ran after the fleeing *chevalier* and yelled at the reeve. "Let him pass!" He knew the reeve wasn't adept enough at defending himself from the *chevalier* and would only be injured or killed if he tried to intercede.

Hearing the command from Odo, the reeve took another step to the side, then crouched slightly, stood side-on to offer a smaller target, and extended his sword defensively. If the opportunity presented itself, he'd bravely have a go at the *chevalier* if he ran close by.

The *chevalier* ran as quickly as he could, he saw the man ahead prepare

------

42 *Karambit knife – Of Asian origin, the Karambit knife resembled a tiger claw with a short, curved blade and handle.*

to defend, but he had no intention of delaying his escape by engaging with him. At the last moment, he veered away, felt the swish of a sword blade as it hissed harmlessly past his side and continued to the bridge and quickly crossed over. Ahead, about twenty paces away, he saw a lone, and unfamiliar knight with sword extended waiting for him. Behind, he heard Odo and the other man following; he was trapped and outnumbered.

Old man Brooker eased himself upright and rose to his feet from against the tree he'd been leaning on. "Right'o lads, time to have a gander at the common. Be at it now." He'd given thought to the *chevalier*'s generous offer and attempt to find this man Odo Brus and his son and decided it was worth pursuing. Finding the peculiar priest was his priority. As the priest wasn't at the stalls or churchyard, he reasoned he must be in the common. "Keep yer eyes open for the priest."

Without waiting for any response from his sons, he began to amble along the main road that would take him past the carriageway that led up the hill to the manor house on his right and Mellester's village on the left. He knew his boys would each take turns pushing the handcart and would follow close behind.

His narrow, small eyes never stopped scanning. Although he kept his head still, his eyes flickered this way or that and missed nothing. For Brooker, observing was survival. He heard a grunt and then the rattle as someone, most likely young Tedric, began pushing the hand cart behind him.

As he approached and then passed by the manor's carriageway, he saw two women and three children, some distance above him, on a grassy bank below the manor house. One woman was hefty, a big girl that he'd seen before when visiting Mellester, the other young woman had long jet-black hair, tied back with a ribbon, and she appeared more youthful and was unfamiliar to him. The big girl held a baby in her arms while the other children played roly-poly on the steep grass-covered slope. They looked to be enjoying the warm sun on a pleasant afternoon. *Spoiled bitches*, he thought and scowled at them. Bert must have motioned to them because he heard the big woman say something, then she waved her arm to shoo them away. Bert responded, and old man Brooker heard him yell, "Doxy[43]!" He chuckled. Bert was always quick with his tongue.

"Bugger off!" Mother Rosa yelled back. She wasn't having any of it from the cheeky boy.

Suddenly, and in response to her rebuke, the boy who yelled at her left the road and began climbing the grassy slope. Young Odo had just rolled down the hill giggling with joy and was nearest the boy. Instantly Rosa heaved herself upright. "Odo! Come here, quickly now!" She turned to her new friend. "Grace, can ye take her?" and handed over her baby daughter, then cautiously began easing herself down the slope to retrieve Odo.

Old man Brooker heard the woman call the boy and clearly heard her yell, "Odo." As a flood of thoughts and incomplete notions filled his head, he stopped. "Bert!" he shouted, "Get yer arse back!" he scolded. Behind him, he heard the handcart grind to a halt and saw Bert reluctantly return. "Stay there!" he told his boys. "Wait!"

Brooker turned back and looked up at the young boy named Odo, who

---

43 *Doxy – A promiscuous woman, or sexual partner of an outlaw.*

was now on all fours, casually trying to climb back up the hill. Could this be the young boy the Frankish knights sought? If the priest, the archer, was Odo Brus, then this could be his son. It was common practice to name children after their parents. Brooker didn't believe in coincidences. Life was either this way or that. Simple. He stared at the boy as he tried to arrive at a solution. The fat purse the Frankian knights offered was tempting…

One way to find out was to ask the boy, perhaps even talk to his mother, the large woman who was having some difficulty finding her way down the hill to her son. Intimidation and threats always loosened tongues, and he'd find out one way or another.

"Samuel, Tedric, move aside, if she tumbles, she'll cause a landslide," yelled Bert with a laugh as he arrived back at the hand cart. His brothers joined in.

Mother Rosa heard the jibe and her temperament only worsened. She spared a look at the three boys on the road. To her surprise, she saw their father begin clambering up the bank towards Odo, who was dawdling. "Odo!" she yelled again in growing alarm. "Hasten! Quickly now."

Old man Brooker wasn't a large man, he was thin, shortish, and very lithe. His occupation demanded he needed to be supple to climb through narrow openings, scale walls, and even run at infrequent times. He spared a quick look to see if anyone was close by and watching. There wasn't, as everyone was focused on the festivities below in the village, and with renewed determination, scrambled up the hill to question the boy and his mother. He wasn't frightened, she was only a woman and offered him no threat.

Seeing their pa race up the hill, the three boys were puzzled about what he was doing and why. His last instruction had been for them to remain with the handcart. They watched and curiously waited.

Mother Rosa calculated she would get to Odo slightly before the man did.

Further up the hill, Grace held Mother Rosa's two girls tightly as she helplessly watched Mother Rosa reach Odo.

Old Man Brooker reached out to grab the boy from the large woman. She was younger than she first appeared and more likely to be forthcoming when threatened, or so he hoped. She twisted out of his way, leaned back and placed Odo on the grass behind her and yelled at him. "Go, Odo ye are in danger. Go to Grace." She then swiped at the man who tried to step around her. He fell, regained his feet, and tried again.

"Who… is … the … boy's… father? …Odo … Brus?" gasped Brooker as he tried to quickly move to the side and clamber up the hill after the boy. The large woman obstinately blocked his path.

Mother Rosa recoiled at hearing the name Odo Brus. She knew with absolute sureness, young Odo's life and that of Priest Oswald were in extreme danger… *If Oswald wasn't already dead*, she thought grimly.

She pushed the man away again, then turned quickly, "Grace, take them to the stables!"

If Rosa was angry before, now she was completely incensed.

"Stand away Sir knight!" Odo yelled. His voice authoritative and commanding.

The young knight was inexperienced and only recently swore fealty to his liege lord, Sir Hyde. He'd spent years as a squire and been yelled at and submitted dutifully to orders from his superiors and betters. Instinctively he obeyed and lowered his sword as the *chevalier* with sword and knife turned away to face the armed priest that ran towards him. His eyes narrowed in consternation as he watched the scene unfold before him.

Chevalier Jacque saw the hardened expression on Odo's face and believed there was only one real option available to him. He couldn't risk fighting the knight behind him; however, he would slay the priest without compassion. He assumed a defensive stance and waited.

Odo wore no armour and had nothing on him that offered any sort of protection from a knife or sword. He was also acutely aware that he hadn't fought with a sword in some years. Although he'd recently practised a little, he had neither the stamina nor quickness he once had, while the *chevalier* he faced was younger, wore chainmail and was better armed. From nowhere, Sir Piers' words resonated in his consciousness. *Acting on emotion may see yer death.* All his training had revolved around discipline. Everything he'd been taught as a Templar knight had emphasised planning, deliberation, consideration, and not to enter a fray with the odds of success stacked in your opponent's favour, for then the outcome would result in death. Sir Piers' words rang true and were wise. But Sir Piers had not likely been in this situation, Odo grimly thought in response.

Odo's skills may have dulled, but his senses were razor sharp. He could smell the air around him, the odour of fear from the *chevalier*. He saw a minute vein near the *chevalier*'s eye twitch, the pores of his skin were enormous and detailed. He heard the scrape of a foot against the dirt path they were on; the sound appeared unnaturally loud. All his senses were heightened, and everything seemed to slow…

He felt Josceline standing beside him watching, and sensed her silent words of love and support. Without fear or thought of his own safety, he unexpectedly sprung forward. Against commonsense and wisdom, and despite all the hours of Templar training and learnings, his body acted on its own accord. Fueled by emotion and pure rage, driven by love for his family, Odo attacked. The *chevalier* was caught completely off guard, and even as he tried to bring his knife-wielding hand to bear, Odo easily swatted it away as he thrust and slashed.

Chevalier Jacque could only step back and parry to defend himself against the onslaught. The speed of thrusts and stabs by the priest were surprising and allowed him no opening to counterattack.

Odo's fury emboldened him, his strength came from faith, and his endurance equalled the endless love he felt for Josceline. He gave the *chevalier* no respite as he drove the Frankian back, step after step. His sword whirled and slashed; his attack relentless and determined. Odo fought with fervour, and the hapless *chevalier* stood not a chance.

Swords clanged together, and they struck with power and force. For the *chevalier*, the battle was already lost. He knew it the moment he tried to deflect the priest's blade and realised it wasn't there. He'd fallen for the clever feint, and his sword slashed only at air. Immediately he felt the unwelcome coldness of steel as it invaded his torso. He felt his body jerk repeatedly as he was struck again and again. With no awareness or cognition, he sunk to his knees with a puzzled expression; he expected to hear singing angels and rejoicing – but there was nothing; the silence deafening as blackness consumed him.

Odo collapsed to his knees in exhaustion as the knight and reeve approached from different directions.

"Priest Oswald!" exclaimed Reeve Norman as he bent down to see if Odo had been injured.

"Pray tell," the young knight spoke. "What wickedness is this?" He shook his head and turned from Odo to look at the fallen *chevalier.*

Odo's chest heaved from the exertion. He looked up at the young knight. "It would serve... ye very well to not speak... of what ye witnessed," he gasped.

The knight's expression hardened. "Would ye care to inform me?"

"Help me," Odo held out his arm and the reeve assisted him to his feet. Odo exhaled and then took another deep breath as he stood and straightened. "If ye choose to tell anyone of this, ye will be responsible fer the deaths of more people. What ye saw, this fight, was the end. The killing stops." Odo met the gaze of the young knight and held it. "If ye tell anyone or yer lord, word will soon spread, and more and more *chevalier*s will come here to this manor, and the killing will continue. Say nothing, and ye save lives of good folk. What say, ye?"

"Who are ye, fer I have seen few men fight with such skill? I have never seen a priest champion a knight."

Odo squared his shoulders and glared at the knight. "I am a priest, but before, I was a Templar knight. These men and others..." he looked at the unmoving form of the *chevalier.* "They brought the devil to Mellester. Now it has ended. Say nothing of this evilness to anyone."

At Odo's mention of the devil, both the knight and the reeve crossed themselves, then the knight dipped his head. "Milord, fergive me, I did not know. I, uh, I will not speak of this."

"Can I be sure?" Odo inclined his head and waited.

"Aye, ye have my word."

"Who is yer liege?"

"Sir Hyde Fortescue."

"If ye break yer word, then I know where to find ye."

The knight shook his head emphatically. "I will not."

"Thank ye." Odo turned to the reeve, I must go to Odo and ensure all is well."

"The bodies?" asked the reeve, concerned about the *chevalier* laying across a boulder at Falls Ende and the dead body beside them. "We cannot leave them here."

"Let's move him to the bushes, and I will remove and bury the two *chevaliers* later," Odo offered.

As the knight slowly walked away scratching his head, Odo and the reeve moved the corpse out of sight behind some bushes and kicked dirt over the congealing blood. Odo discarded his sword and belt then they both made their way towards Sir William's stables at the manor house on the hill.

CHAPTER THIRTY-EIGHT

Huntsman Edgar had quickly walked up the far side of the common with his hounds and turned right onto the road that would lead him to the carriageway and up towards the manor and Sir William's stables. Ahead, on his left and up the bank, he saw a commotion. His eyes narrowed as he surveyed a most peculiar scene. He quickened his pace as he recognised Mother Rosa.

Sir William and his group had tirelessly wandered around the *vigilia* and greeted many people with a welcoming smile and thanked them for attending. He was thirsty and longed to sit with his friends at the manor and be entertained. Already, food was being prepared for him, and a feast and music would highlight the evening before a hunt the following morning.

He and his entourage retraced their route and walked back through the village and towards the manor house when Sir Hyde nudged him and pointed. "See yonder, something is untoward."

Sir William's eyes followed Sir Hyde's outstretched arm, and he paused to stare. "Where is the reeve?"

Knights, lords, and attendants shrugged. "He asked to be excused, milord," someone volunteered.

"Then find him and be quick about it," he insisted.

Out of sight from Sir William and his group, and heading in exactly the same direction behind the stalls and Mellester's buildings, Reeve Norman and Odo strode quickly towards the church, where they would cross the road and then walk up the carriageway to the stables. As they approached the church and could see further, Odo stopped unexpectedly, and his mouth opened in sheer terror. "Nay!" he cried and took off running. "Fetch Godwin!" he yelled over his shoulder to the reeve.

Mother Rosa was absolutely livid. Her face was red from anger, not exertion, and she fought with absolute fury. She'd seen that toad, Brooker, and his three troublesome sons loitering around Mellester on numerous occasions and didn't care for them at all. When he clambered up the bank and reached for young Odo, she saw red. When he asked about Odo Brus, she reacted in a violent rage.

Instead of trying to push him away and fend him off as she'd initially done, she grabbed the skinny, detestable little man and wrapped both her large and powerful hands around his throat and wasn't going to release him. Her actions weren't out of the need to hurt the man because he'd offended her, instead, she genuinely feared for the life of young Odo. She loved the boy; he was like a son to her, and she would protect him with her last dying breath.

Above her, Grace screamed and clutched all three children to her as she slowly eased away, up the bank towards the manor house and safety as Mother Rosa instructed.

Old man Brooker stood no chance. He was outweighed, outsmarted, and more importantly, he'd underestimated the strength and resolve of the substantial young woman. With her hands firmly around his throat and squeezing his windpipe, he couldn't yell for help. He thrashed about and tried to poke, scratch, and punch her. It did little good, her vice-like grip tightened, and he lacked the strength and weight to move her bulk.

Below, on the road, Bert, Samuel and Tedric watched with mouths agape as their father succumbed to a beating. Bert was hopping from one foot to another in anxiousness and desperately wanted to go to his pa and help. Unable to remain at the handcart as instructed, Bert made up his mind.

"I'm going t'help." He said, and abandoning his two brothers, ran towards the bank.

"Bert!" Samuel shouted. "Look!"

Bert paused and looked to where his brother pointed. A man with three large snarling hounds was running towards them.

Their pa had beaten it into them numerous times, "When in doubt, and if ye are gonna be caught, then scarper, run fer it. I'll always find ye later." They had run before and could do so again.

In growing panic, Bert looked in the other direction. He saw a group of knights walking up Mellester's main thoroughfare. Inside the cart were stolen items, including the finely crafted bow and quiver they'd taken from the priest. In moments they'd be trapped and caught, and if they were questioned and the wagon inspected...

"Go, go!" it was Samuel, the quickest thinker, who gave the order. Without waiting, Samuel grabbed the hand cart from Tedric, turned around, and began to run away from the hounds, up the road and away from danger. Tedric followed a step behind, and Bert, with a change of heart, leapt from the bank and followed. If they were quick, they could avoid the knights.

Neither Bert, Samuel, nor Tedric spared their pa a look as they ran as fast as possible. The hand cart bounced over the road as they made it past Mellester's road. The group of knights gave them only a cursory glance as they rushed away.

Mother Rosa wouldn't relent. Only when Brooker finally stopped his thrashing did she release her hold on him. Immediately she looked for Grace and the children and didn't see them and presumed they'd made it to the top and ran to the stables. Her head spun as she heard a shout from below.

She stood with her hands on her broad hips to catch her breath and looked down at the assembled group of men. The body of old man Brooker lay still at her side. She felt no remorse or regret, as far as she was concerned, she'd saved the life of young Odo and done him right.

When she saw Priest Oswald run up the road to join the group, she felt relief. He lived.

"Would someone kindly tell me what is going on here?" bellowed Sir William. "I have a dead man lying on the common, and I want answers!"

They were all gathered inside Mellester Manor's great hall. Reeve Norman, Odo, Mother Rosa, Godwin, Grace, and a handful of knights also stood curiously watching. Sir Hyde was not in attendance, and much to Odo's relief neither was Huntsman Edgar. The young knight who'd witnessed the death of the *chevalier* was not in the hall either and no doubt was with his liege lord, Sir Hyde.

Reeve Norman took a step forward to speak when Odo pushed him aside. "Milord, perhaps it is best if I speak first, and the reeve can speak after."

Sir William looked quizzically at Mellester's priest and held his tongue.

Odo could see the lord's anger festering. He cleared his throat. "Milord, Mother Rosa was protecting the life of Herdsman Godwin's son. Old man Brooker and his godless sons are vagabonds, common thieves, and they came to Mellester to rob and pilfer. They stole food, milord and intended to steal more. Why they wanted to harm Godwin and Hetti Read's son, I know not, milord. But we must offer thanks to Mother Rosa fer saving the lad."

"Then tell me, Priest Oswald, why was the reeve so consumed by other matters and not attending to those, those villains?" Sir William asked and turned his head to give the reeve a cold stare

"Fergive me, milord, fer I must take responsibility," Odo admitted.

"Oh?" Sir William swung his head to face the priest.

"I witnessed some, er, drunken revelry near Falls Ende, milord. I quietly called on the reeve to settle things down, as we both wanted to avoid causing ye or Mellester any embarrassment."

Sir William grunted. "Reeve Norman, what say ye?"

Odo held his breath. Whatever the reeve said now would be telling.

"Uh, milord. It is, as Priest Oswald says. Merchants told me of the pilfering of old man Brooker and his boys. Methinks, Mother Rosa has done us a favour, sire, and rid us of a scourge." The reeve looked down at his feet a moment before continuing. "And milord, there was an incident near Falls Ende, and I was able to, er, help to, er, quell it and prevent things from getting' outa hand. All is well, and I believe it was of no consequence and will be forgotten about." Reeve Norman smiled.

"I was just protecting, wee Odo," loudly stated Mother Rosa.

All heads turned to her. In response, she folded her arms and looked embarrassed after her unexpected outburst.

Sir William paused and briefly gave the matter some thought. He rose from his seat. "Thank ye, Mother Rosa, and I'm sure the herdsman and his woman thank ye too." He turned to the reeve and nodded. "I have things that require my attention. Priest Oswald, Reeve Norman, bury the man and keep yer head on, I don't want bodies piling up in Mellester," he warned, then strode from the hall.

Evening fell over Mellester, and with it came a chill. Reeve Norman and Godwin both carried spades, and Odo, a lengthy coil of rope, and his staff. They remerged from the forest and walked back towards the village. The bodies of three *chevaliers* had been disposed of and would never, ever be found.

Retrieving the *chevalier* from Fall Ende had been challenging, but Godwin had climbed down into the falls many times in the past, and he clambered down while still light enough to see. He tied a rope around the *chevalier*'s body, then the reeve and Odo hoisted him up and carried him away to be buried. Exhausted, the three men quietly walked back to Mellester, each lost to the thoughts of the men who had died.

"Hale to ye!" came a voice from the darkness.

The three of them stopped and were instantly alert. In reflex, Odo repositioned his staff in anticipation of danger.

"Fare ye well?" asked the reeve.

From out of the darkness, a lone knight stepped forward. By moonlight, Odo recognised him immediately. He was the knight who'd witnessed the death of the *chevalier* earlier this afternoon.

"Milord, what brings ye here?" Reeve Norman asked.

The knight managed a laugh. "From what I came to learn, it seems to me ye have a problem," he simply stated.

Odo tensed. "Why would this concern ye?" he asked.

In the darkness, Odo saw the knight raise both hands to show he didn't wield a weapon. "I noticed that behind the church, three fine destriers are tethered. I do wonder as to where their riders are."

Odo took a step closer to the young knight. "Why should ye care? Speak carefully, Sir knight, fer my patience is thin and my temperament unsettled."

The young knight's bravado deflated quickly. "Milord–"

"I am Priest Oswald," Odo corrected him.

"Priest Oswald, I seek only to help and may have a way to ease the burden of the horses fer ye."

Odo was going to take the three destriers, along with his own horse, and ride them away from Mellester during the evening, turn them loose, then return to Mellester before morning. "What do ye have in mind?" he asked.

"I will add those horses to Sir Hyde's, stabled at the manor. If anyone asks, I will say these were purchased privately during the *vigilia*. We will take them with us when we return to Ridgley Manor. Good horses cost more than a shiny penny and have value."

"What will Sir Hyde say to this?" Odo asked.

The knight seemed to relax even more, and his tone changed. "As promised, I have not nor will speak of what I saw this afternoon. But my liege lord, Sir Hyde is not a fool. He knows something happened here today, but not what. He asked questions that I would not answer. I honour my word. However, I spoke with him, only about the horses, and he agreed. But only if I can avow that the horses are not stolen, obtained through deceit or from ill will."

Odo completely understood. In the past, he'd been in similar awkward situations and knew that an astute lord always needed to keep his eyes and mind open. Things happened; sometimes he was required to know, other times it was best he didn't. An even-handed lord knew the difference and when not to ask questions. "Aye, take them, best they be gone from here, soonest." Odo smiled, Ridgley manor's lord just obtained three expensive destriers without paying a penny. "Sir knight, my humble church will require substantial repairs. It is most costly, and I welcome a donation. Perhaps yer lord would care to help the Church fer a most worthy cause?"

The knight grinned. "I will make the suggestion."

"I know not yer name," Odo stated.

“I am Sir Elric, of Legaceaster.”

“Sir Elric, I am sure ye will honour yer word. Are we understood?”

“Aye, Priest Oswald, we are.”

CHAPTER THIRTY-NINE

It was late, and after the events of the day, everyone was exhausted. Reeve Norman wasn't content to end the day without first speaking to the few who fully understood what had transpired at Mellester, and he had something to say.

The reeve called for Mother Rosa, Grace, Godwin and Hetti, to meet at the church so he could talk to them all in the presence of Odo. They all sat expectingly on the hard wooden benches and faced the reeve who stood near the pulpit. It was a reckoning, and he intended to resolve things and make his thoughts known once and for all.

"It must stop, Priest Oswald," he began, his voice and demeanour authoritative. "The death and killings... "He shook his head. "Eventually, Sir William may learn of what has happened, and I'm surely tempted to inform him, as is my duty. Mellester was in danger this day, and the good people here were at risk."

Odo watched and listened. He knew the reeve was correct and

completely agreed. He stood with arms folded and allowed him to continue.

"I know ye have reason to protect the boy, but regardless, it cannot go on like this," the reeve added. "I know ye didn't send those knights here but come they did. I fear your need to seek vengeance may not be in Mellester's interests." Reeve Norman paused and looked toward Odo and waited for him to respond.

"Aye, I have thought on this too," he replied. "Methinks, it will end. There is nothing to prove that the *chevaliers* ever arrived in Mellester. Young Odo is safe, and the killing will stop. I will not go to Frankia and seek retribution, fer I do not want to put anyone's lives in more danger."

Godwin and Hetti sat nervously, with young Odo seated comfortably between them as he slept. They'd talked to each other at great length and feared Odo would take his son from them and leave the village. Odo's declaration put them at ease, and they shared a look of relief.

"And did ye speak to Huntsman Edgar?" asked the reeve.

Odo nodded. "Edgar is keen that the lord does not learn of what the hounds did. He believes the death was his fault. He will say nothing."

Reeve Norman nodded, pleased at the outcome.

"Mellester needs a good priest," Mother Rosa spoke. "And we need ye to be that man, and uh, we can all help to protect Odo," she folded her arms and made eye contact with the reeve.

"Aye, ye have shown that," the reeve laughed.

Mother Rosa frowned; she wasn't yet finished. She looked at Odo. "But ye look after all of us and have no one to look after ye."

Odo shrugged.

"Grace is need'n work. And ye be need'n a hearth wife," she stated.

All heads turned to Grace, who'd tactfully remained silent. Earlier, Grace had understandably asked questions, and Mother Rosa had briefly told her some details, but not all. It was crucial that Grace did not speak of what she had learned, which was why the reeve insisted she come to the meeting at the church.

Odo stared at the young woman with jet black hair. "I, uh–"

"I'll not hear a word against it," Mother Rosa stated with finality after interrupting him. She twisted in her seat to face the young woman who sat beside her. "Grace? Ye will attend to Priest Oswald. Keep him clean and fed and see he has no need fer worry or want. Ye will sleep in the rectory. What say ye?"

Grace looked uncomfortable at Mother Rosa's outspoken and candid outburst. "If, er, Priest Oswald is in agreement?"

Reeve Norman smirked; he didn't want to incur Mother Rosa's anger, while Godwin and Hetti nodded enthusiastically. Odo had no choice and could only agree, Grace would become his hearth wife.

The weeks turned into months, and still, no word arrived about the three *chevaliers* who'd she sent to England. No messages came explaining what had happened to them, and Gisela believed they had died, perished in some unfortunate accident. It wasn't unexpected; she had sent them to Londinium, where it was dangerous for the unwary. She accepted that the possibility existed that Odo Brus had killed them and was most likely in Londinium, where he could hide in obscurity.

However, it was definitely in Londinium, she reasoned, that was where they had fallen victim to some event that saw their deaths. It couldn't have been the tiny hamlet, whatever it was called. The *chevalier*s in a small hamlet could easily fend for themselves, and word would spread if they had died or befallen to some tragic event where many folk were gathered.

It mattered not to her. She had her lands, wealth, title and most importantly, power. Someone somewhere would utter the name Odo Brus, and when they did, she'd be listening. Odo Brus would resurface; when he did, she'd respond accordingly, vengeance was hers, and she'd exact that revenge.

EPILOGUE

Some years later...

The sound of barking hounds woke Odo from his sleep. He stirred and remained in his cot where it was warm, and he thought about the day ahead. After a short while, he rose and quietly stepped outside so as not to disturb Grace. It was bitterly cold, and he pulled his cape tightly around his shoulders to ward off the frigid air.

Already he could see yellow light from tallow candles seeping from beneath doors as villagers woke to go about their business and attend to their daily tasks. Above, the sky was beginning to change, darkness succumbed to light, and dawn would bring a fresh new day to Mellester.

In the distance, he heard the hounds bark again, and he knew that Huntsman Edgar was entering the forest in preparation for Sir William's hunt. Mellester's lord intended to instruct his son, Sir Wystan, and a handful of other young knights, on the finer points of hunting. Odo was envious and quietly wished he could ride a beautiful courser through the forest hunting wild boar.

He ambled down the street, past Cheeseman Gerald's shoppe where he was already hard at work and towards Godwin's cruck house. Mother Rosa and her milkmaids would soon be finished milking and turn the animals out.

Odo paused in a doorway and stopped to reflect. He felt the sadness return. It always did and never left or gave him peace. His son was a short distance away with Godwin, and he longed to share with the boy the paternal love he felt for him. It was like a constant ache, a wound in his chest that never healed. His son had grown into a wonderful young boy, and the feeling of pride was sometimes overwhelming. But those emotions remained suppressed, and he couldn't share them with anyone. To the lad, he was just a cantankerous and fussy old priest.

Odo shivered in the coldness, and as always, his thoughts turned to Josceline, Katherin and William. The pain of their deaths never lessened or diminished, and he carried the burden of guilt with him each and every day.

He moved from the doorway and walked past Godwin's home, and stood in the dark shadow of the byre. He looked skywards; already it was light; he'd been dawdling and daydreaming. Since Hetti's unfortunate passing a few years ago, Godwin and Odo had managed quite well for themselves. Mother Rosa, God bless her, was never far away and adorned Odo with love, kindness, and a firm hand across the back of his head when he put a foot wrong.

He heard voices and then saw Godwin and Odo appear. Godwin had a barrow packed with tools and timber. No doubt they were headed towards Falls Ende to repair a fence. Unseen and in the shadows, he watched as Godwin and young Odo made their way through the pasture.

He heard young Odo's exclaim in a loud voice to Godwin, "I too will be a deierie[44] farmer when I'm old enough." His breath turned white from the cold.

Odo wiped his eyes and smiled; the sadness was temporarily forgotten as he watched his son with pride, running carefree and barefoot in the field.

Suddenly three haunting blasts from Huntsman Edgar's horn interrupted the peacefulness. Odo stared into the blackened darkness of the forest beyond Falls Ende. A boar had been located somewhere in the hills, and Sir William, his son, Sir Wystan, and friends would be eagerly hunting for the beast.

He spared Godwin and Odo another quick look as they prepared to mend the fence at Falls Ende. Recently, a sheep had fallen to its death, and the fence needed urgent attention before others met a similar fate. Already he could hear the distant, excited cries of knights shouting as Sir William's hounds located their quarry.

He turned away and headed back to the rectory where he knew Grace would be up and about. *Thankfully, today will be like any other*, he thought.

---

44 *Deierie - Dairy*

AUTHOR'S NOTES

I attempt to detail historical facts as accurately as possible, but it isn't always easy. Over the years, decades, and centuries, place names have altered, and reported facts are often misinterpreted or are simply inaccurate. This can prove quite challenging for an author, especially when writing about an era that existed over a thousand years ago.

Fortunately, a lot has been written about The Order of The Poor Fellow-Soldiers of Christ and of the Temple of Solomon *(Latin - Pauperes commilitones Christi Templique Salomonici),* or more commonly known as Templars. It's easy to glamorise or misrepresent them, and I have tried to fairly honour their mysterious and lasting legacy.

What must be remembered is that the Templars were a monastic order. They weren't just a group of pious monks who were permitted to wield weapons and protect pilgrims travelling to the holy lands. Most unusually, Pope Innocent II also granted the order a special dispensation that conferred an exemption from obedience to local laws. More importantly, they were exempt from all authority – they answered to no one except the pope, and like all clergy, they were exempt from paying taxes.

However, as powerful as they were, they did have constraints, and all swore obedience to strict vows. The Templars could not own property or receive private correspondence. They could not be betrothed or marry, and most certainly, they could not communicate with any female, even family. Additionally, each Templar took a vow of poverty and could not have debt more than he could pay, and concerning health and disorders, they could not suffer from any vulnerabilities, and, as I wrote in this novel, they were permitted only to eat meat three times a week. Interestingly, for Templars who survived battle, many lived to a ripe old age due mainly to their healthy diet.

Above all, they were fierce and highly disciplined warriors who were forbidden from retreating in battle unless their flag was brought down or when the opposition outnumbered them three–to–one and even then only by order of their commander. There is a lot more to them, and I have listed only a few.

On Friday, 13th October in the year 1307 (Black Friday), King Philip IV ordered the simultaneous arrest of all Templars in France, where they faced charges of worshipping idols, disrespecting the Cross, and a host of other charges that included heresy. On 22nd November 1307, after relenting to pressure from King Phillip, Pope Clement instructed all Christian monarchs in Europe to arrest all Templars and seize their assets. The pope called for papal hearings to determine the Templars' guilt or innocence, and once freed of the Inquisitors' torture, many Templars recanted their coerced confessions. In 1312, Pope Clement disbanded the order and cited the public scandal generated by their confessions as his reason.

And this is where it becomes confusing. In September 2001, a document was discovered in the Vatican Secret Archives, dated 17th - 20th August 1308, that indicated that Pope Clement absolved the leaders of the Templar order. Another document, but this one, well known to historians, dated 20th August 1308 and addressed to Philip IV of France, stated that the Church had granted absolution to all those Templars who'd confessed to heresy and restored them to the Sacraments and to the unity of the Church.

Presently, I believe the Roman Catholic Church has absolved the Templars of any wrongdoing and decreed that their persecution was inequitable and that nothing was inherently wrong with the order or its rule. The modern Church acknowledged that during the Templar inquisition, Pope Clement was unfairly pressured by his relative, King Philip IV, to make a decision because of the enormity of the public scandal.
I thank the enigmatic Templars, they continue to provide ample fodder to feed a creative mind.

William X, Duke of Aquitaine, Duke of Gascony, and the Count of Poitou appears to have been a fascinating person, and history has been most kind to him. In addition to being a competent warrior, he was a prolific poet, a lover of the arts, and was known affectionately as the *Saint*. He probably was a sensitive and creative man, and most undoubtedly amorous, as his previous wives could attest. Many of his poems were said to be quite bawdy.

He died, as I wrote, in *Santiago de Compostela* in northwestern Spain, when on a spiritual pilgrimage, but most unlikely from the hand or influence of the Courteney family.

While his daughter Eleanor would become the Queen Consort of France and later Queen Consort of England, he also had two other children. It was once thought he had a son called Joscelin, but this proved to be untrue. However, it did provide me with an idea to create Josceline.
I think Duke William truly loved his daughter Eleanor, and when on his deathbed, he requested that King Louis VI of France become her protector and find her a suitable husband. The king took this request seriously, became her guardian, and subsequently wasted no time; a week later, he married Eleanor to his son Louis VII. The rest is well-documented history and will continue in another Falls Ende tale.

If you enjoyed *Falls Ende - Quartus*, please leave a review.

With thanks,

Paul W. Feenstra

Books
by
Paul W. Feenstra

Published by Mellester Press.

Boundary

The Breath of God (Book 1 in Moana Rangitira series)

For Want of a Shilling (Book 2 in Moana Rangitira series)

Gunpowder Green

Into the Shade

Falls Ende eBook series
Falls Ende – The Oath   (eBook 1)
Falls Ende – Courser   (eBook 2)
Falls Ende – The King   (eBook 3)

Falls Ende – Primus Book 1
Print version of eBook compilation 1, 2 & 3

Falls Ende – Secundus Book 2

Falls Ende – Tertium Book 3

Falls Ende – Quartus Book 4

www.ingramcontent.com/pod-product-compliance
Lightning Source LLC
Chambersburg PA
CBHW070155120726
47909CB00001B/121